The Case of the Mad Doctor

Paula Lennon was born to Jamaican parents in England. She lived in Jamaica during her teens and developed a great affinity for the island. Although Paula came back to England to study law and was once a London commercial lawyer, she eventually saw sense and returned to live where the weather is more conducive to smiling.

THE CASE of the MAD DOCTOR

P.D. Lennon

First published in the United Kingdom in 2025 by Canelo

This edition published in the United States in 2026 by

Canelo, an imprint of
DK Publishing, a division of Penguin Random House LLC
1745 Broadway, 20th Floor, New York, NY 10019

The authorized representative in the EEA is Dorling Kindersley Verlag GmbH.
Arnulfstr. 124, 80636 Munich, Germany

ISBN 979 8 21726 945 7

Cover design by Blacksheep

Cover images © Shutterstock; Depositphotos

Printed and bound in Great Britain by Clays Ltd, Elcograf S.p.A.

Look for more great books at
www.canelo.co | www.dk.com

1

CHAPTER 1

Bristol, England. July 1772

Isaiah Ollenu's coattails flapped behind his knees as he strutted across the polished boards. He was a tall, broad-shouldered, ebony-hued man of thirty-five years who moved with the agility of one many years younger. After adjusting the ruffled cuffs of his cotton shirt, he fluffed his collar. With one arm waving in the air and the other folded behind his back, he held his nose aloft, inhaling aromatic beeswax in the air, then had to rearrange his horsehair wig that slid sideways.

'If it pleases the Court, My Lord, the defendant, Miss Bailey, is of previous good character. She did not steal multiple pairs of shoes as alleged. It is a grave misunderstanding and I ask the Court to treat the prosecution's preposterous allegation with the contempt it deserves.'

Ollenu spun on his heels and changed his voice, taking on a loftier tone. 'My Lord, My Learned Friend, Mr Dunne, is inexplicably outraged on behalf of a woman who was observed fleeing the area with the bundle of shoes in hand—'

Below Ollenu, the front door slammed with a jolt that shook even the heavy law books on the surrounding shelves. After a swift bow in deference to an empty leather chair, he strode to the library's sash window, wiped away the morning mist and gently slid the window open.

He peered down into Bristol's Broad Street, the thriving centre of trade where prosperous merchants and wealthy customers mingled with tradesmen and labourers on the cobbled streets. Bristol was a city second only to London in commerce and wealth, and second to none in pride and industriousness. The door slammer – a rotund man buttoning his long woollen coat – was Edward Barrow, owner of Paxten Insurance Company. The fat man's ample jowls hung loosely below the pipe he was trying to light, and, although his lips curled temporarily, his demeanour could not properly be described as pleasant.

As far as Ollenu was aware, Jacob Dunne and Mr Barrow were not friends, yet Mr Barrow had visited the barrister's law office three times in recent weeks, and the usually meticulous Mr Dunne had never commented on the visits nor asked for any research to be done thereafter. Mr Barrow, for his part, had never so much as acknowledged Ollenu and merely cast the occasional malignant glance in his direction.

Before Mr Barrow could don his hat, Ollenu snatched up a small bowl of pot pourri, emptied it out of the window and withdrew from the sill. He smiled as the sound of Mr Barrow spluttering and sneezing filtered upwards.

Straightening his jacket, Ollenu resumed a pompous gait. 'My Lord, Mr Wintworth's description of Miss Bailey as "fleeing" is entirely scurrilous and misleading to the Court. I object.'

The amateur actor swerved and flopped into the chair. A croaky voice emerged, as if weakened with age. 'You object to what Mr Dunne? Are you gentlemen not agreed that Miss Bailey was found with the shoes clutched to her stomach? Four pairs if I am correct?'

The library's old oak door creaked and stood ajar. Unaware of the new audience member, Ollenu bounced to his feet and bowed at the now empty chair.

'Why, yes, My Lord is correct. But Mr Wintworth's use of the word "fleeing" is entirely incorrect. The shoes were displayed outside Mr Carberry's shop on Prince Street. As Miss Bailey walked past, she noticed a poorly driven carriage coming perilously close to an immense puddle of water. In a commendable effort to protect the shoes from damage, she gathered as many as she could into her shawl and moved into the shop doorway – next door. Mr Wintworth is quite wrong, she did not flee.'

'This is a most ludicrous defence, My Lord, even by my learned friend's standards. Mr Dunne seeks to confuse the issue and I object!'

Ollenu sat and waved his hand wearily. 'Gentlemen please remember where you are. Now Mr Wintworth, your witness, Mr Carberry, did say he located the girl with the shoes crouched in the doorway of a haberdashery that is, in fact, next door?'

'Yes, your Honour, but—'

'Then your objection is overruled, Mr Wintworth.'

'Thank you, My Lord.' Ollenu stood, gave a deep bow and flourished a hand. 'Mr Wintworth maligns Miss Bailey. She is poor, but not a thief, and there was no intention to deprive the owner of his property. As My Lord agrees it is quite logical to conclude that Miss Bailey intended to return the shoes, he must also agree that the case put forward by the prosecution fails.'

Ollenu sat, narrowed his eyes and rubbed his chin in the manner of a man contemplating the scales of justice with all due seriousness. 'I must say I am leaning towards that ruling, Mr Dunne.'

'My Lord!' The law clerk sprung back on his feet. 'This is the most preposterous piece of storytelling Mr Dunne has presented to date. The suggestion that all a thief need do to get away with theft is lurk in the vicinity for a while and claim she was protecting the victims' goods, intending to put them back, is quite ridiculous. Mr Dunne is a regular Daniel Defoe!'

'And you, Mr Wintworth, are a bumptious cockalorum!'

'I really hate to interrupt your passionate performance, Mr Ollenu.' The library door swung open and a sixty-year-old throat cleared as one grey eyebrow almost disappeared underneath a powdered wig. 'Or should I say *my* passionate performance? Although I could only dream of flitting about with such speed.' Jacob Dunne's bemused angular face was whiskerless, except for enormous sideburns that ran down to his jaw. His silk stockings met knee breeches in an uncomfortable embrace as if both were a size too small. He held two large books against his portly frame. 'Not quite finished filling the shelves, I see?'

Ollenu followed the senior counsellor's gaze and lingered on a cluttered table in the corner. His comfortable personal space where he carried out numerous legal tasks. Books used by the three barristers were piled on the table. Hard leather covers and soft calfskin covers, precious books whose delicate pages he handled each day with loving care. These books, and the knowledge within, were the key to a better life, and over the past five years he had grasped every opportunity to absorb their content.

'My apologies, sir. I was preparing to give the book shelves my utmost attention.' Ollenu spread his arms wide, bent his knees and bounced up and down. 'Must stretch my limbs first.'

'Do dispense with the wig, before Mr Verney sees you.'

With due care, Ollenu returned the borrowed wig to the metal hook, before scratching his closely cropped and now extremely irritated scalp. He turned and dipped his head slightly. 'I am at your disposal, sir.'

Mr Dunne appeared to wince and Ollenu wondered if he was mistaken.

'Do be seated, Mr Ollenu.' A slight frown creased Dunne's already heavily wrinkled brow. 'I must say, I do not recollect ever calling Wintworth a bumptious cock-alorum?'

'The error is mine, sir. That particular term was reserved for Mr Jennings. You said Mr Wintworth was an insentient coxcomb.'

'Aah, yes.'

Mr Dunne placed the two books on Ollenu's table then stood in front of a somewhat faded world map fixed to the panelled wall, his back to his apprentice. 'I shall miss you, Mr Ollenu.'

An uneasy feeling ran through Ollenu's body. Why would Jacob Dunne miss him? He mumbled a curse beneath his breath.

'Hmm? What was that?'

'Nothing, sir.'

Mr Dunne must be about to dismiss him, to extinguish his long-held dream of becoming an attorney and being addressed as esquire. What would Coreen say when he told her that his five years' toil had been in vain? Pregnant Coreen, his beloved wife.

The men had worked together since that period in time when Jacob Dunne was a pre-eminent attorney. Ollenu had celebrated Mr Dunne's educational journey through the Inns of Court and call to the Bar, achieving the rights of advocacy in the higher courts. Their working relationship was a good one, or so he thought.

Ollenu's mind worked feverishly to think of any errors in his tasks. He always checked and double checked every bit of research, and sought alternative views before presenting it to the barristers. Polite was his middle name. He never raised his voice, except to the over-friendly stray cat for rubbing its grubby fur on his stocking-clad ankles. Of one thing he was certain; if he was to be relieved of his cherished position he would not beg or plead, he would listen quietly and leave with dignity intact.

Mr Dunne stole a glance at him and their eyes met for the briefest of moments before the barrister looked away. Ollenu's unease grew in the fertile silence. Unable to sit still any longer, Ollenu rose and stood beside his manager, towering a full head above him, ready to learn his fate, however distressing.

'Mr Dunne, sir. I ask only that you be as generous as possible in your written testimonial for me.' Ollenu patted his stomach in the hope of calming a dull ache. 'Indeed sir, if I might venture, I shall write the testimonial and you may attach your signature?'

Mr Dunne gave no indication that he even heard Ollenu's suggestion. The senior advocate continued to study the world map as if it was new to him, although it had been on that particular wall for years. Ollenu stared at the map, too, but could see nothing to merit such rapt attention. A large flat image of far-away countries and lands, some taken by cannon and gunfire, some yet to be taken. He despised the word 'discovered' as such description conjured up visions of brave pioneers, silenced evidence of brute force, and concealed proof of man's inhumanity to man.

'It is perhaps the fact that I have already provided a generous testimonial that will displease you, Mr Ollenu.' Dunne stroked his prominent sideburn. 'Edward Barrow has all but given up on his own attorney and needs our assistance.'

'Oh, I heard Mr Barrow earlier.'

'You heard him?'

Ollenu was certain this time that Jacob Dunne flinched. Edward Barrow had an overpowering voice that always reverberated through the reception area on arrival. Unfortunately, the oak door to Mr Dunne's private room was so solidly built that not a sound would emanate. Not even Barrow's unbridled bellows. Ollenu had pressed each ear against the cursed door many a time and never caught a single word.

'Heard him leave, sir, and caught a view of him through the window.' Ollenu waited, and as that remark garnered no response he risked probing further. 'I would never eavesdrop, of course, sir. I have seen him a few times this month and assumed something serious was afoot, requiring your esteemed service?'

'Now and then I forget how much you observe and absorb, Mr Ollenu.' Dunne folded his arms behind his back and turned to face his clerk. 'You will be away from Broad Street for a time, but July is never a busy month so we shall get by. You are to work on a fraud project for Mr Barrow. You will be at his disposal for a few months, the exact length of time is uncertain.'

Ollenu expelled a breath, grateful to be relieved of the necessity to deliver bad tidings to his expectant spouse. His burgeoning professional life remained alive and well.

From the corridor came a crash of porcelain, followed by the familiar voices of barristers Tredinnick and Verney lamenting about spilt tea.

'Of course I shall be happy to assist Mr Barrow in whatever way required, sir.'

'You may have to work even harder than usual for your wage, Mr Ollenu.'

'I will do so and expect no extra wage, sir.' A sudden thought crossed the apprentice's mind. 'Of course, I would expect no reduction in wage either?'

'No, of course not. I would absolutely not allow it.' Jacob Dunne fell silent again and resumed his obsession with the wall parchment. He leaned in and ran a mottled finger over the West Indies. 'Yes, I daresay, we shall all miss you.'

Ollenu stared at the bookshelves he often dusted. He would miss Mr Dunne, too. Although not so much the two advocates who availed themselves of his legal skills with barely a generous word. Many late evenings were spent in this room studying cases and statutes, drafting defences, burning candles until the wicks floated on the wax-filled saucers like boats on a lake.

'Tomorrow you shall meet Ruben Ashby at Bristol dock and he will explain all to you. Ashby is Barrow's star agent, a bright fellow, though a bit pious for my sensibilities, always waving a Bible about.'

'And I need to meet this Ruben Ashby at Bristol dock, sir, not at the Paxten building on Corn Street?'

'Pack a strong trunk, Mr Ollenu. You are going to Jamaica.'

Ollenu raised an eyebrow. 'The island of Jamaica?'

'The very same Jamaica, our finest colony of all.'

Ollenu stroked his smooth chin. Jamaica. An island where gunfire, cat-o-nine tails, and worse, ensured the resentful compliance of the enslaved. Where distressed voices of tortured people were ignored, and violent uprisings brutally contained in the name of King and country.

'Sir, I do not believe a visit to that colony would be safe for me at this time.'

'You will be perfectly safe, Mr Ollenu, thanks to your letter of introduction that Ashby carries. Mr Barrow and I prepared the language, and chief watchman Heskel Wilkins endorsed it.'

The law clerk sighed in resignation, painfully aware that even as a man born free, he did not have freedom to pick and choose his tasks. The odyssey to Jamaica was a foregone conclusion and Jacob Dunne could not be deterred.

'You have mastered your training and are a far better apprentice than any certified attorney who has ever instructed me.' Dunne kept his eyes averted. 'Mr Barrow is acquainted with many attorneys who need barristers of my calibre and he will send plenty of business our way if you impress him. He speaks highly of you, and says that you would be ideal for the task.'

Mr Dunne was not known for making jokes – not funny ones, in any event – and Ollenu was unsure whether to smile or maintain a sober appearance. 'Mr Barrow speaks highly of *me*, sir?'

'I am not quiet in my praise of you on the streets of Bristol and the halls of society.' Dunne rocked back on his heels. 'And it is not to flatter you, Mr Ollenu. The goal is always to acquire business from the doubtful.'

'I understand, sir.' Ollenu failed an attempt to suppress anxiety from creeping into his voice. 'But what of Coreen and the children? I cannot abandon my dependants to fend for themselves.'

'They shall be well taken care of, I assure you. Your ship sets sail for Kingston Harbour at eight in the morning. Estimated sailing time is six weeks. Make a good showing in Jamaica and our practice shall be so full of briefs we'll have to reject them. I believe rejecting work from some of the more arrogant attorneys will be your pleasure.'

'I must agree that would be most satisfying,' Ollenu conceded with reluctance. 'And Mr Ashby is content to leave his own family?'

'Ashby is a bachelor of near fifty years of age, though I do understand he has the care of his two nephews since his sister's untimely death and raised them to almost grown men. Recently dispatched them to Cambridge University, I'm told.'

'I see. Sir, what exact matter requires us to voyage to Jamaica without delay?'

'Mr Barrow suspects that a substantial fraud is to be perpetrated by a few of his devious clients, and he is determined that you and Ashby prevent it. Three clients travelled to Jamaica at different times and never returned. One of the missing is my tailor Henry Penket. Do you remember him?'

'Of course, sir. Mr Penket is missing? I assumed he had moved elsewhere in England.'

'He left Bristol for Jamaica near three years ago, and his tailor shop is now adorned with cobwebs.'

'And your bespoke suits have never been as fine as they once were.' Ollenu noted that Dunne did not smile as expected, averting his eyes again, instead. 'Why does Mr

Barrow believe the missing people plan to defraud him, sir?'

'Mr Ashby is better versed than I, Mr Ollenu. He will acquaint you with the details.'

Ollenu fixed his eyes on his familiar corner. 'May I take a few books with me to continue my studies, sir?'

'You will have plenty of fascinating reading material, Mr Ollenu.' Mr Dunne pointed at the books he had placed on the table. 'As neither you nor Ruben Ashby has ever been to Jamaica, I thought those two mighty tomes would be of great use to you. The works of Sir Hans Sloane. They contain great insight into his journey to, and life experienced in, Jamaica.'

Ollenu's tone turned cynical. 'Ah, the gone but never forgotten Sloane. Born 1660, died 1753, physician, philosopher, philanthropist and frequent traveller, who in death has spawned more fawning praise and undeserved adoration than in life.'

'Do try and restrain yourself from such inelegant commentary in polite company, Mr Ollenu,' Jacob Dunne admonished him. 'Sir Hans is strongly admired by most Englishmen.'

'You are quite correct, sir.'

'Much consideration was given to your qualities before the decision was made to send you to Jamaica. You are intelligent and loyal, a keen interrogator, an exceptional recorder of facts and a fine creator of fiction. Brazen and indisputably odd sometimes, you will admit, but we all have our little idiosyncrasies. I trust you, Mr Ollenu.'

Ollenu bowed as pride built up in his chest. 'I will uphold the values and standards of these chambers at all times. You never need doubt that, Mr Dunne.'

To Ollenu's surprise, Jacob Dunne did something he had never done before. He patted the younger man on both shoulders, holding on to them for rather longer than necessary.

'I know, Mr Ollenu, I know. Remember, you are far more intelligent than half the men you encounter on a daily basis. Whatever titles they carry, they are merely men. You have my full support. Do not stand down unless common sense tells you it is prudent to do so.' He blinked, seemingly embarrassed at this fatherly show and headed for the door. 'Carry on… With the shelves, man, not the pantomime acting. And do remember to attribute my chosen insults correctly in the future.'

'Yes, sir.'

'Bon voyage.'

CHAPTER 2

Ollenu would not allow the night before his voyage to be a sombre affair for his family. They had finished eating and remained seated at the dining table. Putting on his best performance, he maintained a cheerful expression as he told them how exciting the sea would be. Although he gave not a hint of any misgivings, he noticed the occasional frown appear on Coreen's face. She could read him well. It was one of the reasons why he adored her so, and had done from the first day they met.

A genuine smile crept over his face as he recalled that fortuitous day. She was admiring colourful ribbons hanging in the window of a dressmaker's shop. A tall, graceful Black woman in a pretty blue dress, with her plaited hair tied back neatly. He crossed the street and stood next to her, pretending an interest in ribbons, as he secretly observed her and wondered what to say. For probably the first time in his life he was lost for words. Weeks later, when they had established a happy twosome, she admitted to having noticed him watching her through a reflection in the glass, and saw him cross the road. As he had taken too long to speak, she had walked on, and purposely dropped her handkerchief so that he could return it to her and introduce himself.

That had been a decade ago. Now they had a family, Fayola, eight years, and Ekon, four years. In the new year, another baby would arrive.

His pleasant reverie was broken as Ekon's spinning top came to a halt when it hit his foot. Ollenu knelt on the stone floor and spun the top himself, while the children crouched beside him and cheered.

'This toy will be most useful to me on my journey, Ekon. I shall play with it often. Thank you for your thoughtful gift.'

As Ollenu began to stand up, Fayola pushed him back down to his knees. 'No, Papa wait. You must wear my gift.'

'Very well, but it will fall off.'

'Let me try, Papa,' she insisted.

Ollenu locked eyes with Coreen who merely grinned and shrugged her shoulders. She could not help him with this matter. As predicted, the bright pink bow refused to stay on Ollenu's head as the quarter inch of hair was insufficient to secure it. Fayola tucked the bow behind her father's ear instead and chuckled.

'What? You would have me walk the streets of Jamaica with this on?'

'You are pretty!' said Fayola.

'Yes, Papa!' Ekon laughed.

'You are supposed to side with me, my son. You would not be seen with a pink bow behind *your* ear.' Ollenu smiled. 'Thank you my dear daughter, but I shall not wear it on my ear. I will keep it in the pocket of my jacket so that it remains close to my heart.'

'That would be a good place, Papa.'

Fayola kissed his cheek and he hugged her. As he rose with her in his arms, he inhaled her warm scent and had to restrain himself from clasping her too tightly and frightening her.

'You both need bed now, it is late.'

'Not yet, Papa,' said Ekon.

Ollenu took Ekon's hand. 'Yes, now, young man. And see that you obey your mother when I am away.' Gently, he pulled the little boy to him and cradled his shoulder. 'I rely on you to look after your mama and sister. You will be sure to do that?'

'Yes, Papa. I will make sure they cook and wash plates and sweep the house.'

Coreen placed her hands on her hips and tilted her head. Ollenu grinned at her and patted Ekon's head. 'Mama will manage all those things without your instruction, son. You must help carry potatoes from the grocer, and gather small pieces of chopped wood to keep everybody warm. At night, you must check that all candles are out, before everyone goes to bed.'

'Yes, Papa,' said Ekon proudly.

Ollenu led the children to their room and tucked them in bed.

Later, as Coreen helped him pack his trunk, he handed her his yellow silk cravat, a gift she had given to him not long after their wedding day.

'You take your cravat with you?' she said with a smile.

'Of course. Tuck it in right there, at the side.'

Coreen folded it with care and followed his request. 'You wear it on special occasions. You believe opportunity will arise to wear it in Jamaica?'

'Perhaps not, dear wife.' Ollenu kissed her cheek. 'But it belongs in my possession at all times.'

'This journey sounds dangerous, Isaiah,' said Coreen. 'Jamaica is not a country for us. If you become separated from this Ruben Ashby, and people do not believe you are who you claim to be, they could treat you terribly. That is my fear for you.'

Ollenu had lied to his wife in the past. Small lies. When she asked him if he thought a blouse she adored was splendid, he agreed that it was, although he did not admire the sleeves. And when her first attempt at baking rye bread meant he had to chew more thoroughly than usual, he had assured her he enjoyed more solid bread. The lie about to leave his lips was not small, but Coreen was with child and he would say nothing to endanger that happy state of affairs.

'I have no fear and you need not fear, beloved. Nothing terrible will affect me, whether Mr Ashby is with me or not. You are fond of Jacob Dunne, are you not? And you know he much admires you. He has made great efforts to ensure that I am formally introduced to Jamaican society and welcomed.'

'I do believe Mr Dunne is a good man,' said Coreen.

'You wait and see.' Ollenu stood behind his wife and placed his palms on her growing middle. His chin rested on her shoulder. 'I shall return to meet our new baby and we shall celebrate a successful mission.'

'I look forward to that day, Isaiah.' Coreen rubbed his arms. 'May it come soon.'

The bedroom door creaked and Ollenu raised his head. Fayola and Ekon entered. Both appeared bashful and hesitant as they silently approached the couple.

Ollenu squeezed Coreen's hand and groaned. 'Oh, to have children who do as they are told.'

'They are Ollenu's,' said Coreen with a smile. 'They were born to do what they believe is right, no matter the consequence.'

'You two are my fault, I am reliably informed,' said Ollenụ indulgently. 'All right, you may come.'

The children shrieked in delight as Ollenu scooped them up and placed them under the sheets. The bed would barely hold four of them, but it would have to do. Many months could pass before he saw any of them again. For tonight, they were all exactly where they belonged.

CHAPTER 3

From his horse-drawn carriage, Ollenu looked out at the majestic passenger ship floating on the cloudy waters of Bristol Harbour, secured to the mooring bollards. The dock teemed with stevedores, merchants and passengers, all jostling for space amidst an array of wooden crates and barrels. A mixed odour of fresh tobacco and raw sugar infiltrated the salty sea air.

Ollenu's emotions fluctuated between optimism and disquiet, but leaned closer to disquiet as the carriage slowed to a halt. The city was experiencing a golden age of wealth and superior commerce, benefitting handsomely from the notorious triangular trade. Bristol ships were known to travel to the Guinea coast carrying mixed cargoes of goods: textiles, beads, trinkets, muskets, pistols, and more, some partly of local manufacture. In Guinea the inanimate goods were off-loaded, replaced by terrified individuals who were taken across the Atlantic to be traded in various islands. Leaving behind the destroyed dreams of thousands of Africans, the ships returned to Bristol with cargoes of sugar, rum, cotton, timber, tobacco and rice.

Ollenu leapt down from the carriage and patted the bay-coloured animal as it nuzzled him appreciatively. The coachman, a miserable character, stood with his rough hand extended and a sneer on his face. Ollenu gave a pointed look at the inside of the carriage then at the man, who merely stared at him, unmoving. Ollenu climbed back into the carriage and dragged out his large trunk before dusting his hands off on his breeches.

'Thank you, sir,' said Ollenu as he paid the driver.

'I wish you a pleasant voyage.' The man's flat tone did not match the sentiment and Ollenu suspected that, for other Englishmen, the statement was delivered with sincerity.

Ollenu watched him depart. Many Bristol citizens were accustomed to seeing people of a darker complexion in the area. True, some Black people were servants, but he had met those gainfully engaged as carpenters, gardeners, weavers and musicians. Despite this, there was always one disgruntled person who thought Ollenu's rightful place was on his knees shining the dirty shoes of his betters.

As footfall on the dock increased, Ollenu dragged his trunk to one side, out of the way of the crewmen, and climbed on top. He wore knee-high boots of fine leather, tailored breeches, a long brown coat covering a crisp white shirt, and carried a certain air about him. His eyes searched the crowd of men and women of all heights and sizes, trying in vain to find a face that matched Mr Dunne's description of Ruben Ashby. When his scalp began to overheat, Ollenu removed his tall hat and tapped it against his thigh as he inspected the populace.

'Mr Ashby!' he shouted. His voice turned many a head, but no one claimed the name. 'Mr Ashby!'

''Ere you, get down orf that luggage!' demanded a longshoreman. 'Damage anything in it an ye'll be whipped.'

'Thank you for your concern. The contents are not so delicate that they will come to any harm.'

'Ooh, 'ear 'im. All lah-di-dah!'

'Drag him orf!'

As the three approached, Ollenu removed his coat, folded it and placed it neatly on a corner of the trunk. He leapt down and rolled up his shirt sleeves to the elbows. 'Gentlemen, I really wish you would not, but if you insist—'

The show of firm muscle had a dampening effect on the seamen's enthusiasm for violence. They hesitated as if trying to decide who should be the first challenger. No one seemed particularly eager to take a swing at the sturdy figure.

'One at a time, men.' Ollenu raised his fists. 'No surreptitious group rush.'

'Mr Ollenu!' A slightly built man bore through the masses, his pale face flushed beneath his hat. Much shorter than Ollenu, his brown hair hung loosely about his ears, almost touching his shoulders, and wayward greying strands lay on his furrowed forehead. Behind him a young, pink-faced lad struggled with a portmanteau.

'Ah, Mr Ashby, I take it?' Ollenu bowed at the aggressive gang. 'I regret you were not able to demonstrate your undeniable strengths, gentlemen. That said, my clothes have, at the very least, been saved unwanted dishevelment and I do hate to appear less than pristine.'

'Is this prattling Negro with ye?' asked a deckhand of Ashby.

'Apparently so,' said Ashby and waved travel tickets at the man. 'His passage is fully paid for as evidenced right here. Is he causing a disturbance?'

' 'E *is* a disturbance.'

'*He* is right here,' said Ollenu. 'And he can speak.'

'Without reserve, it appears,' said Ashby with a frown.

Ollenu stared at Ashby unblinkingly until the investigator turned and beckoned at the youth with the luggage. 'Come along now, lad, do not rest it on the ground. You need to earn your wage.'

As Ollenu studied Ashby a feeling of discomfort crept over him. The first inclination of this man was to assume his companion was wrong, rather than assess the situation and draw reasonable inference. He must be one of those Christians who saw only what they wanted to see and heard only what was music to their ears. It was important that the two get along, but vital that Ashby not entertain feelings of superiority towards him.

'Honoured to make your acquaintance, Mr Ashby.' Ollenu offered his hand.

'Yes, quite.' Ashby held out a limp hand. When it was released he flexed each digit as if in pain. 'I assume everyone calls you Ollie?'

'No. Though should you choose to do so I will call you Ashie or even Rubie. Rubie. The name of a fragrant damsel, no?'

A pink tint crept onto Ashby's cheeks. 'Are all men from Jacob Dunne's chambers so free with their words, Mr Ollenu?'

'I do not know, Mr Ashby, yet what power has a voice that is silent?'

'Your trunk is rather large, I see.' Ashby scowled and eyed Ollenu's fulsome attire. 'I suppose it is laden with clothes?'

'It also contains two books that Mr Dunne insists will be of great advantage to us on our voyage. I must say, your luggage seems particularly small for a few months away from home.'

'Mine contains all the wares I need. I believe there are plenty of charwomen on the island to wash and clean my clothes.'

'Charwomen?' Ollenu held the investigator in a steely gaze. 'I do not believe they go by that mild description, Mr Ashby.'

Ashby clicked his tongue. 'Shall we proceed, Mr Ollenu?'

Ollenu hoisted his trunk onto his shoulder, turned and strode ahead, carving a haphazard route through bodies and cargo that blocked the path to the ship. Ashby ushered the youth along as they followed in the course Ollenu cleared for them. Suddenly, Ollenu came to such an abrupt halt that his entourage almost walked straight into his back. He downed his luggage and clenched his fists. Eyes closed he mumbled, 'Blink twice but you cannot deny that which is certain to the eye.'

'What on earth does that mean, Mr Ollenu?' asked Ashby.

'Nothing, forgive me,' said Ollenu. 'When my nerves are sure to be sorely tested, my natural tendency is to deliver a line of rhyme.'

'You are nervous about sailing? I find you here in your finest dress, taunting angry men, composed and ready to battle, but it is the calm blue sea that makes you nervous?'

'I have never sailed before, yet that is not what burdens me.'

'Then what is it, man?'

'I find it hard to explain, even to myself. A certain fire in my veins, a feeling that something unfortunate will occur, whether to myself or to someone else. This strange feeling last overwhelmed me a month ago as I sat in Brandon Hill park. The following day, in that exact spot, a stone wall collapsed without warning, killed one, and injured passers-by.'

'There are no stone walls on the ship,' said Ashby in a scornful tone. 'Your fire veins are obviously not the precursor to the end of the world, so I will not distress myself.'

'This particular surge was different, more powerful than ever before.' Ollenu wiped his damp forehead with the back of his hand. 'Something is wrong.'

'I never heard of such an unfortunate condition,' said Ashby. 'Perchance, my fate shall be to lose a buckle from my shoe?'

'I hope that is the extent of your distress, Mr Ashby.'

'Let us go aboard,' said Ashby impatiently. 'The *Isabella* awaits.'

'That name,' whispered Ollenu. The name was emblazoned on the vessel's stern and he had been too distracted to notice it. 'The *Isabella* took my ancestors from Africa to Philadelphia in 1684. The tales told in the old journals are not good tales. I have seen drawings of how they travelled, trussed and bound as animals, with no access to sunlight. Their horror is unthinkable.'

'Near a hundred years ago,' said Ashby. 'That *Isabella* is long scuttled or sunk. Besides, this ship takes goods and paying passengers only, rather than trade in mankind. Whatever unease you feel is greatly misplaced. We must board.'

Ollenu inhaled deeply and retrieved his trunk. 'Very well.' Quite possibly nothing frightful would befall them in the future, and the strong sensation he experienced seconds ago was the affliction leaving his body once and for all.

Ashby removed the portmanteau handle from the urchin's fingers and tossed a coin in his direction. The boy's lips set firm, and his face puckered in anger.

'A rotten farthing! Next time carry yer own rubbish, mister!' he shouted, waving a puny fist. 'Tis the likes of ye why me grandda says we'll all be in the poorhouse!' Having said his piece, he turned and dived through the crowd.

'Well!' said Ashby.

Ollenu fought to keep the corners of his lips from curling.

'You believe I am a skinflint, Mr Ollenu?'

Ollenu watched his travel partner struggle under the weight of his luggage and decided that the man was both miserly and a weakling. 'On the contrary, Mr Ashby,' he said lightly. 'I understand you are an exceptional researcher and a numbers man, as well as a devout Christian. I am sure you agreed a fair wage for the work beforehand, so there should be no complaints about remuneration from either side?'

Ashby turned his attention elsewhere. 'Well, ah, that must be Captain Garrick.'

They proceeded up the ramp behind a slow queue of passengers. Ollenu assessed what was to be his new home on the water, noting that the ship was even larger than she appeared from a distance. Giant off-white sails billowed in the strong breeze, held firm to the masts by a confused-looking melee of thick ropes. A small rowing boat was attached to the ship's portside and he assumed that a matching craft was on the starboard side.

Captain Garrick, a stout middle-aged man, wore his rank in blue neckcloth and grey kersey jacket that flapped about his silk stockings, a world away from his crew's coarse canvas and woollen legwear. Briefly, he looked at the tickets presented by Ashby and welcomed him on board with a warm handshake. Casting an intense glare at Ollenu, he inclined his head slightly.

'You're side by side. Tucker here will show you to your quarters, down that way. Take Mr Ashby's trunk, Tucker.'

Thin young Tucker seemed intoxicated as he marched ahead of them, humming and unconcerned with the whereabouts of his passengers.

'You have a letter authorising our mission, I understand?' said Ollenu as they walked.

Ashby patted a folded yellowing paper barely visible from his breast pocket. 'Yes, a sealed letter right here.'

'May I read the content of the letter?'

'It is to be presented to our host Mr Neville Kershaw, who is the deputy provost marshal. I am informed we have authority to access all possible records, and administrators of such records, as may help facilitate our quest to find the disappeared clients.'

'I wish to read for myself.'

'Not even I have read it, Mr Ollenu. Sealed by our chief watchman under the direction of Edward Barrow, having taken instruction from your own magnanimous supervisor. It would be unfortunate were we to dock in Kingston and not be availed a formal welcome for wont of provenance. I will apprise you of all that Mr Barrow and I discussed.'

They descended a steep wooden ladder and continued down a narrow passage. Tucker placed Ashby's trunk at his feet and pointed at the cabins. 'That's yours sir, and that's 'is.'

'Er, thank you.' Ashby hugged his case to his chest and squeezed past Tucker's outstretched palm.

Ollenu wondered if the man was obtuse or indeed a skinflint. Paying the less fortunate for their labours was clearly not a fashionable expedience for Ashby or one he was prepared to contemplate. Ollenu dug into his pocket and handed Tucker tuppence. The sailor took the coin without a word of thanks and turned away.

The two men inspected one another's cabins. Identical rooms supplied with basic, yet comfortable, furnishings. In each, a single feather mattress bed with cotton sheets and woolly pillows, full length mirror mounted against the wall panels, chest of drawers with brass handles and ornamental brass shields, matching writing desk with two candles and a camphor oil lamp. After agreeing to reunite on deck later, they parted company.

Ollenu tossed his coat onto his trunk and placed his hat on top. Through the porthole, he watched the final passengers board. For the first time ever he was leaving England, the country of his birth, leaving the family he loved and colleagues he admired. No more brisk walks beside the River Avon. No more trips with the children to the apothecary to select sweet treats from jars. No more fascinating cases at the court of assizes with Jacob Dunne, possibly for many months.

Ollenu shook off his morose thoughts and headed to the door, noting that, although it closed fast, it could not be bolted from the inside or locked from either side. The two rooms were not identical after all. Anyone could enter and leave his room at will. He frowned and made his way back through the ship up the ladder and onto the deck. As he emerged, a plump overdressed woman called out to him.

'I say, you! Carry this, boy!'

Ollenu smiled and nodded politely. 'Madam, I would be happy to assist were you to ask courteously, otherwise I cannot oblige.'

'You cannot oblige?' The woman's voice went up a decibel. 'You do not know your role?'

'Whatever the merits of my assignment, I assure you it does not include shouldering the burdens of strangers, madam. I bid you good day.'

'You travel as one of us? How is this allowed?'

'Fret not, madam,' whispered Ollenu. 'I promised my good lady wife that I would never lay my head on another woman's pillow.'

With her rolled up parasol clutched to her prominent chest, the woman shrank backwards. 'How dare you!'

A short round man approached her, his pink face anxious. 'What is it, Hannah dear?'

Ashby wandered over to them and directed a look of apprehension at the law clerk. 'What mischief have you brought about, Mr Ollenu?'

Ollenu maintained his composure. It would not do to snap at his colleague although the judgemental man deserved nothing less. 'I made an appearance, Mr Ashby. If such is a mischief.'

The affronted passenger grasped her husband's arm. 'Oh, Nigel, you should hear what he said to me!'

The man glared at Ollenu through thick spectacles that made his eyes appear as pinpricks. He removed his spectacles, polished them with a handkerchief, blew noisily into said cloth, then returned his eyewear above his nose. 'What did that animal say?' he demanded, waving a small fist in Ollenu's direction. 'I shall avenge your honour!'

The woman looked at her tiny husband then lingered on Ollenu before returning to her spouse. 'Oh, never mind, Nigel,' she mumbled. 'My honour does not need avenging.' She gave Ollenu a final appraisal and walked away, nose in the air, pulling her outraged husband along with her.

'You appear flustered, Mr Ollenu, a look I would not have guessed you capable of. You fear she will report you to the captain?'

'Worse than that, I fear she will report to my cabin.' Ollenu stared into the eyes of the investigator, whose expression was one of incredulity.

'Why, I do believe you are quite serious!'

'I am indeed serious and my door has no lock or bolt. We should consider an exchange of rooms, Mr Ashby?'

'No we shall not. We shall not do that at all.'

'This is not the first time I have encountered one such as she,' insisted Ollenu, 'and I fear it will not be the last.'

'Come now, Mr Ollenu, I suspect that you are irresistible only to your own shadow.'

'I tell you when I see that glint in their eyes I know exactly what comes next. I am forbidden fruit and they pretend to be horrified, but are tempted. I do not give in to temptation for I know it would be my end.'

'You have my sympathy,' said Ashby drily.

'You are lucky; you enjoy life without the company of women.'

'That is some assumption, Mr Ollenu.' Ashby's tone was cold. 'Although I am unwed, I have come close to marrying before. It was not to be.'

Ollenu hoped the man would satisfy his extreme curiosity, but it was clear from Ashby's expression that nothing more would be said on the subject of marriage. There was time yet to discover who Ruben Ashby really was, though first impressions left a lot to be desired.

For weeks they journeyed on high seas with a strong wind behind them. Captain Garrick suggested they would make Jamaica in less than six weeks, delighting Ollenu. The sea was not as thrilling as sea-faring tales had led him to believe. There was nothing alluring about being adrift on bottomless water for weeks on end. With not even a tree to look upon, the monotony was both exhausting and nauseating. Some passengers fell sick and spent many hours hanging their pale heads over the ship's sides.

With nowhere to stretch his long legs, Ollenu resorted to running on the spot every morning in his cabin. He longed for the streets of Bristol where he could dart here and there to his heart's content. His arms he strengthened by lying prone in a horizontal position and raising his body multiple times until his joints ached. On occasions, he ventured out onto the upper deck and strode back and forth across the boards earning curious stares. Ashby refused to accompany him for such exercise, viewing it as unnecessary stress that his mature frame could do without. Initially, a few passengers were civil enough to engage Ollenu in small talk, but even they grew weary of it. Soon the daily conversations grew shorter and shorter, descended into a good day or good evening, and finally became a mere head nod.

The crew were by no means dour, and ritually engaged in dice and cards. Ashby surprised Ollenu by participating willingly in the crewmen's activities and proved quite proficient at cards. Ollenu's participation in their games came with well-hidden reluctance. He laughed boisterously when the crew did, cursed when they did, slammed down a fist when they did. One thing he refused to do as they did was cheat, for he knew that his cheating would be unacceptable even if he lost the game. Similarly, to play fairly and win would be the ultimate insult to this rancorous bunch, so Ollenu chose to be an accomplished loser instead, exposing his hand carelessly. All of the sea dogs carried sharp cutlasses in their scabbards and were prone to brandish them when provoked, even in jest. Ollenu had no desire to test anyone's temperament, preferring to praise the unworthy winners for their tact and ingenuity.

In accordance with his newly adopted persona, Ollenu pretended to sip ale from his full tankard before exchanging it with the empty vessel of the nearest drunkard. On the occasions that he and Ashby made eye contact, the insurance man acknowledged the deceit and raised his tankard towards Ollenu. Ashby sank pint after pint of the tepid brew and never appeared drunk. It astounded Ollenu that such a small man could imbibe so much alcohol, yet remain upright and intelligible.

Ashby caught Ollenu watching him and said, 'You find the taste disagreeable?'

'Not at all, Mr Ashby. I am told by those I love, and who I want to continue to love me, that my disposition is not blameless when I drink alcohol, so I surrendered the habit. I do not recall seeing you drink much water. On a journey such as this water is essential for your constitution.'

'There is a reason the good Lord turned water into wine, Mr Ollenu.'

'Into wine, not ale.'

'Do I detect a hint of snobbery? Surely not?'

'I am merely trying to prevent you from becoming one of those passengers who are either clutching their stomachs or precariously balancing their heads over the rails.'

'Your concern is touching,' said Ashby snidely, 'but my insides are soothed by ale, not repulsed by it.'

Ollenu left it at that. Neither Ashby nor anyone else ever enquired about his personal comfort. He had seen and heard workers doing chores for Ashby and fellow passengers, replenishing water and cleaning their cabins. The snub did not bother him as he feared what the workers would do to his belongings in the name of cleaning. Besides, it gave him an excuse to wander the *Isabella*'s interior daily, pretending to be in search of basic necessities as he took the opportunity to check every space.

On one occasion, his nose led him to the large kitchen stocked with barrels of salted pork, beef and cheese. Containers also held dried fruit, dried peas, spices, flour and salt. The absence of flavour in the meals served, indicated that the various spice containers were never opened, to say nothing of being added to any recipe. Kegs of fresh water were plentiful and Ollenu helped himself when necessary, using a tankard to scoop the liquid.

On this day, he left the kitchen and ventured past the captain's spacious quarters. The door was partly open and Ollenu pushed it further. Inside was a wide four-poster bed with hand-carved finials, and fine silk sheets covered the mattress. Velvet-cushioned chairs were arranged on each side of the bed. Frilly lace curtains covered the portholes. Silver tableware and china were stacked on a tall mahogany bureau alongside many bottles of alcohol. It all seemed somewhat gaudy to Ollenu. Still, a man living a wild life on the open seas deserved some comfort, despite the appearance of excess to land dwellers.

At the end of the dark passageway Ollenu came upon a hatch with steps he had not noticed before. He listened and waited before making his way down, way below what he thought was bottom deck. There he found a single cabin. The door was wide open, barely clinging to its frame, and the air smelled fetid as if the space had not been cleaned in weeks. The area held two torn Bibles, as well as ornaments and trinkets that he recognised as Coromantee in origin. Sheets of osnaburg covered the floor and there was no sign of proper bedding. Two wooden chairs in dire states of disrepair lay upturned.

Everything told Ollenu that this room belonged to African men, yet he had never encountered any Black men either above deck or below. What fate had befallen them? Two centuries had passed since the Cartwright decision indicated there was no legal basis for enslavement under English law. The Somerset case concluded only a month ago, and was reported as ending enslavement, yet Lord Mansfield had given such a narrow judgement that already the enslavers had declared they planned to ignore his words. Ollenu had no doubt that on this ship, far from the courts of England, these rough men would have no regard for legal pronouncements that interfered with their plans.

The hairs rose on Ollenu's neck and he backed out of the room, unable to erase a creeping suspicion that something diabolical had happened to the cabin's occupants. This could be what his last rhyme had foretold. His thoughts ran amok as he made his way back up to the sunlight.

'Ah, I wondered what had become of you,' said Ashby when Ollenu reappeared on deck.

'And I wondered if the only people missing are your clients from Bristol.'

'Whatever do you mean by that?'

'Never mind, Mr Ashby.'

'I can assure you Edward Barrow does not view our missing clients as a joke. He is a man who smiles at the thought of money coming *in* to Paxten coffers, not going out.'

'Then Mr Barrow should engage in another line of business, for surely it is the nature of insurance that you take in money and you pay it out?'

'Ah, but only to deserving beneficiaries. Not to those who seek to deceive. If you wish to see Mr Barrow explode, mention the name Giles Mullings. That devious man stayed hidden for near a decade, and Mr Barrow paid his family hundreds of pounds in death benefits. Three years later he discovered that Mullings was living up north in Stockton, and that his newly enriched family had joined him there. Poor Mr Barrow has not managed to reclaim a single penny through the assizes.'

'My, how those jowls must have shaken, eyes protruded and complexion turned tomato red.'

Ashby narrowed his eyes momentarily, and then he appeared to reconsider a response to Ollenu's tart remark. 'Those who plot and scheme to remain hidden in Jamaica for years on end, pretending to be dead, shall not be allowed to take advantage of us.'

'I will do my utmost to assist you in your worthy goal.'

'I am much obliged,' said Ashby. 'Now, let us see what meal is to be served.'

CHAPTER 4

Early one morning Ashby opened his cabin door to Ollenu's knock.

'Good mor—'

'Ah, Mr Ollenu, right on time to further test your knowledge of our clients.'

'I am beginning to feel as if I were the biographer engaged to write their life stories,' murmured Ollenu as he entered. 'Soon I shall know more about them than I do my own kin.'

Ashby gathered his paperwork from the chest of drawers, and turned to see his visitor standing on his head, his polished shoes almost touching the low ceiling. 'What on earth are you doing?'

'Encouraging the growth of my hair, Mr Ashby. I will need hair to fight the harsh sun, and find that wigs irritate my scalp. Horsehair wigs, I ask you. Nothing that flicks so close to an animal's rump should go anywhere near one's head. Do not be surprised if I have lustrous tresses when we finally make land.'

'Is this a joke, Mr Ollenu?'

'It is.' Ollenu sprang upright with a degree of elegance and straightened his clothes. 'I should have known better than to test it on the mirthless.'

Ashby pulled out a chair and sat facing his guest. 'I may yet come to understand your humour. Appreciate it, even.'

Ollenu accepted a document from Ashby's outstretched hand and barely looked at it, before turning it face down. Names, dates, descriptions, things he was tired off. He took a seat on a stool opposite the man.

'The tailor, Henry Penket, left England in April 1769. His absence is a little over three years, and yet his absence causes Mr Barrow such consternation. I fail to see why.'

'I tell you some of these people plan their schemes very thoroughly, Mr Ollenu. His wife began the first chain of the duplicity when she reported him missing. She claims her husband was meant to be away for only nine months. As Mr Barrow says, the clock ticks faster than any of us is keen to witness. Before you blink, the required seven years has passed, and a demand for death benefits arrives. A crafty husband, and an even craftier wife.'

Ollenu rubbed his chin thoughtfully. 'Playing devil's advocate here for a moment—'

'I disapprove of that expression,' grumbled Ashby. 'The Devil has more than enough advocates.'

'Is it beyond the realms of possibility that Mrs Penket is indeed concerned at not having heard from her husband? She last saw him when she waved farewell as he boarded his ship. After that, she received only two letters and sufficient money to last her and their daughter a year.'

'Not once has she mentioned such concerns to any of the watchmen, and the chief watchman received no report from her,' said Ashby. 'The level of underhandedness some people will sink to knows no bounds. The Lord hates a lying tongue.'

Ollenu appeared unconvinced. 'I will keep an open mind as to Mr Penket's behaviour. His wife I do not know, but he was always most polite when he came to measure Jacob Dunne or deliver his suits. It surprises me to hear he is now thought to be a scoundrel.'

'We shall see,' said Ashby. 'Mr Barrow has known this business for far longer than I. He will do anything within his power to prevent being cheated.'

Ollenu sighed. 'Except undertake a long and trying voyage to Jamaica.'

'I'll have you know he is an extremely busy and industrious man, Mr Ollenu.'

'How can it be that the determined Mr Barrow did not commence the search for Mrs Clare Sandie years ago? She is now six years missing.'

'We were only informed of her situation quite recently. Her husband did report her missing to the watchmen over the years. We're told he twice went to Jamaica to search for her, though I believe it more probable the voyage was to reacquaint himself with her in secret. Then he returned to Bristol to keep up the ruse.'

'It seems odd that Mr Sandie, or any man, would marry a young woman less than half his age, and allow her to live apart from him for so long in order to improve their finances,' said Ollenu. 'Their finances appear quite satisfactory.'

'Their brewhouse has no debts, but it is not that profitable an endeavour. You forget that payment to the husband will be substantial with the inclusion of her insured jewels. Even Penket and Dantry insured fine items of jewellery.'

'Oh yes, one must never forget the jewels,' said Ollenu. 'As for Dantry, the ironmonger, may I offer my honest opinion?'

'As unguarded as you tend to be, Mr Ollenu, I would expect nothing less. That man has not been seen for four years.'

'Frankly, I see little reason why Dantry is on your list at all. His wife predeceased him. His business partner continues to successfully manage the ironmonger's in his absence, and did not report him missing. He is estranged from his son who makes no claim, and cannot, being a mere nine years of age.'

'Presently, no guardian has sought to claim on his son's behalf. In a few years they will do so, and we shall be prepared to resist any such claim. Together with the jewellery, we are talking about hundreds of pounds, Mr Ollenu. Enough to buy a homestead and horses and live quite comfortably for many years – in England or in Jamaica.'

Ollenu stroked his chin. 'For the three to remain unseen and unheard of for years suggests they are aided by sympathetic residents.'

'I am prepared to question anyone who may be assisting in the deception, be they merchants or planters or general business folk,' said Ashby. 'I intend to obtain information no matter how painstaking it may be to draw it from their lips.'

'I am quite used to questioning those who hold secret information, so I will do my utmost best with the settlers,' said Ollenu. He sensed a sudden coolness in his companion as their eyes met. 'What concerns you, Mr Ashby? You doubt that I have the skills or intelligence to conduct such interrogations?'

'My dear Mr Ollenu.' Ashby's tone did not indicate to Ollenu that he found him dear at all. 'You do not believe that the questioning of white people in Jamaica is a task for you?'

'Do not be absurd, sir. I must question any man or woman who may help us in our goal to find the missing.' Ollenu frowned. 'Such a task is not new to me. It is what I trained for, and if I must admit it myself, what I excel in.'

'No, Mr Ollenu. I will interview the English men and women; you will interview your brethren.'

'My brethren?'

'The Negroes, the slaves,' said Ashby. 'Surely you were aware that this is the reason you were chosen to accompany me to Jamaica? Why Mr Barrow specifically sought out your services?'

As the insulting words sank in, Ollenu's temples throbbed and his throat grew dry.

Ashby continued, 'The Black people are your domain, Mr Ollenu. You are at liberty to interrogate them at will, even administer corporal punishment if you wish.'

Ollenu clenched his fists so tightly his knuckles strained, and he was unaware that a guttural sound emitted from his throat.

Ashby appeared to realise he had gone too far and took a step back. He spoke so hastily he tripped over his words. 'Of course, if I believe there is something you can add to my questioning of the residents, I will be sure to consult you, Mr Ollenu. You are, after all, a gainfully employed man of law. I have already shared factual information about the missing three, but I will also ensure you are apprised of all knowledge I am able to gather on the island.' Ashby eyed him furtively. 'You see I do not seek to deny your talents at all?'

'To do so would be most unwise, Mr Ashby.'

Not for the first time, Ollenu wished with all fervour that he had pushed open Jacob Dunne's door and listened in on the conversations with Edward Barrow.

'Yes, well, now we understand our positions a little better.' Ashby gave a nervous smile. 'It is good to clear the air; do you not agree?'

'We must hope the air does not become foggy again.'

Ollenu stared long and hard at Ashby, until the investigator rose and walked the few paces to a table. There he reached for a wine bottle before changing his mind. Instead, he poured himself a glass of water which he gulped down and prepared to pour another glass.

'You will take water, Mr Ollenu?'

'Thank you, no.'

Ollenu placed his hands behind his head, closed his eyes and leaned back against the bulkhead. Thoughts of his growing family usually soothed his temper. A vision of Coreen lovingly folding his cravat and tucking it into his trunk filled his mind. He saw Ekon spinning his top, the little boy's face warm with delight, and a giggling Fayola determined to place the pink bow over his ear. He sighed deeply and opened his eyes.

'A voice tells me that this mission is an act of sure folly for me.'

'I believe you worry unduly. Consider it an adventure.'

'I have never seen myself as an adventurer. I was born in Bristol and so were my parents. My grandparents were Coromantee – Akan speakers – and I believe they were brought to England as young free people. I have never ventured further north than Manchester and never further south than Bodmin, never even sat in a moored boat.'

'You could have defied Jacob Dunne and stayed in Bristol.'

'And thrown away everything I trained and worked five years for? Jamaica was not an offer, it was an order, however politely gauged. Whilst it is true no one forced me aboard the ship, Mr Ashby, I assure you I had no choice.'

'How came you to work for Mr Dunne?'

'I wrote a commentary on one of his court cases under the fictitious name of John Dougal and sent it to the newspapers. They would never in a hundred years have published it had they guessed the author's identity. Back then, I worked with an iron merchant and was bored out of my mind. When I learned that Mr Dunne favoured my article, I awaited him outside court and confessed to being the creator.'

Ollenu cleared his throat and changed his tone so as to impersonate Jacob Dunne. 'You? You wrote this? Prove it, sir. So I wrote more commentaries over the following weeks, even dared to criticise him in one piece. Jacob Dunne visited my supervisor and I thought I would be banished from Bristol, but the next instant, I found myself situated at his law office on Broad Street. Over the years I have read and studied and been examined on my knowledge to an extent I believe no one else has ever been subjected to, but I surprised them all – Dunne, Verney, Tredinnick, his fellow partners. I've been interrogated by judges, each trying to perplex me or find some reason to question my character, but in each and every situation I have prevailed.'

'And soon you will complete the notable move from articled clerk to attorney?'

'In two more years and once I have sworn an oath.' Ollenu spoke with pride. 'It could have taken only five years, but I believe it is the undue pressure of his two partners to constantly test and try me that led Mr Dunne to settle on seven years.'

'Seven years training? Goodness! That is how long Jacob toiled for to gain Rachel and was deceived into marrying Leah.'

'Who? Jacob Dunne's wife is Margaret.'

'Different Jacob, Mr Ollenu. Book of Genesis.' Ashby shook his head as if he wished he had not spoken. 'Old Testament story, never mind.'

'I am not a scripture devotee.' Ollenu tilted his head towards the muffled sound of crewmen's voices. 'Had I stayed in England I would not wager on my chances of securing worthwhile occupation ever again. I have washed dishes, lugged coal, beat iron – despite having a good education. The extra two years' apprenticeship is nothing. When it is over I shall add esquire to my name and my family will be more comfortable.'

'You have two children and one to be delivered, I understand?'

'Yes. Fayola is eight. She will ask for me constantly as she is my eager little shadow. The boy, Ekon, is four and clings as a limpet to his mother's ankles. He always finds laughter even when Coreen chastises him. She will be quite tired.'

'Women do tend to get on with daily matters I find, tired or not.'

'That they do.' Ollenu's expression was thoughtful as if filled with memories. 'I hope she remains in good health as the baby grows and is not troubled by anyone.'

'You are undoubtedly a highly favoured apprentice, Mr Ollenu,' said Ashby. 'I am quite sure Jacob Dunne will not allow any misfortune to befall your household in your absence.'

'I only wish—' Ollenu could not finish his sentence. A familiar surge started in his body, slowly at first, before racing through his veins. He closed his eyes and shuddered, then leapt up. 'Secure your paperwork, Mr Ashby. Something happens above.' Ollenu headed straight for the cabin door without waiting for his colleague.

Ashby tucked the bundle of papers into a drawer, and ran behind Ollenu, whose long strides carried him along at a good pace. Ollenu scaled the ladder with ease, pulled Ashby up onto the deck, then lost his footing. Both men collapsed onto the wooden boards. The crew and some passengers watched the pair in a mixture of confusion and astonishment.

'Whatever ails you?' asked Captain Garrick.

Ashby climbed to his feet and brushed off his clothes. 'We were apparently in much need of some fresh air.'

Ollenu hurried towards the portside rails and stared out at the never-ending blue seas glinting under a blazing sun. He closed his eyes, inhaled and gripped the wooden rails.

'What is it, man?' asked Ashby.

Ollenu's eyes sprung open. 'By sea or by sky, someone will die.'

'You there, what the devil are you doing?' The captain descended on Ollenu, who clutched the rail more tightly and turned to face him.

'Draw back!' shouted Ollenu.

'Draw back? I am captain of this ship, Negro. Do not instruct me!'

'Mr Ashby hold tight to the nearest rope,' warned Ollenu.

Ashby's eyes moved from Captain Garrick to Ollenu and back to the captain again. He shifted his feet in discomfort and made no move to grasp any part of the ship's structure.

The captain's lips curled into a sneer. 'And why should he hold tight to anything, you arrogant Negro? What do you see happening? The sky is blue, the sea is calm. Unless you plan to start hopping about doing a war dance?'

The crewmen laughed and made deprecatory noises, hopping from foot to foot, and patting their lips. The passengers, too, tittered, men openly, women behind embroidered fans.

'My profound apologies, Captain Garrick,' said Ashby. 'Mr Ollenu experiences one of his most trying episodes. He will regain his senses directly.'

Ollenu turned slightly and met Ashby's eyes, staring daggers at him. 'Let it not be said that I made no attempt to try and prevent your death.'

The ship suddenly lurched and swayed from side to side catching everyone except Ollenu off guard. Crates and barrels shifted as the immense vessel rocked violently. A long whistling noise brought with it a whirlwind, testing the strength of the canvas sails. Ashby was propelled forward and ended up grasping the rail beside Ollenu. His pale face turned a muddy grey as blood drained away below his skin. Some sailors grabbed the ropes. Those who were too late smashed into their fellow men.

'Whoa! Steady on *Isabella*!'

'Hold her still!'

'All passengers head down below!' ordered Captain Garrick as he struggled to keep his balance.

The passengers' attempt to obey was thwarted by the ship's motion, and their voices rose in screams and shrieks as they skidded in different directions. Some crawled on hands and knees as they struggled to the hatch. Crewmen assisted the lucky few onto the ladder and they disappeared at speed into the body of the vessel.

'The weather has gone mad!' said Ashby as he clung in desperation to a rope.

'The weather is perfectly sane,' said Ollenu. 'This ship is the issue.'

'You are surely not resurrecting your theory that the *Isabella* is some kind of menace?' Ashby's hair slashed across his face scratching his eyes and he threw his head back in pain.

Both the winds and rocking motion came to a sudden stop and the *Isabella* regained her natural position. The sailors laughed nervously as they released themselves from various points of safety. Captain Garrick wiped his brow with a large handkerchief and exhaled his relief as he surveyed the deck.

'Thank God for that,' he breathed. 'Must be some fantastic weather anomaly. Never seen such a thing in all my days.'

'Captain, the danger is not past,' said Ollenu. 'You must all go below deck at once. I must stay here.'

'Giving orders again, eh?' The captain squared his shoulders, but had to look upwards to meet the law clerk's eyes. 'It was but an unusual squall and is now over. The chronometer is barely moved. A few things will have overturned below, but we can right all the furniture and clean up any spills.'

'You speak of spilling water,' said Ollenu. 'I foresee the spilling of blood.'

'Captain Garrick is correct, Mr Ollenu.' Ashby removed a small gold cross from his pocket and kissed it. 'That did give us a tremendous scare, but it is ended. The crew are well equipped to withstand all eventualities that befall us at sea and we all are whole.'

Ollenu ran to the far end of the deck and stared down into the deep. Shadowy shapes rippled the water and clumps of what appeared to be thick seaweed floated towards the surface. Ashby approached Ollenu warily and stared down into the sea.

The figures of Black mermaids emerged from the water, torsos covered with golden armour, thick dread-locked hair held in golden clips. Their lower bodies were fish scales of shimmering orange ending in long tails. Every sylph matched Ollenu's complexion, though their round lavender eyes were twice the size of his.

'What the devil are those?' shouted one crewman.

'God knows! Some kind of giant octopuses!'

The *Isabella* rocked again, more precariously this time, as over a dozen mermaids surrounded the ship and sank long fingernails into the hull. In unison they swung powerful tails, whipping up large waves that crashed over the ship. One desperate sailor could hang on no longer and was flung screaming from the high mast into the sea. As he resurfaced, a mermaid lunged at him, and the pair plunged beneath the water. A group of mermaids pulled even more aggressively on the ship. Their movement sent more crewmen skidding all over the deck, arms thrashing in search of any stable object.

'The ancestors of murdered slaves, cast away at sea, have returned to avenge their loss,' said Ollenu as he struggled to maintain his balance. 'I need to connect with them.'

'Murdered slaves?' said Ashby. 'From over a hundred years ago?'

'A century is but a brief occurrence in time for those who are deceased. They will take the *Isabella* down and all souls aboard her.'

The ship lurched at a sharp angle and another sailor screamed as he soared from high mast to inky sea. He emerged briefly, palms beating the waters, pleading for rescue. Two sylphs appeared on either side of him, seized his upper arms and disappeared below the surface with their captive.

Ashby pulled a small worn Bible from his pocket, closed his eyes and mumbled a short prayer before tucking it away again close to his heart.

Ollenu lost his grip at his safe spot. He fell to the deck and grabbed a piece of rope, pulling himself towards the nearest rail. A dislodged barrel crashed into his shoulder, and he grimaced with pain, but maintained a firm grip. A wave of salty water covered his head and he spat as he struggled to climb over the rail. Soon he was dangling on the rope ladder, hovering above the sea. Water burned his eyes, and for a few moments he could not open them. Fighting against the pain, he blinked and held the gaze of a mermaid. She wore more gold in her hair than her clan, and gold bracelets lined her smooth ebony arms.

'I beg of you, let the ship go!' shouted Ollenu. 'I promise you, my sister, this *Isabella* is not a slave ship.'

The mermaid stared at him, her enlarged eyes roving his strong features. Ollenu tensed as she touched his face, running her cool fingers down his cheek. She screeched and he flinched as the sharp noise, incomparable with any sound he had ever heard before, assaulted his ears.

Ollenu's grip on the rope ladder weakened, and in desperation he tried again. 'This is not the *Isabella* that took our people and caused so much misery, I swear. Do not seize the ship!'

The mermaid turned her head and screeched at the top of her lungs. Almost immediately her followers stopped pulling at the vessel, and it floated back to its original upright position. The mermaids swam from their various positions and gathered in front of their leader on the portside. Ollenu's heart palpitated wildly as he came under the direct scrutiny of many lavender eyes.

'Thank you for showing mercy, sisters.' He lifted a weak hand and waved at them. 'Thank you.'

The leader flipped her tail, dived beneath the depths, and was gone, followed by her faithful clan. He watched as slivers of shimmering orange and gold eventually disappeared into the deep. His energy spent, Ollenu pressed his forehead against the rope rungs and barely held on.

Ashby leaned over the rail then gestured to the crewmen. 'Captain, your men must pull him up!'

'Haul the brute up,' ordered Captain Garrick. 'I intend to have the pleasure of throwing him back over myself.'

The men obeyed the order and Ollenu soon lay panting on the deck. 'The mermaids came for revenge, captain. They believe this to be a ship of kidnappers and murderers,' he said.

'I've seen mermaids, and they do not resemble those coal-coloured creatures.' Captain Garrick stared at Ollenu and spoke in a threatening tone. 'And why would anyone believe we carry kidnappers and murderers on board? You did this, Negro. You summoned those creatures from the sea with your witchcraft. You spoke to them. You roused them to do this!'

Some of the shaken passengers had returned to the deck. All appeared pale and distraught. They spoke in murmurs, their usual confidence extinguished by fear. A few of the crewmen sought to reassure them that all was well. Ollenu remained conscious that all eyes were following him, and none were kind eyes. In fact, many were cruel eyes.

'This was not my doing, captain. I have no power of witchcraft and would do nothing to endanger this vessel.' Ollenu silently tried to communicate his terror to Ashby, a man who was willing to believe the worst of him. For his life to be spared he needed this sanctimonious man now more than ever, but in Ashby's face he saw only an expression of disdain and knew he could not rely on him. 'Mr Ashby, we are on a joint quest, lest you forget. What reason could I have to do this?'

Ashby's sharp eyes flickered below his brow as he appeared to reconsider his approach to the situation. 'Captain Garrick, Mr Ollenu tried to halt the attack and you witnessed him succeed. This man is an ordinary passenger and should face no repercussions.'

'Ordinary?' The captain glared at Ashby. 'He spoke to those dark things. I saw him. You saw him.'

'I am not entirely sure what I witnessed, captain,' said Ashby. 'We all saw that the ship was relieved of its distress once he did speak.'

'Two of my men are dead,' said the captain waving a fist in Ollenu's face.

'Two,' replied Ollenu in a low voice. 'Only two.'

Captain Garrick stormed away and shouted commands to his men. They ran to all sides of the deck righting the overturned containers, realigning the masts and checking for damages. The captain picked up a mop and threw it in Ollenu's direction with a hateful glare. 'You helped create this unholy mess, brute, you clean it.'

Ollenu rolled up his long sleeves and picked up the mop. 'Certainly, captain.' He bent double, hiding the spark of rage in his eyes, and went about his task with gusto.

'You do not object to this filthy work, Mr Ollenu?' said Ashby.

'The deck is wet and needs attention, Mr Ashby. I cannot swim thousands of miles. In the circumstances, it behoves me to do exactly as the captain orders.'

CHAPTER 5

Much later, when Ollenu retreated to his cabin, he found the room in considerable disarray. Silently, he gathered the candles and lamp, pushed the drawers into place and set the chairs upright. Ashby, who Ollenu assumed must have been next door listening out for his return, now appeared under the doorframe and watched his activities, but offered no assistance.

With a worn shirt Ollenu wiped spots of water from his leather trunk, grateful that moisture could not penetrate the tough exterior. The sounds of sea shanties, sung off-tune with raucous voice, echoed from above. Ollenu sank onto the corner of his bed and ignored the immediate spread of water from his soaked clothes to the sheets.

'Hear how the crewmen sing.' Staring at his own wet footprints, he spoke with bitterness. 'When they sing of glories on the high seas my heart is unmoved. When they sing wicked songs, of hanging Negro men and lying with Negro women, my heart burns.'

'They are mere words, Mr Ollenu.'

'They are not mere words.' Ollenu's head jerked upright and his eyes raked over Ashby. 'They are daggers meant to humiliate, to stir fear in those they regard as different and inferior. I wonder what it takes to change a man from peaceable citizen to cruel oppressor.'

'One cannot blame them for being terrified of what they witnessed,' said Ashby in a cold tone. 'They try to calm their nerves in the best way they know how, and singing about dominance is what works for them.'

'Leave me. I beg of you, leave me be.'

'You shall not dismiss me, Mr Ollenu.' Ashby stepped into the cabin and slammed the door behind him. 'The captain is right; you are not ordinary. I did see those strange fish creatures, though I did not care to admit it. Two sailors are dead and, but for the Lord's mercies, we all would have died. You predicted those deaths, you saw danger from sea or sky.'

'I held a certain conviction that death would occur. I knew not who would die, or that mermaids would surface and claim anyone.'

'Those odd creatures were mermaids?'

'Mermaids are not a thing of fairy tales, Mr Ashby. For centuries, both sea farers and the land bound speak of them.'

'Of course I have heard tell of mermaids, but none is described as looking like… that.'

'Like, that?'

'They resemble you,' Ashby flushed, 'except, well… somewhat, grotesque. And you call them sisters.'

'You are a true Englishman, Mr Ashby. You shy from any living thing with an appearance that does not suit your sensibilities. You imagine such beings as beasts and grotesques, frightening beings to be conquered and tamed. You vilify what you do not understand. And, yes, that includes people.'

'You do me a great disservice,' said Ashby.

'The truth when painful is most unwelcome, Mr Ashby. You and I do not look alike. Am I to understand you would not call me your brother?'

'You digress, Mr Ollenu, and I will not be distracted.'

Ollenu massaged his temples, and whispered. 'You did not see the filth-stained cabin way down below.'

'What was that?'

'I said, I could not see a thing from way down below.' Ollenu shook his head. 'I know not why any of this happened.'

'Almighty God, hold me in thy hands.' Ashby pressed his back against the door and briefly closed his eyes. 'I should have cleaved to the monotony of life: work, church, walks, things that rational people do. Instead, here I am, halfway across the world in the company of a fortune teller whose powers are askew.'

'It is heart-warming to hear your favourable opinion of me.'

'Mr Ollenu, I too am in fear for my life.'

Ollenu chose not to respond. They could not share the same fears. His personal trepidation was caused by the many two-legged beings with whom he spent days and nights in close proximity. Armed crewmen, an angry captain, and even this man who stood watching him could, in the blink of an eye, bring about his end. If they wished to prolong his misery they could enslave and humiliate him beforehand. He lay on his back and stared up at the tiny droplets of water clinging to the wooden boards.

'Two years ago, I met a young deckhand at Bristol docks, a man who was once enslaved. He went by the name of Gustuvas Vassa, although his birth name was Olaudah Equiano.'

Ashby turned a chair backwards and sat with his chin resting on the rim. 'You worked as a deckhand? I cannot craft a vision of you in that lowly situation.'

'Never. Sometimes I would go sit by the shore and dream of a better future. That is when I happened upon him. Vassa was a tough man who had been through a lot in his twenty-five years. He was much younger than I, and the tales he had to tell... Aged eleven he was stolen with his sister from his Igbo village. The very idea of it, Mr Ashby. At home tending the house whilst his parents went out to toil and these merchants of misery stole him.'

'A dreadful ordeal, I'm sure.'

'That was only the beginning, for he was destined to be passed from pillar to post. As a youth he lived as the property of a Royal Navy captain, and later that of a Quaker. He changed owners many times over the years and found his sister again once, until they were separated for good. He and over two hundred unwilling Africans were taken across the Atlantic to Barbados. Later he was sent on to the colony of Virginia.' Ollenu rubbed his chest as if to calm an unseen pain. 'Vassa explained how he was named and renamed many times; as Olaudah at birth, as Michael on the slave ship that brought him to Virginia, as Jacob by his first owner.'

'What terrible confusion for all involved,' said Ashby. 'A foolish thing to do.'

'I agree. And then came the fourth name. A Royal Navy lieutenant bought him in Virginia in 1754 and renamed him Gustuvas Vassa. Poor boy. By such time he preferred to be called Jacob and resisted the name change for as long as he was able to withstand the beatings meted out for disobedience. In the end he gave in and accepted the name Gustuvas and now everyone calls him

Gus. It was Gus who first told me stories of the African mermaids.'

'He no longer resides in Bristol?'

'I do not know.' Ollenu shook his head. 'I hope one day he and I shall meet again, and that he is able to reclaim his birth name. Gus both fascinated and frightened me with his doleful tales. I encouraged him to write a memoir, but I know not whether he ever will.' Ollenu's tone became hard and his fingers clenched. 'I changed my name on paper to John Dougal for a frivolous reason, because I wanted my scholarly writings in a newspaper, not because I was beaten or whipped or forced to, to save my life. That is how different my life has fared compared to my enslaved brothers. At times, in my bleakest hours, I dream enslavement befalls me. It could happen, right here on this ship. My identity and freedom stolen from me by men who see themselves as superior and having dominion over me.'

'It shall not come to pass, Mr Ollenu,' insisted Ashby.

Ollenu sat up and stared at him. 'Your voice, as difficult as it was for you to raise it, was all that prevented such outcome this day.'

Ashby shifted in discomfort and fixed his attention on the porthole. 'I have shared quiet words with the captain. No one will imprison you or enslave you or change your name, and they certainly will not throw you overboard. Our destination is near and when we disembark we will be safely received by virtue of our introduction letter.'

With his trust for white men at its lowest ebb, Ollenu felt driven by an overwhelming need to read that very letter, and vowed to discover its location.

'Thank you, Mr Ashby, I am encouraged by your words.' It was early evening, and light outside, but Ollenu yawned and stretched in dramatic fashion so that his shirt sleeves strained against sinewy upper arms. 'Forgive me, I am rather exhausted. You will excuse me whilst I rest my eyes for a minute or two?'

'Yes, of course. I must investigate what damage affects my cabin, tidy up somewhat. We should dine with our fellow passengers on the top deck shortly. Salt pork and beans are to be served.'

'Do Christians not refrain from eating pork? Something about cloven hooves?'

'It tastes pleasing, Mr Ollenu.'

'That is a truth.'

'Now, I shall change out of these damp clothes before dinner,' said Ashby. 'I suggest you do the same.'

Ollenu shut his eyes until he heard the thud of the door. Creeping to the adjoining wall, he listened to the sound of Ashby moving in his cabin. His fingernails ground into his palms as he waited for the investigator to leave. Soon, Ashby's door clicked and his footsteps faded away.

Ollenu looked up and down the dark corridor then quickly headed for Ashby's cabin. He paused, fingers on the door handle, listening. The only sounds to be heard were the creaking of the ship and the jarring laughter of drunken seamen.

The door squeaked as he pushed it open and he winced, even though the sound could not have carried more than a few yards. Inside the cabin, wet clothes were strewn in a corner instead of on the hooks nailed to the wall for that purpose. He flicked through papers on the desk, before turning to the drawers and was disappointed to find only cravats and handkerchiefs. One of Ashby's dinner jackets lay on top of his portmanteau. Ollenu threw it on the chair and hauled the container onto the bed. With his ears cocked for sound, he undid the strap.

Suddenly, there were footsteps. Quiet footsteps, not purposeful footsteps, the movement of someone who wished to avoid discovery. As he stared at the door handle his heart pounded hard against his chest. The creaky sound went past the door and he allowed his breath to gradually escape. A cabin door closed and he assumed it was the one on the far side of his own.

The clothes and shoes inside Ashby's case were in disarray, as if he packed it by tossing each item from a distance. Ollenu searched in the jumble and found nothing. The breast pockets of Ashby's jacket were also empty and when Ollenu returned the portmanteau to its rightful spot, he neglected to place the jacket on top. Kneeling down, he surveyed the area beneath the bed, and found only a pair of fine shoes.

More footsteps came. Carefree footsteps this time, not surreptitious ones. Ollenu lay flat and tried to crawl beneath the bed, but the bedstead was not high enough off the floor to accommodate his muscular structure. He curled up in a fetal position and pulled Ashby's wet jacket over his body. The door opened and Ashby hummed as he entered.

'Ah, that one is more suitable.'

Ollenu could see only Ashby's feet as they moved in the direction of the mirror. He watched as they turned from side to side as if Ashby was checking his reflection. As the door closed again Ollenu exhaled, tossed off the musty jacket, and craned his ears. Ashby's voice filtered in from the corridor.

'Good day,' said Ashby pleasantly. 'Mrs Felton, I do believe? Hannah Felton, wife of Nigel?'

'Yes, that is right, Mr Ashby. Good day.'

Ollenu recognised the agitated voice as the woman who had called him 'boy'. That same voice was often heard on deck, but he had succeeded in his pledge to avoid any further encounters with its owner.

'You must forgive me, Mrs Felton. I should have thanked you long ago for your kind tolerance in not reporting Mr Ollenu to the captain.'

'Oh, no, Mr Ashby, do not apologise. I had forgotten the incident entirely.'

A brief silence ensued before Ashby added, 'That cabin is Mr Ollenu's. I do believe yours is at the far end of this passageway. It is difficult to gain a clear sense of direction on a ship; would you not agree?'

'Good heavens, yes! As soon as I entered I was confused by the absence of my possessions.'

'Do not fret yourself, Mrs Felton. I trust that Mr Ollenu was most polite to you?'

'Thankfully, the cabin is quite empty and I made haste to leave again. You are so right; I really must learn my bearings. Good day, again, sir.'

'I wish you the most pleasant of days, madam.'

Only one set of footsteps disappeared. Ollenu lay flat again, praying that Ashby would leave too. The cabin door re-opened and Ollenu groaned inwardly as Ashby's boots headed in his direction.

'Were I not famished, Mr Ollenu, I would sit at my desk and read, simply to see how much time would elapse before you revealed yourself.'

Ollenu mustered the best guiltless expression that he could and clambered to his feet.

Through gritted teeth Ashby said, 'May I assist you, sir?'

'Mr Ashby, I— Thank you for setting Mrs Felton on the right path.'

The outraged man's eyes swept the room. 'My jacket is not where I left it. Why has it moved?' He waited for an answer that was not forthcoming. 'This is not about you hiding from some poor infatuated woman searching for – how was it you titled yourself? – forbidden fruit? Explain yourself man, your verbosity usually knows no bounds.'

'My letter of introduction, I should read it before arriving in Jamaica.'

'*Your* letter? I was not asked to hand you any letter and I shall not.'

'Every man wishes to hold his fate in his own hands, however impossible that might be. I cannot be alone in that belief, Mr Ashby. It is dangerous to allow another full control of one's destiny.'

'Well, Mr Isaiah Ollenu, Esquire to be,' sneered Ashby. 'You survived your fate for near five weeks. I will not break the seal to satisfy your overactive curiosity.'

'You mock me.' Ollenu approached him, eyes blazing, fists clenched. 'You who have no need for concern that people may judge you by your skin and not by what is written on any paper? You who can travel anywhere on land or sea without being pursued by mistrust? You who is asked questions about me, even when I stand right beside you and can answer for myself?'

'I refuse to let you turn this unforgiveable intrusion back onto me, Mr Ollenu. That is not the behaviour of an English gentleman and you will not guilt me into accepting your presence in my personal quarters. The letter is safe and you shall not have it. Do I make myself clear?'

'Perfectly.' Ollenu bowed slightly, his jaw tight. 'My life is in your hands.'

'That stretches my responsibility rather too far, though I would agree that out of us two, I am the safer pair of hands. Throughout this journey I have found no reason to lock my cabin door, but I shall be sure to do so in future.'

'You have that privilege, I do not. Everyone is free to come and go from my room and, unless they are careless with my belongings, I remain none the wiser.'

'Really, you do make such a fuss, man,' snapped Ashby. 'What is in your cabin that you worry so about a lock?'

'Let me see. For one, Isaiah Ollenu, Esquire to be.'

'Mrs Felton lost her way, Mr Ollenu.'

'Lost her way after all these weeks? You cannot truly believe that?'

'I do.' Ashby retrieved his dinner jacket and as he attempted to slide into it one sleeve turned inside out. He cursed and tried to shrug himself out of his predicament. Ollenu reached out to assist him, but Ashby moved aside and readjusted it himself. 'We must go on deck before Captain Garrick worries we stay down here planning a mutiny.'

'I will change into suitable attire and join you presently,' said Ollenu.

When they left the cabin, Ashby slammed the door shut and made a noisy show of locking it, rocking the handle.

Ollenu entered his own cabin and donned a smart dining suit and fine gloves knowing he would be under even closer scrutiny by captain and crew. He hoped his gentlemanly appearance would constrain any notions they entertained about mistreatment. In his experience, people who found courage to molest the poorly attired, were reluctant to confront the well-dressed. This harrowing journey would end in a few days. Until then, he must appear as human as possible to people who considered him less than.

CHAPTER 6

Edward Barrow pulled his Beaver hat down over his brow and scurried along the busy Bristol street. He passed a flower seller advertising colourful nosegays in a woven hand basket that had seen better days. Avoiding the butcher's eye, he slunk beneath the brass cow head hung above windows where carcasses of ducks, hares and pheasants dangled. The tobacconist on the corner, a place where Barrow made regular visits, would not see his custom today. In the glassmaker's window a beautiful array of flint glass tableware, vases and bottles of all shapes and colours, caught his eye, and he fought against the distraction.

Ahead swung the flag of the Pacific Tavern and he concentrated on reaching that destination. With a furtive glance over both shoulders he entered the establishment. Inside the four dark walls were ale-stained tables that rarely met a clean cloth, chairs damaged by wood-boring insects, and an odour of stale bodies, alcohol and tobacco. The women who served watery ale were as loud and unrestrained as their male customers. Indeed, the buxom woman who ran the tavern was of unsavoury status and rumoured to be more of a madam. What went on upstairs behind closed doors was not for the ears or eyes of the gentry and Barrow had no wish to enquire.

Making his way through the disreputable clientele, Barrow placed his ample behind on a wooden stool. He hated this place with a passion and would not be seen dead in it at the best of times, preferring instead the warmer environment of The Llandoger Trow, his favourite watering hole. Even the smaller Hatchet Inn or The Rummer were better localities, where men of his stature in society were commonly to be found. Today he did not wish to be seen by men of substance. He pulled the hat down further and pretended to be engrossed in his *Bristol Post*.

Barrow checked his pocket watch and hoped his associate would not be delayed. As he looked towards the pub entrance, two thin young boys entered. The smaller boy was at least ten years old. The taller one appeared to be a few years older, yet whiskerless.

A barmaid approached, swinging her hips from side to side. 'Get you a drink, love?' She lowered her generous bosom close to Barrow's face and delivered a winsome smile.

The businessman responded with the weakest of tilts to his lips and drew back. 'Not at the moment, thank you.' He pointed to the boys. 'Children should not be loose in this place.'

'Here you, get out and take your dumb brother with you. There'll be no begging in here today. Go on, clear off!' She turned back to Barrow. 'Sorry, sir, they're always here begging. The little one's deaf and dumb, but the bigger one hears perfectly well. Are you sure you won't take ale?'

'We shall see when my acquaintance arrives,' said Barrow irritably.

As soon as she turned her back, the boys, who had ignored her command, came forward, their threadbare caps held out to Barrow.

'Did you not hear to leave, you unlicked cubs?' said Barrow. 'Leave! Go to school. And if school does not take your fancy there is work aplenty at iron foundries and sugar distilleries.'

The boys continued their meek and mournful journey through the bar. The tall frame of a man appeared at the door and suddenly the mood became muted. He stooped as he entered, and the only customers who spoke or laughed were those whose backs were to the door. The swift sobriety of their compatriots encouraged them to take notice. Thereafter, a range of eyes, brown, green and blue, followed the new arrival. The visitor removed his hat and waved it in the air.

'As you were, good folk of Bristol!' he bellowed and strode towards Barrow.

'All hail chief watchman Wilkins!' shouted a drunkard.

'Long may he watch over us!'

A huge cheer went up, tankards clanked and the merriment resumed, having barely missed a step.

'Good day Edward, sorry to keep you waiting.' Heskel Wilkins was a gangling, clean-shaven man with bulbous eyes that gave him the appearance of being permanently stunned. The officer took a seat opposite Barrow, placed his hat on a spare chair and stretched his long legs away from the table. 'Good day Milly, I'll have a pint of your finest ale. What for you, Edward?'

'Not for me, thank you, Heskel.' Barrow clicked his fingers to gain the woman's attention and gestured in the direction of the urchins. 'Those boys are back again, madam.'

'Ooh! I tell you.' She pointed at the door. 'Clear off you two!'

The boys waved their hands at each other in an exaggerated manner and one left. The younger boy lowered his eyes pitifully and sat at a table beside Barrow. Tears flowed down his soot-stained face and he twisted a torn cap in his dirty hands.

'Poor wee mite. Can't be too hard on him. He has a rough life.' The barmaid lifted his chin. 'Look at me. I'll fetch you bread and beef dripping, is that all right?'

The boy nodded eagerly.

'Say thank you,' said Wilkins.

'Oh, he can't, poor thing,' she said. 'The one that can talk is outside. Gone to harass my customers before they come through the door, I daresay. I'll be back with your ale in an instant, sir.'

The watchman grinned and slapped the barmaid on her bottom. She giggled and sashayed away to fill the order. The young boy dried his tears and pushed his upturned cap towards the officer.

'You're being fed. What more do you want, boy? A night in a cage?'

Barrow shook his head in disgust. 'I fear for the coins in my pockets with these ne'er-do-wells everywhere.'

'Oh, they're not that bad in here. What takes place in the Pacific Tavern stays within these walls, that's why it befits me well and should befit you too.' Wilkins tapped the table three times as he spoke.

Barrow acknowledged the signal by reaching into his breast pocket and removing a small cotton package. He tucked it under the watchman's hat.

Wilkins beamed. 'Soon it will be over, eh, Edward?'

'A few months more, Heskel.' Barrow lowered his voice and surveyed the drinkers. They were heavily involved in their own boisterous conversations and seemed unaware of his presence. 'The *Isabella* sailed for the West Indies over five weeks ago and those two fools will arrive in Jamaica any day now. Pair of idiots are convinced they're searching for deceitful clients and their expensive baubles.'

'I pray they reach dry land hale and hearty,' said Wilkins. 'The wife has her eye on a lovely cottage. Got a thatched roof and wisteria growing up the white walls and a luscious green lawn.'

'Soon she will sew expensive heavy curtains to hang,' said Barrow.

The watchman cast his eyes all over the tavern. 'As much as I do believe Neville Kershaw is a principled fellow, I sometimes wonder if he'll be inclined to forget our pact and betray us.'

'Kershaw is well aware of what can happen to people who cross me,' snarled Barrow. 'Were he even mindful of doing so, I do believe he would resist such temptation. His sole duty is to use the expertise of Ruben Ashby and the Negro Ollenu, to find Mr Francis Dantry, no matter who dies along the way. He is to be well rewarded for his time and trouble.'

'I suppose you're right.' The watchman nodded thoughtfully. 'You suppose they'll find your other two clients as well?'

'Knowing Ashby, he'll discover the whereabouts of Henry Penket and Clare Sandie too, but I have little concern for them. I shall record them as alive and inform their families. They may continue to reside in Jamaica or do as they wish.' Barrow clenched his teeth. 'However,

Francis Dantry must be made to render my money, every single pound note.'

'Whatever goes on in the minds of the likes of Dantry?' The watchman shook his head. 'Why he thought he could stop sending you your share of the slave takings and nothing would ever come of it is beyond me.'

'He's an utter fool,' said Barrow. 'A thousand pounds arrived with a trusted merchant in Easter of last year. Not a shilling since, and I am informed that all scheduled trades from Africa to Jamaica sailed into Kingston untroubled. No piracy befell them, and none were sunk at sea.'

'How does one make such abundant profit, though?' asked Wilkins. 'Surely other registered merchants wait at the dock to buy cargo from the captains?'

'Undermine the competition, price accordingly, and there's a fortune to be made, Heskel. Those merchants are at a disadvantage. They sell the brutes from their bricks and mortar buildings and bear expenses.' Barrow lowered his voice. 'When I sent Dantry the investment monies, it was under the instruction that all slaves be bought and sold as soon as they land. No feeding, no oiling, no transporting, no sheltering. Last year, there were near eighty such sailings, and over fifty so far this year.'

'You're the sharpest businessman I know, Edward.'

Barrow sat upright and puffed out his chest. 'I expect four thousand pounds from Dantry, and I shall not rest until I get what is mine.'

'A blessed fortune,' said Wilkins. 'Sadly, this is what can befall you when you have to use a go-between such as Dantry. He deserves to die if he won't account for your money, Edward.'

'He deserves to die even when he *does* account for my money, and mark my words he will,' said Barrow. 'I expect

Kershaw to torture it out of him, if necessary, and not accept any excuses.'

The watchman shivered. 'I wouldn't want to be in Dantry's shoes.'

'I already miss Ruben Ashby.' Barrow affected a saddened expression. 'A marvellous head for figures, but such a weaselly thing. I cannot fathom how he stands erect with so little backbone. He would never participate in any violence against Dantry. With regret, I have to accept that Ashby may interfere in our plans and may not return from Jamaica.'

'Was there any difficulty convincing Ashby to go on the mission?'

'There would have been, if he thought the pursuit was for only one person. He would have asked far more questions.' Barrow chuckled. 'I provoked him to ire by pointing out there were three clients pretending to be deceased, and a pandemic of fraud claims would be upon us in years to come, wiping out our profits.'

'Here you are, chief.' The barmaid lowered a tankard, taking care not to dislodge the three flasks balanced on her tray. She eyed Barrow. 'Not thirsty yet, sir?'

Barrow shook his head and grunted under his breath, 'I would have to be at death's door.'

'Tell you what though, Edward, over the years Jacob Dunne has caused a lot of criminals to get off lightly.' The watchman wiped froth from his upper lip with the back of his hand. 'My men have to go out and round up the villains Dunne's convinced the judge to set free. He's by no means my favourite person.'

'Now that he has provided us with a useful and expendable Negro, you should adore him, Heskel.'

Both men laughed.

'Well, Kershaw's been given written authority to do whatever he has to do to bring us satisfaction and so be it.' Wilkins sipped his ale. 'That said, I hear that the Negro, Ollenu, is a clever character and useful in court. Will Dunne not demand compensation for him if he dies?'

'Bah! Who cares about the Negro?' said Barrow. 'Arrogant little fool. I should say, arrogant big fool. An overgrown block of meat taking up space in court with fine Englishmen. I flattered that nincompoop Dunne and he sent his man to die. Anyone giving serious thought to the matter would not send a Black to the colonies.'

'You're not wrong there, Edward.'

'In any case, what is one Negro from another? Dunne can get a new one if he is that desperate to have them.' Barrow grinned. 'I would not put work in the hands of Dunne and any Negro even if my company's very existence depended on it.'

The barmaid lowered a plate in front of the beggar boy. He snatched the chunk of bread, tore it in two and took a large bite.

'Chew before you swallow or it'll choke you,' she warned. 'And don't eat it all, there's plenty to share with your brother.' The boy continued to snatch at the food as if afraid it would be taken away before he finished.

'Need anything else, chief?' The woman winked at Wilkins who smiled back and shook his head.

Barrow glowered at her. 'No, be gone with you woman!'

'Don't have to be so gruff about it, sir! I'll be on me way then.'

'You know, Edward, it sobers me to know that people may soon die. I don't quite have the stomach for taking life myself.' The officer retrieved the money bag from under his hat and slipped it into his jacket pocket. 'I once chased a boy thief who jumped over a wall with a ten-yard drop and broke his neck. Horrible it was. Put me off work for a whole day.'

'But you recovered the goods stolen by the little thief?'

'That I did, sir. Pack of pewter buttons.'

'A worthy endeavour.' Barrow sat back in his chair. From beneath the brim of his hat, he watched in disdain as the beggar boy mopped up oily dripping with a piece of bread. 'I must say, I feel heartened by this little talk, Heskel.'

Wilkins raised his empty tankard. 'If the drink were more tasteful I'd get another and raise it to Neville Kershaw.'

'And to the demise of Francis Dantry.' Barrow smiled. 'Even I would drink to that.'

CHAPTER 7

The island of Jamaica emerged from the sea, a breathtaking mass of rolling green hills that from a distance appeared unoccupied and untouched by anything except plant life. Bathed in a fiery sun, the image was as close to a halo crowning the proud land as it could possibly be.

Ashby was captivated by the scenery and overwhelmed by a sense of wonderment. 'What a beautiful island,' he said.

'Impressive indeed,' breathed Ollenu.

As the *Isabella* drifted closer to the elongated arm of land that formed Kingston Harbour, tiny specks of movement became busy people, and indistinct voices were heard as dockworkers prepared to welcome the vessel.

The passengers eagerly made their way to the stern to witness the berth, and women waved lace handkerchiefs at no one in particular. Relieved travellers openly cheered the sight of land. Ashby quietly thanked the Almighty. He could hardly wait to set foot on dry ground, away from the soporific motion of the ship, and away from bawdy sailors and dull passengers. God knew best and must have suitable plans for him ashore.

A hint of excitement was evident in Ashby's voice. 'I am convinced this is to be a great experience, Mr Ollenu.'

'Oh, you are?' said Ollenu drily.

'Been quiet these past few days, I notice,' said Ashby. 'No shivering, no verses and you have not taken on the facial attributes of a demented ass.'

'Jeer if you must, Mr Ashby.'

The passengers disembarked in a hurried fashion, as if they feared the last person off the ship would be forced to remain on board.

Ollenu viewed the almost empty deck. 'The longer I spent on this ship, the more I came to wonder whether Bristol is a city of largely good men, or whether they are mainly bad men wearing masks of goodness.'

'The former thought is right, Mr Ollenu. Bristol is a city of good men. The *Isabella* is a mere anomaly.'

'She is a solid and trusty ship. The fault is not hers that she is beset with evildoers.'

'Beset with evildoers?' repeated Ashby with a look of incredulity. 'Raucous crew members? Yes. An overbearing captain? Yes. Vainglorious passengers? Yes. But… evildoers?'

Ollenu picked up his trunk and headed towards the ramp. 'Things that are done in the dark will surely come to light.'

'Praise be, that was not an ominous rhyme,' said Ashby.

Captain Garrick stood beside the ramp exchanging brief pleasantries with his departing passengers. His rumshot eyes stayed on Ollenu, who gave a tight nod in his direction as he walked past. Ashby shook the captain's hand, and thanked him for delivering them to the island safely.

'Are we to see you again, Mr Ashby?'

'I have not reserved return passage, captain, so I am uncertain whether I will have the pleasure.'

'Best procure one ticket next time,' said the captain, fixing an icy stare at Ollenu, who had stopped halfway down the walkway to await his companion.

Ashby cast a fleeting look at Ollenu and caught a malevolent expression that left him unsure whether he, or Captain Garrick, was the target of such ire. 'I will give that due thought, captain. Good day to you.'

The harbourmaster welcomed all new arrivals to the island with a wave and polite conversation. As Ashby and Ollenu drew closer, the harbourmaster barely looked at the older man, and studied every inch of the younger from pristine felt hat to silver gilt buckled shoes.

'Welcome to Kingston Harbour, sirs. May Jamaica hold everything you seek.' He pointed a stubby finger in the direction that most of the passengers had taken. 'Carriages await. Stagecoaches, single traps, double traps, wagons, something for everyone.'

A few passengers climbed directly aboard saddled horses. Ox-drawn carts were loaded with their personal effects. Scruffy Black boys dragged luggage twice their size, raising the containers over their heads with trembling limbs. Some of the female passengers experienced difficulty climbing into the carriages, their long dresses proving a hindrance to leg movement. The little boys interlinked their fingers to form a step for the women, who made no effort to remove or clean their shoes before stepping on upturned palms.

Ashby asked various coach drivers if they knew the whereabouts of their host, Neville Kershaw. Most men shrugged their shoulders in a careless fashion and offered no suggestions.

'So we are not to receive a rapturous reception, Mr Ashby,' stated Ollenu.

Ashby sensed self-satisfaction in the statement, as if Ollenu was taking malignant pleasure in his failure to locate their host. The opinionated apprentice clearly planned to be as insufferably forthright on land as he was at sea. 'It is simply a matter of finding the right carriage, Mr Ollenu. I would be obliged if you would keep watch over my baggage.'

Ashby disappeared into the crowd while Ollenu stood guard over their luggage. The wharf gradually became less busy until all new arrivals had been escorted inland and the only people left were dockworkers.

A defeated Ashby returned and announced in as cheery a voice as he could muster, 'It would seem we are temporarily forgotten, Mr Ollenu.'

'Need a carriage, sir?'

Ashby was surprised that the strong voice belonged to an elderly man who he guessed was close to three score and ten. Stooping, he hobbled towards the Bristol men. Under his flat cap snowy white hair protruded and his face was covered in matching whiskers.

'Yes, I believe we do,' said Ashby.

The coach driver peered at them closely. 'You and him, sir?'

'Yes, both of us. We expected to be met by Mr Kershaw, the provost marshal's deputy, but it would appear he is delayed?'

'Wouldn't know about that, sir.' The man shook his head and pointed at a carriage. 'That's me over there, sir.'

Ashby was relieved to see a fully enclosed two-horse carriage, as he wished to be spared from the elements, particularly the penetrating sun.

'Gets dark early here, sir. You'd best go to the nearest inn and try to find Kershaw in the morning. That's if he's about. He's usually to be found in the capital, St Jago de la Vega, and I don't see his coach drivers, Johnson and Mortimer, nowhere. Maybe they was sent to fetch you and tumbled into a cask of rum on the way.' The coachman guffawed, exposing tobacco-stained teeth.

Jaded, and in no mood for humour, Ashby fought to stifle his irritation. 'Is there anywhere in particular you would suggest, my good man?'

'The Braeton Inn, past Half-Way Tree, is a decent place for a night or two. Not expensive and the food's not bad.' He grasped Ashby's portmanteau and tilted his body to one side as he led the way. 'Follow me sirs, we won't be too long.'

The two chestnut-brown stallions nodded their heads eagerly as their master and his passengers approached. 'Calm down, boys.' The driver set down Ashby's portmanteau and brushed dust from near each horse's eyes. 'Got the power of yearlings, these two. Wish that I had the strength of a young'un. My old knees be giving me grief all the time.'

'Here, allow me.' Ollenu heaved both trunks into the carriage and pushed them to the far side.

Once Ashby and Ollenu were seated, the driver closed the carriage door and smiled at Ashby. 'Your slave's well-trained, well-dressed too, sir.' He slowly climbed into the driver's seat and took up the reins, seemingly unaware of the injurious effect of his loose words.

A glance at Ollenu told Ashby that the man was seething. Ashby was relieved that the law clerk did not take it upon himself to reproach the driver. With luck, the too readily offended Ollenu would continue to hold his tongue for the duration of their partnership.

The driver shouted a command and cracked his whip. The carriage set off at such a rapid pace that both passengers were almost thrown from their seats. A startled Ollenu was the first to regain his composure. 'For an elderly man to take charge of such powerful horses and large carriage may not be wise.'

'If he continues to ride in this manner we shall arrive battered and bruised.' Clutching his hat, Ashby hung his head out of the window. 'I say, man, slow down!'

'Sorry, sir! My boys love a good run.'

They journeyed at a comfortable pace through the bustling commercial district of Kingston, past haberdasheries, grocers, blacksmiths and tailors as they headed inland. Along the way they crossed paths with wagons drawn by oxen transporting hogsheads of sugar and rum to the port, their wheels raking up slivers of dust as they rolled by. The carts were attended by Black males wearing jackets and trousers that resembled the material of rough sacks. Their straw hats were held down by string tied beneath their chins. Rather more fashionable clothing was worn by overdressed white ladies and gentlemen, carefree British settlers who strolled the newly cut roads. Ashby waved at a few people who tipped their hats. Ollenu made no acknowledging gestures towards anyone.

'My word. But for the heat, you would conclude we were in England,' said Ashby. 'All these shops. I was of the erroneous belief that Jamaica was rather wild and undeveloped.'

Ollenu delivered a sidelong glance. 'With men running everywhere in loin cloths, raw meat dangling from their lips, and naked women tossed over their shoulders?'

'Projecting your personal hopes and beliefs, Mr Ollenu?'

Silence descended upon the carriage and the only sounds were the rhythmic clip-clopping of horses' hooves. About a mile into the journey, Kingston became less inclined to commerce and residential properties now dominated the vista. The rough roads widened. Many areas replicated parts of the motherland as the settlers did their best to make themselves at home.

The large cottages were made of red brick and wood, with generous garden space and trees on the lawns. Most had wooden louvre windows painted in yellow or pale green. A few had white sash windows and white doors. Rosy-cheeked children, overdressed against the sun, played chasing games in yards, and squealed under the watchful eyes of their Black and brown guardians. Their bored mothers sat on front porches sewing, reading or fanning their made-up pink faces.

Eventually, the loud voice of the coach driver brought the horses to a stop in front of a small inn. With its white cobblestone walls and latticed windows it resembled a country cottage in Bristol.

'Here we are, sirs. The Braeton Inn. You'll get a fair night's rest here.' He climbed down and adjusted the bridles of both horses.

Ollenu unloaded their belongings and handed the driver more money than he requested.

'That's most generous. Thank you, sir.' He gave a low bow and climbed back up to his seat. 'Goodnight, gentlemen.'

A handful of carriages occupied the outside of the inn. Their horses, separated from the vehicles, were tethered to wooden poles. The tinny sound of a metal ball hitting a brass plate jingled as the heavy door swung inwards announcing their arrival. The interior was dim, with flickering candles and faint lamplight providing limited illumination. The smell of fresh paint, a mixture of linseed oil and turpentine, lingered, as if the inn had recently been redecorated. A plump woman in a bright blonde wig bustled towards them.

'Come in, come in. Welcome to the Braeton Inn! I'm Miss Sylvie.'

'Good evening, madam,' said Ashby.

'Good evening, Miss Sylvie,' said Ollenu, wiping his feet thoroughly on the coir mat.

The woman examined Ollenu from head to toe and said hesitantly, 'Well, good evening to you.' She turned to Ashby. 'You be wanting a room for the night?'

'Two rooms,' said Ashby.

'Two rooms?' she repeated.

'Yes, two rooms, madam, if you would be so kind.'

The woman shook her head in an exaggerated fashion, yet the stiff curls barely moved. 'I can give you one room. If you want two of you in it, be that on you.'

'Oh, is all accommodation taken?' Ashby looked at his fellow guests. 'Do these people stay overnight too?'

The woman presented a resentful tone. 'None of your business, is it? I said I got one room and one room only, if you want it?'

'With much gratitude,' said Ashby wearily.

The woman brightened up. 'That's two shillings for the night. Dinner and breakfast is extra. We don't take no Spanish coins in here. You can buy ale at the counter. Carl! Carl! Come take the guest's things up to the Lily room. What's your name, sir?'

'Ruben Ashby and this is Isaiah Ollenu. We're from Bristol.'

'Are you a planter, Mr Ashby?'

'No, I'm an insurance agent.' He observed confusion on her face and added, 'I investigate claims from people seeking compensation, and decide when to make payment and when to refuse payment.'

'Oh, I see.' Miss Sylvie nodded. 'Making sure people aren't lying and cheating to claim money they're not entitled to? When they say a place is burned down by Negroes, when it's them merchants that burned it themselves for the cash?'

Ashby smiled. 'You are plainly quite experienced.'

'People get up to all sorts of skulduggery on this island, Mr Ashby. The things I hear would make your hair stand on end.' Miss Sylvie gestured in Ollenu's direction. 'And what's he here for?'

'Mr Ollenu is my… assistant.'

Ollenu stood erect and pointedly cleared his already clear throat.

Miss Sylvie eyed him warily. 'Here, I hope you checked he's in good health before you brought him here?'

'He is in annoyingly good health, I assure you,' said Ashby.

'Hmm, I don't know. I don't really mind them, cause I'm a fair sort. Don't hold feelings against nobody, but my Carl won't be too happy to have him indoors. Says you can't trust them and don't know what they'll get up to.'

Ashby read the tightening in Ollenu's facial features as an indication that the man was struggling with self-control. Night would soon close in and Ashby feared losing this place of refuge. The thought of returning to the unfamiliar roads of Kingston in search of new lodgings was not one he wished to indulge.

'Madam, I will vouch for Mr Ollenu. No one need be the least alarmed by his presence, you have my assurance.'

'Hmm, well I can see you taught him manners 'cause he wiped his feet clean, so maybe he can behave himself. Though I don't know why you're carrying your own luggage when he's got room on his head.'

'Madam, I—' began Ollenu.

'He is trying to grow his hair,' said Ashby quickly and patted Ollenu's arm.

'Oh, here's me husband, Carl.'

The hang-dog expression of the gaunt man suggested he was used to doing his wife's bidding with no say in the matter.

'Not much of a talker is Carl, but he's a good pair of hands so I married him. Now, go and take a seat over there and I'll get some refreshment. What should I serve you?'

'I will try your finest ale,' said Ashby.

'Water, if you would be so kind, Miss Sylvie,' said Ollenu.

Pairs of curious eyes followed the men as they took their seats. Alcohol and conversation so engrossed the remaining customers that they barely noticed the latest guests. Soon a young barmaid appeared. 'There you are, beer and water.' She placed two vessels on the cedarwood table, a tankard of ale and a gourd of water. The water was so cloudy it was impossible to tell whether the darkness was the vessel itself or the filthiness of the content.

As she moved away, a pair of venomous-looking scoundrels in unkempt dress sidled over to Ashby and Ollenu's table. The unwanted company brought with them an air of stale bodies and violence. They bashed overflowing tankards on the table and grinned in the manner of sharks recognising easy prey.

One reprobate had dark greasy hair pulled back into a ponytail revealing a prominent forehead. He bared his teeth, sat, and hacked at the tabletop with a pointed blade. 'So, what brings you two wanderers to these isles, eh?'

The ruffian with him wore short blond locks that clung about his ears, weighted down with perspiration. He threw his dirty jacket over the back of a chair exposing a once white shirt, stained with brown ale. 'Come to seek fame and fortune, 'ave ye?'

Ashby made an effort at politeness. 'Many reasons may bring men to this island. Some come for fame and fortune, others come to learn lessons on how such can be amassed. Then there are those who come merely to experience foreign lands.'

Ollenu swivelled the tainted water and made no attempt to sip. 'Surely, you do not make such enquiry of all men who enter this tavern?' He leaned back in his chair displaying his broad shoulders to their fullest effect. 'Why should you be apprised of our business?'

Silence fell as conversations were cut short and heads turned to stare at the speaker. Ashby's expression was one of pure panic and he tried in vain to catch Ollenu's eye. Instead, Ollenu stared at the knifeman, whose blade glinted in the candlelight.

'Well, I never.' The knife sank into the wood with finality and stood without support. 'The Negro's not only dressed like the lordships, 'e talks like 'em as well.'

'And oo asked 'im anything in the first place?' the blond man sneered.

Ashby urgently waved a hand towards Miss Sylvie who was watching them from the bar. She scuttled over with an empty tray clamped to her side.

'See here, hope you two're behaving yourselves? You better be making Mr Ashby and his man Olloo comfortable?'

'Course we are, Miss Sylvie.'

'Not drinking the water, Olloo?' asked the innkeeper. 'Not to your fancy, is it?'

Ollenu pulled the untouched liquid closer and smiled. 'Thank you, Miss Sylvie, it is quite satisfactory.'

The blond man studied Ollenu with ill-disguised disgust before he addressed Ashby, 'Where'd you get your Negro?'

'I am not his Negro.'

'He is not my Negro.'

'Why'd you teach 'im to talk all proper then? We don't want no Negroes talking good 'ere.'

Miss Sylvie aimed a playful cuff at the aggressive man's ear. 'Mr Ashby's an investigator, and Olloo's his assistant, so I guess he had to learn to talk proper.'

'I don't care if e's Satan himself. You'd best learn to say "Massa", boy.'

'My good man, can you not leave us be?' said Ashby and was startled to find his voice came out in a higher pitch than usual. 'We have no wish to drink with you or engage in further conversation.'

'You'll drink wi' us. And you'll talk.' The blond man grabbed the innkeeper's dress. 'A noggin of rum over here, there's a good lass, Sylvie.'

'Get off, you!' Miss Sylvie tried to shrug him off and he held firm to her garment.

'Release the lady,' said Ollenu.

'Eh? Say something, boy? Did you dare speak to your massa?'

'Do not treat women with such contempt,' said Ollenu. 'Show some respect.'

‘After our women, Negro boy?’ The violator released the woman and concentrated on Ollenu. ‘If you be wanting women, you go pick a few tar savages.’

‘Aye, and the plantations need to birth more baby savages. You’ll serve well for rutting purposes.’

Both trouble-seekers laughed uproariously and clinked their tankards together, sending more pungent ale over the table.

‘Animals rut,’ said Ollenu. ‘Perhaps if you were equipped for rutting purposes, your attempts to woo women would not be so futile.’

Miss Sylvie’s eyes widened. She released a loud burst of laughter and slapped her thigh. Her barmaid gave a snort of derision and clasped her chest.

‘Why you little—’ The knifeman secured his blade and lunged at Ollenu who pushed his chair back and jumped to his feet. A powerful kick to the man’s arm sent the blade flying from his grasp. Each man took a heavy blow from Ollenu, sending both to the floor, with one offender sliding down the wall on his way.

Ashby abandoned his seat and stood back watching the commotion with obvious dismay. Some patrons rubbed their hands together in glee at the extra entertainment. Words of encouragement were shouted and tables bashed in delight. A few less bloodthirsty customers appealed to the men to stop fighting.

‘All’s well, leave them be.’ Miss Sylvie, captivated by the display, waved the dissenters away. ‘Any man intervenes, I’ll break this tray over ’is blooming head!’

The two assailants rushed Ollenu again. One punch sent the first man back to his former position, sliding down the wall, and a dislodged picture frame fell upon him. Ollenu grabbed the standing man by the front of his shirt and by a knee. He lifted him horizontally to head height and threw him on his mate, who was trying to stand up. Both beaten men lay sprawled on the floor panting as Ollenu stood over them.

As Ollenu balled his fist again Ashby moved forward and grabbed his arm, 'Charity, Mr Ollenu. Our Lord wishes us to show charity even to those who would not do the same for us.'

The bruised and embarrassed fighters kept their eyes on Ollenu as they stumbled towards the door, heckled by the boisterous crowd. They raised their fists when a safe distance away.

'Negro devil! Better not let us see you 'ere again.'

'Ye won't get off so lightly next time!'

'Don't forget this.' Miss Sylvie picked up a jacket and tossed it through the door behind them. 'And don't come back here till you learn good manners!'

The customers laughed and clapped in appreciation, then turned their attention back to their conversations, resuming social business as usual.

Ollenu returned the table to its rightful place and arranged the chairs in an orderly fashion. 'Miss Sylvie, I offer you my most sincere apologies for the disturbance. It was not my intent to show disdain for your hospitality.'

'Don't you apologise, Mr Olloo.' She smiled at him as she wiped the table. 'Not your fault, and so brave of you to speak up on my behalf. The men here are too free with their hands and nobody does a thing about it. Here, let me get you some more water. More ale, Mr Ashby?'

Ashby sank onto his chair and let out a sigh of relief. 'I would be obliged, Miss Sylvie, a large one.'

'You need not study me in that manner, Mr Ashby.' Ollenu unfurled his sleeves and sat down. 'I can assure you I am well. In annoyingly good health, as you say.'

'It is not your health I am concerned for, man, it is my own. You near caused my heart to fail me. Why would you choose to engage with those vengeful dogs?'

'I did not *choose* to engage, Mr Ashby, I had to.'

'You had to? How is it I did not feel compelled to show my fists?'

Ollenu shrugged. 'Some men are of calm temperament and can withstand all manner of provocation. Other men cannot and may react in a way that is not in accordance with their natural state of being, but satisfies the most basic instincts.'

'A garrulous way of saying you yearned for a fight?' said Ashby.

'If a knife is headed my way, I will do what is necessary to avoid it connecting with my skin.' Ollenu flexed his fingers and examined his scuffed knuckles. 'The rest was good exercise. I miss my boxing bag at home. Their bodies were nowhere near as sturdy.'

'I am gladdened that you achieved satisfaction, Mr Ollenu,' said Ashby.

Miss Sylvie returned and placed a large tankard in front of Ashby. In front of Ollenu she placed a tall glass of clear water. 'There you are, gentlemen. On the house.' She winked at Ollenu and walked away.

Ollenu took a few grateful sips of the cool liquid.

Ashby put the tankard to his lips and swallowed every drop. Pulling his chair closer to the table, he lowered his head. 'Mr Ollenu, you and I both understand that some people will not favour you. Your very presence will ignite them. They have probably lived here so long they've forgotten that men such as you exist in England. Probably happily forgotten it and have no wish to be reminded. We are here for a matter of months, at worst. Surely you can endure whatever tiresome nonsense they utter until this mission is over?'

'Do be specific, Mr Ashby.' Ollenu's eyes narrowed. 'You would rather I say "massa"? You would rather I answer to "boy"?'

'If it helps us through this trying time, yes.'

'I will not!' Ollenu shouted, then lowered his voice as curious heads lifted. 'Enough, Mr Ashby. I tire of being treated as the lowest of the low. I tire of the expectation that I act the uneducated fool. And believe me, I tire of accepting insults with good grace.'

Ashby sat back in his seat and stared at the oak beam ceiling in silence for a long time. He closed his eyes. 'Dear God, guide us through to blessed morning with clean thoughts and limbs intact.'

'Amen, Mr Ashby.' Ollenu sipped his water. 'Amen.'

CHAPTER 8

Strong sunlight filled the guestroom of the Braeton Inn. As cockerels heralded the dawn of a new morning, Ollenu sat up and twisted from side to side stretching stiff muscles. Ashby slept on, the small gold cross visible between his fingers, his expression serene.

Ollenu pulled his mattress to one corner of the room and leaned it against the wall. Though thin, the mattress proved quite comfortable and was a marked improvement to what greeted them on entry to the room; a single bed next to a pitiful padded mound of large dried leaves.

Ashby had claimed the single bed, a thick mattress on a bedstead spread with soft cotton sheets. Ollenu had resigned himself to the pile of leaves, but before he could lie down, Miss Sylvie pushed the long-suffering Carl through the door with an extra mattress and sheets, insisting their absence was an oversight on Carl's part. Ollenu was sure the replacement bedding was his reward for defending the innkeeper. He had smiled and thanked her profusely for her kindness.

To avoid waking his colleague, Ollenu sat at the bedroom table reading the Jamaican adventures of Hans Sloane. As he read, he played idly with Ekon's spinning top.

Eventually, Ashby stirred behind him and shielded his eyes from the sunlight. 'Is morning arrived so soon?' he asked.

'That, or someone has lit the world's biggest fire torch,' said Ollenu.

Ashby climbed off the bed, inhaled deeply and threw out his chest. 'This is a new glorious day. A day to be confident, to appreciate new things, new people, new experiences.'

'If you say so, Mr Ashby.'

Ashby stretched his arms in the air, winced and quickly returned them to his side. 'Sometimes I forget I am no longer so young that I can make sudden movements and part of my body not complain.'

'And now would be an unfortunate time to acquire any ailments,' said Ollenu.

'Indeed. We must seek out Neville Kershaw as he does not appear to search for us. Now that I recollect, the *Isabella* did berth days early, so he may be unaware of our arrival.' Ashby stared closely at his roommate. 'Without wishing to question your attire, Mr Ollenu, you are aware there is pink fabric behind your ear?'

Ollenu smiled as he put away Fayola's gift. 'Thank you, I near forgot.'

They dressed hurriedly. Ashby tossed his clothes into the trunk, closed it and dragged it close to the door. 'Miss Sylvie's husband can assist us to carry them down when we are ready to depart.'

'I shall take them down, when we are ready, Mr Ashby.' Ollenu placed his trunk beside Ashby's. 'No need to worry poor Carl who labours under a heavy hand. Do not forget to question Miss Sylvie on her arrivals over the years.'

Downstairs, the bar room was deserted and had undergone an impressive transformation. Last night, they retired leaving the dimly lit area littered with beer-stained tables, half-empty plates, upturned tankards and scattered chairs. This morning the open windows allowed light to dominate, and the room was a vision of cleanliness and order. Each table displayed a tiny pot of fresh flowers giving the space a pleasant lilac scent. Miss Sylvie appeared from the rear, wiping her hands on her apron.

'Oh, I knew I heard footsteps. Up with the birds, aren't you, gentlemen? Good morning, Mr Olloo, and to you, Mr Ashby.'

Ollenu nodded at her. 'Good morning, Miss Sylvie.'

'Good morning.' Ashby smiled at her. 'As cheerful as we find your abode, we do not wish to linger. Some morning sustenance first, then we shall be on our way. If we can find what way, that is.'

'If you're going to Kershaw's, you'll travel to St Jago de la Vega,' she said. 'Everybody calls it Spanish Town, by the way, rather than that mouthful. I'll send Carl on the road to find a vacant carriage. In the meantime, we'll get you something to eat. Follow me.'

'That would be most kind,' said Ashby as they trailed behind the innkeeper. She showed them to a corner spot near to an open back door with a view of the outdoors. 'Tell me, Miss Sylvie, there are three people I am keen to find on the island. All of them are known to have sailed into Kingston Harbour over the years and could now be anywhere. I wonder if you've ever heard of them?'

Ollenu studied Miss Sylvie's face as she shook her head at each name that Ashby mentioned.

'The coach drivers often recommend people stay with us as we're known for our hospitality. No better lodgings near here. If that Clare Sandie had come here on her own, I'd remember her, 'cause we don't get women on their own. If, as you say, she's loud and talks a lot, I'd remember her, even if she came here with a man. No woman's allowed to talk a lot in here, except me. Penket and Dantry, I've never heard of. A tailor and an iron-monger eh?' She tilted her head back. 'Carl! Carl? Where have you got to?'

Ashby flinched at the noise. 'Thank you, Miss Sylvie. We shall soon learn whether Mr Kershaw has managed to discover the clients' locations.'

'Though as he is yet to discover ours, it seems most unlikely,' muttered Ollenu.

Miss Sylvie gave him a warm smile followed by a knowing look. 'Between you and me, Mr Olloo, I'm not so sure about that Kershaw. Not above having his palms greased, I'm told, and turns a blind eye when it suits him. Just 'cause he's up there in honourable society, doesn't mean he's all honourable. You heed my words.'

Ollenu stared at Ashby. 'We will be sure to, Miss Sylvie.'

'I'll see how breakfast is coming on, now I'm done tidying up. The maid don't come till the evening, you see. There's a cook in the back, but she isn't finished. Some of them are so lazy.' She stressed the 'them' and sent a quick embarrassed look at Ollenu. 'Won't take too long, Mr Ashby. There's fried dumplings and eggs coming up. How's that sound?'

'I'm sure it will be most appetising,' said Ashby.

'And is that fitting for you, Mr Olloo?'

'Thank you, Miss Sylvie, it sounds highly pleasing.'

'We'll get you some sweet hot tea as well.'

The crackle and odour of hot coconut oil filtered across the kitchen wall behind which Miss Sylvie disappeared.

The tantalising aroma awakened Ollenu's taste buds and he hoped the Braeton's cook was an improvement on the *Isabella*'s cook. A not too difficult accomplishment.

'Miss Sylvie is clearly not enamoured of Mr Kershaw,' said Ollenu.

'People will tittle-tattle to pass time when they have nothing better to do,' said Ashby. 'I cannot imagine Mr Kershaw would hold his position, practically running the island, were he not a man of principle.'

'It is queer that I can, indeed, imagine such a thing.'

Ollenu's mind began to drift. His formerly much trusted mentor, Jacob Dunne, had held meetings with the never to be trusted Edward Barrow, and the two had prepared a letter for the chief watchman to sign. A chief watchman who Ollenu had seen treating the poor with contempt, throwing cold water on beggars.

'Mr Ashby, it would be wise to read the letter you guard so closely.' He held up an open palm as Ashby started to protest. 'I suggest this only so we may satisfy ourselves that all is as it seems. We can assert that the seal was damaged due to unpleasant weather during the voyage.'

'I must say, Mr Ollenu,' sneered Ashby. 'One of your most endearing qualities is your ability to humbly take 'no' for an answer.' He reached for a rolled-up newspaper on the table next to theirs. Opening the *Jamaica Courant* wide, he held it high, so that he could no longer see his fellow diner's face.

'What has your attention?' asked Ollenu at length.

'I see a whole page devoted to seeking the return of runaway slaves and indentured workers, Black and white.' Ashby turned the yellowing pages. 'But I see no mention of missing visitors. Every week a description should be printed, until those unaccounted for are herded from their hiding places. Full descriptions of everyone.'

'What descriptions would you insert?' asked Ollenu.

'Mr Henry Penket, family man, forty-two years, a tailor, stout in girth, medium height, brown greying hair. Mr Francis Dantry, widower, thirty-six years, an iron-monger, tall, broad of chest, pronounced limp, dark blond hair. Mrs Clare Sandie, married woman, twenty-eight years, small frame, long auburn hair, freckled cheeks. All clients of Paxten Insurance Company of Bristol. All believed alive. For a reward, report sightings to Mr Ruben Ashby, care of Mr Neville Kershaw of Spanish Town.'

Ollenu arched an eyebrow. 'I am only surprised you did not add "All believed tricksters".'

'I see nothing wrong with my words.'

'An action in libel can succeed with mere finger pointing. Your words indicate to the world that those people are somehow involved in criminal activity.'

'Hmm, I will forego any thoughts of advertisements,' said Ashby. 'Besides, a public notice may alert them and drive them further to ground.'

The young cook appeared balancing a tray containing two plates of hot food with a savoury aroma, and steaming mugs of tea. Ollenu nodded and smiled politely as she emptied the tray. Cornrows shrouded a face that seemed strained as her dark eyes moved from the plate to Ollenu and back again.

'Thank you.' Ollenu pulled the dish towards him.

'Your food is in the wrong plate,' she burst out and wrung her hands. 'Miss Sylvie will be mad with rage. I will be whipped.'

Ollenu studied his own plate first then Ashby's. Both looked identical. Clean white porcelain with silver cutlery neatly arranged on the edge. His curious eyes met her frightened brown ones and realisation dawned. He leaned towards her and whispered. 'You must not worry. I have found favour with Miss Sylvie and have no need to borrow the dog's plate.'

She gave a pained smile and scurried towards the kitchen. Ollenu noticed Ashby staring at him and waited for the investigator to speak. Ashby grabbed his mug of tea and held it to his lips as if determined to avoid awkward conversation.

Ollenu bit into a fried dumpling and his face registered pleasure as he ate. 'Mmm, this is quite delicious.' He scooped up fried egg, but before it reached his mouth, Ashby interrupted him, and the fork hovered in mid-air.

'No stop!' Ashby narrowed his eyes and picked at his own egg with a fork. He craned his neck and peered into Ollenu's plate. 'See, there are tiny black specks in my egg, Mr Ollenu. Yours too. It resembles dirt. How could the cook do such a thing? I shall complain at once.'

Ollenu placed the egg in his mouth and chewed appreciatively. 'Black pepper.'

'What did you say?'

'Black pepper, Mr Ashby.' Ollenu sighed. 'I can assure you it is perfectly edible and makes the egg flavoursome. Tell me, this is not the first time you have eaten black pepper?'

Ashby tentatively chewed on a mouthful of egg. 'Oh, it is quite tasteful.' He bit through the crisp coat of the dumpling. 'My word, I have eaten *boiled* dumplings... Boiled dumplings in a hot beef stew are extremely gratifying. Never sampled them fried. This is quite splendid too. Who would have thought fried dumplings and peppered eggs could taste as delicious as this?'

'Black people.'

'I see.'

With breakfast finished and their stomachs filled, they strolled outside and into the back garden with its verdant acres.

'Come, let us explore before Carl returns,' said Ashby.

'The air is wondrously clear this morning.' Ollenu stopped walking, raised both arms out to the side and bounced up and down. 'I wish that I could remove my clothes and run through the open fields until I grow tired.'

Ashby looked at him in alarm. 'Were you to dispense with your clothes and run, you may hear and feel a discharge of gunfire courtesy of Carl or some equally outraged man.'

'Were I to keep my clothes *on* and run, I fear my fate will be the same.'

'Then it is agreed you are neither going to remove your clothes nor run, Mr Ollenu?'

Ollenu ceased his bobbing motion. 'Such an idea was, at best, ill-conceived.'

'Thank goodness.' Ashby turned his head to one side and sniffed the air. 'What is that rather peculiar odour?'

'That would be him.'

Ollenu pointed at a thin white man reclining next to a half-built chicken coop with a hammer and saw beside him. The carpenter's eyes were closed. A puff of thick grey smoke emerged from the rolled-up short stick clamped between his chapped lips. Chickens gathered close to his feet pecking at piles of sawdust, searching for minute insects unearthed by his handiwork.

As the two men wandered over, the carpenter blinked and eyed them lazily. 'Miss Sylvie send you to order me back to work, did she? Well, I've been working for two hours and I need my rest.'

'As you were, man,' said Ashby. 'No one sent us to trouble you.'

'You want a smoke?' The man held out the smoking stick, the length of a quill pen, with much wider girth. 'I've got plenty more. Got it from a Negro who hails from St Elizabeth so you know tis the really good kind. He rolled the leaves tight – easier to handle.'

'I have never indulged in smoke of any kind,' said Ashby. 'Although, I must say, I am quite entranced by this scent. What is it?'

'Cannabis sativa, or hemp, if you prefer, sir.'

Ashby sat on the grass next to the man. 'It could do little harm to try one.'

'Not for me, thank you.' Ollenu removed a container of crushed corn kernels from an upturned log and took a seat.

The carpenter lit another cannabis stick and passed it to Ashby, who took a few deep puffs and slouched closer to the man. Soon the two were talking and laughing as if old friends.

'I am experiencing a true feeling of exhilaration, as if I could soar,' gushed Ashby. 'I am on top of the world, with no cares.'

'It will do that for you,' said the carpenter with a chuckle. 'And much more.'

This was the first time Ollenu had seen Ashby appear so elated. The forced laughter, when he played cards with the crewmen, was quite different. Ashby's cheeks now dimpled, his eyes shone and he became almost handsome. Although Ollenu was gratified to see that Ashby could find humour, he was somewhat alarmed that the man had taken the wish to have new experiences too far too soon.

Ollenu stayed out of the conversation. His eyes flicked to and from the inn's back door, hoping to see Miss Sylvie or Carl appear and interrupt the merrymaking before Ashby lost his mental faculties. Somehow he did not believe Jamaica was an island where one could afford to let one's guard down for long.

'Neville Kershaw you're to stay with, you say? He's a strange one. Not stranger than you wandering about with this Negro though.' The carpenter laughed and Ashby joined him.

Ollenu's ears pricked up. 'I understand that some people do not believe Mr Kershaw is entirely trustworthy?'

'Some people, and I bet Miss Sylvie's one of them.' The carpenter guffawed and choked.

Ashby patted him on the back. 'Steady on, my good man.'

Ollenu tried to appear as indifferent as possible. He picked up a handful of chicken feed and threw it towards the birds who spread their wings and ran towards him squawking their delight. 'Are you well acquainted with Mr Kershaw?'

'Can't say I am, but I helped work on his barn. He's a right blatteroon. Says he'll buy land at Montego Bay and build something as grand as Rose Hall.' He peered at Ollenu through reddened eyes. 'You seen what they're building at Rose Hall? Some big mansion way up in the hills overlooking the sea. Kershaw will never earn enough wages for that. He's the marshal's lackey, a simpleton.'

'His wages may be greater than is deserved for his role,' mused Ollenu.

He hoped that Ashby would question the carpenter about the missing clients, but the investigator was interested only in discussing the delights of his new-found narcotic.

'Mr Ashby and I are searching for three people who have been missing for a number of years: Henry Penket, a tailor, Mrs Clare Sandie, a brewer, and Francis Dantry, an ironmonger. Do you know of them?'

'Can't say I do. People often go missing on this island. Rumour has it most of them were last seen in Pedro village.'

'Pedro village?' repeated Ollenu.

The jingle of a bell signalled that the Braeton's front door had opened. Shortly after, Miss Sylvie emerged through the back door with three men behind her.

'Ah, there they are, Mr Kershaw!' bellowed Miss Sylvie. 'Look at them. They're such gentlemen, and Mr Olloo is even helping feed my chickens. Mr Olloo! Mr Ashby!'

Ollenu watched the new arrivals. Even from a distance their expressions seemed hard and unfriendly. He took comfort from the fact that he experienced no tingling feelings or any need to recite strange words. Stretching across the carpenter, Ollenu shook Ashby, who was slumped against the man's shoulder. Ashby roused and blinked a few times, seemingly unaware of his location.

'Here, have this one since you enjoyed it so much.' The carpenter forced a thick roll of hemp into Ashby's jacket pocket as Ollenu hauled him to his feet.

'Thank you, my good man,' slurred Ashby. 'I am sure to enjoy it.'

'See you weren't forgotten after all,' said Miss Sylvie as she walked towards them. 'Your coach driver told Mr

Kershaw you were here. You're looking pale, Mr Ashby. I hope you're not coming down with anything.' She glared at her workman and waved a hand rapidly in front of her face to dismiss the strong aroma. 'Back to work, Podrick. All that smoke and at this time of morning, I ask you!'

'Yes ma'am, right away ma'am,' he murmured.

'You can come and get your things now. I know you're eager to be on your way. Been a delight to have you Mr Olloo, and you, Mr Ashby.'

Ollenu led a wobbly Ashby back towards the inn following in the footsteps of their hostess.

'Gentlemen, so pleased to have found you! I'm Neville Kershaw.' The man was tall, almost as tall as Ollenu, though with a much bulkier figure, borne of food not muscle. Below his curly brown wig lay wide hazel eyes, a long nose, and the thinnest of lips. His handshake was firm and to all appearances sincere, yet Ollenu noticed that the man wiped his palms afterwards, while pretending to adjust his coattail.

Kershaw gestured to his men. 'These are my colleagues, Mr Leonard Mortimer and Mr Albert Johnson.'

Both associates nodded and grunted a greeting. Mortimer was a heavyset fellow with an extremely wide waist and spindly legs that deserved sympathy. Johnson was thin throughout with eyes set too close over a hooked nose, giving him the appearance of a hawk.

'Gladdened to meet you, gentlemen,' said Ollenu. 'I regret; Mr Ashby is rather over-indulged.'

'Mr Ashby,' said Kershaw with a nod.

'Good day,' mumbled Ashby.

Kershaw gave his aides a knowing look. 'Too much cannabis. That's why I stick to snuff myself.' His men laughed with him. 'Now that I've located you, we can be on our way. Do go and gather your belongings, Mr Ollenu.'

Ollenu cast curious eyes over Kershaw's men. 'You are all agents of the provost marshal?'

'Johnson and Mortimer are honorary agents,' said Kershaw with a broad smile. 'I'm an official. You carry your introduction letter from chief watchman Wilkins?'

'Here,' Ashby fumbled in his breast pocket.

'Oh dear, Mr Ashby. Let me assist you.'

Kershaw stepped forward and removed the letter, much to Ollenu's chagrin. All hopes of ever examining the content were now well and truly dashed. The deputy marshal broke the seal and his eyes moved swiftly down the page. He nodded and smiled at his honorary agents.

'It is satisfactory?' mumbled Ashby.

'Quite satisfactory, Mr Ashby. You and Mr Ollenu will receive all the assistance you need. I must apologise for not greeting you last evening. The provost marshal, Mr William Gray, conducts business in the parish of St Thomas in The East, so I carry the weight. We're busy every day and there were a few arrangements to be made. By the time we made them, it was near nightfall and tis not wise to ride at nightfall even when armed.'

As Ollenu headed indoors to collect their luggage, he hoped he was mistaken, and that there was nothing to fear from these escorts whose smiles did not quite reach their eyes.

CHAPTER 9

Neville Kershaw sat opposite Ollenu and Ashby in the carriage, and took pleasure in pointing out places of interest as they travelled along narrow winding roads on route from Kingston to the capital city.

'Welcome to Spanish Town, St Catherine,' Kershaw announced with a flourish of his hand, before leaning out of the carriage and shouting, 'Mortimer, once round the administrative square before we head home, if you will.'

'Right you are, sir.'

'Our rather glorious square is a triumph to architecture, I'm sure you will agree,' said Kershaw.

'Quite so,' murmured Ashby.

The horses slowed to a leisurely trot as they entered the busy square. The elegance of the surrounding buildings made up for the desert appearance of the centre piece, an area that would have benefitted from flowers and trees. Scarlet-coated soldiers, both mounted and on foot, brought an authoritative air to the region. Princely four-wheeled carriages conveyed pampered passengers to and from their appointments. Graceful ladies in lavish silk dresses and velvet coats, faces sheltered behind dainty bonnets and parasols, were escorted by gentlemen in fine tailored suits and tall hats.

'Over here is King's House, the official residence of Governor, Lieutenant John Dalling.' The deputy marshal pointed at an enormous white edifice occupying a large parcel of land to the western side. The grandiose building was styled with a portico set almost four feet above street level and overlaid with marble slabs, surrounded on either side by rows of white louvre windows. A group of well-groomed horses sheltered in the stables adjoining the property.

'What magnificent splendour,' said Ashby in awe.

On the north side, they passed a pretty tavern next to a barber's shop, and the many tethered horses were evidence of each establishment conducting a lively trade.

'Over to the east, facing us, we have the House of Assembly, our Houses of Parliament. Scene of many lively debates between the Governor and the Members, I can tell you. My superior, Mr Gray, occupies an office in there.'

With an upper and lower level, the imposing red brick building dominated the entire eastern side of the square. Across the ground level was a long row of graceful arches, and Ollenu counted at least fifteen such curves. Upstairs a verandah ran the length of the property and was lined from end to end with white jalousie windows. Ollenu formed the opinion that raised voices in the Assembly could quite well carry across the square to the Governor's residence if the windows of both institutions were open.

'How marvellous,' said Ashby. 'I was unaware such striking buildings were here. Rivals any properties I have seen in Bristol, in London even.'

Kershaw indicated a large empty spot occupying the south of the square. 'We are unsure what will be built there, although I've heard talk of a courthouse. I do believe a small courthouse once lay there. Got destroyed in a terrible hurricane,' he explained. 'All sorts of stories abound about Jamaica, about how wickedness causes the hurricanes, but she is our crown jewel. We fought the Spanish for her and will fight any slimy rogues who seek to claim her.'

Ollenu's attention was caught by enslaved men dressed in the osnaburg uniform of labour, absorbed in their tasks of tending horses and sweeping hay. He wondered about their histories; who was born on the island and who was forcibly brought ashore to improve the fortunes of the English. He tried not to perceive himself in their position, subservient, voiceless, and he dreamed of one day helping them find a more fulfilling way of life.

As they left behind the activity of the square, their host pointed again. 'We approach the Cathedral of St Jago de la Vega. Destroyed by a most vicious hurricane in 1712 and lovingly rebuilt in 1714. Inside are some rare medieval-style furnishings that will take your breath away.'

'Exquisite, I hope to see inside one day,' said Ashby. 'Are you a church man, Mr Kershaw?'

'My wife, Lydia, and I go as often as possible. She'll want you to accompany us – both of you.'

Ollenu offered him a brief smile and immediately resumed his interest with the outdoors. In his experience, people who frequented church had no better morals than those who frequented taverns. Many a time the same people did both.

'This is the Middlesex and Surrey County Gaol.' Kershaw spoke with pride as he eyed the giant stone walls surrounding the establishment, keeping the miscreants in and the public out. 'I'm to be found here more often than not, as I help manage the building, for my sins.'

'A sturdy gaol is a necessity,' said Ashby.

'I agree,' said Ollenu. 'One that holds not only the poor or those taking alms, but also finds room for wealthy men of business.'

Ashby scowled. 'Is such talk necessary?'

Kershaw maintained his pleasant bearing. 'Of course, Mr Ollenu, all people are treated equally in the eyes of the law.'

The carriage soon turned off onto a long gravel driveway. Leaning out, Ollenu looked up at the palatial villa whose exterior was bedecked with a climbing wall of pink clematis and surrounded by a generous front garden. Johnson and Mortimer brought the carriage to a halt close to the villa's double front doors.

Kershaw climbed down and held the carriage door wide open. 'Gentlemen, welcome to my home.'

'This delightful place is yours?' gushed Ashby.

'Well, tis a grace and favour house, Crown property you see.'

Ollenu leapt down. He immediately stretched out his arms and bounced up and down, ignoring his host's curious scrutiny.

Ashby, who by now was used to his colleague's daily rituals, merely stepped aside to allow him more space. 'What a fine retreat,' he said.

'It has served well as accommodation for honoured guests and not so honoured guests. You know, people the provost marshal says we need to accommodate if his place is full, or they're not his kind of people.'

Johnson and Mortimer carried the luggage to the front porch. Two small Black boys emerged from the rear of the property and ran towards them, fear etched on their faces. Ollenu winced as Kershaw gave them a look so searing it could separate skin from bone. No doubt the boys were meant to unload the carriage, but did not react swiftly enough to the horses' arrival. Kershaw's expression suddenly changed back to pleasant, as if he remembered he was under scrutiny of a different complexion. Stepping forward, he patted one of the distressed urchins on the shoulder, speaking sweetly.

'Go back to your duties, lads, the bags are seen to. Go on. Tell your mother I said to give you some candied fruit.'

The boys' bare feet seemed oblivious to the gravel as they scampered away and disappeared behind the house.

'Eager little mites,' said Kershaw before turning to Ashby. 'Now, how about I show you the grounds before we go inside? It extends to the rear and covers about six acres in total. I'm fortunate to reside here during my tenure, and I've enjoyed eighteen years so far.'

The large estate had little in the way of agricultural produce: a few coconut trees, some corn and a pumpkin patch. Its extensive lawns were bordered by sumptuous pink and crimson flowering plants. White painted wicker chairs were neatly arranged beneath the leafy trees. Kershaw pointed out an outdoor kitchen, horses' stables, a few cows and a large barn.

'Do you entertain here often?' asked Ashby.

'Not grand affairs, no balls or dances. Tis not suitable for more than a handful of people at a time and they do insist on the most elaborate affairs in Jamaica. In my position, I don't want to be hosting dinner parties week in week out. Relations are wont to get thorny between neighbours at times, and I may be called upon to arbitrate. Tis best to be unbiased, and that is near impossible if either party sees you as a friend.'

'A quite sensible approach,' said Ashby nodding.

'I've arranged for you to attend a grand ball in Montego Bay, St James, on Friday, hosted by Sir Alastair Nicholson. For a Scotsman, he's quite generous and knows how to throw a glamorous event. You and Mr Ollenu can become acquainted with the great and the good.'

Ashby inclined his head. 'We are most grateful.'

'Overjoyed,' said Ollenu.

'At the ball, we can further enquire about our missing clients,' said Ashby. 'I understand from Mr Barrow, that you made vast enquiries yourself, without much success?'

'Greeted with silence, mostly. I've been up and down the land with no luck, but I wish you all the best of it. I shall do everything in my power to help find that rogue, Francis Dantry.'

Ollenu frowned. 'And what of the clients, Henry Penket and Clare Sandie?'

'Oh, of course, those people, too,' said Kershaw hurriedly. 'Penket and Sandie.'

To Ollenu, Kershaw appeared somewhat flustered, as if he had spoken hastily and wished he had chosen better words. The apprentice looked at Ashby, who did not seem to notice anything amiss.

'I've arranged access for you to view registers at King's House tomorrow,' said Kershaw. 'Governor Dalling's aides are expecting you. They keep records of all the ships that come in, names of passengers including the family they brought with them, and details of the areas they were bound for. Not that they won't move about, you understand? But it is a start.'

'You have studied these records yourself?' asked Ashby.

'Yes, though notations are added weekly. You may also view records of people leaving the island, marriage records and death registers.'

Ollenu kept his eyes on the deputy's face. 'Where were Henry Penket and Clare Sandie bound?'

'Er, let me see,' said Kershaw hesitantly. 'It escapes my memory. I believe Mrs Sandie went to Portland, that's in the east. If I'm not mistaken, Mr Penket went to St Mary in the north. Francis Dantry was seen right here in Spanish Town, then went north to St Ann. Can't find any record of him from St Ann's Bay. We searched the entire area for days, and… nothing. Searched every parish where there's been possible sightings of him since then, with no luck.'

'Your search for the missing people is quite recent?' asked Ollenu.

'Well, not so recent.' Kershaw smiled. 'Countless local matters have a call upon my time and there's not enough hours in a day. When I was informed that special investigators would come to assist with the search, I was able to withdraw somewhat.'

'We look forward to resuming the task,' said Ashby.

'And are most keen to commence,' added Ollenu.

'Then that is how it shall be,' said Kershaw. 'Come, gentlemen, let us proceed inside. Lydia looks forward to meeting you both.'

–

The next day, the men were shown into the governor's large study inside King's House. The many shelves were lined with books and papers, including registers dating back to the beginning of the century.

As Ollenu studied lists of deceased people he paused to look at Ashby. 'Mr Kershaw is abreast of Francis Dantry's movements and even went to St Ann's Bay in search of him, yet he can barely remember what parishes Mr Penket or Mrs Sandie were bound for. Do you not find it queer?'

'Not particularly,' replied Ashby absently as he ran a finger down a list of ship passenger departures.

'It appears to me that Mr Dantry is of more interest to him,' said Ollenu. 'Why? Is he the wealthiest of the three?'

'On the contrary, he may be the least wealthy of the three.' Ashby stopped reading and tilted his head in recollection. 'Mr Penket is not only an expert tailor to the gentry and prosperous people, he is also the proud owner of a doublet he sewed, complete with encrusted diamonds, rubies and emeralds. It is of considerable value. When Mrs Sandie's brewhouse was thriving, her husband bought her plenty of jewellery including an emerald necklace. A rather spectacular piece.'

'And Dantry has gold rings and gold cufflinks inherited from his grandparents,' said Ollenu. 'Also worth a lot?'

'Yes, though not worth as much as the others' jewels.' Ashby turned his attention to a departures list. 'As an ironmonger, Mr Dantry has good custom in England, but he also has plenty of competition. He came to Jamaica in the hope of supplying his wares to additional markets on the island.'

Ollenu's tone was sharp. 'Iron tools for the slaves to work with, chains for their necks, fetters for their ankles.'

Ashby flushed. 'I daresay someone has to supply them, so I cannot blame him for wishing to be involved.'

'I can,' said Ollenu.

Ashby continued running his forefinger down the list. 'When we are finished here, we should ask Johnson to stop and set us down close to a few shops so that we can investigate further.'

'I am heartened to hear you say *we*,' said Ollenu. 'You no longer object to my asking questions of the settlers?'

Ashby shuffled uncomfortably. 'I conceded long ago that you are good at what you do. Nevertheless, there will be occasions when I insist that you follow my lead.'

'I am sure there will be,' mumbled Ollenu.

Upon leaving King's House later that day, they made frequent stops in the horse-drawn carriage and entered various places of business. A burly grocer was amiable, but could offer no useful information. A tailor was very interested to hear of a fellow tailor in Mr Penket, but swore he had never met him and did not recognise the description. A drunkard at a tavern overheard their requests for information. He insisted that his wife of ten years was Clare Sandie in disguise, and demanded a reward for handing her over.

'Disguised she may be, sir, but she is not Clare Sandie,' said Ollenu. 'Thank you for your time.'

'I daresay his poor wife would disclaim him with equal fervour,' said Ashby as they left the man clutching his pint.

Outside the tavern, Ashby headed towards a group of soldiers as they stood grooming their horses. The officers knew nothing of the three missing people, and promised to be on the alert.

'We should try the barber across the square,' said Ollenu as he squinted at a wooden sign. 'Leon Graham.'

'Yes,' said Ashby. 'I will know where to return for grooming.'

The barber was engaged in conversation with a male client as he cut his hair. A young blond boy swept up tresses throughout the shop with a coarse broom. As Ashby introduced himself and Ollenu, the barber peered through his window at the horse-drawn carriage.

'Oh, I see Johnson brought you. You're with Kershaw, then?'

'Yes, that is where we expect to remain for most of our time in Jamaica,' said Ashby.

'Kershaw never paid me for the last two hair-cuts I gave him. When I demanded payment, he lied and said he already paid. My shop was broken into the very night we had a row, and many of my tools went missing. I wager he had something to do with it.'

The customer frowned and kept his head steady. 'I've always found Kershaw an affable fellow to deal with. I'll not be quick to believe ill of him.'

'He can't fool everybody,' said the barber. He removed the cloak protecting his customer and brushed off the man's shoulders. 'Reckons he's entitled to favours. I suppose he does right by some people, especially the merchants, or he'd have been forced out by now.'

After the customer bid them farewell, the barber cleaned his combs and muttered, 'Then he has the nerve to come here enquiring about a missing man.'

'He mentioned only one man?' asked Ollenu. 'Not two men and a woman?'

'One man,' insisted the barber. 'Francis Dantry.'

Ollenu gave Ashby a knowing look, and met a frown.

'Do you know the whereabouts of Francis Dantry?' asked Ashby.

'Maybe I do. And maybe I don't. Tell Kershaw I've not forgotten he owes me my money. It's hard making a living when people refuse to do right by you.'

Ollenu studied the man's red face and overall demeanour. Years of training, of interviewing reluctant witnesses, indicated that the man could indeed have more information. He stared into Ashby's eyes. 'Mr Ashby longs for a neat trim. Now seems a convenient time?'

Ashby scowled. 'Well, I er… yes, I suppose so.'

The hair stylist's face brightened. 'Do take a seat, Mr Ashby.' He removed a fresh apron from the clothes rack and draped it across the reluctant man's shoulders.

'A little off the ends,' mumbled Ashby as he slumped into the chair.

'And the whiskers, sir?'

'There is barely a sprout. When next I visit, it can be attended to.'

'Very good, sir, my charge be only sixpence.'

Ollenu examined the small space. It was clean and the equipment was neatly arranged. The chairs seemed comfortable, and the mirrors shone. Clearly Mr Graham took pride in his surroundings. 'Such a charming environment, so well-appointed and pristine.'

'We do our best with the place.' The barber beamed as he snipped Ashby's hair in an expert manner. 'You'll never find me working in slovenly conditions as some tradesmen do.'

'I know an esteemed gentleman who would take delight in having his name associated with a fine place such as this. My employer, Jacob Dunne. One of the finest barristers in England.'

'I've heard of him, he's in Bristol,' said the barber. 'You hold steady, Mr Ashby. Soon be done with you.'

'I shall be sure to inform him of the excellent service you provide. How impressive, were you to have a prominent sign etched with the words "Highly recommended by Mr Jacob Dunne, Esquire, Barrister of Bristol".'

The barber's eyes shone. 'My word!'

The youth paused sweeping and looked excited at the prospect. 'That would be rather grand, Father. I would polish the sign every day.'

Ollenu seized on the new information. 'Instead of Leon Graham, it could read Leon Graham & Son.'

'You can make this be, Mr Ollenu?' said the excited barber.

'Before the year ends, the sign can be shipped to Jamaica,' said Ollenu. 'However, we do need to hear what you know of Francis Dantry.'

'Go see Tom the blacksmith on the edge of the city. Everybody knows Tom; Johnson can take you over there. Tell Tom I sent you, or he won't utter a word about Dantry.' He finished trimming Ashby's hair ends and admired his handiwork. 'Dantry rented a room from him for months, then disappeared.'

Ollenu watched as Ashby handed the barber sixpence and shook his head. The miser would never learn. With an apologetic smile, Ollenu added another sixpence to the barber's palm and the man grinned in delight.

'I wish you a very pleasant evening, Mr Ollenu.'

As they left the barber Ashby looked askance at Ollenu. 'Whilst I prefer to determine my own grooming needs, I accept that your intervention proved most opportune.'

'And your hair has never looked more alluring, sir.'

Ashby ignored his colleague's grin and fixed his hat. 'We must ask Mr Johnson to take us to Tom the blacksmith right away.'

Ollenu shook his head. 'That may not be wise, in the circumstances.'

'What circumstances? Darkness shall not be upon us for hours?'

'Tomorrow, after Mr Kershaw has left for the gaol, we must go unaccompanied,' said Ollenu. 'We should not inform him, or his assistants, or his wife, of our plans.'

Ashby frowned. 'Your mistrust of our host is grave.'

'Some voices say he is good; others suggest he is unprincipled. He has shown interest in finding only one man. Should we locate Mr Francis Dantry, prudence suggests we hold a secret conference with him, before we notify Mr Kershaw of our success.'

'As you wish,' grumbled Ashby. 'Be aware that I put my trust in God to guide us, rather than in you.'

CHAPTER 10

In the morning, the two Bristol men sat at opposite ends of a cedar table in the Kershaw's drawing room. The strong aroma of fresh coffee emitted from a large jug in the centre.

Ollenu wound the spinning top and set it loose on the table, guiding its movements to ensure it did not fall off. Kershaw had long set off for the gaol and Ollenu was keen to leave the house. Apart from anything else, he wanted to avoid the effervescent Lydia Kershaw, who had taken a fancy to him and would use any excuse to be at his side.

'Should we leave before two hours has passed our departure will appear suspicious,' whispered Ashby as he cradled his mug of coffee.

'The mistress,' Ollenu mouthed. 'She listens beyond the door.'

Ashby opened one of Hans Sloane's tomes and pushed the second volume across the table to his associate. He raised his voice. '*A voyage to the Islands Madera, Barbados, Nieves, St Christopher and Jamaica*. I pray we conclude this Jamaican adventure in the shortest possible time, so we can move on with our lives, just as Sir Hans did. Albeit, Sir Hans endured a whole fifteen months on the island.'

Ollenu stopped spinning the toy and let it rest on the table. Keeping his eyes on the closed wooden door, he spoke loudly. 'I wonder, was Sloane ever tempted to remain in the tropical climes?'

'He could hardly remain in Jamaica, Mr Ollenu. Remember that our illustrious expert on botany, minerals and medicine had to attend to aristocratic clients all over the world including London and Paris. Evidently he had fingers in many pies.'

'Of pies, I have no knowledge. His supporters claim he invented chocolate milk and I say, a likely story.' Ollenu sipped his coffee. 'Scholars, who have conducted more vigorous research than I, insist that humans drank chocolate with eggs, sugar and milk for centuries in various countries – since Before Christ, even. It is rather predictable that "inventions" and "discoveries" are associated with European people, particularly white English men.'

'His family is Ulster-Scots.'

'I do not concede my point. All of a sudden, Sloane's particular recipe is adjudged a medicinal elixir and lauded in every newspaper in the land.'

'You remain a cynic, I see.'

'I am in good company, Mr Ashby. Sir Isaac Newton once described Sloane as a very tricking fellow – hardly a compliment.'

'You, of all people, should know that we cannot be admired by everyone, Mr Ollenu.'

'I choose to believe you meant that in a truly agreeable way?'

'How else?' Ashby flicked through the book's pages. 'I could write no more than a few simple pages about my voyage to Jamaica. There are over six hundred pages here. Calculating numbers is my fascination, not devising words.'

Ollenu opened the second book and slowly turned the pages, occasionally looking up at the door as if expecting to see it ajar. He caught Ashby's eye and mouthed. 'She is still there.'

Ashby nodded and continued reading in silence.

Ollenu unfolded a newspaper report tucked within the book's pages and flattened out the creases. 'This report concerns Sloane's search for encouragement to take on the Jamaican appointment: "*It is said that, before consenting to accompany Albemarle, the newly appointed governor, to Jamaica in 1687, he consulted Sydenham on the subject, and that the father of English medicine told him that he had better drown himself in Rosamond's Pond, a sheet of water in St James's Park, which was then a fashionable resort for intending suicides.*"'

'Now that is troubling.' Ashby adjusted his reading glasses. 'One has to be suicidal to depart for Jamaica?'

'In 1687, Mr Ashby. The island has recovered some of her dignity since then.'

'And the world thanks Sir Hans for not committing suicide.'

'I am thankful that Mr Dunne does not work with only one class of people.' Ollenu appeared wistful. 'He advocates for every citizen: rich, comfortable, barely surviving. One gets the opportunity to assess how their varied backgrounds affect their perceptions of justice and the actual justice, or injustice, they receive.'

'You mean it is a good opportunity for Jacob Dunne to claim the headlines in the law reports by testing out his outrageous defences.'

'Outrageous effective defences,' said Ollenu proudly. 'I drafted many of these, night after night. Some defences work and some do not, but testing the court's indulgence is a good mental challenge.'

'Having spent considerable time with you, Mr Ollenu, I can quite see where some of these brazen defences came from. And there I was, as I'm sure were many readers, of the belief that the audaciousness was purely Jacob Dunne.'

'I accept the compliment, Mr Ashby.'

'I assure you, I offered none.'

'I should add that the insults thrown at the prosecutors are entirely Mr Dunne's and he guards them most fiercely.'

'You are proud that criminals get released to prey on the good citizens of Bristol?' said Ashby in a pompous voice. 'What lawyers do is lie on a daily basis, causing thieves and vagabonds to walk free.'

'Everybody lies, Mr Ashby.'

'But your lies are legitimised by wigs and gowns and haughty tones in the hallowed halls of the courts. Do you not feel any remorse? Your clients are common criminals.'

'There is no such thing as a common criminal. The criminal you call "common" is so called for he does not wear top hat and tie and has no gilt-edged suit in his closet. The only difference between the two is that the Crown is reluctant to prosecute one, however nefarious his misdeeds.'

'Your reflection on society and your profession is somewhat clouded, Mr Ollenu.'

'Then look to your own profession. Do insurance agents not lie? Are their calculations not based on fabrications about risks and the costs of such risks? Of course, they are. Your clients are deceived into paying more than is equitable for the service received and most will never recover a shilling. Everybody lies, Mr Ashby.'

'I regret having interrupted your criticism of Sir Hans,' grumbled Ashby.

'I am happy to continue,' said Ollenu. 'Sloane left no real medical papers, not of substance in any event. Only one medical publication I have ever heard of, and that was published a few years before his death. The old man died at ninety-two. If he was such an illustrious doctor, where are the medical writings for the fifty years before that? Nowhere. He was too busy travelling the islands, writing tales, fraternising with pirates, collecting mementos and drinking chocolate. If not rum, too.'

Ashby stared over his glasses in annoyance. 'Such a free-flowing fount of criticism. Admit you despise him merely because he married into a slave-owning family.'

'Such knowledge does not endear him, I agree. You may not wish to hear it, but Sloane's fame is not based on achievements in his own profession or on contributions to natural science, rather it is a result of astute investments.'

'Oh, be still, Mr Ollenu.' Annoyed, Ashby leaned forward, nose almost touching the pages to avoid seeing the law clerk's face. 'No one decreed you purveyor of suitable endeavours for noblemen.'

Ollenu turned his attention to the sturdy grandfather clock, admiring its highly polished long wooden case and shiny silver face. The loud ticking and melodic chimes were somewhat soothing, and he was content to listen to the comforting sounds of time passing by as they waited.

-

The strong odour of burning steel and heat was overwhelming as they approached the blacksmith's shop. Ollenu understood why this trade was established so far from the centre of activity. Fellow shop owners would object to the smells and temperature, and possible danger from out-of-control fires. A large cottage was the closest building to the shop, and, from a collection of tools in the front yard, Ollenu guessed that the cottage was also the blacksmith's home.

The brawny man lowered his hammer and wiped dripping sweat from his forehead with the back of his darkened hand. 'Yes, he lodged here in a furnished room, and was free to go about anywhere inside. Only me and the wife live there, and I'm over in here most of the time.'

A slender woman entered the shop with a tankard of ale that she handed to her husband. 'I noticed a carriage arrive. Who are these, Tom?'

'Don't mind them, Evie, they're all right. Barber Leon sent them. Mr Ashby's a fraud investigator and Mr Ollenu's an apprentice lawyer.'

As the woman greeted them, the blacksmith swallowed a mouthful of ale.

'They're looking for Francis Dantry,' he said and wiped froth from his lips.

'As well as Henry Penket, a tailor, and Clare Sandie, a brewer,' added Ashby.

The woman scowled. 'I don't know nothing about them two, but Francis Dantry owes us a fair bit of money. Fooled me, he did. Just upped and left. You never know people nowadays.'

'Would you permit us to see his room?' asked Ollenu.

The woman looked at her husband, who nodded. 'Won't hurt to let them see his place. We be needing to get it cleared out and look for a new lodger.'

Inside the spacious room was a wide bed spread with floral sheets and pillows, a set of drawers, a table and two chairs. White lace curtains hung from the small window. Reading material lay scattered on the table beside a lamp.

An array of clothes – suits and shirts – hung from an open rack. Pairs of shoes and boots were neatly arranged in a corner.

'Your lodger planned to return,' said Ollenu.

'So it would appear,' said Ashby with a frown.

'All I know is, he said he was off to some village with a Spanish boy's name. Could be Pablo or something.'

Ollenu stared at her. 'Pedro, perhaps? I heard mention of that place before.'

'I do not recall ever hearing of Pedro?' said Ashby.

'No, you would not.' Ollenu eyed him with distaste. 'If memory serves me right, you were soaring above earth when Miss Sylvie's carpenter mentioned it.'

Ashby's cheeks crimsoned. 'Oh, yes, well—'

'He also said that rumour has it people have disappeared in Pedro,' added Ollenu. 'Where on the island is that village?'

'I believe it's in St Ann in the north,' said the woman. 'Not far from St Ann's Bay.'

Ashby's eyes widened. 'St Ann's Bay is where Mr Kershaw said he searched for Dantry without success. Do you know why Dantry chose to go to Pedro in particular?'

The woman shrugged. 'To sell more iron tools I suppose. Tom bought some from him. He often had a case of iron things he carried about.'

'Dantry came to the island four years ago,' said Ashby. 'When did you first meet him?'

'He may have come to Jamaica four years ago, but he came to live with us here last year, March, and left this February. We haven't seen a penny since February.'

'Mr Kershaw must surely be aware that Dantry was last seen alive and well six months ago?' said Ollenu. 'Right under his nose in Spanish Town. How can it be that Edward Barrow is not also aware of this information?'

'Something is clearly amiss,' said Ashby. 'May we inspect his possessions?'

'I've got no objection. Need to finish me washing as rain be on the way.'

As Ollenu flicked through the books and papers on top of the table, Ashby searched through one of the drawers. He removed a stack of documents and read each with speed. Soon he lifted a single leaf of paper.

'Look at this letter from Edward Barrow to Francis Dantry dated last year.' The colour drained from Ashby's face as he whispered, 'Barrow knew that Dantry lived here in Spanish Town. The story that Dantry was in hiding and preparing to commit a fraud against our company is untrue.'

Ollenu walked over to the chest of drawers and studied some of the papers. 'Barrow is a prolific slave trader,' he murmured.

'I was unaware that he had joined the Society of Merchant Venturers.' A frown deepened on Ashby's brow as he read. 'He never uttered a single word about such membership. Dantry is Barrow's licensed agent, collecting money on his behalf.'

'In this letter, he thanks Dantry and acknowledges receipt of one thousand pounds,' said Ollenu. 'He states that he anticipates many more successful trades of African cargoes.'

Ashby rubbed his chest and looked about to faint. 'I wonder how long this arrangement has been in existence and how many cargoes?'

'The hostilities commenced at the end of last year. See, in this letter Barrow enquires why the money has not arrived, and in this one he demands the sale proceeds.' Ollenu inhaled deeply. 'I now understand why Kershaw is so interested in Dantry and cares little for the wellbeing of anyone else. Blood money.'

'It explains why Barrow has spoken of buying a second estate in London,' said Ashby. 'Our business finances are sound, but he has personally achieved significant earnings from this African trade.'

'Mr Ashby, I believe Neville Kershaw expects us to find Dantry and the missing money. Barrow has promised Kershaw a share of his wealth.'

'But where is Dantry?' said Ashby. 'Is he hiding somewhere on the island with the money? He does not appear on lists of departures from Jamaica. And you did not see his name on any register of deaths.'

'If Pedro is the place where people go missing, then Pedro must be our next destination,' said Ollenu. 'And we shall not inform Kershaw.'

'I'm not at all certain that Kershaw is a part of this deception.' Ashby stroked his chin, deep in thought. 'He, too, could be labouring under a misconception, exactly as we were.'

'You are hard to convince, Mr Ashby. If only we had set eyes on that letter of introduction – or whatever the letter truly was.'

Ashby closed the drawer and rubbed his eyes. 'What on earth shall I say to Kershaw this afternoon, by way of conversation?'

'You say that after we tired of reading indoors, we had a pleasant walk through the city,' suggested Ollenu. 'In fact, a good long walk is exactly what we should do directly.'

CHAPTER 11

Ashby had to admit he enjoyed walking through the dust-strewn streets of the capital. Walks provided more enlightenment than carriage rides, as they afforded time to admire stylish monuments built by the artistic Spanish and talk to the English settlers. He also needed to try and clear his befuddled mind.

The settlers, who acted as guides, pointed out where handsome Spanish structures had once stood until demolished by the new conquerors. Ashby had to concede that the English could be unnecessarily vindictive; a view Ollenu was all too keen to embrace.

They ventured along a wide dirt road shared by pedestrians and horse-drawn carriages. Children skipped and giggled, seemingly unaffected by the heat. Adults strolled under their parasols, engaged in conversation with their neighbours. Ox-drawn carts trundled by, laden with casks of alcohol. Everything seemed in order to Ashby. He was about to comment on the peace and serenity of it all when the atmosphere suddenly changed.

A cloud of dust at the far end of the street grew in height and width as it rapidly headed towards them. Stirring up the cloud was a huge dapple grey horse, with thick legs of solid muscle that ended in immense hooves. Carriages and sole riders hurriedly moved out of its path. The animal galloped at a furious pace, its hooves making a tremendous noise and causing the earth to vibrate as it drew closer. The rider was obscured, revealing only scant views of a dark billowing cloak and knee-high boots.

Ashby found to his dismay that his legs lost all power of movement as terror anchored him to the spot. His wild eyes turned to Ollenu, who grabbed him with both hands and pulled him out of harm's way, barely in time to avoid the deadly hooves. Both men lay sprawled in the dry dirt.

Ollenu was first to stand. 'Take my hand.'

'Good Lord!' A breathless Ashby clung to his colleague and struggled to his feet. 'That was far too close for comfort. Thank you, Mr Ollenu.'

Shopkeepers and merchants rushed from their business premises and assisted Ashby, fussing over him and ensuring he was unharmed. A bystander recovered Ashby's hat.

'Thank you, I am shaken but otherwise perfectly whole.' Ashby coughed to release the dust particles trapped in his throat. 'Can anyone identify that lunatic?'

No one in the small crowd of concerned pink faces could identify either the horse or the rider. They commiserated with Ashby on his misfortune as the animal faded into the distance. Not one person tended to Ollenu, who blinked through stinging eyes and wiped dust from his face. Recovering his own hat, he flicked specks of embedded gravel from the brim.

Ashby brushed at his scuffed jacket sleeve, then did the same with a knee. 'Whoever it was, rode as if he were astride one of the Four Horses of the Apocalypse.'

'An insolent rider,' said Ollenu as he dusted off his breeches. 'Someone who does not care whether I live or die.'

'You believe it was you he sought to harm?' said Ashby. 'Yet you did not become rooted to the spot, and I heard no verse escape your lips?'

'I cannot rhyme to order, Mr Ashby. A burst of lightning will cause me to flinch as it would any man and I do not recite poem.' Satisfied that he was uninjured, Ollenu fixed his hat. 'My genteel attire may have provoked such rage that the rider desired my end. Had he asked, I would be delighted to inform him where I purchased my suit and hat.'

'Hmm, I have never heard of clothes rage, Mr Ollenu. We cannot let this unfortunate mishap spoil the afternoon. Let us proceed with caution.'

They passed through an area that served as an informal market place where the air was rich with the odour of fresh produce. An array of vegetables displayed on barrows and carts created a riot of colours. Citrus fruits were stacked in wooden boxes of various sizes. Tarpaulin spread on the ground was covered with tomatoes, pumpkin and cabbages, all recognisable products to Ashby. He assumed the unidentifiable produce were unique to the West Indies.

Prudent shoppers advised them what price to pay, and warned how to avoid being taken advantage of. A kind man explained how to differentiate between innocent bruising and worm-infested produce.

Ashby poked at round purple fruits, smooth and shiny as apples, with the soft texture of plums. 'I wonder what these queer things are?'

'Star apples,' said a female voice.

Beside them stood a mature English woman. She wore a cream-coloured bonnet and a lilac dress that nipped in at the waist and flared at the ankles. Her raven hair hung in curls about her shoulders, and her hazel eyes were warm. 'They're rather tasteful, I assure you.'

'Why, thank you, madam.' Ashby gave a polite nod. 'Star apples. I do not believe I have ever heard of such things.'

'I remember you two gentlemen from yesterday,' she said.

'Er, yesterday?'

'Do you not recall, sir? You nodded at me as you entered the parish church and I waved back. I stayed in the corner replenishing the flowers.'

'Oh, of course,' said Ashby. He did recall a handful of parishioners were in the church, although he had been too absorbed admiring the stately interior to do more than briefly nod at them.

Her mischievous eyes fell on Ollenu. 'You, sir, said the disagreeable odour of the pulpit reflected the sins laid there.'

'Forgive me, madam.' Ollenu removed his hat and bowed. 'Sometimes words flow before my brain has given the subject matter due consideration.'

'I can attest to that,' said Ashby.

'Here try one of mine.' She snapped a star apple in half. The interior revealed succulent white juice surrounding pulpy pale flesh.

Ashby hesitated for a moment then stretched out his hand. 'I must say I am not accustomed to eating on the roadside.'

'I understand, sir.' She laughed and her eyes sparkled. 'Once, I was the same. In Jamaica you're entitled to become less reserved, indeed it is expected.' She took a mouthful of white flesh and soon removed a black seed, the size of a cashew nut, and tossed it aside. 'Heavenly.'

Ashby followed her actions. 'Why, yes. It is rather luscious and sweet. Thank you.' He removed his hat and held it awkwardly at his waist. 'I'm Ruben Ashby. This is Isaiah Ollenu.'

'Eleanor Lamont.' She smiled, curtseyed, and then handed the fruit seller some coins. 'I know who you are. I heard that a rather odd pairing had arrived on the island. You two entered the church and matched the description perfectly. I noticed you wore a rather attractive pink bow in your pocket, Mr Ollenu.'

Ollenu bowed. 'A gift from my young daughter. It cannot stay on my head so I wear it on my chest.'

'That is quite charming,' she said. 'How are you finding the island, Mr Ashby?'

'It is quite a revelation, Miss Lamont. Most people are extremely courteous. The meals are heavily spiced and delicious. The sun is much warmer than I am accustomed to, but the air smells wonderfully clean compared to the smoke and fog of Bristol. If only the biting insects would ignore me, I would be quite happy exploring the land.' With a broad smile he added, 'Apparently the Rio Cobre lies ahead and we were determined to find it. Would you care to join us?'

'I would be honoured, Mr Ashby,' she said with another curtsey.

'Do continue your walk with Miss Lamont, Mr Ashby,' said Ollenu quickly. 'I passed some rather interesting yellow fruits and the fragrance called out to me.'

'Why, I am sure we can wait for your return, Mr Ollenu,' said the lady, unaware of Ashby's sudden frown.

'I see clouds in the distance, threatening the sun, so you must not delay.' Ollenu met Ashby's gaze, smiled and then bowed at his female companion. 'A pleasure to meet you, Miss Lamont. I bid you good day.'

'Good day, Mr Ollenu.' As he strode away she said, 'Is he safe to walk alone?'

'Believe me, he looks after himself on roads and in taverns. He will also be quite safe at the Kershaw's, provided he avoids Mrs Kershaw.'

'Oh, does Lydia Kershaw treat him unkindly?'

'On the contrary,' Ashby chuckled. 'Mrs Kershaw wishes to treat him very kindly indeed, if only he would allow her that opportunity. It amuses me to watch the obvious consternation she invokes in him. As much as it entertains me, I do politely intrude as would any dutiful chaperone when she becomes too affectionate.'

'Oh, poor Mr Ollenu.' Eleanor smiled. 'I am sure he appreciates you as his guardian.'

'It is the only occasion he shows any appreciation whatsoever.'

Much to Ashby's delight, Eleanor Lamont linked her arm through his and twirled her parasol above her bonnet. As they walked he stole a glance at her. She was undeniably attractive. Her light voice charmed him as she pointed out various individuals and relayed choice bits of information about them. It crossed Ashby's mind that few things were secret in Jamaica, despite the vast expanse of lands that separated some properties.

A vision of the lady he had once loved and lost passed before his eyes. Hettie was a quiet woman who enjoyed her work as a midwife and willingly accompanied him to church. She had loved him despite his faults. Everyone expected them to announce a forthcoming marriage. If only he had not driven her away.

'By the way, I should inform you that I am Mrs Lamont not Miss.'

The unexpected words shook Ashby out of his reverie, and a feeling of disappointment replaced the warmth that had engulfed him moments earlier. 'Oh.'

'I am a widow, Mr Ashby. My husband succumbed to fever over a year ago. I will return to England eventually, once our estate is sold. We had no children and there is nothing to keep me here now.'

'I am sorry to hear this.' Ashby patted her soft hand. 'I would not have thought the island a good place for a lady, such as you, to be alone?'

Her eyes twinkled. 'Such as me?'

Ashby blushed and stuttered, 'You are quite a charming lady, Mrs Lamont.'

'Compliments do not come easily to you, do they Mr Ashby?'

'You noticed. Do forgive my awkwardness.'

'You are a perfect gentleman, Ruben.' She squeezed his arm. 'I simply cannot continue to address you as Mister now that we are friends, can I? Do call me Eleanor.'

'I am honoured, Eleanor.'

'My sister, Franny, is in England at present and her husband lives in a property close to mine. My brother-in-law keeps a watchful eye over me so I have no fear. I live a quiet life, although if there is anywhere distant I really need to visit, I may use a footman as escort.'

'I am pleased that you attend to your safety, Eleanor.'

They came upon the Rio Cobre, a striking expanse of blue-green water. Thick layers of verdant vegetation arose from either side of the banks and presided over the gently flowing water. Broad-leaved trees cast welcome, cooling, shadows over the couple as they walked the narrow path beside the river.

'They say the river is over thirty miles long and runs from way up in the hills all the way down to Kingston Harbour,' said Eleanor.

Eyes filled with wonder, Ashby admired the water's beauty. 'How perfect.'

'It would be perfect if it had a bridge,' she said wistfully. 'I would love to stand on it and cast flowers over the edge, run to the other side, and watch them float downstream.'

'Yes, that would be an agreeable pastime,' said Ashby. A vision of them both, side by side, casting flowers into the water swept through his mind. He took the opportunity to study her side view, her pink cheeks and cute button nose, her dark bouncing hair. The thought that she enjoyed his company was something he regarded with wonderment and gratitude.

'Did you enjoy your time at church yesterday?' asked Eleanor.

'I did. It helped me feel closer to the Lord.' Ashby stared at the dark waters. 'Although I must say, I am concerned that what I witness day to day, does not accord with the preachings of the Gospel.'

'You are so right, Ruben. People adapt those parts of the Bible that suit them and disavow the rest.'

Ashby nodded. 'I have no wish to disparage the island, as I am but a newly landed visitor, but I pray that more encouraging signs await me.'

'After you left the church yesterday, my curiosity led me to ask a few questions,' said Eleanor. 'I understand you're in search of disappeared clients?'

Taken by surprise both at the direct question and the sudden movement of her eyes straight to his, Ashby stuttered. 'Oh, I, yes that is so.'

'Then I hope they are discovered without too much ado.'

As they walked alongside the river, Ashby patted her warm hand. 'Tell me, Eleanor, do you know of a village in St Ann called Pedro?'

'Why, yes. Very few people live in Pedro, but a much spoken of Scottish fellow is settled there. Doctor Lewis Hutchinson. He lives in a place he calls Edinburgh Castle.'

'My word, I have not yet come across any castles in Jamaica. Edinburgh Castle sounds rather grand.'

'I cannot say, as I have never attended that village.' Eleanor stopped walking and turned to him. 'You do not appear to be armed Ruben?'

'No, I am not keen on firearms.' Puzzled, Ashby scratched his chin. 'Why would you mention such a thing? I do not anticipate a violent confrontation with anyone during the course of my mission; a mission authorised from England.'

'I have no wish to alarm you, Ruben, but one should always anticipate violence in this land, from all sides.' Eleanor voice reflected her concern. 'Even the priests and pastors are armed. If you change your mind, I have a store of guns and ammunition.'

'I must say, you do not give the impression of being a weapons devotee.'

Eleanor laughed and tightened her grip on his arm. 'Stanley, my husband, was a great gun enthusiast. He could slay a rat at a hundred feet.'

'I pray it will not come to that,' said Ashby. 'Though I daresay it is better to confront rats than drunken rascals or wilful mermaids.'

'Oh, you have seen the mermaids?' Eleanor seemed delighted. 'I am told they sit on the shiny stones of the Rio Cobre when no one is near, and comb long yellow hair with gold combs. They are shy, gay sprites who, if startled, vanish into the deep.'

Ashby frowned at the recollection. 'I believe we are referring to rather different beings, Eleanor. Not a yellow curl in sight, and they certainly were not shy.'

Mrs Lamont fell quiet and Ashby sensed a change in her countenance. 'What troubles you, Eleanor?'

'I am no flibbertigibbet, but when you mentioned Pedro my mind went to the rumours concerning Doctor Hutchinson.' Her smile was bashful. 'That's why I mentioned guns. It is said, he has shot and killed people. No proof of such acts has ever been obtained, and he seems largely unaffected by the gossips.'

'Mr Ollenu and I plan to visit that village, but it may be wise to avoid the doctor if he is prone to violence?'

'The rumours may just be rumours, Ruben. I met Doctor Hutchinson a few times, and he was most charming and polite. In fact, I am sure to see him tomorrow in Montego Bay at Sir Alastair Nicholson's ball. He attended last year's ball and proved himself a thoroughly engaging character.'

'Ah, then I shall see you at the ball, Eleanor, how splendid! Mr Kershaw arranged invitations for myself and Mr Ollenu.'

'Half of the island is invited,' she said. 'Well, those with wealth or connections to grant them esteem. I believe my invitations to grand events come by virtue of my late husband's connections not my own. He was an Assembly-man and quite popular with the titled set.'

'Oh, I see,' said Ashby somewhat distracted by her radiant face.

Eleanor took his arm again. 'I sincerely pray that you and Mr Ollenu do not put yourselves in danger, Ruben.'

'I shall be sure to warn him of the rumours surrounding the doctor.'

'I wish Mr Kershaw would perform his role to greater effect,' said Eleanor. 'He has a large gaol with many cells, yet it holds only petty thieves, pickpockets and vagrants, some of whom cannot even remember their own names.'

'You have been inside the gaol?'

'Yes, with the local deacons some Sundays. Many detainees are starved of someone to show an interest in their cause and wellbeing. Meanwhile, the so-called respectable people duel over disputed land, treat their slaves abominably, assault women of all complexions, and are never so much as cautioned, to say nothing of being shown inside a cell.'

'I have spent the past few weeks suffering lectures from Mr Ollenu that a two-tiered system of justice exists in England, though things sound more brutal here in Jamaica.' Ashby sighed. 'I do wonder whether God is too busy to address the ills of this island.'

'He does have much to contend with, Ruben,' she said with a smile.

Ashby stared at her reddened cheeks and bright eyes. She was a goddess and it was a long time since he had admired a woman so. 'Do you attend church often, Eleanor?'

'Not weekly, for I am not that keen to kneel and mingle with parishioners who masquerade as Christians. Your Mr

Ollenu was right about the church. The flowers can be changed. The people, I fear, cannot.'

'Oh, people can change, Eleanor, if they really want to.' Ashby watched as a gull swooped and claimed its struggling prey from the dark waters. Had he changed his ways with alacrity all those years ago, he could well be a happily married man minding his own business in Bristol. He smiled wryly. Or he could be a divorced man, or a widower.

'We can examine them on our return if you wish, Ruben, the church flowers?'

'I welcome the opportunity, Eleanor. I shall also kneel and say a prayer that all goes smoothly in Montego Bay tomorrow.'

CHAPTER 12

The carriage arrived at Sir Alastair Nicholson's mansion in Montego Bay, St James, before sunset. A large blue flag with a white saltire fluttered proudly from the gable roof. Below the roof was a white facade and multi-paned arch windows. Acres of well-kept green lawns surrounded the approach, broken only by a wide pathway cut to accommodate multiple conveyances. The elevation provided a scenic view of the Caribbean Sea and densely packed wild forest that lined the coastline.

An African footman immediately appeared at the carriage door and opened it with a deep bow. His neat blue jacket was buttoned to the collar and his matching breeches ended in long white stockings and shiny buckled shoes. Mortimer stayed on top of the carriage and tipped his hat at Ashby and Ollenu. Johnson jumped from the top seat and stood with hands on hips, watching them alight.

'Will you stay too, gentlemen?' asked Ashby.

'Oh no, Mr Ashby,' said Johnson politely. 'We're bound for The Goose boarding house in the town centre. Everyone knows it. Just send word when you need to be on your way again tomorrow. If you stay any longer, you'll have to hire a carriage to take you back to Spanish Town.'

'Thank you, Mr Johnson, we shall be sure to follow your instructions,' said Ashby.

The pristine footman stood to attention, and, after soliciting their names in a well-rehearsed line, he escorted the two new guests up the stately stone steps.

Ollenu stared in awe as they crossed the threshold. Inside the expansive hallway were floor to ceiling tapestries, interspersed with tall floral vases on large mahogany sideboards and life-size portraits of haughty men. Branching off from the hallway on either side were the highest panelled double doors he had ever seen, each decorated with gold handles.

Indistinct voices floated from beyond one set of open doors, light-hearted female giggles, intermingled with the more sonorous tones of males. A piano played an unrecognisable tune out of key, as if someone was practising their skills. Not for the first time, Ollenu was taken aback by the two completely different sets of lives being lived on the island, the decadent and the despairing. The majority of people who resembled him were not on the right side of decadence.

'I wonder which one is Doctor Lewis Hutchinson?' murmured Ollenu as they proceeded down the hallway.

'I look forward to that discovery,' said Ashby.

Their steward threw back his shoulders and shouted, 'Mr Ruben Ashby and Mr Isaiah Ollenu from Bristol, England!'

As Sir Alastair Nicholson strode towards them across a sparkling marble floor, Ollenu studied him critically. The nobleman had a long face ending with a sharp chin, dark brown eyes and matching hair with flecks of grey throughout. He was identical to his portrait, except for a significant bulge to his stomach. Either the man had overindulged in recent months or the artist had purposely sought to flatter his sitter.

'Delighted to meet you, Mr Ashby.' He shook Ashby's hand with vigour then turned to Ollenu, grasping his hand with equal enthusiasm. 'Mr Ollenu, I hear Jacob Dunne speaks very highly of you. It is a pleasure to make your acquaintance at last.'

Ollenu bowed. 'The pleasure is all mine, Sir Alastair.'

Sir Alastair turned and beckoned to a tiny footboy in an oversized suit whose natural black coils were closely trimmed to his scalp. 'Come take these bags upstairs Toby.'

The boy rushed forward and snatched the bags from the men. He balanced one on each of his thin shoulders. 'Welcome Mr Ashby, and Mr Ollenu,' he announced boisterously. 'I am at your service.'

Sir Alastair winced and shook his head. 'The aim, Toby, is to relieve each guest of his burden, not to remove his humerus from his scapula. On the next occasion, welcome the guests first, then politely hold out your hands and let them offer the bags to you.'

'Yes, Sir Alastair.'

The boy bowed and his small body was soon concealed behind intricately carved banisters as he clambered up the wide stairway. The aristocrat smiled after him with some affection. 'He is only seven, but he has the right attitude and will be proficient in a few years.'

'I should assist him,' suggested Ollenu. 'The bags contain leather boots and are heavier than they look.'

'He is strong, believe me,' said Sir Alastair. 'Bit rough about the ears, but he can manage anything thrown at him. I may even permit him to open carriage doors and escort my guests up the steps.'

'Of course you will teach him how to read?' said Ollenu.

'How to read? Why ever would I do that?'

'Even you must admit that none of us is getting any younger, Sir Alastair. In years to come, when our eyes grow dim and our hands frail, it would be a blessing to have a youth close by to read for us. Even to write for us when our hands shake.'

'Why, you are so right, Mr Ollenu. Do you know, it had never crossed my mind?'

'Oh, but it would have, I am sure, sir,' said Ollenu. 'You had already identified his potential. It would be only a matter of time before you saw even greater promise.'

'Yes, quite. He shall start English lessons first thing tomorrow.' Sir Alastair beamed and looked on all sides of the hall. 'My good lady wife is probably arranging for the service of more beverages, or playing chaperone somewhere. Come and meet your fellow guests.' He indicated that they follow him and strode on ahead.

'So, the boy will learn to read and write?' whispered Ashby.

Ollenu lowered his voice. 'And sign his freedom papers with a flourish.'

They entered an enormous ballroom. The panelled walls were lined with silver candelabra and portraits of Scottish kings, and the ceiling decorated with mosaic as homage to the Sistine Chapel. A gentle evening breeze blew through open windows, surrounded by heavy red velvet curtains. Ladies waved colourful fans as speedily as hummingbirds' wings, both to stave off heat and to appear demure. Plump settees of soft leather were aligned on opposite walls and low side tables conveniently arranged in between.

General gaiety and universal good humour possessed everyone in this space, but dismay settled upon Ollenu as he surveyed the ballroom. Not a single ebony complexionedface, male or female, on any person that was not in a subservient role. The English took Jamaica from the Spanish in 1655. How could it possibly be that over a hundred years later not even a mulatto resident was considered worthy enough for an invitation to this spectacular event?

Anger surged through Ollenu, creasing his brow. He swiped a glass of Madeira from the passing waiter and drained it.

Ashby collected a glass for himself. 'Mr Ollenu, I thought you had forsaken alcohol?'

'I had. It welcomed me back with open arms.'

'Everyone is so engrossed,' said Sir Alastair as he stretched his neck to see above the many heads. Using his chin, he indicated various dignitaries, naming each one.

Ollenu grew impatient as anecdotes relating to each face tripped lightly from their host's tongue. Finally, it became too much. 'Sir Alastair, would you be kind enough to indicate the doctor, Lewis Hutchinson?'

'Hmm, Doctor Hutchinson. He is definitely here, but he may be in the drawing room or somewhere quieter.' Sir Alastair waved a hand. 'Ah, there is Sir and Lady Webster. Lovely people. Their home is to be erected on an estate a mile from here. I am heartened that Montego Bay is developing at pace. Not good to have too much wild land in between estates.'

'Indeed, sir,' agreed Ashby. 'Good neighbours can be a blessing.'

Someone hailed Sir Alastair and he waved towards the voice. 'Do excuse me, gentlemen. You must eat as you mingle. My wife says formal seating does not allow for proper interaction so we're trying it her way. Oh, if the

Madeira is not to your taste, there are trays with Menzies and Morrison's bitters or spicy rum.'

At the far end of the room, a long ornate table was set with low-burning candles that kept the lighting appropriately muted. Whole roasted chickens were laid out, together with suckling pig, fried fishes and rolls of cornbread. A plum pudding, darkened with fruit, rum and molasses, was smothered in a buttery sauce. In between the foods, lay bottles of wine and flasks of alcohol.

Extravagantly dressed housemen stepped forward to aid the guests with their dishes, then quickly retreated to the sidelines. Some merry guests were happy to load their own plates without expert assistance. As a result, a scattering of bread rolls and chicken legs languished beneath the overladen table. Ollenu and Ashby made their selections from the feast.

'It would be quite a revelation if we discovered that Francis Dantry rents a room at the doctor's castle,' said Ashby. 'Paying substantial rent in order for his location to remain a secret.'

'It is possible,' said Ollenu as he sampled the cornbread. 'If Pedro is as remote as suggested, he could avoid prying eyes, even Kershaw's prying eyes, and live in comfort.'

Ashby nodded in agreement. 'Safe in the knowledge that he, and his fortune, are unlikely to be found.'

'It is also possible that, if Doctor Hutchinson is indeed a murderer, and Dantry came upon him, Dantry is dead.'

'I prefer not to entertain such a ghastly thought, Mr Ollenu.'

As they ate and wandered the floor, the men engaged in polite conversation with friendly guests. Each time Ollenu's name was mentioned, it was accompanied with the words 'apprenticed to Mr Jacob Dunne Esquire', a statement that encouraged warm looks and impressed nods in his direction.

'I see no one with a shock of red hair, red beard, slender, of forty years, who could be our Scotsman,' said Ollenu.

'It would appear he is not yet arrived.' Ashby looked at the array of guests. 'Doctors are not known for keeping good time and Doctor Hutchinson may be no different.'

A gentleman who overheard their conversation said, 'I have not seen Doctor Hutchinson, Mr Ashby. Perchance, he makes no appearance, because Doctor Hutton may be in attendance.'

'Who is Doctor Hutton?' asked Ashby.

The man smiled and tapped his prominent nose. 'A fellow doctor, a neighbour, who Doctor Hutchinson attacked. Left him with a steel pin in his head.'

'How atrocious!' said Ashby.

'Indeed, but nothing ever came of that incident,' said the gentleman. 'Doctor Hutchinson claimed self-defence and his word was accepted. The matter was hushed up and is rarely mentioned. People whisper that he has actually killed before. Shot a number of people dead.'

'How many people are said to have met their fate at his hands?' asked Ollenu.

'In a twelve-year period, some suggest forty, others say as many as sixty.'

'Sixty!' Ollenu repeated and coughed so hard his eyes watered. An alert waiter rushed over and handed him a glass of water.

'That is too fantastic, sir!' said Ashby. 'Whoever heard of such a diabolical thing?'

'As you say, it does seem too fantastic,' agreed the guest.

'It seems akin to madness,' said Ollenu.

'Funnily enough, people take great pleasure in referring to him as the Mad Doctor and the Mad Master, when he may well be perfectly innocent.' The gentleman craned his neck and peered into the distance. 'Do excuse me, I must go and rescue my good friend Giles from those overzealous spinsters.'

'This is most concerning,' said Ashby and took a mouthful of wine. 'The doctor has apparently demonstrated violence against a fellow physician, yet I cannot believe that he has killed scores of people. No one could commit such crimes for years on end unchallenged.'

'On this island? I do believe it,' said Ollenu with a frown. 'It is beginning to seem more likely that Francis Dantry is no longer among the living.'

'Do not be completely swayed by that gentleman's words, Mr Ollenu. One must keep an open mind. The Bible says "judge not, lest ye be judged".'

'Mr Ashby, the Bible also says "thou shalt not kill".'

The two men continued circulating among the guests, participating in innocuous, friendly dialogue. In due course, Ollenu felt Ashby's elbow in his side and followed his colleague's gaze. The object of attention was a lean man with a short red beard whose vivid red hair was tied back with brown ribbon. Immaculately dressed in evening suit, he was at ease speaking to two younger gentlemen who seemed intrigued by his words.

'Are you suffering any peculiar vibrations, Mr Ollenu?' whispered Ashby. 'Is a rhyme to be expected?'

'I do not suffer peculiar vibrations, Mr Ashby. And you are most welcome to devise a verse of your own, if you require such entertainment.'

They moved closer. Ashby paused near the man's shoulders and started a conversation with a venerable couple. Ollenu studied the man's features. His thick red eyebrows were almost joined to form a monobrow and the grey-green eyes fixed on his listeners were sharp and penetrating. He wore no jewellery of any kind, not even a pocket watch in his waistcoat. The red-headed man adjusted his position to accommodate the new arrivals as the two groups were drawn into mutual conversation.

'Ruben Ashby from Bristol.' Ashby grasped the man's hand and shook firmly.

'Doctor Lewis Hutchinson from Pedro, St Ann.'

'And this is my colleague, Isaiah Ollenu.'

Doctor Hutchinson smiled as they shook hands. 'I heard your announcement earlier, although I could not see the persons being introduced.'

'Pleased to make your acquaintance,' said Ollenu. Nothing about this affable man suggested he could break another man's skull, much less shoot anyone.

The doctor took a sip of wine, his eyes fixed on the law clerk. 'I did wonder at the name Ollenu; it is unknown to me.'

'My lineage goes back to the Coromantee region of Africa. The name is more familiar there. In my Bristol home live four of us, including my wife and children. Four and a half to be precise.'

'Another one of you on the way, how charming.' The words purred from the doctor's thin lips.

Unable to deduce whether the comment was genuine politeness or a subtle taunt, Ollenu responded graciously. 'I look forward to being charmed, if that is what being kept awake all night means.'

'And what brings you good gentlemen to Jamaica?' asked Doctor Hutchinson. He led the way as the three men wandered across a seemingly endless checkerboard marble floor that formed part of the extensive balcony, supported by solid white pillars.

'I wish I could say it was the bright weather and fine food,' said Ashby, 'but I work in the insurance industry and am always on the lookout for clients, new and old.'

'And you, Mr Ollenu?'

'I work closely with Mr Ashby – seeking clients. I am also in training to become an attorney.'

'A man of law.' Doctor Hutchinson inclined his head slightly. 'A noble profession. And you enjoy your work?'

'Certainly, it keeps my brain active, introduces me to people I would never have crossed paths with, and gives me opportunities to help drive the law in the right direction. Change will only occur if those in the field of law propel it.'

The doctor nodded as he studied Ollenu. 'An idealist, I find that most impressive.'

'On our voyage, we read the adventures of Sir Hans Sloane, such a revered man with so many avenues to his work, a great doctor by all accounts,' said Ashby. 'How do you fare as a physician in Jamaica?'

'Yes, Sir Hans was a man of great versatility.' The doctor smiled warmly. 'I made these shores twelve years ago and could never pretend to be in his esteem. He resided here for only fifteen months, yet he found time to explore the island as well as play doctor to the Duke of Albemarle.'

'Before the good Duke unfortunately drank himself to death,' added Ollenu. 'Celebrating the birth of a new baby to James the Second, I believe?'

Hutchinson grinned. 'Thirsts were well and truly quenched at that celebration. Alas, I am never requested to provide medical services to the nobility, although I await the call.'

'You have many patients?' asked Ashby.

'Not a single one.'

'Not a single one?' said Ollenu.

'Pah!' The doctor shrugged his narrow shoulders. 'I am rather out of the way at Edinburgh Castle. Pedro is a tiny settlement with few houses and I do not receive many visitors. My living is made mainly from my extensive herd of cattle.'

A solemn waiter appeared and refilled all their glasses with wine.

'Edinburgh Castle sounds such a delightful place,' said Ashby.

'It is, and I would be honoured to show you both my residence. You must come with me this very night. Get away from these pompous, boastful people.'

Ashby laughed conspiratorially and shook his head. 'We are at Sir Alastair's pleasure this night, but thank you Doctor Hutchinson. If you could facilitate a visit tomorrow, during daylight hours, we would be gladdened to accept.'

Hutchinson smiled and grasped Ashby's hand. 'Then it is done.'

'Surely, Doctor, you do not intend to ride back to Pedro in the dead of night?' asked Ollenu.

'I enjoy nighttime, when it is cool and dark and only owls speak. I relish the freedom of movement when no people walk or ride. My horse, too, loves to gallop at night and needs no encouragement from a whip.'

'May I propose noonday for our visit, doctor?' said Ashby.

'That will give us enough time to see Pedro, and then travel back to Montego Bay before nightfall,' added Ollenu.

'Noonday it is, gentlemen. Your coach drivers will find me with ease. That was Johnson and Mortimer I saw on your carriage, was it not?'

'The very same pair,' said Ashby.

'Odd men those,' said the doctor. 'They are neither planters nor watchmen, yet they are at Neville Kershaw's right hand and accompany him everywhere.'

'Quite possibly they are bodyguards,' mused Ollenu.

'Possibly.' The doctor raised a glass at someone inside the hall. 'We should return indoors for fear of offending Sir Alastair. Not many people extend invitations to me, nowadays, so I can ill afford to insult those that do. I believe he shows such generosity because he too has Scottish roots and is more trusting than the arrogant English.' Doctor Hutchinson looked at Ollenu. 'Imagine, the English sailed here armed to the teeth with cannon, informed the occupying Spaniards that *they* were the foreigners, and drove them out. The audacity!'

'Audacious indeed,' said Ollenu, nodding in support.

The doctor bowed and departed, his stylish slippers silent on the floor.

'There, he is not at all disagreeable or threatening.' Ashby sounded somewhat relieved. 'I would go further and suggest he is quite sincere.'

'He is unacquainted with truth, Mr Ashby. He did not see us arrive, yet he saw Johnson and Mortimer on our carriage?' Ollenu looked askance at his colleague. 'You would do well not to believe everything he says.'

As they re-entered the ballroom, Sir Alastair accosted them and introduced them to his wife, Lady Victoria Nicholson. She was an elegant woman whose wholesome figure was contained in a fine blue gown, with a diamond tiara sat upon her dark upswept hair.

'Mr Ollenu, I understand you play the piano?' she said sweetly.

'I do, my lady, although it is many weeks since I last applied these fingers to the keys.'

'I wonder; would you be good enough to play a few tunes for us?' She touched his arm gently and whispered, 'Some of our guests, the ones who can play, arrived early and swallowed wine as if the island is near to run dry. They are not fit to play anything. You must save me.'

'Of course, Lady Nicholson. I will not let you down.'

She led the way to the piano. The guests clapped expectantly as Ollenu flapped up the tail of his immaculate jacket and positioned himself on the padded stool. Ashby's eyes widened as one melodious tune after the other flowed from the piano. The impressed guests hummed and swayed in pleasure.

When Ollenu paused, stood and bowed he was immediately pressed back into his seat by Sir Alastair with the entreaty, 'One more, Mr Ollenu!'

When Sir Alastair was otherwise engaged, his wife brought requests of tunes to Ollenu. Playing the upbeat melodies brought welcome peace and comfort to his spirit. Couples took to the floor, prancing and twirling, and Ollenu conceded to each request, despite his tired fingers. Although in need of rest, he appreciated the need to keep everyone enraptured. The audience consisted of people of influence, people who would surely remember him if he ever had to call upon them for assistance.

He was happy to see Ashby engaged in conversation with Eleanor Lamont. His smile grew wider as the investigator led Eleanor onto the floor and the two began dancing. Ruben Ashby needed a living human being to believe in, rather than a god and a gold cross.

'Would you play Bach's "Toccata in D Minor"?' whispered Lady Nicholson who had sidled over to him unnoticed. 'Special request from a guest.'

'Of course.'

'Toccata' was a strange request in the midst of such light-hearted pieces, and Ollenu wondered who could have selected it. As the tune did not sound so bleak when played with speed, he resolved to increase the tempo. Nodding to enthusiastic claps, he finished his current piece and bowed to Lady Nicholson.

As soon as Ollenu's fingers hit the keys for 'Toccata', it was as if each hand had acquired an extra pound in weight. The sounds that emitted from the piano were slow and hard, the tune taking on an even more chilling tone when played so sluggishly. He raised his head and looked up at the audience, all of whom merged into a blur of shapes and faces he could not identify. The candles on the walls flickered, the shutters bashed and windows shook. Ollenu's unrestrainable fingers continued to punish the keys despite his efforts to stop.

Suddenly, a pair of pale hands pressed into his, bringing an abrupt end to the musical offence. Ashby gave an embarrassed laugh as he loosened his grip and stood up straight. 'Now we'll have something gay by Handel, Mr Ollenu. We deserved Bach's darkest piece for our hubris.'

Some guests appeared ruffled. Most brushed off the unfortunate incident with good grace, and a few seemed too intoxicated to have noticed anything unusual.

Ollenu blinked repeatedly and inhaled as much air as his lungs would allow. The room haze lifted and all guests were now clearly visible. He resumed playing with controlled passion, choosing the pleasant notes of Vivaldi's Summer. Ashby returned to the side of Eleanor Lamont, who nodded at Ollenu and clapped her encouragement. Gradually, indistinct chatter and laughter filled the room again.

As perspiration poured from his brow and soaked his skin, Ollenu played what he determined must be his last tune, rose and bowed slowly to all sides of the room. Enthusiastic claps followed him as he pursued a waiter holding a tray with glasses of water. Along the way, he was stopped many times to shake hands and accept congratulations, and he acknowledged their praise with humility and humour. He grasped the glass of water and downed it in one go, before lifting another one that he drank with more dignity.

Ashby approached him, clapping heartily. He shook Ollenu's hand and patted his shoulder and declared, 'Well done, Mr Ollenu! Great show, man!' He then lowered his voice to a whisper. 'What happened to you?'

Ollenu appeared confused. 'What happened to the whole room?'

'You were playing so brilliantly. We were enthralled and then you went off into that... That... Whatever it was. It sounded as if you were trying to raise the dead, man. Whatever possessed you?'

'Are you deaf and blind, Mr Ashby? Did you not hear the windows rattle, hear the shutters bang against the panes, see the candlelight dim?'

'I saw and heard nothing of the sort, Mr Ollenu, and I can assure you, neither did anyone else. The windows and doors are wide open. No windows rattled, no shutters banged, and no lights dimmed.'

Ollenu stared at the windows. It was as Ashby said. Not even the curtains had moved. His insides churned and he wiped moist palms on his tailored jacket. The illusion could only be attributed to the long journey, lack of sleep, or second glass of Madeira that he should not have imbibed.

He rubbed his pulsating temple. 'The wine is warm and may have produced a disagreeable effect.'

'Then you should, once again, forsake wine, Mr Ollenu.'

'You should not forsake the widow Lamont. She looks this way.'

'Oh, er, yes.'

'Well, go on, Mr Ashby.'

'A thought occurred to me earlier, Mr Ollenu. Let us say, my clients, in dire need of money, started selling their valuables. I have observed the guests to see if anyone wears our insured jewellery.' He leaned closer to Ollenu. 'Behind you is a lady with an emerald set necklace that I must inspect further. A close inspection should reveal the provenance. I shall return shortly.'

Before Ollenu could challenge this questionable line of thought, Ashby had ambled over to the woman and her female friend. Ollenu saw that Eleanor Lamont was keenly watching Ashby's assignation with an expression that one could only acquaint with jealousy. As discreetly as he could, he made his way across the floor towards her. 'Mrs Lamont, such a pleasure to see you again.'

'Good night, Mr Ollenu.' She barely looked at him, her attention taken with his colleague.

'Mr Ashby's company has mislaid three clients in Jamaica, as well as their expensive jewels. He is a thorough researcher. He will do whatever is necessary to recover them – both people and property.'

'Mary Blanchard is not mislaid, Mr Ollenu. She lives mere miles from Spanish Town. I would not mourn should she become mislaid.'

'Ah, you are intimately acquainted with the lady?' said Ollenu.

'No, my husband was. Intimately acquainted that is.' She gave a wry smile. 'I am sorry to unnerve you, Mr Ollenu. It all remains very raw. I, too, am given to speaking before my brain has thought of polite sentences.'

'I am so sorry this happened to you, Mrs Lamont.'

'You know you may call me Eleanor?'

'You will forgive me, but to address you without formality would incur the wrath of less civil minds and result in my undoing.'

'I understand. Believe me I do.' She continued to watch Ashby. 'It does not become a man of religion to philander with so many women.'

'Oh, I am sure Mr Ashby has faith foremost in mind, regardless of what questions he asks of those ladies.'

'Perhaps you are correct, although he admits that doubts have begun to cloud his religious beliefs.'

'Eleanor.' The voice came from a soldier who waved at her from a distance.

'Do excuse me, Mr Ollenu.'

'Of course, Mrs Lamont.'

He watched her walk away then turned to look at Ashby. The investigator smiled and bowed at the ladies before he returned to Ollenu's side. 'False alarm.'

'You ought to be more alarmed by what is going on over there, Mr Ashby.' Ollenu waved a water glass in Eleanor's direction. 'By giving those women your utmost attention, you seem to have lost hers.'

Eleanor's back was to them as she chatted to a strapping gentleman dressed in full soldiers' uniform.

'Do not look so forlorn,' said Ollenu. 'All is not lost. Go over there and interrupt. Regain your rightful place at her side.'

'I cannot do so, Mr Ollenu. She is deeply engaged, and may not wish to be interrupted.'

'Oh, you do not know women. She pretends to be engaged because you offended her by placing your nose in another woman's bosom.'

Ashby flushed pink. 'Mr Ollenu, your choice of words is entirely inappropriate.'

A man of aristocratic bearing approached them. 'Mr Ashby, Mr Ollenu.' He smiled broadly and shook their hands. 'So good to have real talent on the island. I'm Charles Cadogan, and most delighted to meet you.'

'Likewise, Mr Cadogan,' said Ashby. 'I can pretend no particular talent. My gifted associate here is the talented one, as you have seen and heard.'

'Simply marvellous skills, Mr Ollenu! And the best dressed man too! I adore that golden cravat, sir, it goes exceptionally well with your colour.' In one of Cadogan's hands was a burning tobacco pipe. With the unoccupied hand, he tweaked Ollenu's cravat as only a person not used to asking permission could do. 'You don't happen to possess a spare cravat, Mr Ollenu? Wouldn't look as splendid on me, of course, but I desire to brighten my appearance.'

'Unfortunately, I do not, sir.' Ollenu touched the cravat lovingly. 'My dear wife gave this to me, and it is a treasure I could never part with. Should you pass through Bristol, I would be delighted to introduce you to a superior tie-maker who I am sure would be eager to show you his wares.'

'I would be most obliged,' said Charles Cadogan.

Ollenu smiled at the bombastic man. The face was not familiar, but the name certainly was. As the man was so friendly, he decided to be forward. 'You are Earl Cadogan are you not? Son of Lord Cadogan and Lady Elizabeth Sloane Cadogan? That would make you the grandson of Sir Hans Sloane?'

'Why, yes I am.' The man seemed surprised and pleased. 'I try not to flatter myself with titles unless I'm in England, as people allow me to be myself in Jamaica. In England, I live under the burden of the Sloane and Cadogan names. Here, I can be Charles or Charlie.'

'You should not be embarrassed by your good name, My Lord,' said Ollenu.

'Charles, will do, Ollenu. I take little pleasure in the Lord and Earl monikers. I cannot pretend to have any skill except for managing my parents' estates and I'm not exceptional at that. I fail to visit more than once a year.'

'Your grandfather was a great man, Charles. We enjoyed reading his books on the subject of his voyages and adventures. Mr Ashby and I were speaking about him earlier. It takes a distinguished and brave man to accomplish all that Sir Hans accomplished. His was such a marvellous contribution to the world.'

As Ashby's eyebrows surged up his forehead, Ollenu gave the investigator a brazen smile.

'Yes, the old man was a right one.' The earl grinned. 'He gained the trust of kings and lords, and even a bloodthirsty pirate such as Henry Morgan. I could only aspire to be compared to Grandfather.' He flicked back a brown curl from his brow. 'My mother told me so many stories about him, and it is to my eternal regret that I never met him.'

Ollenu nodded. 'Although it would be wonderful for you to hear his actual voice, you are so fortunate that he left behind a legacy. Many fascinating pages for you to read about his life.'

'Yes, books and countless things that he passed on to the British Museum. I am grateful.' The earl puffed on his pipe. 'Gentlemen, you remain on the island indefinitely?'

'We hope our investigations conclude in the shortest possible time,' said Ashby. 'We are trying to find missing clients of mine. You may have heard mention of them: Henry Penket, Clare Sandie, Francis Dantry?'

'I regret, I have not. Discreet enquiries on my part may provide some clues. You stay here with Sir Alastair?'

'We do plan to spend a night or two with Sir Alastair,' said Ollenu.

'Our base is in Spanish Town with Neville Kershaw,' said Ashby. 'Tomorrow, for a few hours, we shall be in Pedro, St Ann, at the home of Doctor Lewis Hutchinson.'

'We return to Montego Bay long before nightfall tomorrow,' said Ollenu with confidence.

'We must all ride together across my lands,' said Charles Cadogan warmly. 'My valet will find you, wherever you are on the island. Everybody knows everybody's whereabouts in Jamaica, and who's bedding who. Be mindful. Even when you assume no one is watching, they are.'

CHAPTER 13

Jacob Dunne walked along the cobbled streets of Bristol under the faint glint of moonlight and flickering oil lamps. His hat and long coat were enough to absorb the light drops of rain. Thankfully, he needed no umbrella; they were heavy cumbersome things that usually ended up forgotten in a corner far from home.

The barrister had just left The Hatchet Inn – a charming Tudor-style public house that, despite being over a hundred and fifty years old, showed no signs of losing its popularity. Twice weekly, he enjoyed meeting there with business associates, attorneys and fellow barristers, even those he disliked, such as Messrs Jennings and Wintworth. The fighting talk of court was the fighting talk of court. Outside that combative arena the men would drink, smoke, play card games and, of course, discuss professional performances.

A good tale was always to be told or heard, often embellished, depending upon the character of the teller. Tales of drunken judges nodding off mid trial, of scheming witnesses confused by their own lies, of defendants leaping from the dock and avoiding the clerks, stories that evoked heartfelt laughter. These recollections were often followed by more sombre tales of outrageous verdicts and, even worse, of lenient sentences, leading to much criticism and shaking of grey heads. Win or lose Mr Dunne was always prepared to rebuff any attacks on his own courtroom performances, an exercise he shouldered with good nature.

The Hatchet Inn was a place where business took place, too, and he would sometimes be retained by a new attorney seeking representation for a defendant. Very rarely would he refuse any request, after all everybody deserved an advocate. Some of the accused, who at first appeared guilty, were nothing of the sort. Many were in the wrong place at the wrong time or victims of mistaken identity or impersonation. He had come across a few who, down on their luck, had agreed to accept payment in return for confessing to crimes they could not have committed. And yes, some were guilty as charged. Usually the guilty had an eyebrow-raising excuse that not even Ollenu's remarkable imagination and creativity could turn into a sound defence.

The judges who alternated at the Bristol courts of assize practised contrary policies. Some would happily sentence anyone who pleaded guilty and move on. Others would make further enquiries of the barristers and refuse to accept a nonsensical plea. Mr Dunne was adept at navigating the whims of those august gentlemen, though he wished his trusted right-hand man was available to help sway the lordships' minds.

He missed Isaiah Ollenu more than he had ever thought possible. Even the impertinent pantomime performances, ruthless in their mocking tone. The memory of how Ollenu's appointment had scandalised society made him smile. He recalled that shocked attorneys had predicted the ruin of his chambers. Even fellow barristers, who he considered friends, had warned him it was a grave error to bring a Negro into the fold. He remembered the sceptical snorts of his partners, Tredinnick and Verney, when he first introduced Ollenu, and now, five years later both gentlemen stared forlornly at Ollenu's vacant corner in the library and lamented his absence.

As Mr Dunne made his way through the city centre, he passed lecherous men and loose women stumbling out of taverns and gambling dens looking worse for wear. Loud voices. Curses, mixed with beseeching words, echoed in his ears. Men sang indecent tunes, encouraged by their rowdy comrades. With head slightly lowered, his eyes were alert for opportunistic pickpockets and trouble seekers.

Soon he was ambling alongside the River Avon, where courting couples met and became lost in their own worlds. It was a longer route home to Clifton, but he cherished the calming feel of the waterside environment as he left the bustle of the city centre. Less grime, less noise. Peace and solitude of the nighttime differed in the extreme from that of daytime disorder.

The tranquillity was pierced by a loud splash, followed by a scream and shouts for help from a ragged boy who ran up and down the footpath in front of the splashing victim. 'Help him! He can't swim.'

The barrister increased his pace and leaned over the algae-streaked river wall. The person in the water made no calls for help, but a bobbing head was visible in the dim moonlight and the splashing indicated a panicked reaction.

'Help me little brother! Somebody help him.'

Jacob Dunne waited to see who, out of the younger men escorting their sweethearts, would do something to assist the victim. Not one of them seemed moved by the spectacle of a helpless child and some merely murmured dismissive comments. The boy on dry land screamed again and the barrister could no more ignore the heartfelt wail than he could ignore the pitiful mews of a lost kitten.

'What is his name? Call to him. Tell him to stop kicking and lay on his back.'

'He can't hear or talk!' shouted the boy. 'His name's Seb. Help him, mister! I can't swim.'

'Neither can I, young man.' Mr Dunne spotted a small boat moored to a thick tree stump. Without pausing to give the situation further thought, he descended the iron ladder fixed to the river wall and wavered as the boat rocked beneath him.

The boy onshore screamed again, 'Don't let him drown!'

The advocate grabbed the oars and threw all his might behind each stroke. He had not rowed in the thirty years since his days at Oxford, and his arms ached from the effort, but the boat moved in the right direction so he had not lost his touch.

'Hang on, young Seb!' he shouted.

The drowning boy thrashed the water and Mr Dunne was afraid the oar would hit him. As the boy's head disappeared below the water, the rescuer reached in up to his armpit and seized the blond hair. He pulled with all his strength and Seb emerged from the water coughing. The boat wobbled dangerously and Mr Dunne grabbed the boy's shirt collar, keeping his head above water.

'Hold onto the side whilst I catch my breath, Seb, I cannot lift you yet.'

The boy showed no sign of understanding and Mr Dunne remembered that he could not hear. He secured the oars, kneeled down and reached out both arms to the boy. His head was sinking, but the whites of his pleading eyes were visible. The child grabbed his hands. 'That's right. Good boy, Seb. Look at me, I will pull you up.'

Mr Dunne felt as if his arm sockets were being stretched by a torture machine. His favourite beaver hat slipped from his head and floated away, but he concentrated on his task. He hauled Seb partway out of the water with one hand. When his tiny waist emerged, he used the other hand to grip the boy's trouser waistband. With a firm tug, he pulled the child onto the deck where he lay spewing water as tears poured down his face. Mr Dunne smoothed back the hair from the waif's eyes. 'All right Seb, never mind. I'll take you to your brother. You are whole, thank goodness.'

Slowly the barrister rowed back to the river wall. Although his arms hurt he lifted the boy, who could not have weighed more than fifty pounds, and placed him on the ladder. 'Up you go, young man.'

Following the boy up, he clambered over the wall and staggered to a wooden bench. Some of the bystanders congratulated the rescuer, but their praise was muted by the louder censure of opinionated watchers.

'Who'd risk their necks for them? Little beggars were lucky not to drown.'

'They wouldn't be missed, except by the night watchmen.'

'Be back to bag snatching in no time, thanks to you, counsellor!'

The prejudiced men and women drifted away, leaving the barrister and the two boys. Mr Dunne wheezed as he fought to catch his breath. A sharp pain pierced the area below his ribs and he pressed a fist into the spot in an attempt to dull its force. Tomorrow, he would be unable to turn in his bed, much less climb out of it. Margaret would chide him for endangering his health and wellbeing in such an impulsive act. He should have insisted that those men half his age take the lead. Now he was sure to suffer aches and pains for weeks.

'What on earth brings you two out here at this time of night?' he said roughly. 'Your parents must be frantic.'

The older boy sat on the cold, damp, ground cradling the younger one's head. 'What's frantic mean?'

'It means you should be home in bed fast asleep, not drowning in the river.'

The boy squinted at him. 'You're Mr Jacob Dunne. I seen you down the court many a time when we was begging outside.'

The law man was aware of an endless stream of young beggars that wandered the city, but to him they were all invisible faces and he had no recollection of ever seeing either of these boys.

'Begging at night will bring you no end of trouble. What if some drunkard had tossed you in there with Seb? That would have been the end of you both,' Mr Dunne scolded. 'Whilst I would not recommend begging as a form of employment, I do suggest you end your monetary endeavours before the sun goes down.'

The boy shook his head. 'Can't be giving up so early, sir. I'm the man of our house.'

Mr Dunne sighed. 'It is quite late and high time you took yourselves off to said house.'

'Well it's not no house, really. It's a caravan.'

'Whatever it is, you must make your way there without further ado.'

'Ma will be fuming if we come back without enough money.' He stroked his young brother's cheek. 'Don't matter what time o'clock. No money, no dinner.'

The barrister's annoyance dissipated as he stared at the urchins. Both were noticeably gaunt and their clothes riddled with holes. 'What's your name, young man?'

'Billy.'

'Well, Billy, can I assist you to get home? I do not see a watchman and one may not pass this way for quite some time.'

'We don't want no watchman, sir. They despise us and we hate them. They're always chasing us.' Billy sniffed and wiped his nose with his sleeve. 'We need to beg some more money, then I'll take Seb home to Ma.'

'Take this.' Mr Dunne handed Billy all the coins in his pocket: three shillings and four pence. 'Your ma will be satisfied. No more excuses, go directly home at once.'

'Cor! Thanks, Mr Dunne.' Awash with excitement, Billy showed Seb their earnings.

Seb gesticulated and his thin mouth emitted muffled grunts that Mr Dunne could not interpret. Billy responded to the sign language with hand and facial gestures of his own and it was apparent that they both understood these movements. The barrister frowned and grew more concerned by the changing expression on the older boy's face.

'Whatever is the matter, Billy? Does Seb no longer feel well?'

'He says that friendly Black man who gives us tuppence and sweets sometimes belongs to you, and you sent him to Jamaica to die.'

Jacob Dunne's eyes bulged and the pain in his side seemed to move, striking him in the chest as a dagger.

'What in heaven's name made you utter such slanderous words, young fellow? Wherever did you get that monstrous idea?'

'S'not no idea. Seb heard it in the Pacific Tavern.'

'Is that so?' sneered the law man. 'You forget; you say he cannot hear.'

'Aye, but he can read your mouth most times, unless you cover your lips. And talk with his hands. He remembers things he's seen and heard, even months afterwards, and he don't lie, sir. Barrow, that miserable gollumpus from Corn Street, took drink with old Wilkins. I seen them together meself.'

Billy recanted a disjointed tale. As Jacob Dunne stared into the youth's earnest face he was never more certain that he was listening to the voice of an honest witness, even though any judge would throw out such testimony as hearsay. These young imps could not have invented such an elaborate story, and they knew all the names, Ollenu, Ashby, Kershaw, Dantry. Elements of the story were confusing, but two things were certain. No new briefs would come to his chambers courtesy of Edward Barrow, and Isaiah Ollenu would not be fending off work from impressed attorneys. In fact, if Ollenu – who he had instructed not to stand down – stayed alive it would be a miracle.

Mr Dunne massaged his throbbing temples with both hands, but the action brought little comfort. The evening's events could be in his imagination. Maybe he was not at the River Avon in reality. He was heading home where Margaret would be in the drawing room, waiting to offer him a hot cup of tea and discuss the day's events before they retired to bed. Now he was walking towards his front gate. Paddy, the dog, was running down the front path to greet him, standing on two legs at the gate, his fluffy tail wagging furiously.

'Mr Dunne, you awake, sir?'

'Unfortunately, yes.' The barrister blinked. 'Yes I am, Billy. But evidently I have been asleep for months now. What a fool I am.'

'You're not no fool, Mr Dunne. You're a hero. You saved Seb.'

The counsellor stared out at the rippling dark river waves. 'Young man, if anyone ever suggests to you a plan of action that sounds advantageous, you must demand the fine details. Then consider the pros and cons before you agree to anything.'

'Consider the what, sir?'

'All the reasons why such plan is a good idea, and all the reasons why such plan is a bad idea.'

Billy nodded thoughtfully. 'To beg money is a pro, cos we get money. To stop begging before sunset is a con, cos we get less money?'

'I cannot fault you for not taking advice from me, Billy.' Mr Dunne sighed and hung his head. 'I am but an easily swayed ninnyhammer.'

Seb's fingers flew again and his brow creased, then he clutched his rescuer's hand and pressed his damp head onto the lawman's shoulder.

'Seb says you're the best, and he don't believe you sent your Black man off to die in Jamaica.'

'Oh, but I did, young Seb.' Mr Dunne patted the mute boy's head. 'To my eternal shame, that is exactly what I did.'

CHAPTER 14

The horse-drawn carriage took Ashby and Ollenu along an easterly route, away from Montego Bay. The coastal road was lined with giant mahoe trees and lush vegetation that had, so far, survived the rapid development of the colony. The air smelled salty, though not overpoweringly so, and the temperature was pleasantly mild for most of the journey. After leaving the parish of St James they crossed through Trelawny, before finally entering St Ann. Soon the carriage was trundling alongside the glorious blue waters of St Ann's Bay, where small fishing vessels battled strong waves to avoid being smashed against the rocky outcrop.

The indistinct voices of Mortimer and Johnson could be heard over the sound of the carriage wheels crunching along uneven dirt and stones. Both men seemed to be of good cheer. The carriage turned off the main road onto a narrow track with a sign pointing uphill, indicating that Pedro lay ahead. The road was almost deserted, with only two or three small houses set far apart on vast swathes of land. To Ashby, the tiny village of Pedro was as different from Spanish Town as oranges were from star apples. Acres of leafy trees on untamed land gave it a refreshingly rural appearance. He was about to express his thoughts on the rough beauty of the scenery when Ollenu spoke first.

'I find nothing attractive about this isolated place.'

'Another of your endearing qualities, Mr Ollenu, is your eagerness to appreciate the wonder of God's creations.'

'One of us must reflect upon what it could mean to visit a dwelling that cannot be observed from afar by the public.'

'Harm cannot reasonably be expected to befall us in broad daylight.'

'My fervent hope is that you are correct, Mr Ashby.'

The horses slowed their pace as they climbed the slight hill and eventually Mortimer brought them to a halt. He leaned down and bellowed, 'Edinburgh Castle, gentlemen!'

'That is it?' Ollenu descended and stood, hands on hips. 'Not much of a castle.'

Ashby too had expected something more impressive than this edifice. Not, of course, a magnificent structure comparable to Bristol Castle – a Norman castle built in medieval times to withstand all approaches – but certainly more than what stood before them. It was barely a castle at all with little of the opulence associated with buildings afforded such description. The only aspects similar to castles were the two circular looped holed towers at the front, set at opposite corners. At best it was an unremarkable large house of bleak grey stones with narrow windows, a house set in the middle of nowhere.

'This does not resemble a dwelling where people could hide for years,' said Ashby.

'Live people, no,' murmured Ollenu. 'Dead people, yes.'

Ashby ignored his colleague and ran his eyes all over the estate. In the distance were a few huts of wattle and daub. Near to the huts, Black males tended cattle, while those with cutlasses in hand slashed at corn stalks.

Johnson picked at his teeth with a twig. 'You two be asking Doctor Hutchinson about those missing people then?'

'It is a question we ask most people we meet,' said Ollenu.

'Just so you know, Mr Kershaw already spoke to the doctor, and he knows absolutely nothing,' said Mortimer. 'He'd never lie to us.'

'I'm sure you are correct, Mr Johnson.' Ashby bowed and straightened his jacket. 'Do return for us in a few hours, if you would be so kind, gentlemen.'

Beneath his hooked nose Johnson's smile was almost a sneer. He shook the horses' reins and waved farewell before departing. Mortimer turned and gave them a bright smile and a hearty salute.

'That was the quietest "yes, sir" I have ever heard,' mumbled Ollenu as he watched the dust billow in the disappearing carriage's wake.

A young girl with plaits dangling about her shoulders knelt on the stone steps, a bucket of water by her side. With both hands to a cloth she scrubbed vigorously, her small shoulders rocking back and forth. As the visitors approached, she grabbed her rag and bucket, and fled towards the rear of the premises.

'Our host comes to greet us,' said Ashby. 'I saw a flash of red hair disappear from an upstairs window. At the very least, we know that he does not shoot on sight.'

'Do we, Mr Ashby?'

'See that you remember my instructions, Mr Ollenu. I intend to conduct this interrogation and I expect you to follow my lead.'

'Very well.'

Doctor Hutchinson waved a hand in the air as he approached them, and slapped a cane against his thigh. He greeted them warmly and shook hands. 'Mr Ashby, Mr Ollenu, delighted to have you.'

'We would not miss the opportunity,' said Ashby with a smile.

Ollenu stretched his arms and bent his knees repeatedly as he twisted from side to side.

Doctor Hutchinson regarded him with curiosity. 'Is there a medical reason why you flap in that manner, Mr Ollenu?'

'Merely awakening my limbs, doctor.'

'Have no concern,' said Ashby. 'His limbs seem not to resent the frequent punishment he bestows on them.'

'You walk with the cane?' asked Ollenu.

'Oh no, I carry it in the event my Negroes fall prey to laziness. Wave it in the air a few times, and that usually concentrates their minds.'

Ollenu stared at him. 'And if it does not… concentrate their minds?'

'Then I can always find… other ways.' With one swift motion Doctor Hutchinson tossed the cane over his shoulder then rubbed his pale hands together. 'Come, we must go indoors where the air is much cooler. I would not wish for you to collapse in this infernal heat. Jamaica has a most vengeful sun.'

As they approached the arched front entrance, Ashby observed that the two statues flanking the door that seemed so innocuous from a distance were gargoyles. Hideous gothic creatures that some people found fashionable, but were the last thing in outdoor embellishment that Ashby would wish for.

The temperature plunged as they crossed the threshold. The high vaulted ceiling failed to cast much light on the dark entrance hall. The hall was sparsely furnished with only a few wooden chairs for guests to rest their legs or change out of their boots. Charcoal etchings, drawings of macabre figures, hung from the walls. Dark corridors led off from the hall, and although the building appeared modest from outside, the inside felt cavernous as if it contained more rooms than it could possibly hold. A gun cabinet with different-sized weapons was in clear view. Beside it a plump black cat yawned and stretched, its yellow eyes casually considering the new arrivals before it curled up again.

The curtains in the drawing room were barely opened, yet the lack of light did not appear to concern the doctor. Ashby observed a large fireplace stacked with unlit chunks of wood and wondered if there could ever be need for an indoor fire in Jamaica. A sideboard held a tray with a pitcher of water and glasses, surrounded by opaque bottles of what appeared to be wine.

A flattering portrait of the doctor hung on the wall above a large desk. Behind the desk ran a whole wall of books, fiction and non-fiction: Voltaire, Milton, Swift, Defoe. Upon the desk was a block of wood embedded with a row of short spikes topped with what appeared to be the dried-out skulls of cats.

Ashby let out a yelp of horror and stepped backwards, forcing Ollenu to raise his arms and save himself from being knocked off-balance. 'Whatever is it, Mr Ashby?'

Ashby could not speak and pointed a trembling hand. Ollenu walked towards the desk, lowered his head and peered at the objects. 'Miniature dried pumpkins, with charcoal eyes.'

Doctor Hutchinson cackled loudly, a sinister sound that echoed inside the four walls. He drew aside the curtains and light flooded the room.

'Really, gentlemen, what did you expect?' He gestured them to sit as he ambled over to the sideboard. 'It is such innocent trifles that cause nonsensical rumours to spread. I am sure my house Negroes have told the whole parish that I strangle their missing kittens. Ah, the burdens I bear.'

Ashby sank into a chair and clutched his heaving chest. He wondered if the doctor's shocking notion of humour was born from the indignity of being accused of heinous crimes, or whether taking pleasure in scaring visitors was his natural propensity. Either way it was a most unappealing characteristic.

'Of what nonsensical rumours do you speak, doctor?' said Ollenu.

'That I am intent on evil. That I have killed people. I know gossips will have mentioned it at the ball, they cannot help themselves. Such absurd accusations.' Doctor Hutchinson held Ollenu in a penetrating stare. 'Tell me honestly, do I resemble my latest moniker – the Mad Master of Edinburgh Castle?'

'You do not,' said Ashby with a quick glance at his silent colleague.

'And what is your opinion, Mr Ollenu?' With rum glass in hand, the doctor executed a perfect pirouette as if he were a ballet dancer. 'Evil mad master or not?'

Ollenu sat on a chair next to Ashby. 'During the course of my work, I come across many evil people. You, sir, certainly do not give the appearance of a killer.'

The doctor smiled and sipped his rum.

'Nevertheless, looks do deceive even the best of minds as I am sure you are aware,' continued Ollenu. 'Healthy patients feign illness, cough and splutter and pretend to be at death's door. And then there are those who appear to be in exceptional health, but are rotting away inside, down to their very souls.'

The doctor's eyes narrowed. 'You are rather peculiar, Mr Ollenu.'

Ashby cast a look of extreme annoyance at Ollenu. 'He is far more than that.'

'Gentlemen, a drink? Wine, rum, water or I can send for fresh tea or coffee?'

Both men declined. The doctor downed another mouthful of rum then took a seat behind the desk. He crushed a small piece of paper into a ball and tossed it in the direction of the door. The cat pounced in delight and smacked the toy with its paws, chasing it along the stone floor.

'I do adore cats,' said the doctor.

'Sweet little thing,' said Ashby, before assuming a rather forthright expression. 'Doctor Hutchinson, I wonder if you would favour me by answering a few questions?'

'Of course, Mr Ashby. I guessed you had questions. Do go ahead.'

'Three people are missing. All of them came to Jamaica in recent years and none returned to England. Francis Dantry, Clare Sandie, Henry Penket. Have you ever seen or heard of them?' Ashby provided detailed descriptions of each and information of their business endeavours.

'I had learned of your search for them from guests at the ball.' The doctor maintained eye contact with his inquisitor. 'Henry Penket passed through here over two years ago. That gracious man even measured me for a suit, but I never saw him again, I'm afraid. When he departed, I do believe he was bound for the parish of St David.'

'And what of Mrs Sandie and Mr Dantry?'

'No. Mrs Sandie is not familiar. If she is on the island to pursue opportunities for a new brewhouse, Port Royal would be a more fitting place than St Ann.' The doctor stroked his bushy beard. 'As for Mr Dantry, I would remember an ironmonger. I always have use for ironware and would welcome such visit. Understand that some who come here may stop for a glass of water and be served by my slaves without ever coming into my vision. I am most hospitable to everyone and insist that my workers show the same grace.'

A shabbily dressed male appeared in the doorway and rapped on the open door.

Doctor Hutchinson's monobrow became v-shaped as he stared in the direction of the intruder. 'What is it, boy?'

'Massa, the cow having calf and Atta say it not going well, sir.'

'Blast! Can Arthur do nothing by himself?' As the doctor headed towards the door he pointed a finger at the sideboard. 'I should not be delayed long, gentlemen. If your thirst has returned, do help yourselves to cool refreshments.'

When the footsteps of Doctor Hutchinson and his bondsman grew faint, an irritated Ashby said, 'Must you seek to provoke him, Mr Ollenu?'

'It is important to have him drop his guard, so he forgets his prepared responses. Then one can study his mannerisms, and seek to detect what is truth and what is deceit.'

'And what exactly did you detect?'

'A blank look overcame him when he spoke of Clare Sandie. Truth or deceit? I am unsure. When you mentioned Francis Dantry, he could not look at you. His eyes went to the fireplace, then to the ceiling. I believe Dantry was here, and possibly still is here.' Ollenu frowned deeply. 'It was hard to read the doctor's mind when he spoke of Henry Penket, since he readily admitted to their meeting. I wonder if Penket did go on to St David, or not.'

'I saw no revelations in his appearance or voice,' said Ashby. 'He may be entirely truthful.'

'And he may not.' Ollenu rose and walked to the sideboard. 'We should begin a search for signs that the doctor has possession of your clients insured jewels.' He ran his fingers along the many shelves, shuffled the books and checked behind each of them.

'I must say his environment is not at all welcoming.' Ashby opened a small brass box on the desk that resembled a jewellery box, but it contained only buttons and coins. 'Everything is so dark and dreary; it creates an eerie impression. Why anyone would wish to plunge their visitors into discomfort is beyond comprehension.'

'I doubt if Doctor Hutchinson does anything without due consideration,' said Ollenu.

Beside the sideboard was a chest of drawers. Upon it stood a candle with wick burned low, a small model of a ship, and a bowl of green berries. As Ollenu rummaged through the drawers, he raised his head every few seconds and cocked an ear for the return of footsteps.

'This appears to be his main living quarters.' Ollenu ran his fingers over the stones surrounding a wall candle and checked if any were loose. 'If he hid valuable jewels it is probably unlikely he hid them here, unless there are secret compartments in the walls.'

'He is unaware that I know the jewels and perhaps would not hide them from me.' Ashby rose and slowly studied each wall. 'He could well leave precious items dangling in plain sight.'

'I suspect the doctor has avoided censure all these years by leaving nothing to chance,' said Ollenu. 'He was happy to invite us here, yet not at all keen to show us the grounds. Instead, he escorted us inside, probably concerned that we would see or hear something outside. That girl on the steps was terrified. She may worry that blood will spill before the day ends.'

'Blood will spill?' Ashby shuddered. 'Do you mind, Mr Ollenu?'

'Merely giving voice to my thoughts, Mr Ashby. We must investigate the castle grounds.'

'So be it.'

They headed down the dark passage watched by gruesome wall drawings whose chalk eyes followed every movement. Ollenu stopped occasionally to check behind picture frames and plaques. A stone gargoyle, head impaled with a candle so that it resembled a horn, caught his attention.

'The statue's eyes shine, Mr Ashby.'

Ashby rubbed the front of his neck and shivered as he leaned in for a closer inspection. 'Glass, not precious stones.'

The black cat plodded along in front of them as they continued down the corridor, then threw itself down in an inconvenient spot.

Ollenu peered at the feline as he stepped over it. 'That blue collar about the cat's neck sparkles. What is your opinion? Jewels?'

'Let me see.' As Ashby took a step towards the animal it growled, sprang onto all fours, and ran in the opposite direction.

'Quick, catch it!' said Ollenu and gave chase.

Ashby moved aside and let Ollenu take the lead. 'Do go.'

An African woman sweeping the corridor, hurriedly stepped aside as the two men raced past, and stared after them in surprise.

Ollenu cornered the cat, whispered kind words, and stroked its smooth fur. Tail rigid, it hissed and lay flat.

Ashby panted as he caught up with them. 'I cannot imagine what excuse I would offer if Doctor Hutchinson caught me chasing his princely pet.'

'That you were determined to make friends with Prince and would not be dissuaded despite its obvious reluctance?'

'How would I fare without your wealth of suggestions, Mr Ollenu?'

Ashby crouched low and examined the sparkling collar. 'Bless my soul! These two pieces are decorative glass, but these three are indeed gems, diamonds.' Putting on his glasses, he examined them more closely. 'I daresay these look very similar to the ones that Henry Penket stitched into his doublet.'

'Remove the collar,' said Ollenu.

The cat spat at Ashby and wriggled away. Before Ollenu could catch it, the animal leapt high up on a window ledge and set about cleaning itself, keeping wary eyes on its abductors.

'We shall never get near it again,' groaned Ashby.

'Maybe it is as well,' said Ollenu. 'The doctor is greatly fond of the cat and would notice the collar missing. We must continue to search further for indisputable evidence. Let us see if the young girl can be found.'

The men exited through the back door and observed a group of slaves in the distance, with Hutchinson conspicuous as the sole white man. The doctor's shirt sleeves were rolled up and his arms covered in blood. A cow bellowed and writhed on the ground.

'The doctor does have at least one patient,' said Ollenu. 'An animal with no choice in the matter.' A sharp neigh came from one side of the castle and Ollenu pointed. 'Look there, that large grey horse. It reminds me of the beast that near trampled us to death in Spanish Town.'

'Horses look alike,' said Ashby.

'So you would not object, and I am free to enquire of the doctor whether he was in the capital?'

'You are a free man, you come to take us from Massa, sir?' The question came in a whisper from a tremulous female voice. The speaker was the same girl who had scrubbed the front steps earlier, and could be no more than fifteen years of age. The piece of damp rag was clutched to her chest.

'Do you need to be taken from him?' asked Ollenu softly.

The frightened girl fell silent and fixed her attention on Ashby.

'Speak up, girl,' said Ashby. 'We shall not harm you. Your master will not either, I promise.'

Ollenu frowned and shook his head. 'You cannot make that promise, Mr Ashby.'

She wrung the filthy cloth in her hands, looked at the doctor in the distance and then back at Ollenu. 'Massa treats the animals with more kindness than us. He is cruel and will not let us talk to strangers.'

'What is your name?' asked Ollenu.

'They call me Rosa. Though Massa calls me vermin and virus, those are not my names. If he sees that we talk he will kill me. You will buy me?'

'We will not buy anybody,' said Ashby impatiently.

Ollenu shot Ashby a death glare before turning his attention back to the girl. 'Rosa, where are your relatives, your mother, father?'

'My grandmother lives there, and my cousins Simeon and Malachi there.' She pointed to the huts at the far end of the estate. 'I do not know where are all my family. Everyone was sold when I was small. Nanna Della says they may not be in Jamaica; they may be on islands or as far as America. I do not know where America is, but everyone says it is far, far, away. I am afraid Nanna Della will soon die and I will be by myself. She wants me taken to where it is safe. People die here because of Massa. White people and Black people. Nanna knows.'

'Doctor Hutchinson looks this way,' warned Ashby, and with a forced smile waved at the Scotsman.

'Rosa, quick, clean my boots,' ordered Ollenu. He mimicked Ashby in smiling and waving at Hutchinson.

The girl knelt down and dabbed at the pristine leather footwear. Hutchinson scrutinised the three for a while longer, before the renewed bellows of the anguished cow forced him back into physician mode.

'Stay down Rosa,' whispered Ollenu. 'We must meet Nanna Della.'

The girl shook her head and dabbed at Ashby's shoes. 'Massa will never allow us to speak. When we try, he beats us until we bleed. The last time, before the marshal came, Massa gathered all the field slaves and whipped us. No one would speak to the marshal. Massa says we spread rumours and lies and he won't… tolerate it.' She looked up at Ollenu as if to check if she had used the right word and seemed gratified when he nodded. 'He will use the hot poker on our flesh and salt our skins if we speak.'

'Good heavens,' said Ashby and loosened his shirt collar.

'You will help, sir?' Rosa's pleading brown eyes bored into Ashby who looked distinctly uncomfortable.

'We will do our utmost best to help,' said Ollenu.

'It is not our position to assist slaves, although we have great sympathy,' said Ashby. 'Our instructions are explicit.'

'Our instructions are not explicit, Mr Ashby,' snapped Ollenu. 'I remain confused as to Jacob Dunne's role in this whole sordid affair. You have already proved that Edward Barrow outright lied. Kershaw is probably an accomplished liar too. I will not mindlessly follow your lead. Do as you wish, but I will do whatever I can to discover what happens on this estate.'

'This is not our fight.' Ashby's tone was severe. 'We cannot go off on a frolic of our own. This is not our country and we have no role in its governance. Anything we do will be seen as unwarranted interference, however noble.'

'So, Mr Ashby.' Ollenu gave him a scathing smile. 'You are one of those pork-eating, ale-drinking, Bible-spouting, hypocritical Christians? You will next say that slavery was meant to be? That servitude is their lot?'

'No, I do not say that, Mr Ollenu. You deliberately misunderstand me. The slaves must make a report to a law officer if they are being assaulted.'

'If?' repeated Ollenu with incredulity. 'She said they were beaten before the marshal arrived and dared not say anything. They are often tortured. Do you believe they can ride off to Spanish Town and report it to someone else? And to whom? Is Governor Dalling to grant them an audience at King's House?'

Ashby flushed deep pink and fell silent.

'Massa comes,' announced Rosa in alarm. She leapt to her feet and sped away.

Sweat darkened Doctor Hutchinson's shirt. Blood and slime dripped from his hands. He dried his palms on his breeches leaving bold red splotches on the fabric, then pushed back his hair. His tone indicated a foul mood. 'Is that vermin pestering you?'

'Not at all,' said Ashby.

'Rosa was kind enough to clean the dust from our shoes.' Ollenu lifted a spotless shoe and twirled it in the air. 'Such thorough attention and expertise, you are fortunate to have her service.'

Hutchinson's cold eyes moved slowly between the two men. Ashby wilted below the penetrating look and swallowed warm air.

'The calf is dead,' declared the doctor. 'The cow was a cherished animal, but I had to break her neck. If she cannot birth live calves, she is of no use to me. As for these blasted slaves, one cannot get them to do their jobs and tend to the beasts. Useless Negroes every single one of them.'

A hesitant man approached with a jug of water. 'You wash your arms, Massa?'

'Go on, pour!' said Hutchinson roughly. After washing his arms under the steady flow of water he pushed the empty jug away. 'Too much to ask to bring a towel, eh, boy?'

The man lowered terrified eyes and studied the soil.

The doctor stared stone-faced in the direction of the unfortunate stillbirth. 'Go dig a hole! And ensure it is more than six feet deep or vultures will be drawn to the land from afar.'

'I am so sorry for the loss of your animals, Doctor Hutchinson,' said Ollenu. 'Mr Ashby and I intend to wander the grounds, stretch our legs. You do not have to accompany us, of course, for I see you are quite busy.'

'No, we shall go fishing by the river presently,' said the doctor as if he was speaking to a young child. 'When evening is upon us, we shall dine and play brag or your preferred card game.'

'Oh, but evening will not find us here, doctor,' said Ashby.

'There shall be no wandering over my land by yourselves. I am a host and must carry out my duties as expected. We will dine and discuss anything you wish before you retire. When the cock crows at dawn, you may view the entire estate in my company.'

'Doctor Hutchinson, although your generosity is appreciated, we shall not stay overnight,' said Ollenu politely. 'Our carriage returns in an hour or so.'

A change came over the physician's face, the smouldering anger replaced by obvious amusement. 'I can assure you, your carriage will not return this afternoon, Mr Ollenu. There is no lodging house anywhere near for Johnson and Mortimer to relax. If they had planned to return you to Montego Bay, they would have stayed right here and waited.'

'But surely you can provide transportation should they not return?' said Ashby, aware that panic had crept into his voice.

'Sir Alastair expects our return this night, doctor, and our change of clothing is there,' said Ollenu sharply. 'We will, of course, pay your coach driver generously.'

'I own no carriage, Mr Ollenu. I have four horses. Three are quite overworked and only one is in prime condition. I will not chance breaking any of their limbs on these rugged tracks, you do understand?'

Neither of the men answered the question.

'Pedro is a tiny village,' continued Hutchinson. 'The residents may have fit horses, but they will not lend them for a journey to Montego Bay. Besides, I would not wager on your safe arrival at a neighbour's house. The surrounding swamps are rife with crocodile and wild boar. Should you take a wrong turn, you could lose a leg, if not your life.'

The doctor rubbed his hands together as if celebrating a momentous achievement. 'Now, gentlemen, a wonderful afternoon lies ahead of us. Do follow me.'

CHAPTER 15

The afternoon at Edinburgh Castle may well have proved enjoyable for Ollenu, had the host not been a suspected mass-murderer. Despite the forced civility all round, tension marred their outdoor activities. Keeping them at Edinburgh Castle, albeit not under lock and key, amounted to abduction in Ollenu's mind, yet after the initial shock Ashby seemed to be coping with the turn of events with great fortitude. This observation served only to increase Ollenu's personal unease.

Doctor Hutchinson gave them fishing rods and escorted them to the small river that ran alongside a boundary of his property. 'One has to be patient to catch the big fish,' he said. 'Patient and guileful, would you not agree, Mr Ollenu?'

'Entirely,' said Ollenu. 'Many are shrewd enough to escape, but it takes one error, one wrong move, and they are hooked. And, of course, one must haul them in with caution, for the truly desperate may yet break free.'

'It is as you say,' agreed the doctor.

They fished for an hour. Doctor Hutchinson caught the largest fishes and delighted in showing off each specimen before placing them, tails flickering, in a large pail of cold water. He seemed to take great pleasure watching their bodies struggle to stay below the surface, the fins and gills bouncing against one another.

'A splendid haul.' The doctor waved a hand at the bucket. 'Do choose your meals, gentlemen.'

Ashby pointed at a wriggling aqua-blue body. 'That one is a fine fellow, he will suffice.'

'A parrot fish, quite delectable. And for you, Mr Ollenu?'

Ollenu had little interest in food. His appetite deserted him the moment it learned that a night under the doctor's roof was inevitable. 'I am not much of a fish enthusiast, doctor. I will be satisfied with any one you select.'

'Oh no, Mr Ollenu, I would not dream of imposing my tastes upon you. Do go ahead and choose your fancy.'

Ollenu chose a large pink fish with a silver belly.

'A wise choice, the snapper has a delightful flavour.' The doctor removed the snapper fish from the bucket with his bare hand and dangled it high by the tail so that it was level with Ollenu's gaze. 'Do you wish to disembowel it yourself?'

'I fear I would make a disgusting mess, doctor. I ask the fishmonger to remove the offal when I buy them.'

As Doctor Hutchinson ran a sharp carving knife cleanly through the belly of the fish, he stared into Ollenu's eyes. 'But it is so, so satisfactory a task.'

The fish's eye bulged in desperation as a mass of blood and giblets were expelled in a gruesome gush.

'We all differ in what satisfies us, doctor,' said Ollenu. 'To watch an animal, any animal, die brings me no cheer.'

'Ah, a man who sympathises with the voiceless.' Doctor Hutchinson washed the bloodied fish in the flowing river water before placing it in an empty bowl. 'An admirable quality.' He reached for Ashby's fish. 'What about you, Mr Ashby. Do you wish to do the honours?'

'Er, I would rather not.' Ashby patted his blanched cheeks with a handkerchief and kept his eyes elsewhere. 'Whilst I am thankful God sent fish to feed us, I would rather an expert prepare them for their fate.'

Once he had cleaned six fishes the doctor covered the entrails in a mound of soil and pressed the area underfoot. 'I will take these to the kitchen for the cook to scrape. I loathe the way scales take flight and cling wherever they fall. The cook will turn them into something delicious, I promise you. Carry on fishing if you wish.'

As the doctor headed through the tall grass, back towards the castle, the men stared after him in silence. Finally, Ashby said, 'Our host is quite fanatical about the art of fishing.'

'Mr Ashby.' Ollenu spoke with weariness. 'I do not believe we discussed marine life.'

'You read far too much into his words, Mr Ollenu.'

'You clearly do not read enough. Keep in mind the cat's diamond collar.'

Ashby took a few steps closer to the crystal-clear water and stared down. Ollenu joined him and asked, 'What has your attention now?'

'I hoped to see mermaids with golden hair and gold combs.' Ashby sighed. 'It would be wondrous to observe them emerge, sit on smooth stones, and bask in the sun's warmth.'

'Golden hair and gold combs?' Ollenu raised an eyebrow as he stepped back from banking. 'Your ideal vision of fair mermaids may well materialise, Mr Ashby. I suspect the African mermaids have more pressing business on their minds than sun worship and coiffure. Justice being one of them.'

Ashby scowled. 'You walking malcontent. You cannot bring yourself to admire the joyful aspects of life. God is on our side and does not wish us to continually entertain dismal thoughts.'

'There are no dogs.' Ollenu stared at the mound of soft dirt where the fish entrails were buried. 'On an estate the size of this, not even a mongrel.'

'Dog ownership is not compulsory in Jamaica. It is not compulsory in England either, for that matter. I see no reason why failure to own a mongrel should lead you to draw any adverse inference.'

'Dogs dig things up, Mr Ashby. They have keen noses and delight in excavation. That is why Doctor Hutchinson has no dogs.'

'I remain unconvinced, Mr Ollenu.'

Ollenu moved away from the water and stared at the rough ground. He jabbed a long branch into the soil as he walked, and with his boot, scuffed at suspicious mounds of earth. Crouching down, he poked into deep holes and peered under dark crevices. He had underestimated the extent of Hutchinson's domain. The land surrounding the castle was extensive and wild, far too vast to undergo an intensive search in a day. He stared off in the direction of the enslaved community, the small mass of huts home to those who existed on the bottom rung of the ladder. The people who watched him through fearful eyes, their bodies tense with mistrust, could possibly lead him to exactly where he needed to go.

'Well? Found anything?' asked Ashby.

'We must speak to Rosa's grandmother, Nanna Della.'

'Look, the doctor returns.' An alarmed Ashby used his foot to smooth out a wide patch of earth that Ollenu had disturbed. 'Quick, throw away that stick, man!'

'I do not propose to strike him with it, Mr Ashby.'

Ashby's voice rose to a high pitch. 'He carries firearms!'

'Two tucked under his arm, one in his hands,' said Ollenu, squinting in the direction of their host. 'No need to grow anxious, Mr Ashby. See how he looks at the skies? I do believe he intends to start shooting, but we are not his targets.'

To an unaware observer, the doctor was a thoughtful host finding interesting ways to entertain honoured guests. To Ollenu, bird shooting was another deliberate demonstration of their abductor's expertise with targets small and large. A clear display of his dominance with all manner of lethal weapons. First a sharp blade to gut the fishes, now lead balls to blast the birds.

'Here you are, gentlemen.' The jolly doctor presented Ashby with a musket. 'Your prowess shall be revealed this day courtesy of this Brown Bess.'

'I have little prowess with guns, doctor,' said Ashby.

'You will soon master your aim, Mr Ashby. The birds are quite unassuming, flying easily, singing gaily, expecting nothing and then… For them, there is nothing.'

Doctor Hutchinson handed a musket to Ollenu and although Ollenu laid fingers on it, the doctor maintained his own grip for longer than necessary. 'A sheer plummet, a gentle thud, instant oblivion.' The doctor finally released his grasp with an ominous smile at his guest.

With the doctor's probing eyes lingering on him, Ollenu made sure to hit any bird that came within his range. Under no circumstances could he show fear or weakness, and he was well aware the doctor sought to bring forth such emotions.

Ollenu noticed that Ashby never hit a single target. He had long observed that Ashby preferred to shy at biting insects and rodents, rather than crush them. Now he wondered whether the investigator's actions were deliberate, out of sympathy for the simple creatures, or whether he was a terrible shot. Ollenu was sure the doctor was also mindful of his colleague's poor performance, and would soon rule out Ashby as any possible threat to his liberty.

The sound of breaking branches diverted Ollenu's attention towards two casually dressed white men who appeared from the dense undergrowth and strolled onto the grounds unchallenged. With pistols held at their sides they approached the Scotsman and exchanged warm greetings.

Doctor Hutchinson introduced them as his nearest neighbours, the planters James Walker and Roger Maddix. Ollenu guessed they were the same age as the doctor.

Maddix was a long-necked, burly man, clean shaven, with thinning brown hair that hung limply on his shoulders. 'We heard explosions and decided to come and make sure everything was as it should be, doctor,' he said.

Walker was shorter than Maddix, and more slender. Prominent ears protruded beneath hair that seemed prematurely grey for his boyish features. 'Yes, you can never be too vigilant.' He stared at Ollenu as he spoke. 'So much disquiet in the air with the restless Negroes burning plantations and threatening to start rebellions over the slightest of issues.'

'Many issues that appear slight are not slight when fully examined,' said Ollenu.

'Is that so now?' said Walker with a noticeable narrowing of his eyes.

'Mr Ashby and Mr Ollenu were contemplating whether my neighbours could accommodate them. I took it upon myself to advise them they would be much more comfortable here.'

'And so right you are, doctor.' Walker smiled – an insincere attempt that barely curled his lips. 'I've only got one extra room and the place is small I'm afraid, although I've plans to build additional rooms. Wouldn't suit you at all, gentlemen.'

'Mine neither,' said Maddix. 'Besides, Dorcas – that's the wife – snores so badly I oftentimes take to the spare room myself to escape her thundering.'

He laughed loudly and his friends joined in. Even Ashby managed a nervous twitch of the mouth.

Ollenu viewed the discourse as private code, as if the three Pedro residents were communicating some secret understanding amongst themselves. Beneath the civility of many Englishmen lay a cruel and ruthless undercurrent, and these jovial planters could be accomplices, helping the doctor hide his heinous behaviour behind a cloak of respectability. The comfortable way Maddix and Walker held their guns made Ollenu thankful that he and Ashby had not gone in search of the neighbouring estates. Wild boar and crocodile would have been the least of their worries.

'Pleased to see that all is well, doctor,' said Walker.

'And all is well, is it not, Mr Ashby?' Doctor Hutchinson delivered his warmest smile with the coldest glare.

'Yes, quite so,' said Ashby.

'Mr Ollenu, what say you?' The challenge in the doctor's low voice was apparent to Ollenu, if to no one else. The grey-green eyes refused to leave his dark brown ones and Ollenu was forced to blink first.

'I say, yes, gentlemen.'

'Splendid!' The doctor clapped his hands in glee. 'Both of my guests are quite comfortable.'

Maddix and Walker, satisfied that peace reigned at Edinburgh Castle, bid them farewell and disappeared back into the dense thicket. As the doctor led the visitors towards the castle, he whipped out a dust cloth, polished his weapon and chattered about the quality of his armoury. With growing disquiet Ollenu witnessed the sun's retreat and the lengthening of shadows.

-

The long dining table took up most of the room, and seemed out of place for a house unaccustomed to visitors. A candle at either end of the table offered sparse light. As he surveyed his surroundings, Ollenu took a long drink from a glass of water, but the effort failed to calm his nerves. A house slave approached and set hot aromatic dishes before them.

Ashby stared at a painting on the wall. 'What a magnificent galleon, doctor.'

'Yes, I do admire ships, particularly large intricately designed ones, so majestic as they ride the waves.' Doctor Hutchinson handed Ashby a long-handled fork. 'Did you enjoy your voyage? It was the *Isabella* you say you arrived on?'

'Yes, the voyage was tolerable, though fairly monotonous,' said Ashby. 'Frankly, I was quite relieved to arrive in Kingston Harbour.'

Ollenu listened as the doctor and Ashby engaged in light chatter. The roasted fish had absorbed the smoke of a wood fire that heightened both the smell and the taste, but the law clerk barely registered either. He watched as

Ashby cleared his plate with indecent speed, seeming to savour both the spicy food and the doctor's conversation. Ollenu sensed that Ashby had grown more relaxed after the meeting with Maddix and Walker. The arrival of other white Englishmen seemed to help the white Englishman feel at ease, and Ollenu despaired of convincing the investigator that action was necessary that very night.

Doctor Hutchinson told tales of the island and behaved as if he appreciated the company of his new guests. His tone was light-hearted and friendly at all times, even towards the enslaved people who came in and out during the course of the meal, a clear sign to Ollenu that the Scotsman was putting on an elaborate show for his visitors.

'Ah, gentlemen, the aristocracy of Jamaica are rich in worldly goods, but will always be unsettled in mind, always in want of more,' said the doctor. 'In the words of the great Voltaire, "It must the greatest king confound, with all his courtiers circled round, amidst a splendid court to find, that grandeur can't give peace of mind." Such fascinating insight. Do you appreciate good poetry, Mr Ollenu?'

'Alas, I am no judge of good poetry, doctor. I can barely form a decent rhyme; a fact I am sure Mr Ashby will support.'

'I fancy you speak with modesty,' purred the doctor.

'Modesty is not his forte,' said Ashby.

'You appear not to have maintained much of a Scottish dialect, doctor,' said Ollenu.

'I took countless elocution lessons to rid myself of my cursed accent, Mr Ollenu, so I am rather relieved to hear that it was money well spent.'

Ollenu nodded politely. Despite the thinly veiled threats levelled by the doctor outdoors, he now seemed keen to cultivate the impression of a cultured intellectual, a misunderstood wanderer, a lost soul who had sought and found a comfortable place on a tropical island to live out his days. The cat's shiny collar stayed at the forefront of Ollenu's mind as a stark reminder that Lewis Hutchinson was perhaps far more than a wronged physician.

The host sat forward and placed his elbows on the dining table, the backs of his folded hands under his chin. The skin on his knuckles was thin and grey under the dim candlelight.

'Do you enjoy Jamaica, Mr Ollenu? Feel welcome thus far?'

Ollenu met the doctor's bemused look. 'I was attacked by two ignorant scoundrels in a boarding house and I was near trampled to death by a huge horse with an unknown rider. Welcome is not quite how I would describe my feelings.'

'People can be so cruel in words and deeds.' The doctor nodded as if he empathised. 'They say I steal cattle, as if I were some form of cowboy cattle rustler. Can you visualise me stealing cattle, Mr Ollenu?'

'I cannot.' The law clerk considered his words with care before he continued, 'To steal cattle would require far more effort than you would care to exert. For you, the work must be quick, clean, easy.'

Doctor Hutchinson frowned as he picked up his wine goblet. Slowly, he turned the neck of the vessel in a circular motion. 'It appears, Mr Ollenu, that you and I are quite similar.'

'Oh?'

'We are treated as outsiders, often ostracised by society, despite our natural wish to fit in and be appreciated for who we are.'

'And yet you avoid our most conspicuous difference?' said Ollenu.

'Ah, you refer to our colour? You, a most favourable shade of brown, and I as pale as a cloud?'

'I refer to our hair. I have barely any. Yours is long and wavy. Long hair, both in England and in Jamaica, is quite fashionable.'

Hutchinson pursed thin lips. 'You ridicule me, Mr Ollenu?'

'Not at all, doctor, I would not dream of it.'

The cat pressed itself against Ollenu's leg, startling him. He avoided staring at its valuable collar. Instead he leaned over and dropped a piece of fish tail onto the stone floor. The feline ignored it and stared up at him, disdain evident in the yellow slit eyes.

'You do not consider us alike, Mr Ollenu?'

Ollenu turned his attention away from the spite-filled animal, and pushed at the food on his half-full plate. 'Our positions in life are quite different, doctor.'

'I must disagree. The titled class see me as lower than an Englishman, a mere Scotsman who should not be allowed to achieve the lofty heights of English doctors, who should never be permitted to tend to dukes and lords and earls.'

'I am not a doctor and have never dreamed of being a doctor to the aristocracy,' said Ollenu.

'Ah, but you aspire to work as their lawyer, to be thought of as esteemed enough to hear them confess their darkest secrets, and advise them? Am I not right, Mr Ollenu? You wish for your opinion to be considered no less than any pre-eminent mind?'

'That is the wish of most men in most professions,' Ollenu conceded.

'I agree,' added Ashby.

The doctor considered Ashby with a mere flick of his eyes as if he had forgotten the man's presence and saw no value in it. 'We both want what we believe society owes us, Mr Ollenu: respect, a voice, a presence, a life at the front, not restricted to the outside looking in. When we do not get what we deserve we become angry at the world.'

'But perhaps we are not prepared to take the same actions to satisfy our anger?' suggested Ollenu.

'Oh yes, we are. You may say otherwise, but given the right circumstances and opportunity…' The doctor let his words trail off. 'We all have an edge, Mr Ollenu. Sometimes we do not know what we are capable of until pushed towards it.'

Ashby looked at each man in turn, lowered his fork, and gulped his wine rather hurriedly.

'Could I be a hangman; I sometimes ask myself?' Hutchinson's voice took on a deep sonorous tone. 'Could I tie a noose about the neck of my fellow man and pull until he is quite dead? Could I watch his tortured eyes, the screams trapped in his throat as he kicks and struggles to reclaim the breath that drains from his soul?'

This was as close to a confession as Ollenu had ever heard, and he stared into the doctor's eyes. 'Indeed, you could be a hangman, Doctor Hutchinson. A man who kills innocent animals, breaking their necks because, through no fault of their own, they fail to please him, would not be averse to breaking the neck of his fellow man.'

Ashby dropped his wine glass and the stem broke. Claret splashed over the wooden table and dripped onto the floor. The yellow-eyed cat meowed and ran aside, licking wine from its fur with a distasteful shake of its head.

'I am terribly sorry, doctor,' said Ashby, as he attempted to mop up the spill with his napkin.

'Leave it!' snapped the doctor, flapping a dismissive hand at Ashby. 'You pretend that I am the only one so predisposed, Mr Ollenu. Do you say that since you docked in Jamaica, you have not met a soul, not a single soul, who looks virtuous to outward appearances, yet who you would shoot if given the chance and feel not a tinge of regret?'

Ollenu's mind drifted to the works of Sir Hans Sloane. The physician recorded in gory detail the variety of punishments inflicted on Black people in Jamaica. Rebellion was punished by nailing the slaves to the ground, applying fire to their feet and hands, gradually burning them up to the head. Spurious crimes resulted in castration or mutilation, chopping off half the victim's foot was the usual practice. Any presumed negligence would result in victims being whipped until their flesh was raw. Masters smeared pepper and salt on the wounds, and evil owners dripped melted wax on them, all to heighten the sufferer's torment. Ollenu despised the men of no conscience who committed such atrocities and was sure he had met a number of them. Would he shoot them if he could?

'Well, Mr Ollenu?'

'I cannot truthfully say I would not seize such opportunity, doctor.'

'It is as I say, Mr Ollenu.' The doctor gave a satisfied smile. 'We are quite alike.'

'And yet,' added Ollenu, 'if one of us were to mortally wound the other, only one would hang from the gallows. The free man would continue to inflict havoc upon the population.'

Doctor Hutchinson fell completely still and his pale skin grew greyer under the almost extinguished candlelight. Shadows flickered on the walls and a chill descended in the atmosphere.

Ashby grabbed a pitcher and poured red wine into another glass. 'I say, this wine is marvellous. May I pour for you, doctor?'

'Yes, if you would, Mr Ashby.' Holding up his empty goblet, the doctor maintained his fixation on the law apprentice.

'Mr Ollenu?' Ashby waved the pitcher at his comrade, desperation apparent in his eyes.

'Not for me, thank you.'

'Are you sure?' asked Ashby. 'It really is perfectly divine, much better than the Madeira imbibed last evening?'

'Quite sure, Mr Ashby.'

'You play the piano exquisitely, Mr Ollenu,' said Doctor Hutchinson. 'Particularly "Toccata". I am only sorry I do not have one here for your usage.'

'You have been more than generous in providing for my entertainment, doctor. The fishing, the shooting, the conversation.'

'Nevertheless, a piano would be a fine addition to Edinburgh Castle. I shall make enquiries about where I can purchase such an instrument.'

'I am acquainted with a lady in Spanish Town who may be able to assist you there,' said Ashby. 'A truly enchanting lady named Eleanor Lamont, a widow.'

'Ah, you enjoy Jamaica, Mr Ashby.' The doctor smiled warmly and appeared to take a keen interest. 'Do tell me more about your lady friend.'

Ollenu was relieved that the doctor was drawn by Ashby's romantic assignations. Although he fought to hide his inner feelings from the doctor, he could not hide from himself the fact that he feared the man. Poor Rosa and her family had good cause to fear him too, as did the rest of the Africans at Edinburgh Castle. These oppressed people were depending on him to take action.

This night, with or without Ashby's help, he would discover whether murder was indeed the secondary profession of Doctor Lewis Hutchinson.

CHAPTER 16

The small, windowless, guestroom was drab in its appearance and lack of diversion. A bed, a chair and a table. Not a painting, not a plaque, not even a mirror. A large candle flickered in solitude on the bare wall. Ollenu considered extinguishing it before he left, but could not bear the thought of returning to a pitch black space.

On the bed lay a clean night shirt, placed there by a house slave. As it was too large for Hutchinson, Ollenu wondered if it could have been worn by Henry Penket or Francis Dantry, or some other deceased person. He would never change into that nightwear and would not rest on that bed, not for a few hours yet. He tied his yellow silk cravat about his neck for good luck, and prayed that no rhyme would escape his lips tonight.

The castle walls were too thick to hear Ashby next door. Ollenu hoped Ashby had not fallen asleep, as the man was lagging in resolve, having succumbed to Hutchinson's charms, wine and heat. At the stroke of midnight Ollenu pushed Ashby's door and winced as it gave a low squeak. Under the faint candlelight Ashby pulled on his boots. He gave Ollenu the merest of nods then picked up the candle in its holder.

Nothing stirred as the men crept silently down the dark corridor. Ollenu paused momentarily outside their host's bedroom door and listened to the sound of deep breathing from within. He signalled Ashby to continue and they descended the stone staircase. Soon they were beside the glass gun cabinet. Ashby held the candle high as Ollenu slowly opened the door and removed two weapons. He checked they were loaded with shot.

Ashby wiped moist hands before accepting a gun. 'As you must have witnessed, I am not adept at handling weapons, even for sport.'

'I could not fail to notice,' said Ollenu. 'Hutchinson *is* expert at handling weapons for sport, and, I would wager, expert at activities no sane man would call sport. He will not take me by surprise.'

'How I let you persuade me to engage in this fool's errand, I'll never know.'

'This fool's errand is the reason I am in Jamaica, if I recall rightly. What was it you said? My duty is to interview my brethren?'

'I did not consider such duty would be conducted after midnight.'

Behind them the cat growled and arched its back. Ollenu turned and stared at it. 'Not even a sparkle. The collar is gone.'

'So it is,' said Ashby. 'The woman who swept the hall saw us with the cat.'

'We must forgo all distraction,' said Ollenu. 'Help me with the door.'

Together the men struggled to move a heavy block of wood that secured the rear door. Once outside, they headed for the cluster of distant huts, the community of the enslaved. Moonlight broke through the tall trees as they crept along.

'Rosa's hut is that way.' Ollenu pointed. 'This ground is rugged, beware of ridges and holes. If you are unsteady, hold the back of my shirt and follow my footsteps.'

In the semi-darkness, Ollenu struggled to stay upright as he led the way towards their destination. The silence of the journey was broken occasionally when owls hooted and toads croaked, peeved by the presence of night intruders.

'Ooh, what's that?' Ashby snatched at something that flew by his ear. He opened his palm and revealed an insect resembling a beetle with a luminous glowing underside. He held it aloft between his fingers. 'What a fine little creature. It must be some form of firefly. There's a bright light close to its tail. Hear it click as it tries to escape my grasp.'

Ollenu turned and barely glanced at it. 'They appear to be plentiful, Mr Ashby. Delightful they may be, but useful only if you can gather a thousand of them to help light the way. I suggest you let it fly on.'

Ashby reluctantly released the object of his admiration and grabbed the tail of Ollenu's shirt. More than once he tripped and Ollenu saved him from hitting the ground.

'Not far now,' whispered Ollenu.

Turning to see why Ashby had released his shirt, he found the gleaming blade of a cutlass within touching distance of his own nose. He blinked and drew his head back slightly in an effort to prevent connection. A shocked Ashby stood motionless with cold metal pressed against his pale throat.

The two assailants were unclothed from the waist up and barefooted. Their cutlasses remained pointed at the intruders as words flew from their lips at a rapid pace. Their bellicose tones suggested an intense argument between the pair.

'They speak Akan,' murmured Ollenu.

'What do they say?' asked Ashby.

'I have no idea.'

'You mean, you do not speak the language of your Fathers?'

'I was taught Latin,' hissed Ollenu.

'You speak Latin?'

'I said I was taught it, not that I learned it.'

The two Africans continued quarrelling as if Ollenu and Ashby did not exist, although their blades remained so close to the trespassers that any movement from either would draw blood. Ollenu took a tentative step backwards and gained a few inches of space.

'When I was very young my parents tried to teach me Akan, but it was forbidden by the English,' he said. 'My parents continued to try, but whenever they threatened to punish me for some silly misdeed, I threatened to inform the authorities and get them punished. Eventually, they gave up trying.'

'And they say children are a blessing.'

'There are always exceptions. As I grew older I realised the value of learning Akan, but no one would teach me. I catch a few odd words here and there.'

'You, Negro!' snapped one of the men in good English, albeit with a strong West African accent. He pushed the blade close to Ollenu's forehead, much to the law clerk's chagrin. 'So you cannot speak as we do? What are you?'

Ollenu put his hands up in the air in surrender. 'A spoiled boy who grew up to be a spoiled man.'

'You come here to die, Negro!'

'Oh no, sir! No, that was not my intention,' said Ollenu. 'I beg you to listen. We are here only to talk, upon my oath.'

'Your guns have small mouths and a lot to say.'

Ollenu gulped as the assailant tugged the gun out of his waistband.

'For you.' Ashby withdrew his firearm with shaking hands and held out the handle towards the man's ally. 'Take it.'

As he watched the exchange, Ollenu was reminded how unattractive guns were with the barrels pointed in the wrong direction. It would be most bad fortune to escape the clutches of Hutchinson only to be brought down by some aggressive kinsmen. 'Will you let us pass through now that we pose no threat?' he asked.

'No threat at all,' stammered Ashby. 'We never were a threat, honestly.'

'Danger and death share your shoes, white man. Where you go, they go.'

'Your skin is ours.' The cutlass point flicked Ollenu's shirt collar. 'Your clothes and voice are theirs. No one who shares our skin fishes and shoots with Massa. No one speaks to us without Massa here.'

'Doctor Hutchinson does not know we are here.' Ollenu tried to keep his voice even. 'He certainly does not want us to speak to you.'

'It is a trick. Massa sent them to trick us to say wrong things, and be whipped.' The man's face moved closer to Ashby's. 'So you can watch and laugh as we are lashed and cooked in hot wax.'

'We must kill them, now, quick,' said his companion.

'No, wait!' Ollenu tried to remember the Akan language, but even the most basic words deserted his memory. 'Rosa said she lives with Nanna Della, and her cousins Simeon and Malachi live nearby. She told us that the master beat you all and threatened you about speaking out. She asked for our help and I promised her we would help.'

The armed men shared looks of frustration and slowly lowered their many weapons.

'That girl never listens, Malachi. What did I tell you?'

'It is you she will not obey, Simeon. You are soft with her.'

'Follow us,' said Simeon.

Soon they were shown to the hut of Nanna Della and Rosa, both of whom had to be roused from their slumber. Malachi lit a fire torch that flooded the hut with light. Rosa sprang from her modest bedding in an instant, her eyes shining with undisguised delight at the visitors.

'You came, Mr Ollenu! You came!'

Ollenu smiled and put a finger to his lips. 'Ssshh!'

She hugged his arm. 'You met my cousins, Simeon and Malachi?'

Ollenu cast nervous eyes at her male relatives. 'Er, yes, they introduced themselves in rather spectacular fashion.'

'This is the man you speak of, child?' Nanna Della sat up and peered at them through a gaze clouded by age. Her thin body was concealed beneath an osnaburg sheet and thick grey plaits hung under a tattered brown headscarf. 'You were right when you said he and a white man would come. Who is the white man?'

'Mr Ashby is trustworthy, I swear,' said Ollenu. 'We must know what Doctor Hutchinson has done to visitors who came to Edinburgh Castle.'

Rosa rubbed her grandmother's arm. 'We must talk Nanna. They will listen.'

'Speak, you need not fear,' said Ashby.

'The people who rule care not that he murders, even their own.' The old woman pulled her sheet over her shoulders. 'No one heeds our voices.'

'We will heed your voice.' Ollenu crouched beside her. 'Tell us what you know.'

'A young white man came here on his way to Trelawny, but he became sick. Then, I was a house worker and saw everything. Massa took him in and made us nurse him. In three days the visitor was better, eating and walking without help. One afternoon they ate food and played card games and laughed. Massa showed the man how to play the lute. Later, when the man was ready to depart, Massa sent us to pack his belongings.' Her voice caught in her throat and Rosa rubbed her arm again. 'Massa embraced the young man and bid him farewell. I watched as the man rode away, so happy he came to no harm.' She closed her eyes briefly. 'A loud bang. A red hole in the back of his shirt, a shirt I had washed and dried. He fell from the horse, dead.'

'Do you know who the man was?' asked Ashby as he loosened his collar.

The old woman shook her head. 'A child of God who was murdered.'

'What happened to the body?' asked Ollenu.

Nanna Della shrugged. 'I ran and hid. The housemen are loyal to Massa. I am sure they help him, but they do not admit it. Three of them work inside that house and I do not trust any.'

Ashby removed a broad piece of dried leaf from Rosa's bed and fanned as if he were on fire.

Ollenu rubbed his dry throat. He wondered how many victims knew they were about to die before they perished. Mercifully, some did not know. He had no doubt Hutchinson taunted his guests before killing them, just as he had taunted himself and Ashby during their outdoor pursuits. 'Do you know what became of a tailor named Henry Penket?'

'I do not know that name, but a tailor was here two years ago. He made Massa stand on a box and measured his legs with a paper strip. That man did not leave here. The next day we saw his horse wandering with no saddle. We do not know what became of that man.'

'What about an ironmonger named Francis Dantry?' asked Ollenu. 'He walks with a limp. Did he ever rent lodgings here?'

Nanna Della shook her head. 'No white man or woman has ever lived inside with Massa. He lives alone.'

'What is an ironmonger?' asked Rosa.

'The ones on this island sell wares made from iron, farm tools, and er… other items,' explained Ashby.

'Ankle, arm, neck chains, fetters and shackles,' said Ollenu.

Rosa's brow furrowed. 'Is a limp a name for a piece of wood, as Massa's cane?'

'No, a limp is a way of walking when there is damage to the leg,' said Ashby. 'Some people who limp do use a cane. Francis Dantry does not.'

'There was a man who Massa walked through the lands with. I stared at them because the man walked this way.' Rosa put her left leg forward and dragged her right leg behind, rocking from side to side as she moved a few paces. 'When Massa saw me, he said he would buy iron bracelets for me. They both laughed and I ran.'

Ollenu's face burned with rage as he looked at Ashby. 'Dantry?'

Ashby nodded. 'Left leg firm, right leg lazy. Same rocking motion.'

'Many have passed through this land in hope of food and rest and he has shot them,' said the old woman. 'He has killed both white and Black, but nobody cares if the Negro dies. We thought they would care if those of their own skins die, yet no one comes to take him.'

'We have heard only rumours that people have died here at his hands,' said Ashby. 'We need proof of such slaughter.'

'You do not believe?' asked Malachi in a combative tone.

'That is not what he said, Malachi,' said Rosa. 'He said proof. Remember when you said I stole your bread? I said I did not take it. You found crumbs on my dress. Proof I did take it.'

'And you said no,' said Malachi. 'You lied.'

'Solid proof will overcome denial and lies,' said Ollenu.

'An item that belongs to a victim is a good start,' said Ashby. 'A necklace, a watch, a ring, cufflinks.'

'We have proof,' said Rosa. 'The hole is there.'

'We do not talk of that place, girl.' Simeon's eyes grew wide. 'Duppies walk there.'

'Duppies?' Ashby frowned. 'A new species of animal?'

'A duppy is a ghost,' explained Ollenu. 'You know, ghosts? White burial shrouds? Wooo! What hole is it you speak of?'

Malachi's voice was filled with fear. 'A deep, deep hole that must lead to Hell. Dead bodies are there.'

'You must show us this hole,' insisted Ollenu.

Nanna Della looked concerned, but Rosa hugged her frail shoulders. 'You said you want me to be free Nanna.'

The old woman touched her granddaughter's soft cheek, then turned to Simeon. 'Take them. Take them to that terrible place. I will pray for you all.'

'I go, too,' said Rosa climbing to her feet.

'No, stay here,' ordered Simeon. 'You will listen to me now, girl. You will stay. I get the long rope and we go.'

Simeon and Malachi, each armed with a fire torch, led the way through the thick brush, helping Ollenu and Ashby when they stumbled. Ollenu made no comment when he noticed long gleaming scars on the backs and limbs of the cousins, but his heart ached.

'I trust we shall not fall into that deep hole with the bodies,' said Ashby nervously.

'You will not fall into that deep hole,' said Simeon. 'Deep holes with no bodies, you will fall into them.'

'Oh.' Ashby came to a halt and squinted at the mass of dense vegetation that disguised sharp rocks and crevices.

'Walk,' ordered Malachi. 'If you fall in, we pull you out.'

Ollenu hoped that the prickle running through his body was a natural surge rather than an inkling of forthcoming danger, and he wished he could differentiate between the two. No unstoppable words came from his lips, and for that he was grateful. He peered over his shoulder and listened, but could hear nothing except chirping insects and hooting owls.

On they went until Malachi gestured that they stop. He took a few steps forward holding the torch aloft and pointed, his pupils distended in evident terror. 'It is there, see.'

The hole was about four by six feet wide and it was impossible to see far into the murky depths.

Ollenu rolled up his sleeves. 'Hold the rope firm; I must go down.'

'Are you insane?' cried Ashby. 'That pit is akin to the Black Hole of Calcutta. Descend and you may never rise.'

Ollenu tried to repel his fear as he peered into the pit of darkness, wondering what horrors awaited him. 'We cannot expect these men to risk their lives as we keep ours safe from harm. We are no better and no more entitled to life than they.'

Simeon and Malachi turned steely eyes on Ashby as if challenging him to dispute the statement, but the investigator fell silent and scowled in the dark.

Suddenly, the earth rumbled and it was as if a herd of animals were on the loose. Something bellowed and Ollenu realised that whatever was causing the tumult was approaching from the surrounding land. All eyes turned to the undergrowth as the roaring grew louder. The brush parted and a horned beast emerged, a giant bull, its hide thick as a rhinoceros. Sharp horns pointed skywards and red glaring eyes studied its targets as steam fired from its wide nostrils. Heavy chains clanked on its torso. The creature raked the ground with massive hooves and swung its head from side to side as if contemplating who to attack first.

'Great God above!' murmured Ashby.

'Rolling Calf!' shouted Simeon.

Malachi threw the rope to the ground. 'Calf, come!'

The two cousins unleashed a string of words in their own language and both scrambled into the trees, tossing the fire torches and weapons to the ground as they climbed.

Ashby crouched low and fumbled in his pocket for his Bible. Pressing the book to his lips, he whispered, 'Yea, though I walk through the valley of the shadow of death, I will fear no evil: for thou art with me—'

Ollenu snatched a discarded fire torch and held it at arm's length, narrowing his eyes as he watched the bull. The creature leapt forward. Sweat seeped from every pore in Ollenu's body and he assumed a boxer's stance, feet apart, aware that he would be thrown off balance when the vast muscle hit him, determined that he would injure the thing before it claimed his life. At the last instant, a terrified Ollenu closed his eyes and it was as if the animal passed straight through him. He swayed, knocked off-balance by the force of wind brought with it. The bull galloped away into the distance, huge tail whipping from side to side.

Ashby scrambled to his feet. 'We must flee, at once!'

'No, we cannot let the creature divert us! We came seeking evidence and that is what we must find.'

Simeon and Malachi slid down from the trees, grabbed the guns and ran as fast as their legs could carry them.

'Simeon! Malachi! Come back!' called Ollenu. 'We need you, come back!'

The two men disappeared without a backward glance, screaming as they went.

'They are sensible,' said Ashby. 'We must leave before we are killed!'

'We have come too far to turn back now, Mr Ashby. You came in search of your clients and this may be their final resting place. If this hole contains solid evidence, we can bring an end to Doctor Hutchinson's killing ways.'

'That thing could return at any moment,' said a shaky Ashby. 'Next time, it will ensure we are crushed or burned to death.'

'It looks and sounds real, but its steam does not burn.' Ollenu stared in the direction of the departing bull, his heart palpitating wildly. 'It must be a form of phantom. I will make haste before it returns.' He grabbed the discarded rope and tied one end to the thick trunk of a nearby tree. 'Should it start to unravel, I expect you to drop the torch and hold onto the rope.'

'I am not strong enough for this,' said Ashby. 'My arms are all a flutter. I have never been so frightened in my entire life. This cannot be what the Lord planned for me.'

'Whatever happened to "the Lord works in mysterious ways"?' Ollenu stared into the investigator's frightened eyes. 'Do not release the rope. I am trusting you with my life, Mr Ashby. Consider that when you consider letting go.'

Ollenu lowered himself into the hole, descending slowly. The further he went the more the stench of death and decay crept up to irritate his nose and test his stomach. Above, he could see Ashby's silhouette and the waving torch. Part way down, he paused as fear claimed his strength. He dangled precariously, wondering if he would ever see the light of day again. Despite what he said about trusting Ashby, he did not have faith that the horrified man would remain in place if the beast returned.

Taking a deep breath of putrid air, Ollenu continued downwards praying that the rope would hold. The depth of the pit astounded him. As he was about to run out of rope he gave a start as his feet hit something uneven that crackled.

'Mr Ollenu, is all well down there?' shouted Ashby his voice echoing into the void.

'Yes! Have care and throw me a torch.'

Seconds later a flaming torch landed at his feet. Holding it aloft, his stomach churned. The remains crumbling beneath his feet were indeed skeletons, man not animal. His stomach groaned, threatening to send bile to his lips. Taking great gulps of stale air, he fought to collect his thoughts. Some of these souls were probably not yet reported missing. He picked up a piece of delicate textile no bigger than two inches wide. The lace edge of a petticoat. Many women had clothes adorned with similar lace, even his wife, Coreen. At best, only one deceased woman lay beneath his feet. Clare Sandie.

Fighting nausea, he retrieved some of the bones and forced them under his shirt. The touch of human remains against his skin was repulsive, yet he could not leave the appalling evidence behind.

He was about to quench the torch when he noticed an object snagged against the wall, a silver watch hanging from a chain. The glass face was cracked, time frozen, and it was speckled with dried blood. The watch's weight suggested it was an expensive object. He crushed the torch flames underfoot, then pushed the broken timepiece deep into his boot.

'I rise!' he shouted and began the ascent, desperate to get away from the cursed hole.

'Make haste!' shouted Ashby. 'I hear something!'

Once Ollenu's shoulders were visible, Ashby leaned over and dragged him out. Ollenu collapsed on the ground and tried to lay flat on his stomach. The evidence under his shirt reminded him of its presence and he was forced to sit upright.

'That place is full of human bones,' whispered Ollenu. 'Many, many bones. I have some of them.'

'Something comes,' said Ashby, trembling. 'I am sure of it!'

'Come on!' Ollenu leapt to his feet. 'Run!'

'In what direction?' shouted Ashby.

Ollenu grabbed Ashby's arm and ran, following the lead taken by their runaway escorts, Simeon and Malachi.

'I cannot hear anything,' panted Ollenu. 'It could be a wild boar or a stray horse.'

'It's behind us!' said Ashby. 'I see a bright light.'

Ollenu swerved blindly and ran in a different direction, mindful that his slower partner was struggling to keep up. Soon he lost all sense of location and was unaware of whether they were running towards safety or straight back to the hole. Nowhere appeared safe to hide.

A distinct crackle of dry twigs caught Ollenu's attention, and he spun to see the ball of yellow fire headed towards them with speed. Ashby fell to his knees, buried his head in his hands, and began to pray.

'I found you, Mr Ollenu! Mr Ashby, why do you hide your face?'

Rosa held her fire torch high and stared at the astounded men.

'Oh, thank God it is only you,' said Ashby clutching his chest.

'Young lady, were you not told to stay behind?' said a breathless Ollenu.

'Boys give too many orders. I never listen to what Simeon says.'

Rosa led them safely back to her quarters where they collapsed outside Nanna Della's hut. The entire community was awake, although some were afraid to leave their huts, having heard that demons were again running loose on the estate. The braver ones ventured out to see what was left of the new visitors to Edinburgh Castle. Incense burned and African prayers were uttered, interspersed with chants. Some danced and gyrated, while one put on a cow-head mask and pranced about bellowing. As the activity grew more frenzied, the people writhed and twisted, contorted their faces and made haunting sounds.

Trembling, Ashby sat and clutched his Bible as he watched the dramatic exhibition. 'As soon as day breaks, we must get away from this cursed place,' he whispered.

Ollenu sat next to him and brought his knees up to his chest. The dancing and exuberant carry-on did not concern him in the least. To a white man it might appear that the participants were little better than the snorting apparition they encountered earlier, but this was not maniacal activity.

'Do you remember what you said, about the *Isabella* crewmen's behaviour? You suggested that their cruel singing was done out of fear and to calm their nerves?'

'I do recall,' said Ashby.

'The slaves are frightened people,' said Ollenu. 'This active, part religious ritual is done in the hope of driving away evil spirits and protecting themselves. They do as their ancestors showed them to do to survive.'

A firm hand squeezed Ollenu's upper arm from behind. He gratefully accepted a calabash bowl of hot dark brew from a man, and muttered thanks over his shoulder. The smell was akin to peppermint, the taste much harsher, and he relished the warmth if not the flavour as it slid down his throat. Many herbal infusions had a bitter taste, but were effective and rewarded those who partook with better health. After emptying the content, he licked his lips and placed the bowl on the ground.

'I needed that,' he said.

Ashby clasped his bowl with both hands, sniffed at the steamy aroma and grimaced. The enslaved man nodded and encouraged him to drink by gesturing towards his mouth.

Without swallowing a drop, Ashby carried out the motion then lowered his vessel. 'Dear Lord, I know you see all things,' he whispered. 'I know you will help those who call upon you with genuine hearts.'

Nanna Della chanted in her own language and threw faded cloth over their shaking shoulders. Ashby clasped his makeshift shawl and bemoaned the awful events of the night. He poked his unusually silent colleague with his foot. 'Do you hear me, Mr Ollenu?'

Somewhere in the back of Ollenu's mind he was aware that Ashby had spoken, but he barely heard a thing. The Africans singing also diminished, and although he could move his lips he could not answer. The images grew blurred and became a massive blend of browns and greys. Soon Ollenu saw and heard nothing at all.

CHAPTER 17

Slivers of soft sunlight penetrated the thatched roof, extending to the bed of dried leaves where Ollenu lay. The sounds of lowing cattle, together with crowing roosters, filtered through the wattle and daub walls of Nanna Della's hut. A concerned Rosa gently raised Ollenu's head and held a gourd of hot dark liquid to his parched lips.

'Rolling Calf did this,' said Simeon.

Malachi nodded in agreement. 'Calf will kill.'

'Poison did it,' said Rosa irritably. 'Nanna said so.'

'Poison?' Ashby searched Ollenu's eyes for signs of recognition and saw none.

'Poison, Mr Ashby.' The old woman stared down at Ollenu. 'Someone gave him bad bush to drink last night.'

'That foul brew,' Ashby wrinkled his nose. 'The odour alone discouraged my thirst. I emptied mine on the ground.'

'Today you would be dead,' she said.

Ashby wiped his forehead with shaking fingers and peered into a steaming pot. The scent was mild, pleasant even. 'What is that mixture you give him, Rosa?'

'We call it bissy tea,' said Rosa.

'Made from the seed of kola nut and good for poisons,' said Nanna Della. 'The second pot is cerassie tea. It will pull heat from his skin.'

'He barely moves, and he certainly does not drink,' said Ashby. 'Stop, Rosa. See it runs down his neck, not into his mouth.'

'He must swallow,' insisted Nanna, 'or he will die before the sun climbs above the hills.'

Ashby knelt beside Ollenu and dragged him into an upright seated position. 'Ollenu, can you hear me, man?' There was no response, although Ollenu's eyes were partly open. Ashby propped him up into the curve of his shoulder and used one hand to tip the law clerk's chin. 'Head up, you have to drink. Try again, Rosa.'

She poured again and Ashby watched with relief as the patient's throat contracted. When the gourd was empty Ashby resettled Ollenu down in his original position.

'Della, the thing we saw last night – the Rolling Calf – what is it? Where did it come from?'

'I have heard of Rolling Calf since I was a child,' said the elderly woman. 'It is a kind of duppy, the spirit of a very evil dead person – a butcher of animals or a murderer of man. Not everyone can see it. A group may be near it, yet only one or two see it. Some hear bellows, others hear silence. Some feel the earth shake, others feel nothing. People may fall sick if it passes close to them.'

'A human being's spirit within a ghostly bull?'

'Spirits take many forms, Mr Ashby. For it to be so angry though—' She shrugged frail shoulders. 'They say the calf is quick to sense evil. Massa is evil and often he goes to that hole. Maybe the calf came in search of Massa, to attack him, and found only you.'

'My word, a duppy intent on being the sole evil thing on the land.' Ashby looked over at his unconscious colleague and tried to banish the Rolling Calf's image from his mind. 'Della, tell me, do you know what afflicts

Mr Ollenu? No, not poison. Sometimes he does not move or he shudders and mumbles a rhyme. Minutes, hours, days later, some unfortunate event occurs, usually something horrible. He says he cannot see exactly what will happen, but he knows that calamity awaits.'

Nanna Della frowned. 'First a rhyme, then a disaster?'

'Yes, vague words of doom. I have twice witnessed it, but on the latter occasion two sailors died.'

'When I was a child, people in my village could foresee danger; it is not new. They saw floods and dry times and even the coming of the white man. People spoke in unknown tongues, but I know of none who would rhyme. One man would first lie on the ground twisting as a snake and another would howl as a dog.'

'I say with certainty that Ollenu will never writhe on the ground. A pristine appearance is his delight. I sincerely pray he never howls.'

The strains of a familiar voice nearing the hut, unnerved the occupants. Simeon and Malachi ran for the exit. 'We must go!'

'Come Nanna!' said Rosa, poised to scamper.

'I will not run from him.' The medicine woman shook her head. 'I am too old to run and no longer afraid. Go with your cousins, quick, my child.'

Rosa hesitated and looked at Ashby.

'Go on, Rosa,' he said as he climbed to his feet. 'I will look after Nanna Della and Mr Ollenu, I promise.'

The girl snatched up the hem of her dress and fled behind the departing cousins.

Doctor Lewis Hutchinson strolled into the hut, tapping his cane on his side. His bottom lip fell and he stared at Ashby, as if surprised that the man was standing.

Recovering his composure, he beamed at his guest. 'Mr Ashby, you arose early. Do you fare well this morning?'

'In the circumstances, yes.' Moisture crept through Ashby's palms and he wiped them slowly against his sides. He hoped his voice sounded firm and confident, although he felt nothing of the sort.

'Pray tell, you did not spend the night down here with these Negro brutes?'

'I did.'

'Oh dear, whatever ails Mr Ollenu? I warned you not to venture out unaccompanied by me.' The doctor crouched close to Ollenu whose eyes were now closed. 'So he has expired, how unfortunate.'

Ashby's eyes widened in alarm. He immediately put his hands under Ollenu's arms and dragged his colleague's heavy body from the makeshift bed. With Ollenu propped up against the wall, Ashby tapped the man's cheeks urgently with both hands. 'Ollenu? Come back, man. Ollenu!'

The glazed brown eyes slowly flickered back open.

'Ah, he lives after all,' announced Doctor Hutchinson with a degree of nonchalance. 'Or do you have the power to raise Lazarus, Mr Ashby? I should examine my ailing guest further.'

The doctor knelt beside Ashby, his head so close to Ollenu that his long nose almost touched the invalid's cheek. To Ashby it seemed as if Hutchinson was sniffing the victim, as a wild animal would do before sampling flesh. Ashby studied Ollenu for signs of distress, noting that the law clerk seemed conscious and struggling to move his body. The patient's arms and legs were motionless, but his fingers unfurled in tiny increments and a crease appeared on his brow. His lips parted. Ashby sensed that if Ollenu could speak he would deliver a poetic verse to rival that of Alexander Pope.

'That will not be necessary, Doctor Hutchinson,' said Ashby. 'Do not trouble yourself. He has taken medicine.'

'Taken medicine you say?' The doctor sat back on his heels. 'And who administered such treatment?'

'It was I,' said Nanna Della in a strong voice.

'You?' With the help of his cane, the doctor rose, his face rigid with anger. 'You with all your hocus pocus and spells? You suppose I failed to hear your accursed noise last night? It is a wonder you live, yet here you are purporting to be a doctor when you cannot even read a book. You treated him? Pah!'

The matriarch held his gaze and showed no fear. 'I do not know what poison it is, but I know the signs. We have treated poisons for years and years. My parents and their parents knew what to do. Some of my children would have learned too, had I been allowed to teach them, had they not been stolen away.' Her expression became pained, as if recalling memories she had long fought to quash.

'Wherever your miserable children live, I can assure you they are not doctors,' sneered Hutchinson. 'No Negro knows a thing about treating people. Eating people? Oh, yes. I'm quite sure you're well versed at that.'

'Our medicines were given to us by the land,' she replied. 'The land teaches us to live in harmony with it, to learn from it, and heed its voice. The white man never learns to understand the land, nor live in harmony with it, or with the many different people who walk upon it.'

'You dare to back-talk me, you crone? Had your tongue been removed when it should have been, you would not prattle in this insolent manner.' He raised the cane in her direction.

Ashby stepped in front of the elderly woman. 'Doctor Hutchinson, control yourself, man.'

The doctor lowered the cane. His temples throbbed and eyes blazed as he stared at the object of his hatred.

'The old woman has tried her best to help Mr Ollenu,' said Ashby. 'It is unconscionable that she should be attacked for that noble effort, whether or not it succeeds.'

Doctor Hutchinson pointed his cane at Ollenu. 'He must be returned inside the castle where he can rest on a suitable bed and recover.'

Ashby watched as the crease on Ollenu's brow grew deeper. 'Thank you, but he does not yearn for an improved bed.'

'So, you have come to believe that the mumbo jumbo of these Negroes is true?' The red monobrow went up. 'They are little more than savages. Mr Ollenu is a sturdy man, with a sound constitution, but should he survive his illness it will be by sheer chance. No, it shall not be said that this gentleman came all the way from England to die in a mud hut on my estate.'

Ollenu's fingertips reached out and lightly brushed against Ashby's elbow, before his slack arm fell to his side.

'You will not return inside that place, Mr Ollenu,' said Ashby firmly. 'We will depart from here and go back to Montego Bay.'

'That is not his destiny,' stated Hutchinson with a smile.

From a distance came the sound of horses' hooves. The doctor moved to the hut's entrance and shaded his eyes with his hands as he looked towards the three riders. Their horses came to a stop at the castle's front steps. 'Damnation,' he muttered and set off to meet the new visitors.

Ashby peered outside the hut and was elated at the sight of the three familiar men. 'Help is at hand, Ollenu,' he whispered and squeezed Ollenu's shoulder.

Shortly thereafter, footsteps approached and into the hut strode Neville Kershaw with his allies Johnson and Mortimer, followed by an unperturbed Doctor Hutchinson.

'Well now, what goes on here?' asked Kershaw.

'Mr Kershaw, thank goodness,' said Ashby. 'We must leave this place at once. Mr Ollenu is terribly ill and, I fear, will not survive without proper medical attention.'

'What ails him?' asked Kershaw in a tone that suggested no concern whatsoever. 'His face looks swollen, and I'm sure those lips are thicker than usual.'

'The Negroes apparently poisoned him,' said the doctor. 'Although I am yet to fully examine him myself. The old witch herself admitted it.'

'You see, Mr Ashby, this is why we stay far from them.' Kershaw shook his head. 'You're fresh from England. Your poor stomach will not withstand the things they eat. They boil cows' feet. Urgh! You should fear them.'

'My fear of them is surpassed by my fear of the man who stands beside you,' said Ashby.

Kershaw arched his eyebrows. 'Don't talk nonsense, Mr Ashby. A smart man can't be believing slave lies about the good doctor. They're the cause of all the silly rumours against him. Now, we should get the Negro indoors for an examination. If the doctor finds he's as bad as you believe, we'll fetch the carriage to take him.'

'Inside the castle would be a cooler place for him to lie,' said Ashby with hesitation. 'But only until such time as the carriage arrives.'

'My slaves will carry him,' said Doctor Hutchinson as he left the hut.

'Why did you not bring the carriage with you, Mr Kershaw? You knew we were left here by Johnson and Mortimer yesterday? Left against our will, I should add.'

'See here, I'm entitled to my rest and can't be at your beck and call all hours,' said Johnson roughly. 'All I got for carrying you and the Negro about is a sore backside and insect bites.'

'Aye,' said Mortimer. 'You go from happy to find your own carriage and travel about Spanish Town, to be wanting us to wait in desolate Pedro, for you and that savage.'

'Gentlemen,' said Kershaw and raised a palm at his aggrieved men. 'Mr Ashby, a wheel on the carriage is being repaired. I thought you would enjoy a stay on this abundant estate, where there's fishing and hunting to be done. Had I known your Negro would take ill, I would have seen to the wheel immediately.'

Ashby swallowed dry air and tried to hide his discomfort from this hostile posse. When Ollenu was alert the men were polite to a fault. Now that the law clerk was seriously ill, they did not try to hide their disdain, and could not bring themselves to use his name. Now he was a Negro and a savage.

Startled, Ashby watched Kershaw deliver a sharp kick to Ollenu's knee. The victim gave no response. 'He's out of it. Not quite dead, but out of it.'

'Mr Kershaw, such behaviour is completely unwarranted,' said Ashby weakly. 'Your boot will not assist his recovery.'

Kershaw's eyes narrowed. 'He is a Negro, not one of us. Their bodies can withstand a lot of treatment that ours cannot.'

Ashby licked dry lips. 'I must insist you fetch your carriage, or any available carriage, without further delay. Mr Ollenu's condition worsens.'

Doctor Hutchinson re-entered the hut with two muscular house slaves behind him.

'Come now, Mr Ashby,' said Kershaw. 'Makes sense that the Negro stays right here under the doctor's care, rather than us haul him away, as there's no doctor for many miles.'

'I was informed that a Doctor Hutton lives near here?' said Ashby.

Hutchinson smiled. 'Ah, he moved to Kingston, after our little… skirmish.'

'Mr Kershaw, I tell you we must be away from this estate entirely.' Ashby's voice rose in dismay. 'Strange spirits roam at nightfall. A fiery bull, a huge creature that could bring down any man, bore down upon us and then… it was gone.'

'I see your creature.' Johnson picked up a cow mask, placed it on his head, mooed and danced in an exaggerated manner. 'Rolling Calf come!'

Mortimer picked up a dried cow's skin and spread it across Johnson's shoulder. 'That's a better look, more bullish.' He and his accomplices laughed.

'I can't believe you let slaves convince you to engage in superstitious foolish talk,' said Kershaw.

'I speak not about a cow mask or skin,' said Ashby in frustration. 'I know what I saw. A great hulking beast with red eyes and steam from its nostrils. It shook the very earth to its core when it ran, and then it vanished.'

'Mr Ashby,' said Kershaw patiently. 'You saw a wild bull. More than a few of them wander about here. Besides, we also get frequent earth tremors on the island. There are many explanations for what occurred last night. Perhaps you partook too wholeheartedly in the doctor's wines?'

'Sir, I am not impaired. I understand an angry Rolling Calf can sense evil. I do believe Doctor Hutchinson is well aware of what evil goes on here.'

'Oh, and what evil goes on here?' asked the doctor with menace.

Ashby took two strides to the corner. 'Here, gentlemen, here is evidence of the doctor's nefarious deeds. This is what Mr Ollenu unearthed last night on this very land.'

Kershaw walked over to the spot where four bones of different sizes lay. Johnson and Mortimer moved forward and looked over his shoulder at the objects.

'Looks human,' muttered Johnson. 'Where are these from?'

'A very deep hole at the edge of the estate,' said Ashby.

'How did you find them?' asked Mortimer.

'The slaves led us to the hole last night. It holds evidence that people have died right here, Mr Kershaw.'

'Slaves are killers.' Kershaw straightened up and rubbed his chin. 'Seems to me the killers led you to their victims, Mr Ashby.'

'My people did not kill them,' said Nanna Della.

'Do not speak!' said Hutchinson.

'The slaves did no such thing, Mr Kershaw,' said Ashby.

He rubbed his neck, wishing he could be anywhere but in front of these aggressive men of no compassion. God had many calls upon His mercies, and was not answering His sheep's prayers.

'I do not want to believe any of this possible, but after what I saw and heard last night I realise I have been naive. It is simply not credible that slaves could kill people on this estate, kill white and Black people, and Doctor Hutchinson not be aware that bodies lie on his land.'

'Well, doctor, do bodies lie here?' asked Kershaw.

'But of course.' The doctor beamed at the deputy marshal. 'Mr Ashby and Mr Ollenu have rather let their imaginations run away with them. These are indeed human bones, and I believe Mr Ollenu recovered them from a deep pit. I put them there myself, though I did have assistance from time to time.'

Ashby was taken aback by this admission. 'The bones of Clare Sandie, Henry Penket and Francis Dantry,' he murmured.

'As I told you before, Mr Ashby, the only one I met was Henry Penket – two years ago.' The doctor laughed and slapped his cane on his thigh. 'The bones are from cadavers, sir. Cadavers I purchased from an undertaker in Port Royal. All were very dead when they came into my possession.'

Ashby held up part of a humerus. 'Cadavers with gunshot holes?'

Hutchinson blinked, then curled his thin lips. 'Why yes, Mr Ashby, I daresay some bones do show signs of violent assault. Such cruelty takes place on this beautiful little island far more often than we wish to concede. Men are always shooting themselves over dice and ale and women and land.'

'I do not believe you,' said Ashby hesitantly.

'Then you need only consult the undertaker, Mr Ashby, for I do not lie. I hold a fascination for bones. I examine specimens, try to find out why some bones are brittle and some strong, to discover what causes such porosity. It is all completely innocent. Once I am finished… Well, what am I to do with the bones afterwards? They were all unclaimed bodies with no one to mourn them. The best I could do for them is bury the remains so deep they would remain untouched.'

'Well, that's that then,' said Kershaw with a satisfied look. 'Seems a perfectly reasonable explanation to me.'

'Gentlemen, surely we should consult this undertaker?' said Ashby.

'What?' Kershaw gave Ashby a look of admonishment. 'You expect us to question the word of a doctor, a gentleman, because of Negro gossips? Surely you would not expect us to do that Mr Ashby?'

Ashby drew up his shoulders. 'Yes, sir, that is exactly what I expect. For you to do your duty and follow the evidence wherever it takes you.'

'So, Mr Ashby, you want to educate me about my job?' Kershaw's expression darkened. 'You want me to rush and get my carriage after you insult me? You'll stay right here with the Negro under Doctor Hutchinson's care.'

'Mr Ollenu will not survive a carriage journey,' said Nanna Della. 'Let him stay with me until he is recovered.'

'Your master told you to be quiet, old fool.' Johnson slapped Nanna's mouth, an assault that jerked her head.

'See, that advice comes from the mouth of a Negro you trust, Mr Ashby,' said Kershaw with a broad smile. 'She says the Black should not travel in any carriage. Once he recovers – if he recovers – Mr Johnson and Mr Mortimer will be back to take you onto your next destination.'

Ashby fell silent. His heart thudded as realisation of where his trusting nature had led him sank in. Yet again Isaiah Ollenu had been proved right. Neville Kershaw was not the person he thought him to be, and Johnson and Mortimer were no better. He attributed their aggression to growing frustration that the whereabouts of Francis Dantry and the much-sought slavery money was still unknown.

Kershaw headed to the exit. 'We'll be on our way then, doctor.'

'Thank you for your understanding, gentlemen.' The Scotsman smoothed back his flowing red mane and clapped at his slave men. 'Take him inside.'

Ashby followed behind the bondsmen who half-carried, half-dragged Ollenu. He suspected that one of them was the poisoner, that one of Ollenu's own people had done this to him. Yet these slave men were not Ollenu's people. He, Ruben Ashby, was now Ollenu's people. This new-found knowledge was a revelation that brought on a sense of hopelessness. On this island existed the unchallenged assumption that colonists were on the side of right and Negroes on the side of wrong. Even though his own eyes confirmed the assumption to be a fallacy, he was in no position to take action. He could not save Isaiah Ollenu, could not protect him from the likes of Lewis Hutchinson or Neville Kershaw for that matter.

Dejected, Ashby thrust his hands deep into his jacket pockets. He wondered what the bulky object beneath his fingers was, until he held it before his eyes – a long fat roll of cannabis. A parting gift from the friendly carpenter at Braeton Inn. A substance powerful enough to send him into blissful oblivion and blot out the impossibility of his predicament. A substance that would render him incapable of making any choices, good or bad. He uttered a silent prayer of thanks to an otherwise preoccupied God.

CHAPTER 18

Ollenu found himself in a room within Edinburgh Castle that he did not recognise. The space was completely devoid of furnishings, except that piece where he lay – a stripped bed standing in the middle of the floor. High up on the grey stone wall, sunlight entered through a narrow aperture, an arrow-slit in the shape of a cross to facilitate both a crossbow and a longbow. Scratch marks on the stone suggested to Ollenu that at some stage a ladder had leaned against it. A place where Hutchinson could launch attacks on unsuspecting visitors by arrow if he tired of using guns.

Although his arms were heavy and his fingers flexed with difficulty, Ollenu was relieved that he could move again. For that, he owed his unending gratitude to Nanna Della and her all-natural potion. Running weak fingers along his face, he checked that his nose and mouth were intact. His jaw creaked as he opened his lips, and dried saliva cracked at the sides of his mouth. He tried to call out, but no sound emerged.

Gingerly he sat up. His legs moved, too slowly, but any movement was good and he inched off the bed, grimacing in pain. Although his legs were awake, his feet could not withstand his weight and he sank to the ground. The stone floor was cold and damp, the odour rank. Without doubt the enslaved house workers never cleaned this room. Either they were unaware it existed or forbidden from entering. An image came to mind of the mad doctor spending hours there, looking out for vulnerable targets, and urinating where he stood.

Disgusted by the thought, Ollenu clutched the bed frame and hauled himself off the floor. Thankfully, he was not chained, the doctor possibly confident that his prisoner would never rise again or function coherently, the expectation being a swift death.

His bleary eyes swept the room. The stone wall contained cracks and crevices, places where bits of damaged stone had broken away. The remains of iron fetters were embedded in the stone, some with chains attached to them. A large bow and arrow hung from a hook nailed in a corner. He did not have the strength to take them down, much less to draw the bowstring.

The door was ajar. Even if by some miracle he dragged his body outdoors, he would be seen by those loyal to the doctor. Kershaw had kicked him and spoken of him as if he were inhuman, and the mad master would happily treat him as such. Hutchinson would take great pleasure in watching his captive crawl like a wounded dog, before turning the miserable event into gun sport.

Pain and heartbreak overcame Ollenu as he remembered his final conversation with his mentor Jacob Dunne. The talk was of Ollenu helping Barrow for a few months. Dunne had wished him bon voyage. How could the barrister have sent him away to help recover a slave trader's wealth, knowing all too well that he despised the bloody trade? A trade Dunne himself claimed to despise.

Ollenu strained his ears as voices came from the passageway. Ashby and Hutchinson in unintelligible conversation. Ashby was laughing and Ollenu could think of no comforting reason for the investigator to be in good humour. Suspicion returned to his already dull brain, clouding it, and a deep furrow formed in his brow. As the voices drew closer Ollenu, struggled to move back into the middle of the bed. He resumed his former supine position, arms close at his sides, legs stretched in front.

Ashby entered ahead of the doctor who closed the door behind him and strolled over to his prisoner. Ollenu breathed evenly and did not stir. A new and markedly different odour enveloped the filthy room. An odour he had last encountered in Kingston, courtesy of the carpenter.

Something sharp plunged into the soft skin of Ollenu's cheek. In his fevered mind he saw a knife that would soon impale him to the bed. Fear of being murdered in such a painful manner forced his eyes open. The pointed fingernail of Doctor Hutchinson pressed deeper into his skin.

'Ah, so you have not left us Isaiah Ollenu?' said the doctor. 'Good. I have plans for you.'

'Mr Ollenu, my dear, dear man,' said Ashby cheerfully. 'Praise God, you're back with us.'

Between Ashby's fingers was the end of a cannabis roll and in his eyes an expression of vacancy. All thoughts of engaging Ashby in an escape plan made a rapid and steady exodus from Ollenu's mind, leaving him in a state of confusion. The Christian catastrophe could barely stand, and weaved unsteadily on his feet.

Hutchinson peered into Ollenu's eyes and spoke in a jocular tone. 'I wonder, should I examine your eyes for cataracts? Eyes are not my forte, but I do have instruments

I could pierce them with. Soon you will have little need for sight, good or bad.'

Ollenu blinked and tried to remain rigid, though his heart beat at a rapid pace as terror overwhelmed him.

'It pleases me to find you alert, Mr Ollenu. Will you speak at all? No? A pity, for Ruben tells me you rhyme when you foreshadow a death, and I hoped to critique your effort.' Hutchinson drew himself up to his full height. 'You have rejected my hospitality, unlike Ruben here who was clearly led astray by you and your fellow Negroes. He is now aware that this is what your scheming kind do. Is that not so Ruben?'

'It is quite so, Lewis,' Ashby chuckled. 'Depraved and scheming Negroes.'

'You did not succeed, Mr Ollenu. Until you came here, the unsubstantiated rumours merely floated in tankards, but now you insist on proving malfeasance where there is none. You would sully my name further, and isolate me from the great and good. You wish them to exclude me from their gatherings, to shun me in public. You want to see me hang. Well, your cadaver hunt proved nothing and look where it got you.' He jabbed a fingernail back into Ollenu's face, closer to his watering eye.

Ollenu tried to gather his frightening thoughts. If he could secure a firm hold on the doctor's arm, he might bring him to ground and subdue him with sheer body-weight. He dismissed the idea almost as soon as it came to him. Even if he pinned the doctor down, he had no strength to crush the life out of him, and Ashby would be of no assistance now that he was on first name terms with the killer. In his despair, Ollenu wondered why death was toying with him in this manner, making the end so torturous and drawn out, allowing the white men to mock him until they grew tired of persecution games.

Doctor Hutchinson circled the bed, all the time keeping his eyes on the invalid. 'You, Mr Ollenu, will be disposed of. You have no value, monetary or otherwise, despite your pridefulness. You died from poison administered by those degenerate slaves. No one shall know any different.'

Hutchinson smiled a slow sinister smile. 'How does it feel, Mr Ollenu? How does it feel to know that mine is the last face you shall ever see? That you will perish right here in a dingy attic and no one will ever know?' He punched Ollenu in the stomach and seemed angered that there was little movement. 'You do not feel?' He aimed for Ollenu's face and the blow jerked his head to one side. A trickle of blood ran down his nose onto his bold yellow cravat and his eyes watered. 'Hah! You can feel.'

The doctor drew back, rubbed his fist and looked at Ashby. 'Your turn, Ruben. Strike him.'

Ashby looked perplexed momentarily. 'Peace be unto all men, even Negroes.'

The doctor resurrected his tone for dealing with small children. 'But we must teach this one a lesson for his abhorrent behaviour, Ruben. He has caused a stir on my once peaceful land. This is no time to spare the rod, strike him.'

'Spare the rod, spoil the Negro.' Ashby clenched the hemp roll remnant between his teeth, balled his hand into a fist and punched Ollenu on the jaw. 'Ooh, that hurt!'

'You can do much better, Ruben. Harder this time, spill some more blood. Negroes have plenty, and this one has no further need of any.'

Ashby repeated the action and rubbed his hand, grinning through the pain. 'A jaw of steel.'

Doctor Hutchinson cackled, 'Or so he believes. Jawbones can be broken.'

'I wonder, should I get into fighting, Lewis?' Ashby slapped Ollenu on the shoulder and laughed. 'See, I can fight too, Ollenu my man. I should have stood up in the Braeton Inn and knocked out those greasy scoundrels.' He pranced about, boxed at shadows and lost the last nub of hemp in the process.

Hutchinson pressed his pointed nose close to the law clerk's ear and sniffed. 'I smell death, Mr Ollenu.'

The sound of horses' hooves filtered in from outside. 'Who the devil is that now? It is barely noonday and my castle is overrun with intruders.' Hutchinson sent a hostile glare towards Ollenu as he headed through the door. 'The sooner I return you to that cadaver pit the better.'

Ollenu listened to the braying horses and tried not to become too hopeful. Neville Kershaw and his henchmen could have returned, or maybe Roger Maddix and James Walker had come to do the neighbourly thing and assist the doctor with his live burial. The doctor would not let Ashby live, but the investigator was either too high to realise that his life was about to end, or he knew it, and opted to expire in a cloud of serenity.

'I could soar as a bird!' declared Ashby. He crushed the smouldering dregs underfoot and looked towards the open door. 'I wonder if Lewis has any of these delightful dried leaves secreted away somewhere? I say, Lewis, Lewis!' he called and staggered out into the dark corridor.

Ollenu forced himself upright. It sounded as if many horses had arrived, yet there were not many accompanying voices. Crisp male English accents intermingled with those of a young enslaved man. A voice, with a distinct aristocratic accent, was one he had heard before and his heart lifted. There must be some means to get the attention of this man.

Hutchinson had said this was an attic, so Ollenu reasoned the castle must have a third floor. The access point was probably concealed from general view and most probably barricaded. Ollenu squinted at a dark corner where stood an array of small opaque bottles. The objects next to the bottles resembled hollow reeds, the size of quill pens, with one end honed to a sharp point. His stomach churned. Whatever toxic substance was in those bottles could be plunged into his body with the reeds. The end of his life, in this filthy torture chamber, would include unbearable pain.

He stared at the arrow-slit about ten feet above him. Beginning the climb, he placed his feet in the broken fetters. Fetters he had avoided all of his life. He clawed at the bare wall, scraping the skin on his fingers, and inched upwards, breaking his fingernails along the way. Blood seeped from his damaged skin, but he ignored the throbbing pain. His legs felt as if someone had tied a hundredweight to each and he lifted them with great effort. Faint grunts, purporting to be shouts, came from his lips.

Soon he could see through the opening. The only thing visible was blue sky, not salvation. The wall was at least two feet thick, similar to a proper castle and although the opening was wide enough for his hand to go through, it was not wide enough for his head. He clutched a chunk of stone wall with one hand and used the other to try and break a piece off, but the stone remained solid. In desperation he pulled the yellow cravat from his neck, pressed his temple against the cold wall and stretched his arm as far as it could go. As he waved the cloth he prayed that it would be seen by the right person, but there were no acknowledging calls from below.

In a final effort to attract attention, he released the fabric and raised an eye to check that it had gone. Part of the material fluttered outside the castle, but part snagged onto a piece of uneven stone.

Filled with despair, Ollenu closed his eyes and slid down the wall, collapsing into a heap on the floor. A crunch in his boot, followed by glass stabbing his ankle, came as a sharp reminder of the watch recovered from the death hole. The watch and his bleeding ankle were the least of his cares. The tears that coursed down his face were not brought about by flesh pains, for he barely noticed his injuries. Time was of the essence and now there was no more time.

His shoulders shook as he thought of Coreen raising the children alone in poverty, having never received a single farthing from deceitful Dunne. A pang wrenched his soul when he remembered that he had left the children's presents – Ekon's spinning top and Fayola's bow – at the Kershaw home in Spanish Town. Thankfully, his offspring would never know he had not kept those precious gifts close to his heart. He thought of the baby he would never meet. His new daughter. And it would be a daughter, as he always guessed right each time. They planned to name her Amara. Her mother would tell her of who he dreamed to be: Isaiah Ollenu, Esquire, attorney at law. He hoped Amara would be satisfied with who he became in the end.

–

'Good day, Doctor Hutchinson.' Earl Charles Cadogan, dressed in all his finery, dismounted and stood beside his majestic black horse. His equally smart groomsman also alighted from his steed and held the reins of two spare riderless horses.

'Good day, My Lord.' Doctor Hutchinson executed an elaborate low bow. 'What brings you to Edinburgh Castle may I ask?'

'Ah, Mr Ashby.' The earl peered past the doctor's shoulders. 'So you are here after all? That silly stripling told me you had taken your leave.'

'I am here.' Ashby tottered towards the new arrivals. 'Oh, I say, I remember you – Charlie from the party!'

The earl studied him with some concern. 'Are you entirely well, Mr Ashby?'

'Never so improved of health, Charlie. St Ann is a most worthy parish and Pedro a village with much to admire. I tell you it has flaming, vengeful, monsters and—'

'I am so sorry, My Lord.' Doctor Hutchinson hugged Ashby's shoulders and smiled at the earl. 'Mr Ashby has rather overindulged on dried herbs and his imagination runs amok.'

'That thing runs amok.' Ashby made grunting noises and trod the ground where he stood. 'A Rolling Calf they call it, except it was colossal for a calf.'

'I will ensure that Mr Ashby stays out of extreme sunlight for the day,' said a nervous Hutchinson.

The earl's expression alternated between confused and amused. 'I took the liberty of bringing horses so that we could ride together as promised. Whatever has become of Mr Ollenu?'

'Mr Ollenu is not to be found, I'm afraid,' said Hutchinson digging his nails into Ashby's shoulders.

'Oh, I looked forward to our meeting again,' said Cadogan, disappointment evident in his voice. 'Such a good fellow. Articulate, discerning and knowledgeable. I rather took to him.'

'Last night, he proceeded down that path.' The doctor pointed towards the enslaved Africans huts. 'This morning, I was informed that he must have departed.'

The nobleman frowned and pushed back his curly fringe. 'That is most regretful. Has there been a disagreement between you?'

'Hah, disagree with that old doomsayer?' said Ashby. 'He would insist on having the last word.'

The doctor clapped in the direction of a slave boy hovering nearby, increasing the look of apprehension already apparent on the youth's face. 'You! Come escort Mr Ashby upstairs to his room at once.'

Ashby sidled away as the youth appeared at his side. 'I will remain right here and converse with Charlie from the party.'

'The intention was for you to ride with me, but you do not seem in any condition to do so,' said the earl sternly. 'Were Mr Ollenu available, I would have welcomed his company. You will see him again soon, Mr Ashby?'

'Oh, be sure, I *will* see him again soon,' laughed Ashby.

Cadogan signalled to his valet, who handed the earl a bundle of papers. 'See that he gets these documents, if you would be so kind, Mr Ashby. They are my grandfather's papers, that I found within my mother's possessions on her estate. I thought he may wish to read more of Grandfather's exploits and adventures, unique events that were not recorded in his published books.'

'Whatever would old Rhyming Doom want with more papers? He's tired of reading papers.' Ashby snatched the bundle from the earl's outstretched hand and threw it up into the air. 'See how the pages rain!'

Charles Cadogan exclaimed in annoyance and looked to the heavens as his family papers went up and slowly floated back to earth. A sudden rush of breeze released Ollenu's cravat and it drifted downwards, coming to rest on a tall bush barely above the visitors' heads. Amongst a cluster of green leaves, it was noticeable only as a large golden leaf, tinged with red.

'Oh dear, how unfortunate, My Lord,' Doctor Hutchinson mumbled.

The earl's groomsman swiftly gathered the strewn papers together. He stood on tiptoes and retrieved one of the pages from the bush, without noticing the cravat dangling beside it. After dusting off all the pages he returned them to his aggrieved master.

'Mr Ashby, I am quite shocked by this unfortunate display of bad manners. My grandfather's writings have lasted for decades and never been treated in such a scandalous manner.'

'My Lord, do accept my profuse apologies on behalf of Mr Ashby,' said the doctor, his tone subservient. 'If you would be kind enough to let me take the writings, I would be most appreciative. As a fellow physician, I have always had a keen interest in Sir Hans' work.'

'As you wish.' The earl handed over the bundle. He beckoned to his groomsman and climbed back onto his horse. 'Good day to you both and I do hope Mr Ashby regains his senses sometime soon.'

'Good day, My Lord.' Hutchinson touched his forelock in deference.

'Wait, Charlie from the party, do not take your leave. I have not finished describing the great bull that chased us. It was twice this wide…' Ashby spread his arms apart. 'Much bigger than this puny horse.' He delivered a hard slap to the flank of the earl's horse. The animal neighed and kicked out with its hind legs, an action that sent Ashby tumbling into the bush.

'What the blazes!' shouted Cadogan as he clutched the reins and fought to stay in the saddle.

'Here, come on, boy.' The groomsman reached across his own steed to pat the earl's horse. 'Steady now.'

The cravat became dislodged from the bush and fell to the soil. The earl's agitated horse stepped forward and covered most of the fabric under a large front hoof. The animal breathed heavily through flared nostrils and tossed its head.

'All right, boy, gently does it.' The shaken nobleman dismounted and adjusted the bridle. As he patted the stallion, it took a step forward to nuzzle its owner.

'Sir, what is that red material underfoot?' asked the valet. 'Did it fall from your pocket?'

Cadogan picked up the cravat, now stained red with blood and brown with Nanna Della's elixir. As the earl straightened out the necktie his appearance changed from angry to suspicious. He looked at Ashby, who was using the bush as a prop to stay upright, then stared at Doctor Hutchinson who was glaring at his troublesome guest.

'Do not move, either of you,' warned the earl as he reached into his holster.

'Come, come, My Lord.' The doctor's eyes widened as he stared into the barrel of the aristocrat's pistol. 'What can this mean?'

The earl gestured to his aide, who immediately drew his own weapon.

'Where is Isaiah Ollenu?' demanded Cadogan. 'Great sentimental value is attached to this cravat and he would never part with it. Yet here it lies stained with blood that I am inclined to believe is his blood.'

An uncomfortable silence was finally broken by the grinning Bristol man. 'It is a secret, but I will share it with you, Charlie. He is hidden upstairs. You should see him, he cannot even speak!' Ashby burst out into peals of laughter and waved his arms at his sides. 'Usually he bobs up and down as a Jack-in-the-box, or struts haughty as a peacock, but now his clothes are all filthy and he can barely move his legs!'

Cadogan looked from the doctor to Ashby and back again, his face incredulous. 'You planned to murder Mr Ollenu?'

'Not I, My Lord.' The doctor stood tall and pointed at Ashby. 'It is he who attacked Mr Ollenu. Look at his hands. Look at mine.' The doctor held out his unblemished thin hands, twisting them back and forth.

Ashby looked down at his own hands. The knuckles of his right hand were bruised red and had already begun to swell. 'Look at this,' he chuckled holding out the injured hand. 'How did that happen, Lewis?'

The doctor squirmed beneath the aristocrat's cold glare. 'My fault was to try and help poor Mr Ollenu recover in secret, so that Mr Ashby would avoid sanction for beating the man.'

'I will hear what Mr Ollenu has to say.' The earl levelled his pistol at both men. 'Take me to him, now. Go on, I will follow.'

The reluctant doctor led the way up two flights of stairs and down a narrow passage, glancing over his shoulder from time to time. The collarless yellow-eyed cat watched the procession with interest, then ran to catch up with its master and rubbed against his ankles. Doctor Hutchinson pointed to the partly open cell door.

'Good God!' Cadogan handed his weapon to his valet. He rushed over to Ollenu and pulled him off the floor, placing him to sit at the foot of the bed. 'Can you speak, Mr Ollenu? Can you hear me?'

Ollenu said nothing and watched through barely open eyes as Doctor Hutchinson approached the bed.

The earl glared at the doctor. 'If Ashby did this to him, why did you not intervene? Are you not a man of medicine? Could you not assist him?'

Doctor Hutchinson made a half-hearted attempt at sounding remorseful. 'It appeared Mr Ollenu was too far gone, My Lord.'

Hutchinson lowered his head close to Ollenu's face to scrutinise him. Quick as a flash Ollenu plunged a dirty bloodied finger into the doctor's eye. The man howled and stepped backwards, spinning wildly and clutching his face. The cat's unguarded tail was caught by the master's shoe and the unhappy feline yowled in pain and fled.

'Mr Ollenu, thank goodness I find you not on the precipice of death!' declared Cadogan. 'Who did this to you? The doctor or Ashby?'

Ollenu grunted and pointed at the cursing madman, who was bent double tending his weeping eye with a handkerchief.

'You shall come with me, Ollenu. You too, Ashby.' The earl spoke in a tone that showed no fear of contradiction. 'Doctor Hutchinson, you shall not impede us.'

'I would not dream of it, My Lord,' the doctor simpered.

As Cadogan walked past the doctor he snatched the bundle from the man's breast pocket. 'I will take my grandfather's papers.'

The nobleman and his aide escorted Ollenu slowly down the stairs, followed by an unsteady Ashby.

'We are to leave?' said Ashby with regret. He looked back at the doctor. 'Wait, Lewis, do you happen to possess anything delightful to smoke?'

Doctor Lewis Hutchinson glowered and his whole body trembled. Although his lips moved, it was as if he could not trust himself to speak.

CHAPTER 19

The Bristol men were shown great courtesy at Earl Cadogan's Spanish Town estate. His palatial mansion occupied an enviable parcel of flourishing land with no immediate neighbours, and as many servants as it had rooms.

Three days had passed since the journey from St Ann back to St Catherine, a journey that had almost claimed Ollenu's life. A combination of poison, heat and over-exertion had pushed the law clerk into a rambling fever from which he was only now recovering.

Ashby helped nurse Ollenu daily and kept a watchful eye on whoever entered his room. It was a luxurious space with all the comforts one could wish for: a four-poster bed, soft sheets, and plush feathered pillows. The tin bath was replenished twice each day, and surrounded with fresh towels and soap.

The investigator became so irrational that he examined any food or water prepared for Ollenu, before letting the patient eat or drink. Although aware that this behaviour vexed the servants, Ashby was past caring about the emotions of anyone else, such was his shame at his sinful actions towards the law clerk. There was no doubt in his mind that Hutchinson had murdered his clients, and would have murdered Ollenu too. As Ollenu had made no mention of any event that occurred in the castle, Ashby prayed that God would continue to block the law clerk's memory.

On this morning, Ollenu, propped up in bed, dipped his silver spoon into a bowl of maize porridge, then paused with it mid-air. 'You, Mr Ashby, have a ruinous effect upon my appetite. I cannot sup whilst you continue to stare at me.'

'I apologise, force of habit.' Ashby looked away, cleared his throat and shuffled on his chair. 'Eleanor came to call upon you yesterday, but you slept and I thought it best not to awaken you. She asked that I pass on her heartfelt wish that you are soon much mended.'

'To call upon *me*?' Ollenu's tone was one of amusement. 'I sincerely hope you found a topic of mutual interest for discussion, and not me?' On receiving no response, Ollenu added, 'It would be remiss of you to let the enchanting Mrs Lamont slip through your fingers, Mr Ashby.'

'I fear I have nothing much to offer her.' Ashby sounded as doleful as he looked. 'Her husband appears to have been a man of adventure, fearless and popular. What am I, Mr Ollenu? A dull insurance agent, afraid to stray far from my natural environment. Not much better than a comfortable pair of slippers.'

'Everyone welcomes a comfortable pair of slippers. Besides, I suspect she would give anything for a man who appreciates home life. One who is not tempted to stray into villages where he has no business.'

'Hmm? Whatever do you mean?'

'I mean that perhaps you are exactly what Eleanor Lamont desires. It is conceivable that what she had before was not exceptional. You know, it is not a sin to ask her about him?'

Ashby flushed. 'I could not possibly do so.'

'Of course you could, Mr Ashby. When it comes to matters of the heart, embarrassment is a part of life. There is no reason why the good lady would ride a whole mile without escort, were she not interested in spending her day with you.'

'When in her company, I barely know what to say,' said Ashby. 'I am a youth of fifteen years again. It is years since I met a lady I genuinely admire, yet I fear the ghost of another man may prove too hard to vanquish.'

'You said it, ghost. He is gone. I do not wish to appear cold, but you are here, flesh and blood.'

'At Sir Alastair's ball she was much occupied with a soldier. She seemed dazzled by him, all tall and official-looking. The sort who always seem to have no shortage of women fussing at their side. I cannot hope to compete.'

'If you continue to talk in that manner, I would have to agree. Listen, soon you will return to England. She plans to return to England once she has settled her estate. If you do nothing else before you leave Jamaica, Mr Ashby, you must tell her you would be extremely honoured to call upon her in England, and enquire where she will reside.'

'Eat your porridge.'

Ashby walked to the window where he idly fiddled with the shutters and stared out at the extensive green pastures.

'You are not the coward you pretend to be.' Ollenu placed the empty bowl on a side table and stared at Ashby's back. His tone turned cold. 'You will be a worthy protector for Eleanor. When called upon to shield her, you can unleash your fists. I will attest that your blows have effect.'

Ashby stiffened and briefly closed his eyes. God had not answered his prayers after all. The trauma Ollenu had suffered at his hands was not forgotten. With reluctance, Ashby turned to face his accuser.

'I am so sorry, Mr Ollenu. You cannot know how deeply I regret my disgraceful actions.'

'When you slammed your fist into my jaw, you were aware that the doctor was a person of evil, yet you showed no restraint. You took pleasure in it.'

Ashby wrung moist hands as he spoke. 'It is difficult for me to fully express my emotions of that day.'

'Oh? Do try.' Ollenu sat up straight, his eyes boring through the man. 'I lay in pain, desperate for you to knock him senseless. Hoping you would attempt to save us. And yes, I said *us*. Not you, saving Ruben Ashby. And I, saving myself.'

'I was overwhelmed by the events of that morning and the awful night before. When I found the cannabis stick, the smoke brought relief from my woes. I chose to seek pleasure by any means possible – even hitting you made me feel admired and appreciated.' Ashby fiddled with his already loose collar. 'For an hour or so, I felt extreme happiness. As if I were on the side of the righteous, and all was well with the world.'

'On the side of the righteous,' stated Ollenu with bitterness. 'Hutchinson, Kershaw, Mortimer, Johnson.'

'I was weak; I could not see my way to oppose them.' Ashby hung his head. 'And I knew that his watchful neighbours Maddix and Walker could appear at any moment, guns drawn, ready to defend him. I should have awaited the Lord's guidance.'

'Yes, and the Lord's guidance was riding to the castle with spare horses for us,' seethed Ollenu. 'Can you even begin to understand how I felt, believing I would never see Coreen or my children again? That I would never meet my new baby?'

'Your thoughts would have driven a lesser man to madness. I swear, you cannot hold me in greater contempt than I hold myself.'

'If Doctor Hutchinson had ordered you to shoot me, you would have obeyed. Will you deny it? Well?'

'I wish to believe I would not raise any weapon against you, but I am a simple mortal and my mind was in a wretched place.'

Silence occupied the guestroom. With shoulders slumped, Ashby resumed his preoccupation with the view through the window, though, in his sorrow, he saw nothing except a blur of blue and green.

At length Ollenu said, 'Once I was dead, he could not let you live.'

Ashby mopped his dripping brow. 'I am forever thankful you did not die.'

'Likewise.' Ollenu settled back into the bed and stared up at the intricately designed ceiling cornice. 'To dwell on my missed appointment with death will not aid my journey to health, so I shall not. I intend to be fully restored in time to witness that fiend Hutchinson hang.'

Ashby gave him a look of dismay mixed with embarrassment.

'They have arrested Doctor Hutchinson, have they not?' asked Ollenu. 'He is in gaol?'

'No. He continues to reside at Edinburgh Castle, at leisure.'

'How can that be?' Ollenu sat bolt upright. 'What of the human bones? I heard his preposterous explanation about an undertaker. Surely no one believes he bought cadavers from an undertaker?'

'Either it is true, or the doctor's reach is strong and powerful. There is an undertaker in Port Royal who confirms he sold cadavers to him.'

'He was bribed. It is a lie. A damn abominable lie!'

'Be calm, Mr Ollenu.' Ashby gently pushed the patient backwards and tucked the pillow under his head. 'Your recovery will become undone should you exert yourself in this manner.'

'Wait, there was a watch.' Ollenu sat up again and peered into each corner of the room. 'A heavy silver watch hung in the shaft. I pushed it into my boot. The glass broke and cut my ankle, but it lies inside my boot. See if you recognise it as the property of one of your clients.'

Ashby frowned and shook his head. 'Your ankle was cut, but were there a broken watch in your boot, I would have seen it.'

'The servants must have it. You must ask them!'

'Of course, I will, Mr Ollenu, be calm.'

'I cannot understand how he remains at liberty.' Ollenu threw his head back against the pillow in frustration. 'Charles Cadogan found me crippled in that loathsome death chamber. He is a witness, the ideal witness. No court in the land would accuse him of falsehoods.'

Ashby scratched the back of his neck and wished to be anywhere else but in front of Ollenu. 'The earl is aware that both Hutchinson and I attacked you. I admitted to my role.'

'You were under the influence of a mind-altering substance. What is Hutchinson's excuse?'

Ashby cleared his throat. 'If the doctor is to be charged with assault or attempted murder, it is almost certain that I will join him in the dock.'

'Then perhaps you should join him in the dock?'

Ashby lowered his eyes. He retrieved the empty porridge bowl and made his way to the door. 'I shall leave you to rest.'

'Oh, and Mr Ashby?'

Slowly Ashby turned, braced for a cutting remark.

'Do express my sincere gratitude to Mrs Lamont for her kind wishes, and inform her that, should she decide to call upon me again, I will be delighted to receive her.'

Ashby gave his patient a hesitant smile and closed the door.

CHAPTER 20

Two weeks had passed since the life-threatening events at Edinburgh Castle and Ollenu's health continued to improve. From being barely able to use his limbs, he could now do double-handed body lifts and jump on the spot.

He sat on a settee on the upstairs verandah that circled Earl Cadogan's home, providing stunning views of the surrounding hills. Lost in thought, he idly played with his son's spinning top. Hearing footsteps behind, he turned to see Ashby approaching. The investigator placed a saucer holding a cup of tea on the wicker table, and balanced his own cup in his palm.

'Should we inform Charles of the cat and the diamonds?'

'No.' Ollenu shook his head decisively. 'We have neither cat, nor diamonds. If word gets out, Edinburgh Castle may be overrun with all manner of scoundrels believing riches are to be had.'

'The earl says he has a surprise for us, and the surprise should arrive within the next half hour.'

Ollenu sipped his hot tea. 'What sort of surprise?'

'A carriage will arrive presently,' said Ashby. 'I wonder, has he found an acclaimed doctor to provide you with a thorough examination?'

'I suppose he will insist upon it, despite my assurances. I tried to convince him that a doctor is unnecessary, as I am much improved. Alas, I await to be poked and prodded, and given a clean bill of health.' Ollenu frowned and squeezed the wooden toy top until his knuckles strained. 'It is an abominable state of affairs that the mad doctor is free to ply his evil trade.'

'Try to refrain from any mention of him when you are examined by the new physician,' warned Ashby. 'Your whole bearing changes, and he may well conclude you are not at all mended.'

'Only on this island would such a person remain at liberty, and we both know it is only because the latest victim is I, a mere Negro. No real enquiries will be made despite the earl's best efforts; of that I am sure. All atrocities will be brushed aside as if they never occurred.'

'Surely not, Mr Ollenu? The field slaves saw people enter that castle, people Hutchinson denied ever seeing. If allowed to speak, they will tell what they know. And once the house slaves are convinced that he cannot exact retribution, they will surely speak too.'

'Have you not paid heed, Mr Ashby? No one cares what Negroes see or hear. The slaves are merely goods, stocks, property. Those tormented beings who toil as animals under a severe sun, have no stories worth telling and no tales worth listening to.'

'Jamaica cannot be one hundred per cent lawless, have faith. We are in the home of Charles Cadogan, an earl, someone with great social and, I wager, political standing on this island and in England. That must equate to something when it comes to challenging Doctor Hutchinson.'

'I believe Earl Cadogan is true of heart, but he does not reside here and probably knows less about this place than we do. I fear he may be too trusting of the established leaders.'

'He dispatched his valet and footman to collect our possessions from Kershaw, who is forbidden from setting foot on this property. We must trust the earl.'

Earl Cadogan strutted onto the verandah, immaculate in a three-piece suit and polished, knee-high boots. 'Do I hear my name?'

'Oh, er, we were admiring your taste with these handsome couches.' Ashby patted the purple velvet furniture with rolled arms the same height as the back, and decorated with deep button tufting.

'Ah yes.' Cadogan smiled. 'Saw them at the home of the Earl of Chesterfield, Philip Stanhope, and made haste to order some myself. Now they are much sought after furnishings and we refer to them as Chesterfield's. Servants say it is a burden to remove dust out of the buttons.'

Ollenu raised an eyebrow, drummed his fingers on his knees and glared at Ashby.

'Is there news of the possible arrest of Doctor Hutchinson?' asked Ashby quickly.

Cadogan shook his head, sank into the adjacent Chesterfield and stretched out his legs. 'My man and I visited Governor Dalling's office earlier. He is returned from Barbados and well aware of the rumours surrounding Hutchinson. I informed him of the events in Pedro, but it did not have the effect I had hoped. The officials have accepted Hutchinson's explanation for the cadavers and believe them to be legitimately obtained bones.'

'Did I not predict this reaction?' Ollenu mumbled and cast an aggrieved look towards Ashby. 'There was a timepiece in that hole, a fine watch. Have you ever seen a cadaver wear a watch?'

'The old pastor at the cathedral?' said Ashby.

'Oh, so now you choose to jest, Mr Ashby?' Ollenu threw up his hands and spoke passionately, 'One of the slaves must have thrown the watch away. He or she may be of the mistaken belief that they broke it when they removed my boot. Fear of being whipped and beaten led them to dispose of it and deny all knowledge.'

Charles Cadogan's genial look vanished, replaced by a hard stare. 'My dear Mr Ollenu, I realise you experienced many dreadful things, that literally left a very bad taste in your mouth, however, the conclusion you reach is quite false. My servants are not whipped or beaten, and have no reason to perjure themselves. Countless civilised people reside on this island, I will have you know.'

'Forgive me,' said Ollenu and rubbed his temples. 'It pains me that my word as a Negro means nothing.'

'It is not merely a matter of your word.' Cadogan rose and walked to the edge of the balcony. He lit his pipe and stared off into the distance. 'I see the carriage arrives, right on time. Stay seated, gentlemen, I will return presently.'

Once his footsteps could no longer be heard, Ollenu turned to Ashby. 'The old pastor in the cathedral? You are an accomplished wit after all, Mr Ashby.'

'I shall forever remain in your shadow, Mr Ollenu.'

The horses brayed as the carriage was brought to a stop. Shortly, thereafter, a woman's voice could be heard coming up the stairs with the earl.

'A female doctor in Jamaica?' said Ollenu.

'I know of only one in England, and do not believe that fair lady would ever leave those shores for these,' said Ashby.

The footsteps continued along the hallway and the voices grew louder. The woman kept up a stream of chatter that the earl was unable to interrupt.

Ashby leapt to his feet and spilled tea in his haste to return the cup to the small table. His eyes widened as he stared at the small woman, with long auburn hair and freckled cheeks. 'Mrs Clare Sandie! As I live and breathe!'

'Good day to you too, Mr Ashby,' the woman beamed. 'I hear told you and your Mr Ollenu have been searching high and low for me.'

A startled Ollenu stood and bowed. 'Mrs Sandie, I am charmed, and grateful to see you alive and well.'

'I cannot quite believe my eyes,' said Ashby.

'It's my husband who's been causing all this fuss for years on end. Never should have married him, but that's what happens when you're young and foolish. I was down on my luck. He had money and the brewhouse. I don't plan to waste what remains of my youth looking after him in cold, grey Bristol.' She took the seat vacated by the earl and removed her bonnet. 'I must say, it weren't my intention not to go back at first. I did go round the island looking for a good place for a brewhouse, but changed my mind. Found me a fellow and decided to stay with him instead. And don't give me that look, Mr Ashby. I'm not the only one that's done it. I know one woman that's reported as missing and she's working at an alehouse in Port Royal under a different name. She's happy to be considered dead – prefers the debauchery of Port Royal over a mundane life in Liverpool. And there's another supposedly missing woman I heard of who's said to be living in a village in Trelawny with a free Black man. And it's not just the women, men do it too. Lots of—'

As she continued her stream of chatter, a stunned Ollenu used his empty tea cup to cover his lips and whispered. 'I see what you mean.'

'Quite,' murmured Ashby.

The earl finally interrupted her monologue. 'What Mrs Sandie relates is quite so. As I said, Mr Ollenu, the problem is not merely your voice. Some people reported as missing or dead are neither. Even last week, a married fellow long thought to be deceased was found very much alive. He had deserted his wife and absconded with a mulatto to the parish of St Thomas in the East. His identity was revealed when the registrar saw his name as the father of new twins.'

'My word,' said Ashby.

'This whole affair is even more convoluted than first appears,' sighed Ollenu. 'But I remain certain that the mad doctor is guilty of many murders.'

Cadogan puffed on his pipe. 'The rulers of this island will not accuse Doctor Lewis Hutchinson of a crime as heinous as murder, when the supposed corpses are secretly living the gay life all over the island.'

'Indeed, it is a dilemma,' said Ashby.

Mrs Sandie studied their faces. 'Who's this Doctor Lewis Hutchinson?'

'Madam, I am truly thankful for your sake that you never encountered him,' said Ollenu. 'His greetings may include the use of a bow and arrow.'

'He's a Scottish doctor who lives in Pedro, St Ann,' explained Ashby. 'We feared you met your demise at his hands. We are certain that other women were far less fortunate.'

'Oh!' Mrs Sandie blanched, rubbed the front of her neck and for once seemed lost for words.

'Over the past two weeks, my men have searched far and wide for your clients.' The earl smiled at the woman's pale face. 'Mrs Sandie was the only one they traced and, with a little persuasion, she was gracious enough to come forward.'

'Mrs Sandie, have you met one Henry Penket, or Francis Dantry during your time on the island?' asked Ollenu.

She shook her head. 'No, I remember Mr Penket from back in Bristol. A very good tailor who sewed for my husband. Never met Francis Dantry. Wouldn't know him if I walked straight into him. Listen, I don't want my husband looking for me. It's been six years. I go by Clare, but I use another surname now. And no, I won't tell a soul where I've been or where I live. He should have found some woman to comfort him by now.'

'You remain wife to a husband,' said Ashby.

'Not in my mind, and I'm never going back to England. You tell him that when you set eyes on him.'

'I shall be sure to pass on your kindest regards,' said Ashby in resignation. 'Edward Barrow can close one suspected fraud case.'

'I regret, I also bring bad tidings,' said the earl. 'That old woman, Nanna Della you call her? She passed away two nights ago, peacefully I understand. You say she told many tales of death at Edinburgh Castle, but you will never again hear them from her lips.'

'She held on to life for as long as she was able, for her granddaughter.' Ollenu let out a low moan and covered his face with his palms. 'She thought Rosa would be safe from Hutchinson now that I am here, and she finally let go, but no one is safe. I failed them both.'

'Be not of faint heart, Mr Ollenu,' said the earl. 'Change may yet occur.'

'You have done much to assist, Charles,' said Ashby. 'More than most men seem to have done in the twelve years since Hutchinson has lived here.'

'Yes, I too thank you, Charles. My frustrations are not with you, yet it is upon you that I unburden myself. We need an audience with Governor Dalling. He cannot continue to close his ears to the truth and must be made to see reason.' Ollenu stared at his colleague. 'If I cannot speak, Mr Ashby can relate in his own words exactly what we saw and heard in Pedro.'

Ashby shuffled in discomfort. 'I do believe it important that my suspicions of Doctor Hutchinson's transgressions be formally recorded for posterity.'

'And?' encouraged Ollenu.

Ashby inhaled deeply. 'I do not wish to sound impertinent, Charles, but could you possibly prevail upon the governor to spare us a moment of his time?'

'We would forever be in your debt, My Lord,' added Ollenu.

Cadogan nodded in a sombre manner. 'I will do my utmost best, gentlemen.'

'That doctor sounds a right horrible person.' Mrs Sandie took a small embroidered fan from her purse and fluttered it about her face. 'See that's why I keep myself away from this side of Jamaica. Nobody gets murdered where I am. We enjoy tasty foods, drink ale and entertain ourselves with no troublemaking. Speaking about drink, I don't suppose I could get a dash of cool rum, my dear earl? I've been in that carriage since dawn and my throat is all parched.'

'Why, of course, Mrs Sandie.' The earl rose and allowed her to take his arm as she stood. 'We shall retire to the drawing room. You can rest on a comfortable chaise longue and catch your breath. Do excuse us, gentlemen.'

Echoes of Mrs Sandie's voice could be heard long after the pair disappeared from view.

'I am gladdened that she is accounted for,' said Ashby. 'The men are surely deceased. And now, poor Nanna Della, though I thank God she went peacefully.'

'I fear for Rosa's family,' Ollenu said in a sombre voice. He rose and leaned against the balcony, staring down at the earl's servants as they cleared the front path of weeds. 'She has Simeon and Malachi, but she loved that old lady with all her heart. Their lives are unbearable. Too many people suffer all over an island where it is commonplace to abuse and humiliate and torture.'

'We cannot save them all, Mr Ollenu.'

'We must do what we can, Mr Ashby.'

'There is little time to do anything. You are near mended and we should set sail for England as soon as we can. I understand that the *Isabella* will pass through these waters presently, but I shall not arrange passage on her. The *Marianne* leaves Kingston early next week. We are welcome to stay here with the earl until then. I am satisfied that Henry Penket and Francis Dantry are dead, though it is clear the authorities will not yet record them as such. If I can, I will prevail upon the governor to do so. We have done as much as could be expected of us by Barrow and Dunne.'

'Curse Barrow and Dunne!' said Ollenu bitterly. 'I do not wish to set eyes upon Jacob Dunne again as long as I live. Tell me, you shall not return to work with Edward Barrow?'

'Well, I—' Ashby stammered.

'I cannot believe it.'

'But what would you have me do Mr Ollenu? It is all the life I have ever known. I am in fair health and, although I am getting on, have no wish to retire. My savings will not cover my keep and I… owe a few debts.'

'I will find a means to support my family that does not involve Dunne,' said Ollenu forcefully. 'I will do whatever I must to get by, and I will help those whose goals are to improve the lives of Black people on the islands. The abolitionist movement is growing and Granville Sharp welcomes more supporters. For now, I must surrender my goal of becoming an attorney, and it wounds me more than I can ever truly express.'

'Please, no rash decisions, Mr Ollenu. I beg you, wait until you are fully recovered to consider your position further.'

'I am fully recovered, Mr Ashby.' Ollenu turned cold eyes on his partner. 'I have had sufficient time to harness my wandering thoughts in my luxurious surroundings. It is so easy for you, is it not? This whole distasteful mission has barely touched you?'

'That is not true!'

'Do you not see what is before you? The suffering of the many people?'

'The ones on this estate hardly suffer. They seem well cared for. The earl spoke the truth. I have not seen a man with a whip or heard a single cry from any worker.'

'You believe the fact that everyone here is called a servant and not a slave makes their positions joyful? You believe that only whips and pokers can ravage the soul?'

'You deliberately misunderstand me yet again, Mr Ollenu.'

'You intend to slide back into the comforting arms of Bristol society as if nothing has happened,' sneered

Ollenu. 'Despite bearing witness to horrors, you will not spare even a shilling for the abolitionists.'

'It is not easy for me to reconcile life, as I find it in Jamaica, with the teachings of the Bible,' said Ashby. 'I have lived a sheltered life for near fifty years, and my faith is now challenged in ways I did not conceive. I know I cannot remain ignorant to what goes on in an island many miles from home. I try to find the right path, Mr Ollenu. I may proceed in a halting manner, but I do try.'

'What goes on, as you say, is inhumane treatment, brutality, demeaning of souls, a loss of ancestry. To concede such would spoil your perfectly structured life and throw you off the path you so blindly trod.'

Ashby got to his feet, his face crimson. 'I shall listen to no more of this!'

'Go on. Run away, Mr Ashby.'

Ashby bit his lip. With some clear effort at will he retook his seat and spoke through gritted teeth. 'You have no right to speak to me in such a manner, no right at all.'

'After what you did to me, I earned the right to speak to you in any manner.'

'I expressed my great sorrow, Mr Ollenu. Although it can never be enough, I know not what else to say.'

'Say nothing else, Mr Ashby. The time is nigh for action.'

CHAPTER 21

Dressed in their finest suits, Ollenu and Ashby rode Earl Cadogan's horses towards Spanish Town square, accompanied by one of his senior servants. The restored yellow cravat was safely tucked away in Ollenu's trunk at the mansion, while the pink bow protruded from his jacket pocket.

True to his word, the earl had procured a hearing before Governor Dalling at King's House. The initial agreement was for him to escort them to their destination and make the introductions. The plan went awry when, at dawn, word was received that one of the Cadogan estates was aflame. Although drawn to the jaunty aristocrat, Ollenu realised the man could not comprehend how or why anyone toiling his lands might not be entirely thrilled with their lot.

Aware that the King's House meeting was meant for Ashby only, Ollenu tried to prepare mentally for the snub. Despite his knowledge and experience of Doctor Hutchinson, he was warned of a strong chance he would be forbidden from speaking on the matter. Although irate, Ollenu conceded that there was only so much that the nobleman could do when it came to the laws of the island, as he too was a stranger. He had thanked the earl for his efforts and tried to be of hopeful disposition. As they rode on, Ashby's voice broke through his thoughts.

'Where did you learn to play the piano, Mr Ollenu?'

'When I was ten my mother worked for an ambassador's wife. The lady gave etiquette and deportment lessons to young girls at her home. She was also an excellent seamstress and taught Mama to sew hems and linings. I accompanied her and made such a nuisance of myself that I was ordered to stand in a corner of the music room as punishment.'

'I gather you removed yourself from the corner?' said Ashby.

'Indeed, I did,' said Ollenu. 'There was a cello, a harp, a flute, some small instruments, and in the middle a fine piano. From the time I first touched a key I was enthralled. I created my own tunes and played. The lady did not favour me, but she was so impressed by my pleasant tunes that she taught me to read sheet music and play properly. Her husband, the ambassador, travelled all over Europe and attended live piano recitals. He knew nothing of me. One day, upon his return, she sat me at the piano. I suppose he expected me to clean the keys. It gave her great pleasure to watch his incredulous expression.'

'I imagine it was much of a shock,' Ashby smiled, 'though a welcome one.'

'Yes, she enjoyed astounding people,' said Ollenu. 'She taught me to read English at a level beyond my years, purely for her own amusement, rather than an interest in my education. It amused her greatly to present me at her dinner parties and surprise her friends by having me read long selections from difficult books, or recite from memory. She would boast that she had the brightest Negro boy in England, yet never once did she offer me as much as a candy. Some English people are singularly perplexing.'

'I cannot disagree.' Ashby patted his neighing horse. 'There, there, boy. Whatever became of the ambassador's wife?'

'I know not. After three years my mother ceased her visits and never took me back to that house.'

'But why ever not? You obviously benefitted exceptionally from the experience, even if the lady did not embrace you?'

'I did wonder,' said Ollenu. 'It was not until I was an adult, and even then after much persuasion, that Mama finally confessed. She decided not to return after the ambassador abandoned his spouse for an Italian soprano.'

'Unfortunate that may be, Mr Ollenu, but she is not the first wife to be deserted by a delinquent husband.'

'She is the only wife Mama ever happened upon who packed up all her husband's clothing to send on to him in Milan. Mama discovered many new scissor-holes in delicate clothes that were not improved by the addition of holes.'

Ashby nodded. 'Your mother's judgement is irreproachable.'

'Quite so.'

As they approached the busy square, Ollenu watched with interest as various scarlet-coated men rode past on horseback and in carriages, headed for the House of Assembly opposite the King's House.

Mentioning their presence to Ashby, he received no response, and saw that the distracted investigator was staring at a nearby soldier. Although only a side profile was visible, he recognised the soldier as the man seen being over-attentive to Eleanor at Sir Alastair Nicholson's ball. Ollenu decided not to raise the subject for fear of damaging Ashby's already frail self-esteem. Tiny green-throated birds sang in the trees overhead and Ollenu hoped their sweet music heralded a new turn of events this day.

They dismounted and led their horses under the shelter of leafy trees next to the King's House, away from the strong sunlight. Word must have spread throughout much of Spanish Town that the governor was back in residence, having returned from Barbados. A large crowd of merchants and settlers, men and women, raised their voices and argued with his guards, demanding to see the ruler.

'I believe we are a little early,' said Ashby. 'We must await our turn with patience.'

Ollenu watched Ashby as he secured the horse's rein to a wooden post. Now was as good a time as any to ask the investigator a question that occupied his mind.

'You made a comment about having a few debts, Mr Ashby. Forgive me, but you do not have the appearance of one with debts. You are a numbers man. How does an expert in financial matters acquire debts?'

'Very little is missed by you, Mr Ollenu.' Ashby fell silent for a moment.

'I missed your answer.'

'I was once a gambling man – and I mean real, high-risk gambling. You look surprised. I lied when you enquired about my expertise on the *Isabella*. I pretended as if it were mere good fortune, and having keen instructors amongst the crewmen. Truth is, I used to wager large sums and near lost my home as a result. It is the reason I lost the lady to whom I was affianced.'

'Ah, I did wonder about that. I am sorry, Mr Ashby.'

'No, the fault is entirely my own. It was many years before I learned to constrain my destructive habit. I finally ceased a few years ago and began settling my debts. I do throw the occasional dice, but never again for banknotes, purely for amusement.'

'You shall not lose another lady; of that I am sure. You have spoken with Eleanor Lamont?'

'On occasion.'

'Come now, Mr Ashby. You know exactly what I wish to hear.'

'I know also that you do not need to hear everything, Mr Ollenu.'

'To lose her would be an offence against romance, and no Bible verse will ever provide consolation for your guilt.'

Ashby averted his eyes. 'Let us see if we can make our entrance.'

Both guards kept their muskets pointed downwards as Ashby and Ollenu squeezed through the muttering crowd. They removed their tall hats and climbed the few steps of the imposing building.

'Good day, sirs. Ruben Ashby from Bristol, and this is my assistant, Isaiah Ollenu.'

'Good day, sirs,' said Ollenu with a low bow.

'Is Earl Cadogan arrived yet?' asked Ashby. 'Regrettably, an unexpected diversion drew his attention elsewhere earlier.'

'Not yet, Mr Ashby. The governor is expecting you directly, you may proceed.' The guards moved aside and allowed both men to enter.

'Was my greeting to your satisfaction?' whispered Ollenu as they strode through the sumptuous marble-tiled hallway.

'I made no request that you place your head to your knee,' said Ashby. 'I asked only that you be at your most courteous. That you do not sit unless offered a chair, and that you hold your tongue unless questioned.'

'You ask so little of me.'

Walking towards them was a tall man whose burgundy coat and waistcoat were lined with gold trimming and many gold buttons. His pale face bore patches of pink that Ollenu assumed were caused by heat, rather than the application of ladies' rouge.

'Mr Ruben Ashby?' The man did not smile as he held out a sunburnt hand. 'Governor Dalling. We are acquainted at last.'

'Good day, Governor Dalling. I do thank you most sincerely for your time.'

The governor studied Ollenu who bowed low. 'Good day, Governor Dalling.'

'Yes, well. Follow me.'

The walls of the large meeting room were lined with oil paintings of long dead kings and queens of England. In the middle was a polished oval table, and seated on throne chairs were two men. The governor introduced them.

'The provost marshal, Mr William Gray.'

Ollenu looked at Gray who acknowledged his name with a slight nod. Kershaw's manager was a thin man in a dark suit that swallowed him. As his owlish eyes stayed on Ollenu, the law clerk wondered if the man was as morally challenged as his deputy, or an honest man.

'And Mr Jeremiah Partridge, the custos rotulorum for our parish.'

The elderly custos wore a long robe around his well-fed frame. He smiled amiably, and his plump cheeks almost covered his small eyes.

Ashby sat. As the white men grunted greetings to each other, Ollenu stood behind Ashby's chair and studied them. Governor Dalling poured red wine into goblets. Five goblets, Ollenu noted, surprised that they intended to offer him refreshment. Then he recalled that Earl Cadogan was expected and must be the fifth guest. This explanation lingered less than a minute before the door opened. To Ollenu's extreme surprise and considerable dismay, in walked Neville Kershaw.

'Gentlemen,' he said as he bowed at the gathering. His eyes followed Ollenu's, a look of menace apparent.

Ollenu shivered, and as an unpleasant tingle ran through his body he murmured, 'Their hands held high, a time to die.'

Ashby directed a worried look at the deputy marshal as the man took his seat. 'I was unaware that Mr Kershaw would make an appearance, governor.'

'He is Mr Gray's right hand,' said Governor Dalling. 'Of course he must be here to provide his side of the story. Surely you see the fairness in that?'

'I understand your position, sir,' said Ashby with a frown.

'I believe Earl Cadogan will join us presently, but in the meantime we are willing to hear your concerns, Mr Ashby,' said the governor. 'We understand you are most displeased with the behaviour of Doctor Lewis Hutchinson.'

Ollenu crushed the brim of his hat under his fingers. Displeased?

'Some matter of bones?' said William Gray. 'Mr Kershaw has assured me that all enquiries were completed to his full satisfaction. The cadavers came from an undertaker in Port Royal, as the doctor explained.'

'Exactly so, sir,' said Kershaw. 'There is no reason to believe either gentleman told falsehoods.'

'Hutchinson may indeed have purchased a number of bones from the undertaker to conceal his misdeeds, but not all,' said Ashby. 'The doctor shot and disposed of people who visited Edinburgh Castle on horseback or on foot. Living breathing people. The Negroes saw them.'

'I questioned the slaves months ago and they denied having seen or heard anyone being shot,' said Kershaw. 'You arrive, and of course they spout a whole lot of nonsense again.'

The provost marshal massaged his chin as he studied Ashby. 'You wish us to believe the Negroes, over the word of an honourable doctor?'

'Mr Gray, his profession does not define his morals. My client, Henry Penket, was on that estate and never left alive. I do not believe Mr Kershaw has ever questioned the doctor in regard to Penket, despite rumour having abounded for years about Edinburgh Castle. I ask you to heed my words and search for Penket's remains. Allow him a decent burial and add his name to your records of the deceased.'

'I understand that up until quite recently, you claimed he killed one Mrs Sandie?' said Governor Dalling. 'Yet I am told by the earl that not only is she alive, but the only way to silence her chatter is to give her rum.'

The governor laughed and was joined in his merriment by the custos, the provost marshal and his deputy. Meanwhile, Ollenu's temples throbbed, and he continued to roughly mishandle his hat.

'The conclusion as regards Clare Sandie was reached in error,' said Ashby earnestly. 'The disappearance of the male clients remains to be resolved.'

'I've done everything I can in accordance with this letter from Bristol's own chief watchman, Wilkins.'

Kershaw took the document from his breast pocket and waved it in the air, tantalising Ollenu. 'My carriage brought them wherever they wanted to go. Mr Ashby, you must agree?'

'I believe your motivation does not accord with ours,' said Ashby.

Kershaw's eyes narrowed. 'And what does that mean?'

Ashby ignored Kershaw's scrutiny and returned his attention to Governor Dalling. 'Even should you dismiss the matter of the bones; you are aware, are you not, that a watch was found in that pit?' he said. 'From its description, an expensive piece.'

'It is alleged that a watch was found, Mr Ashby,' said the governor. 'Is that not the truth of the matter?'

'Governor Dalling, the truth is, *I* found a watch in that stinking pit. Pieces of lace from a petticoat also rot down there with God knows how many women and men, Black and white. The people who owned those items were murdered by Doctor Lewis Hutchinson. He must be apprehended forthwith.'

Silence filled the space. Ashby closed his eyes briefly, and groaned.

'Here speaks the Negro about whom I have heard so much,' said Gray in disdain. 'Mr Kershaw mentioned that you have much to say for yourself.'

'My name is Isaiah Ollenu, sir, and any words I say for myself, or in regard to anyone else, are true to the best of my knowledge.'

The governor raised an eyebrow. 'You aspire to tread the hallowed halls of court I understand, complete with wig and gown?'

The men, except Ashby, laughed at this statement. Ashby poured himself another glass of wine and downed it in a swift motion.

'I understand he is Jacob Dunne's man,' said the custos with an encouraging smile. 'He already walks with him in court, though surely not in wig and gown. Speak, Mr Ollenu, but have care what you say about a dignified doctor.'

Ollenu raised his broad shoulders and straightened his posture. 'I am a witness of fact to the existence of the watch that you refuse to consider. An old slave woman who was a witness of fact to at least one murder is deceased, therefore I accept I can offer only hearsay about actual murders. That said, I implore you to desist from allowing Doctor Hutchinson a grace he does not deserve. Take him into custody and commit your resources to a thorough search of the entire estate.'

'Mr Ashby, your assistant is not reticent to share advice,' said the provost marshal in a sour tone.

'His advice has great merit,' said Ashby. 'Gentlemen, I, too, have heard from many slaves on the estate how the doctor treats visitors. Hearsay notwithstanding, I listened to Hutchinson's words and watched his behaviour. I believe he murdered two of my clients and many innocent souls. I also believe evidence of their worldly goods will be found on the doctor's estate. I beg you to take heed.'

Governor Dalling kneaded his fingers. 'It will bring you relief to know that, after my talk with the earl last evening, I agreed we would send able yeoman John Callendar to Pedro for an audience with Doctor Hutchinson. He will shortly be on his way.'

'One yeoman?' said Ollenu in disbelief.

'A preliminary measure,' said the custos. 'And well in accordance with good practice when dealing with persons alleged to have committed misdeeds.'

Ollenu raised his voice. 'Sir, you must send many armed soldiers, not a single yeoman, however noble he might be. The ironmonger, Francis Dantry, was seen walking with the doctor on his land, selling shackles and fetters. No one knows what became of him.'

Kershaw sat forward, his interest clearly piqued. 'The doctor denies that Dantry was ever on his property and I saw no evidence whatsoever that he was there. Who says he was?'

'The slaves saw him,' said Ollenu.

'Hah! The slaves,' laughed Kershaw. 'This again.'

Ashby slammed an open palm on the table. 'The ironmonger is well known to me. He has a pronounced limp. One of the slaves demonstrated his gait perfectly, without instruction from me. Francis Dantry hobbled across the grounds of Edinburgh Castle until Doctor Hutchinson put him beneath the ground. I would swear to it.'

Kershaw's grin disappeared, replaced by a deep frown. 'Why, that lying, Scottish—'

'Governor, send your soldiers to the castle without delay. Ransack the entire structure. Tear it down stone by stone, if necessary,' said Ollenu with passion. 'To approach the doctor with politeness, because it is considered civil practice, will satisfy your etiquette, but resolve nothing. You are meant to be the law of the land – act thus!'

The governor crimsoned. 'How dare you!'

'Our Father who art in Heaven,' whispered Ashby, eyes closed. 'Could you not stay his tongue?'

'The Negro must leave this chamber at once!' said the provost marshal rising to his feet.

'See what I told you, Mr Gray?' said Kershaw in a smug tone.

'Our generosity in allowing you a voice was misguided,' muttered the custos glaring at Ollenu.

'Wait, gentlemen,' said Ashby. 'We should tell you about the cat.'

'Of what cat do you speak?' asked the provost marshal.

'The cat is black, yellow-eyed, and of foul temper.' Ollenu straightened his damaged hat. 'Should any of you cowards find your way to Edinburgh Castle, I hope it sinks its teeth into your buttocks.'

'I say!'

'How dare you!'

'The audacity! Well, I never!'

Ollenu turned on his heels and headed for the door, head held high. A flushed Ashby murmured apologies and followed behind the law clerk. Ollenu strode down the corridor, out of the building and past the two guards. As he descended the steps Charles Cadogan rode towards him and dismounted.

'Oh, I am sorry to be late, Mr Ollenu. Your audience has ended?'

A boiling Ollenu bit his lip and did not respond.

'The meeting did not progress quite as planned, Charles,' said Ashby. 'Your presence may bring favour to my pleas. We should return to beseech them again.'

Before the earl could respond, the sound of horses' hooves rumbled in the distance. Soon a cloud of dust hovered in the air as the three riders arrived and brought their horses to a stop. Ollenu immediately recognised Rosa's cousins, Simeon and Malachi, astride Hutchinson's horses. The man in front was one of Earl Cadogan's servants.

'Let them through!' shouted the earl and gestured to his servant.

'Sir, these slaves came in search of Mr Ollenu and Mr Ashby,' said the servant. 'Trouble is in Pedro.'

'Simeon, Malachi, what trouble is this?' said Ollenu.

The young men dismounted and walked towards the Bristol men. They halted suddenly as Neville Kershaw appeared out of the building and approached his waiting henchmen, Mortimer and Johnson.

'Come closer, both of you,' said Ashby. 'Mr Kershaw will not be permitted to harm you.'

The governor, provost marshal and custos, drawn by the commotion, now appeared on the steps of King's House. Despite the protestations of the two guards, a growing crowd of settlers who had amassed in hope of speaking to the governor, surged forward, surrounding them. Voices of varying pitches were raised. Attracted by the noisy gathering, a group of, at most, a dozen soldiers near the House of Assembly, headed across the square.

'Quiet!' shouted Earl Cadogan, and waved a hand in the air.

'The Devil-man has Rosa,' said a breathless Simeon.

'What Devil-man?' asked Cadogan.

'Otherwise known as Doctor Lewis Hutchinson, the Mad Master of Edinburgh Castle,' said Ollenu.

'He holds her inside the castle, and will not return her to us,' said Malachi. 'He says he will kill her first and give us her dead body.'

'Help us, please!' begged Simeon. 'You said you would help.'

Ollenu's conscience went into battle with common sense. He was neither taught nor trained to apprehend violent killers, that was a job for watchmen and their ilk.

He cast a withering glare at the governor. None of these men would raise a finger to save the life of a Negro girl. Yet to place his own life at risk, when he had a growing family to care for, was illogical.

Ollenu locked eyes with Governor Dalling. 'A Scotsman now rules the colony of an Englishman!' he shouted. 'Soon your governor will raise the saltire.'

Voices grew in a babble of sound as the beleaguered governor faced a flurry of questions from curious citizens. He scowled, stood on tiptoes, and peered over the crowd. 'Where is the yeoman, John Callendar?'

'I am here, sir, and ready to depart.'

'Go now. Remain civil in your discourse with Doctor Hutchinson. Find out exactly what has come to pass at Edinburgh Castle and report to me.'

'Yes, Governor Dalling.'

The provost marshal beckoned to a soldier. 'Accompany Mr Callendar. Allow him to speak to the doctor without the need for a display of arms.'

'Yes, sir.'

'This is preposterous.' Ollenu shook his head in disbelief. He looked at Ashby. 'You must have heard my verse. Something terrible is sure to occur soon. This day? Tomorrow? I do not know, but I must ride to Pedro. Will you stay, or will you ride?'

'I heard.' Ashby blanched and inhaled deeply. 'May the Lord watch over us. I will ride.'

'I had faith that you would. The Lord, I am not so sure about.' Ollenu smiled at him then turned to the aristocrat. 'Earl— Charles, I must leave directly.'

The earl waved at his servant. 'Untie those two horses.'

'You allow him to ride your horse?' said Governor Dalling.

'Mr Ollenu is highly talented,' said the earl, 'but not even he can run from St Catherine to St Ann.'

As Ollenu and Ashby climbed onto their horses, Ashby reached inside the pocket of his saddle and pulled out a pistol. 'I have another. You take this.'

'Wherever did you obtain guns?' asked an incredulous Ollenu.

'Eleanor. She insisted I take them and ammunition. For a long time, I have refused to contemplate the need, but now I consider them a necessity.'

'I told you, you found a great woman in Mrs Lamont, did I not?'

'You did. Do you never tire of being right, Mr Ollenu?'

'Clare Sandie was an error.'

'Mine too.'

'Follow us,' said Malachi. 'The way we take, we get to Massa's land before them.'

'Lead the way,' said Ollenu. 'The madman will not be peaceful. He and I do have one thing in common, the need to remain free at all costs.'

'Kershaw follows with Johnson and Mortimer,' said Ashby, glancing over his shoulder. 'I believe he finally accepts that Hutchinson killed Dantry, and is now rabid with thoughts of hoards of banknotes somewhere at Edinburgh Castle.'

'He rides for banknotes,' said Ollenu. 'We ride for Rosa.'

CHAPTER 22

Lead by Simeon and Malachi, the group journeyed at a rapid pace under an unyielding sun. Ollenu had no doubt that the overgrown narrow lanes and perilous tracks taken could not be followed by other riders.

As they travelled, the heat and strenuous events of the day took a toll on Ollenu's recently recovered body. He had ridden Jacob Dunne's horse many times before, accompanying the barrister all over the county, but never for long hours and never when his body felt sore. Every muscle strained, but no aches would deter him from making the trek to Pedro. He questioned their leaders from time to time, impatient to progress.

'We are close,' said Malachi at length. 'Soon we reach Massa's land.'

From the undergrowth came a sudden rustle of leaves and the disturbed horses whinnied in alarm. Simeon urged his horse into the dense bushes and swung his cutlass in swift slashes. The frantic squeals of a wild boar filled the air and, shortly after, the man emerged jubilant, trailing red liquid from his blade.

'Ugh!' Ashby wrinkled his nose in disgust. 'Must we kill everything?'

'Better than the hog kill us or a horse,' said Ollenu.

They rode on to the grounds of Edinburgh Castle through the enslaved community, watched by field workers. Some seemed wary, a few waved at them.

'We go this way,' said Malachi, pointing towards their huts.

'What lies that way?' asked Ollenu.

'Guns,' said Simeon. 'We must prepare.'

Simeon and Malachi led them to Rosa's hut. Inside, they moved aside the sparse bedding and wooden chair. Digging up shallow earth, they removed a cloth bundle containing guns and ammunition that they shared amongst themselves, two guns each. The African men also exchanged their cutlasses for much sharper blades that they slid through their waistbands.

'Rebellion comes this very day,' said Malachi. 'Many of us collect weapons. No longer will we live as we do.'

'When we find Rosa, we go,' said Simeon. 'It is time to join our brothers and fight for freedom.'

Ashby held his pistol at his side. 'I do not know if I can do this,' he whispered.

'You see even a wisp of red hair, shoot,' said Ollenu. 'Before he does. For he will.'

As they emerged from the hut, Ashby peered into the thick brush. 'The Rolling Calf may lurk unseen.'

'The Calf appears only at night,' Ollenu assured him. 'In this sunlight we are safe from ghostly spirits and beasts.'

In the distance, Ollenu observed that the heavy wooden door of Hutchinson's castle was closed. As they crept towards the building, taking shelter under the many trees, he envisioned the doctor poised with a musket in the urine-soaked attic, waiting for one of his targets to appear on the horizon. Up at a window, he saw a flash of red hair.

'He's there,' said Ollenu pointing.

'I hope we are not visible to him,' said Ashby.

An arrow from a crossbow landed in a tree with a tremendous thwack right next to Ashby's head, dashing such hope almost immediately. The investigator yelped and threw himself to the ground.

'Get off my land!' shouted Doctor Hutchinson.

A gun shot rang out and a puff of grey smoke billowed from one of the castle's apertures, followed quickly by another one from a different window. The men retreated further into the bushes.

Ollenu crouched beside Ashby. 'He does not fire alone.'

'Four house Negroes defend him,' said Malachi.

'Then they have an advantage,' said a trembling Ashby. 'We should await the soldier's arrival.'

'A single soldier will not much alter the odds,' said Ollenu.

He worried that Hutchinson could have already committed one heinous deed this day, but he would not share such fears in front of Rosa's cousins. There was still a chance she might be alive and chained in the attic.

Searching the various arrow-slits for signs of movement, he saw none. Eventually, he cupped his lips and shouted, 'Release Rosa and step outside!'

Silence followed. Over the course of the next half hour, both Ollenu and Ashby demanded, pleaded and cajoled, but were met with only explosions.

Ashby whispered, 'Mr Ollenu, perchance he cannot hear?'

'He hears,' Ollenu frowned. 'He no longer wishes to talk. Now his sole aim is to kill.'

'Rather than surrender, he could take his own life?' suggested Ashby.

'Never. And certainly not before he has taken mine. I embarrassed and humiliated him in his domain. I will not be forgiven.'

Eventually, came the sound of horses' hooves. The yeoman John Callendar rode onto the grounds accompanied by the soldier. Long before the two men were close enough to the castle to dismount, a loud explosion resounded and a pall of grey smoke came from a slit in the castle wall. The yeoman clutched his chest and toppled from his horse. The soldier shouted out in alarm, leapt from his steed and ran to the aid of the fallen man.

Ashen-faced, the officer waved a fist at the castle. 'You have killed John Callendar!'

The response was a bigger blast and plume of dark smoke. The soldier abandoned both horses and dragged the dead man into the thick brush, hidden behind the trees.

'That poor soul,' whispered Ashby. 'May the Lord embrace him.'

'The madman has lost all reason and become desperate,' said Ollenu. 'He must be aware that his liberty ends this very day.'

A bang struck a tree perilously close and Ollenu threw himself flat on the soil. Returning fire would accomplish little. Piercing the thick stone walls was almost impossible, and even a highly trained marksman would find it difficult to aim a shot between the arrow-slits.

'I must get inside the castle. When I run to the door, you fire at any place you see movement.'

'Are you sure this is a sound idea?'

'It is the only idea to form. The shooters cannot angle their weapons towards the door through those narrow windows.' He stared at the investigator who now held a gun in each hand. 'I depend upon you, Mr Ashby. You will prevail.'

Crouching low, Ollenu ran as fast as he could towards the door, and raced up the steps. Ashby fired a shot in the direction of the attic window. He fired the second gun at one of the lower windows.

Ollenu slammed his fists on the heavy wooden door, then launched his shoulder at the frame. There was barely any movement. He signalled to Simeon and Malachi in the bushes. The slave men crouched and ran forward as the castle's defenders discharged more rounds in their direction. All three men pressed against the door, but although it rocked, it remained firm.

The law clerk looked over to where Ashby had hidden and could no longer see the investigator. He frowned as his eyes searched the surrounding undergrowth, but there was no sign of him. Surely Ashby could not have lost heart and abandoned the mission? Yet the man who had disavowed any further use of cannabis would no longer feel invincible, and must have opted to flee instead.

'Something strong is needed to break the door,' said Simeon, as he rubbed his shoulder. 'Come Malachi.'

As the lithe bare feet of the two African men took to the undergrowth, Ollenu slammed a fist on the door in exasperation. What they needed was a battering ram, but such heavy equipment was not a feature of this estate.

Soon, he heard more horses' hooves and turned to see three riders racing in. His heart sank and a sickening chill enveloped him as his eyes met those of the deputy provost marshal, Neville Kershaw. Beside him were Mortimer and Johnson. They dismounted and stood in front of Ollenu, whose back was pressed against the castle's solid door.

Ollenu contemplated his next move. There would be no opportunity to reload his guns. The distance between himself and the men was at most twelve feet. He could beat all three rogues at hand-to-hand combat without suffering a bruise, if he could get close enough.

As if reading his mind Kershaw pulled a pistol from his waistband and calmly stated, 'Make any sudden move and I will blast your skull into the heavens. Drop that gun and put your hands up. And the one at your side.'

Mortimer and Johnson, following their master's actions, drew their weapons. Slowly, Ollenu tossed both guns to the ground and raised his hands above his head.

'Edward Barrow is quite right.' Kershaw grinned. 'You and Ashby make the perfect team for this little enterprise. I waited on your expertise to lead me to Dantry, and never realised, until our meeting this morning, that you already had.'

'If only we'd known,' said Johnson. 'We'd have found our money by now.'

'Did you find a stack of banknotes inside the castle?' asked Kershaw.

'We made no search for money dripping with the blood of slaves,' said Ollenu bitterly. 'Nor did we recover any.'

'Bloody or not, slavery money is just as good as any other money,' said Mortimer.

'Better even,' said Johnson. 'There's much more of it.'

The three cronies laughed.

'Today you die, Negro,' announced Kershaw. 'You really are a nuisance. Do you know I have permission to kill you, if you get in my way?'

Ollenu frowned and licked dry lips.

Kershaw retrieved a paper from his breast pocket. 'I am sure you wish to know what this letter says?'

'I am sure it will give you great pleasure to inform me.'

'It instructs me to welcome you with open arms and give you reasonable assistance in your search for Mr Henry Penket and Mrs Clare Sandie. In regard to Mr Francis Dantry, ironmonger of Bristol, "all efforts must be taken to locate and apprehend him, including manual restraint".' Kershaw gave a broad smile. 'It's the last line that warms my heart. "Whatever the outcome of this mission, no penalty shall be applied and no action, whether civil or criminal, shall be taken against Neville Kershaw, or against any person who assists the said Neville Kershaw, should any harm, mortal or otherwise, befall Ruben Ashby or Isaiah Ollenu." See, that's the sort of permission I appreciate.'

Mortimer spat a chewed twig at his feet. 'Kill anybody who gets in the way.'

Anger coursed through Ollenu's veins. Jacob Dunne and Edward Barrow were the stewards of this outrage. Now here he was, about to die, at the hands of their host. A man, charged with their wellbeing, who would not be punished for their deaths.

'Would you agree that I have done my utmost to assist you?' said Kershaw in a mocking tone.

'For certain, your dear wife, Lydia, tried to assist me. I would not let her.'

Kershaw's smile disappeared and his eyes narrowed. 'What's that about my wife?'

'She deserves so much better than you, poor lady. I hope, for her sake, that someday, someone comes to lodge in her home, who shows her the love and affection she craves, and eventually takes her away.'

'Well I'll be—' said Mortimer.

'The nerve!' breathed Johnson.

Kershaw's face reddened and his words grated from his lips. 'I would say it was pleasant knowing you, but that would be a lie, savage. Barrow will be informed that both you and Ashby got in the way. Where is dear Ashby?'

'Right here, Mr Kershaw.' Ashby appeared from the side of the house, with a pistol outstretched in his trembling hand, and a small Bible clutched to his chest in the other.

'Go back, man,' Ollenu hissed. 'Run!'

Ashby continued walking until he stood directly in front of Ollenu.

'Drop that gun, Mr Ashby,' warned Johnson. 'You don't have enough shot to harm three.'

'Aye,' said Mortimer. 'The Bible won't be much good either, but hold it if you must.'

'Leave him be. He couldn't shoot straight if he tried,' sneered Kershaw. 'That's a convenient position to stand in, Ashby. One lead ball will go straight through you and straight through your Negro.'

'He is not my N—'

'Not now, Mr Ashby,' said Ollenu.

'Tell me first, what made you this way?' said Ashby lowering his weapon. 'You hold a good position. You earn your keep, have a fine grace and favour home, and yet you pursue us with thoughts only of finding wealth and committing murder.'

'Well, I weren't planning to keep all of the money for myself,' said Kershaw. 'Some is for Johnson and Mortimer here, and of course, the bulk goes to Edward Barrow. I suppose he'll have to share it with the chief watchman and Jacob Dunne.'

Ashby glanced at Ollenu. 'These gentlemen have a point, Ollie. Surely, you must see it?'

The law clerk frowned and remained silent.

'You do see their point, Ollie?'

Eventually, Ollenu nodded. 'Yes, Ashie, clear and sharp.'

'Mr Kershaw, what if Doctor Hutchinson says he is unaware of Dantry's filthy lucre, and it is not hidden inside or anywhere on the estate?' said Ashby. 'What then? Will you kill him also?'

'If I have to,' said Kershaw flatly. 'I was in the doctor's corner, but now I know he's led me a merry dance for months, I'm not about to show him mercy.'

'Quite so.' Johnson nodded. 'Imagine he welcomed us, all innocent like butter wouldn't melt.'

'And lied that he'd never set eyes on Francis Dantry, when he'd already killed him,' said Mortimer shaking his head.

'We need doctors,' said Kershaw, 'but Hutchinson we can do without. Now, do you wish to say a prayer before you meet your maker, Mr Ashby?'

Ollenu moved aside so that Ashby no longer provided a shield. He spread his arms wide, bent his knees and bounced up and down.

The Spanish Town alliance chuckled heartily as they watched him. Johnson and Mortimer even mimicked the law clerk's motions.

'A moving target, is still a good target,' said Kershaw. 'And you, Negro, are quite a large one.'

Ollenu stopped bouncing and pointed behind Kershaw. 'If you shoot, you answer to them.'

'Them?' repeated Johnson. 'Who would "them" be? Your Rolling Calf and his mates?'

Again, the three men laughed.

Kershaw said, 'And I suppose if I look behind me, I'll see something fearsome, something that will have my knees a knocking?'

'That depends entirely upon your mental constitution,' said Ollenu.

A scowling Johnson was the first of the three assailants to look over his shoulder. 'Ooh-er!' he exclaimed.

Mortimer and Kershaw turned slowly in unison.

Malachi waved the sharp point of his cutlass under Kershaw's nose. He, and Simeon, stood mere feet behind the white men, and behind them stood more than fifty Africans. The throng of silent men and women, in torn and dirty osnaburg clothing, many barefoot, were armed with cutlasses or pistols, some with both.

'Weapons down one and all,' said the alarmed deputy marshal as he tossed his gun to the ground. 'No need for this. Everybody keep calm.'

Johnson and Mortimer quickly threw their weapons aside.

Ollenu's heart soared. The majority of these people were unknown to him. Some of the men were of bigger build than himself. Powerful, angry, enslaved men were better than a battering ram. He guessed that most of these saviours had recently escaped from plantations, or already lived in the hills. Simeon was right, a rebellion was underway, a rebellion that he thoroughly hoped would succeed.

Simeon and Malachi collected the men's discarded weapons. Screams resounded as a group of slaves began to beat and drag the three white men towards the bushes.

'Here is money.' A shaking Kershaw dipped one hand into his pocket, using the other hand to try and protect his face from blows. 'Take this!'

'Mr Ashby are you not a Christian?' Johnson screamed. 'Call off the savages!'

Ashby pointed at Johnson. 'Simeon, that person is an extreme savage. He slapped Nanna Della's face.'

A cursing Simeon immediately advanced on Johnson, followed by Malachi. The man howled in pain and begged for help as furious blows rained down on him.

'Wait!' shouted Ollenu.

'You go to his aid?' asked Ashby in surprise.

'I go to help myself,' said Ollenu. He grabbed onto Kershaw's jacket and snatched the letter from his pocket. 'As you were, gentlemen.'

'Mr Ollenu!' shouted Kershaw. 'I beg you, sir. Have mercy!'

'Whatever happened to Negro and savage?' Ollenu pushed the letter into his pocket and turned his attention elsewhere. 'Help us with this door!'

Some of the burly men attacked the door with rippling shoulder muscles until gradually, it splintered. Ollenu was certain that the African men would do everything in their power to get Hutchinson today, to avenge years of mistreatment and torture. If he knew this for a fact, Hutchinson also must know that he could not win and would need the slaves to show mercy. Thus the shooting from inside had long ceased.

As the door collapsed inwards, the men roared in celebration and ran inside, followed by many women. At the same time, the house slaves threw down their weapons and cowered, begging forgiveness. The intruders ignored them. With cutlasses aloft, they chopped at the tables and chairs, and pushed over the bookshelves. Some smashed the gun cabinet and collected arms. Ollenu reloaded his weapon and advanced up the stairs with Ashby close behind him.

'I believe the doctor is inside the attic. Prepare to shoot.'

'Oh, I am prepared,' said Ashby.

'Tell me...' Ollenu turned to stare long and hard at him. 'Did you see our rescuers approaching when you chose to stand in my defence?'

'No. In all honesty, I did not believe Kershaw would shoot. When I realised he certainly would do so, a retreat was impossible. I accepted that my time on this earth must end.'

'But not quite yet, I am relieved to say.' Ollenu resumed his strides up the stairs. 'And I thank you, Mr Ashby.'

'I am unsure that I would act in that manner again,' said Ashby hesitantly.

'That you were willing to do it once is enough. Rosa!'

'Doctor Hutchinson!'

Silence greeted them. They broke through the hidden door leading to the attic and headed up the secret steps. Beneath them came jeers and chants as the Africans continued to destroy the doctor's possessions. Screams for mercy indicated that the house slaves, who had sought to guard and protect their master, were being beaten. Ollenu could not bring himself to despise them for having chosen the wrong path, but he vowed not to come to their aid.

'Rosa!'

'Doctor!'

Terrified of what lay behind, Ollenu stood outside the closed attic door. Memories of the place where he was held and tormented threatened to overwhelm him.

'Hear that?' said Ashby. 'Someone is inside.'

Ollenu nodded. 'I hear.'

He inhaled deeply. With all his being, he hoped that the person whose death his verse proclaimed earlier was not the brave girl who had saved his life. 'Open the door,' he demanded. 'Come in peace or those slaves whose lives you have made an eternal misery will take your life, and I will not deny them.'

'Doctor, you must do as we say,' said Ashby. 'Come with us and have your day in court. Fight and you will be killed.'

The distinct scrape of a bolt being drawn was heard.

'Do not shoot!' said a firm voice. 'My weapon is down.'

Ollenu frowned. The familiar voice was male, and not that of Doctor Hutchinson.

'We're coming out,' said another male voice that Ollenu also remembered.

Ollenu kicked the door and it smacked against the inside wall. There stood a burly man whose thinning brown hair lay on his long neck, and a shorter prematurely grey man with protruding ears. Hutchinson's overprotective neighbours, Roger Maddix and James Walker. Their guns, bows and arrows, lay on the dirty stone floor.

'Where is he?' demanded Ollenu.

'What, no pleasantries?' sneered Maddix. 'That's no way to speak to old acquaintances.'

'We hear you've been harassing the good doctor, making all sorts of unsubstantiated accusations,' said Walker. 'And now this.'

Ashby winced as he trampled on the withered stem of his cannabis stick, lying exactly where he had crushed it weeks ago. 'I implore you, tell us where to find the doctor. He has taken a slave girl, Rosa.'

'Good for him,' said Maddix. 'Everyone needs a good slave.'

Ollenu balled his fist and punched Maddix in the nose, knocking him to the ground. The man cursed and held his bloodied nose.

Walker hurriedly took two steps back. 'Damnable savage! You will never find him. Never.'

Rubbing his fist, Ollenu turned and ran back down the stairs, followed by Ashby.

'The doctor took flight long ago,' said Ollenu. 'That is why he did not answer me. His loyal friends held us at bay to aid his escape. We must learn where he is destined before it is too late.'

Downstairs they found a house slave cowering on the floor with Simeon and Malachi standing over him. Ollenu stared down at the brawny man whose eyes bulged with fear. The same man had tapped his arm and handed him a bowl of hot bitter liquid, a poison that had almost claimed his life.

'Where is Rosa and that madman?' demanded Ollenu.

The man's eyes flitted between Ashby and Ollenu, but he remained stubbornly silent.

'Listen, you fool, if you wish to die today, it shall be done.' Ollenu grabbed the man's neck. 'Your master killed a yeoman sent by the governor. A whole army will return for you. They will boil you alive if you do not speak. What has Hutchinson done with Rosa? Where is he?'

The man trembled uncontrollably and his eyes widened. 'He rides to Old Harbour Bay. He has one horse, a big grey, with both him and Rosa.'

'Get out,' said Ollenu roughly. 'And do not let me ever see you again.'

Once outside, Ollenu and Ashby saw the soldier on horseback, leading a horse with the body of the dead yeoman draped over the saddle.

'I shall return to Spanish Town at once,' he said, his voice distraught.

Ashby placed a hand on the victim's back and uttered a short prayer. When finished he said, 'I am filled with much sorrow.'

'I, too, have much sorrow,' said Ollenu. 'This travesty should never have come to pass.'

'You tried to prevent it,' said the soldier. 'I heard you speak earlier. The governor did not heed your warning.'

'We must travel to Old Harbour Bay for that is where Hutchinson rides,' said Ollenu.

The soldier nodded. 'That is down on the southern coast. Not too distant from Spanish Town.'

'Once there, where might he go?' asked Ollenu.

'He may plan to escape at sea,' said the soldier, 'though I know of no ships on course to leave that bay this day.'

'We cannot allow him to leave the island,' said Ollenu.

'If that killer becomes sea bound you will need the navy's assistance.' The soldier wiped his eyes as he turned away. 'Admiral Rodney and his men are at Old Harbour Bay. They will assist you. I wish you Godspeed.'

'Godspeed,' said Ashby.

As Ollenu and Ashby headed towards their horses, a loud shot rang out. Ollenu turned to see a slave man sprawled on the ground, pistol in hand, blood flowing freely on the soil. The deceased was the same man he had interrogated inside. The determined man had tried to murder him a second time. Loyal to the mad master with his last breath, he now lay dead, killed by one of his own. Ollenu mouthed a silent thank you to another barefooted man, the alert shooter.

'You were right, Mr Ashby. We cannot save them all.'

CHAPTER 23

Ollenu was eager to set out for Old Harbour Bay at once, as were Simeon and Malachi, but Ashby provided the sole voice of reason.

'Mr Ollenu, we must allow the horses rest. They will never ride all the way to the south coast without rest.'

'We cannot delay,' said a frustrated Ollenu. 'Hutchinson has a good start.'

'He also has Rosa, and the weight of the two upon the animal will surely prevent him making great headway.' Ashby sank onto the grassy ground and stretched his legs. 'As there are no ships for him to sail aboard, he must stay hidden. We have time to find him. If we are too hasty, our horses will collapse before even halfway to our destination, and we shall remain in the middle of nowhere.'

'We need fresh horses,' said Ollenu.

'Maddix has three good horses on his land,' said an agitated Simeon.

'Walker has two,' said Malachi. 'Every day they and Massa are together. They help him move bodies. We take their horses?'

Ollenu's eyes lingered on the castle's peak. 'Missing animals is the least of their troubles. If they know what is good for them, they will stay hidden in the attic. Should fortune favour them, the soldiers will come to their rescue by tomorrow.'

He looked down at the resting Ashby. The horses were tired, and so was Ashby. Although he was loath to admit it, he too was tired, and knew that rest was important, if only for a short time. Simeon and Malachi, he was sure, were not permitted intermission from labour, and he wondered at the level of pain and agony inflicted on their bodies over the years. Nothing would make them now be still. Until Rosa was returned to the fold the two would be relentless.

'Yes, fetch the horses,' said Ollenu as he sat on the ground. 'Be alert, their women may have firearms.'

As he watched them run he prayed with all his heart that their efforts to find Rosa safe and sound would not be in vain.

'Age rather creeps up on you.' Ashby massaged his lower back. 'On occasion, I feel a burning sensation that is not assisted by time in the saddle.'

'Yet you do not complain?'

'I have learned much whilst in your company, Mr Ollenu. You have endured much pain, with far more grace than I ever could. My aches pale in comparison. There are people here who have suffered unimaginable indignities, and continue to suffer in silence. In the circumstances, I would be ashamed to voice any complaint. I should be one to whom they bring their complaints, without fear. My voice should be heard on their behalf.'

Ollenu stared at him. 'I… I am speechless.'

'Something of an achievement on my part,' said Ashby with a smile.

'Mr Ashby, were you a lady, I would embrace you.'

'Were you a lady, Mr Ollenu, I would allow you.'

Sounds of Edinburgh Castle being ransacked filled the air and both men flinched. The cries of the deputy marshal and his men could no longer be heard, but Ollenu found it hard to care whether they lived or died. Though it was not his place to restrict the vengeful slaves, he hoped they would not set fire to the castle, and destroy any possible evidence of the doctor's hideous crimes. Had he been treated as atrociously as they were, his first inclination might be to raze the place to ashes. In any event, the gruesome sinkhole remained, and a thorough search in daylight was bound to reveal more terrible secrets within.

Ollenu retrieved the introduction letter from his pocket and his expression became steely. 'So, Barrow and Dunne did not affix their signatures to this death warrant, only Heskel Wilkins.'

Ashby reached for the letter and shook his head as he read. 'You were so right. I should have broken the seal before we boarded the *Isabella*. I should also have asked many more questions of Barrow. Forgive me.'

'There is no need to seek forgiveness, Mr Ashby. True, we would not have boarded the ship. However, we would not be here now, in a position to stop a crazed man from continuing his murderous pursuits. No one else on the island has the stomach for it.'

'God really does work in mysterious ways,' said Ashby.

'I do wonder if Hutchinson had knowledge that Dantry was involved in the slave trade, and in possession of thousands of pounds?' mused Ollenu. 'The madman displays no obvious signs of wealth anywhere, so I am doubtful he stole it.'

'Dantry had no reason to bring any banknotes to the castle, and he left none with Tom the blacksmith,' said Ashby. 'Conceivably, the doctor is oblivious that the guest he murdered was not a mere ironmonger, but also a person that a ruthless Bristol man relied upon for his own wealth.'

'Meaning there is no hoard of blood money for Kershaw, Johnson and Mortimer to find,' said Ollenu grimly. 'They rode all the way here for a much-deserved and thorough beating.'

'May the Lord forgive me for having no sympathy.'

'Wherever the money lies, there may it rot.'

Ashby nodded. 'Amen.'

Soon Simeon and Malachi returned riding newly stolen horses. With them were two fine brown stallions that neighed and trod the ground, seemingly eager to run. Ollenu quickly stood and pulled Ashby to his feet. He cast one final lingering look at the castle.

'Now, onwards to Old Harbour Bay.'

-

Old Harbour Bay was a small port with a tavern and scattering of shops. Set amongst a vast range of untamed trees, its barren appearance was improved by an expanse of brown sand and the unending Caribbean Sea. A handful of unmanned fishing vessels occupied the coastline.

'Simeon, you and Malachi search through the trees and any huts,' said Ollenu. 'Avoid the houses, for the owners may be armed. Alert us if you see his grey horse.'

Ollenu and Ashby proceeded towards the shoreline. As they neared the water's edge, Ollenu observed a naval ship anchored close to shore. Amidst the gathering of uniformed men stood one imposing man in a long ivory wig, blue breeches, and matching knee-length jacket with gold buttons. He introduced himself as naval commander Admiral George Rodney.

'Doctor Hutchinson is a Scotsman, forty years, slim, red hair, red beard,' explained Ashby. 'He is astride a large grey horse, and has a young slave girl with him.'

'A murderer in our midst?' Using a telescope, the admiral scanned the sea. 'Doctor Hutchinson has not sought to depart, for no vessels have sailed since yesterday. I see only what appears to be a merchant ship way out yonder.'

'I see no ship,' said Ashby squinting.

Ollenu searched the waters too, but his unaided eyes could see nothing distant except the sea meeting the sun on the horizon in a blend of brilliant colour. Shadows would soon be upon the land. An all too familiar feeling coursed through Ollenu's body and he became awash with fear. With eyes closed he mumbled.

'Death is on hand, at sea or on land.'

Ashby retrieved his Bible and kissed it. He reached for his pistol and checked that it was ready to fire.

Another soul was sure to perish this very day, and with sinking heart, Ollenu feared for young Rosa. Approaching Admiral Rodney, he gave a short bow. 'Admiral, sir, I earnestly ask that you direct some of your officers to search the houses.'

The naval commander looked down his pointed nose. 'Mr Ashby, who did you say he was?'

'I did not,' said Ashby with a scowl. 'My colleague introduced himself to you, sir, quite eloquently.'

'Again, I am Isaiah Ollenu, Admiral. Whatever my qualifications and connections, the only importance is that we apprehend the murderer Hutchinson. He has slaughtered many and will slay more.'

The admiral contemplated Ollenu as if surprised that he dared offer any instruction. Far too accustomed to the look, Ollenu held his shoulders high as he spoke.

'Admiral Rodney, the mad doctor killed yeoman John Callendar this same morning. Shot him dead with no provocation. He tried to kill the soldier escort. Hutchinson has nothing to lose, and will not hesitate to slaughter the brave men of the King's navy. Together, we must stop him.'

The admiral turned to his men. 'Vaughan, Ingram, take some men and check the houses. Do not let Doctor Hutchinson evade you. Turnbull, release the boats. Be ready if he takes to sea.'

'At once, sir,' said the naval officer.

While the naval men studied the sea and others ventured inland to the houses, Ollenu and Ashby entered the surrounding dense undergrowth with pistols raised. Ollenu's attention fluctuated between clearing a path through the wild land and watching the rapidly setting sun.

A high-pitched neigh caught their attention. They headed for the sound and found themselves in a small clearing. A riderless dapple-grey horse plodded aimlessly on the spot, its saddle strapped with weapons. A coiled rope hung from its side.

Silently, the two men approached the animal. Ashby pulled a gun from its saddle pouch. Ollenu stroked its thick mane, and reassured it with soothing words. He unhooked the rope, formed a noose and again cast his eyes about the thick bushes for the animal's master.

Pointing ahead, Ollenu traipsed further inland and became concerned as dry brambles crackled beneath their feet. If Hutchinson was close by, he too could hear them. He placed a hand on Ashby's arm and indicated that he not move. Silence reigned, interrupted only by occasional bursts of birdsong.

Suddenly, the distinct sound of a trapped scream echoed in the trees.

'Hear that?' hissed Ollenu.

Ashby pointed. 'I believe it came from over there.'

Pushing aside sharp branches, they trudged on. Ollenu's heart pumped at an unnatural pace as he spun in a circular motion, ears straining for another cry.

'No one is here,' said Ashby peering into the thicket. 'But I am certain the wail came from here.'

With a final glint of orange, the sun disappeared. In less than an hour darkness would fall upon the land. As the birdsong changed swiftly from cheerful to disturbed, Ollenu looked up to see what roused the bird. Cloth billowed from a branch above his head. It resembled a black sheet, but on closer inspection was revealed to be a silk cloak. Ollenu leapt high into the air and snatched at the garment. The cloak fell away revealing Lewis Hutchinson covering the mouth of a struggling Rosa. The doctor pushed the girl violently towards Ollenu, who dropped his gun and caught her light frame before she hit the ground.

Hutchinson cursed, leapt from the tree, and ran.

'Look after Rosa,' shouted Ollenu and pushed her towards Ashby.

Ollenu set off after his quarry. The doctor was nimble and determined, but the terrain was treacherous and he stumbled many times. With speed, Ollenu swung the noose high into the air and lassoed Hutchinson's neck. The Scotsman let out a piercing cry as he fell to the soil. In an instant he was back on his feet. Before Ollenu could pull him in, the doctor tore the rope from his neck and ran through the bushes, in the direction of the open sea.

Rosa grabbed a chunk of wood and ran past Ollenu, ignoring his pleas to run to safety.

Doctor Hutchinson burst through the low hanging trees and onto the exposed sandy shore, his fiery hair trailing behind him. To Ollenu's horror, Rosa was closing in on Hutchinson and at the same time a naval officer was taking aim at the fugitive.

'Do not shoot! You will hit the girl, do not shoot!' Ollenu ran at the officer and knocked him off balance as the shot went astray.

'Hold fire!' shouted Admiral Rodney. 'This man must be taken alive. We shall avenge the life of poor John Callendar in the right setting!'

Rosa tripped over the hem of her dress and fell onto wet sand. Hutchinson continued his path and leapt into a small fishing boat. He raised the oars and began to row with considerable power.

Admiral Rodney beckoned to his man. 'Get him, Officer Turnbull.'

'Yes, sir.'

As the officer and two navy men jumped into the boat, Ollenu climbed in with them. He rolled up his long sleeves and grabbed one of the four oars before anyone else. Turnbull picked up his own oar and eyed the law clerk with some suspicion.

'It is a long story, sir,' said Ollenu. 'For now, let us row.'

'Row, gentlemen!' ordered Turnbull.

As their boat travelled across the waters, it made no gain on the doctor and despair threatened to overwhelm Ollenu. Ahead, he could now see a distant ship – the ship Admiral Rodney must have seen through his telescope. Doctor Hutchinson was making good progress towards it. Ollenu knew not whether that ship was friend or foe. If the vessel was an enemy of the King's navy, their tiny boat could be sunk by cannon within an instant.

Suddenly, the calm sea began to ripple and small waves rapidly grew into larger more violent ones. A wind whipped up from nowhere and battered the row boats. Hutchinson continued to row, but his boat too ceased to make any further progress. To Ollenu they all seemed to be rowing at a standstill.

Hutchinson looked behind at Ollenu's naval boat, and then ahead at the unidentified large ship. Ollenu gazed at the ship too and could now make out the name, *Isabella*.

The sea again sent huge waves into the air, rocking both tiny vessels so hard their sterns tilted skywards. 'Hold on tight, men!' shouted Turnbull as he clung to the side.

Ollenu held firm and stared down into the sea. 'The mermaids have returned.' He watched the sleek figures swim past, their long black locks floating behind, and their tails swishing. The mermaids headed directly for Hutchinson's boat.

The Scotsman screamed, 'Get back, Negro fiends!' He lifted the oars and desperately tried to strike them. 'Get away!'

The mermaids' agile bodies dodged the wooden blades, and the doctor made no connection. As his boat rocked from side to side he struggled to stay seated. With pistol in hand he fired blindly at the water, then threw the empty gun at one of his tormentors.

'Go back to the bowels where you belong!' he shouted. 'Cursed coal vermin!'

A colossal wave upturned the doctor's boat and Hutchinson plunged overboard. For a moment he was completely submerged in the water, then as his head breached the surface he screamed.

'Stay away from me, disgustful monstrosities!'

The doctor floundered and struggled to stay afloat. Despite the perilous rocking of his own boat, Ollenu readied himself to dive in. To his dismay, two mermaids caught up with Hutchinson first and pulled him under water.

'No! Do not take him!'

With renewed strength, Ollenu inhaled, dived into the water and swam towards the nymphs. The largest mermaid turned to face him and a look of recognition passed between them. He grabbed hold of Hutchinson and stared into her huge lavender eyes, silently pleading for her to let go. Swishing her powerful tail from side to side, she glared at Ollenu. He touched her bare silky shoulder hoping to appease her. With his breath tightening in his chest, he tugged on Hutchinson one last time. The mermaid screeched as she released the captive, and her assistant followed her lead.

Ollenu swam upwards dragging the doctor and gasped when he broke the surface. Meanwhile, the sea continued to toss them like rag dolls. He clutched Hutchinson's hair and pulled the doctor's head back so that his mouth and nose were above water. The man spluttered and struggled to escape the law clerk's grasp.

Ollenu peered into the turbulent water below where a group of mermaids continued to swim, watching him, as if wondering whether to reclaim the white man.

'Justice awaits this killer, my sisters!' he shouted as he continued to wrestle with the doctor. 'Upon my oath!'

In unity, the mermaids turned their heads in one direction. Through burning eyes, Ollenu watched as they shrieked then headed out towards the *Isabella*. As soon as they streaked away, the waters fell calm.

'Do not touch me! Would that I drown than be taken by the likes of you.'

'That is not your destiny,' said Ollenu. 'What awaits you is the gallows.' He dragged the man's head back above the surface and, summoning as much strength as he could muster, punched him in the jaw.

The doctor gave up the fight and collapsed into Ollenu's arms. Officer Turnbull urged the naval boat towards them, reached over the bow and seized the dazed Hutchinson. The navy men hauled the doctor into the boat and pulled the apprentice up after him.

Ollenu panted as he stared at the defeated madman, who now bore a close resemblance to a wet rat. 'Doctor Lewis Hutchinson, King of Edinburgh Castle, quoter of Voltaire, killer of the innocent.'

'I should have blasted your brains from your skull at my dinner table,' whispered a shaking Hutchinson.

'As you have done in the past. Maybe as many as sixty times.'

One of the naval officers pointed out to sea. 'What goes on over yonder?'

All heads turned to look at the distressed *Isabella* being tossed as if she were a toy in the hands of a giant. Ollenu remembered the dark cabin from his voyage and it struck him that the mermaids were not mistaken in pursuing the modern *Isabella* after all. They knew it was not a centuries-old slave ship. Their brothers were murdered on the new ship and revenge would be theirs.

Screams of terrified sailors echoed in the air. The ship's masts toppled in a slow painful motion and soon the vessel disappeared from view as it sank into the deep.

'Vengeance goes on over yonder,' said Ollenu. 'Much delayed vengeance.'

CHAPTER 24

The sky was a cloudless blue and the bright morning sun shone on Kingston Harbour, where the good ship *Marianne* floated awaiting her passengers. The harbourmaster bellowed boarding instructions as deckhands dragged heavy trunks and chests up the ramp.

Ollenu and Ashby stood side by side at the rear of a long queue of passengers. Heightened voices, some tearful, others cheerful, were engaged in indistinct conversations, as they prepared to leave Jamaica.

'Where is that little boy?' Ashby's eyes roved through the array of bodies surrounding him. 'Ah, there he is. Come here, young man. I near forgot to give you this.'

Ollenu's eyebrows stayed raised as he watched Ashby cheerfully hand a coin to the child who had carried his trunk.

'You do realise that was a sixpence, not tuppence?' said Ollenu.

'I made no error, Ollenu,' said Ashby with a grin. 'Do not appear so astounded. I have come to believe that everyone – and in particular those who undertake strenuous labour on my behalf – deserves ample compensation.'

'I agree, most wholeheartedly,' said Ollenu. 'And that was quite generous of you.'

Ashby took a deep breath of salty air and stared out to sea. 'I wonder how angry the Mad Doctor of Edinburgh Castle must be, now that he is incarcerated. They say he is wont to scream that a giant bull breathes fire and rattles chains outside his cell at night. The guards patrol the gaol grounds, but it remains invisible to them.'

'It brings me great joy to learn that a Rolling Calf is his company,' said Ollenu. 'I regret it cannot torment him during daylight hours as well – he deserves no less.'

'I must admit to relief that Kershaw, Johnson and Mortimer were spared,' said Ashby. 'When they are fully recovered from their injuries, I pray they turn to God and forgo the Devil's leadership.'

'You are more generous of spirit than I. Had they died, I would not care to throw ashes on their graves.' Ollenu turned for a final look at the island. 'Is that not the lovely lady Lamont I see?'

'Oh, yes. What a welcome surprise.' Ashby attempted a wave at Eleanor, but quickly lowered his hand as if burned by an unseen flame.

'Surprise? She appears not to have any luggage, so surely she must be here to bid someone farewell?' said Ollenu slyly. As this comment garnered no response he added, 'Oh, come now, you must have informed her you would depart today on the *Marianne*?'

'I may have mentioned it.'

'Coincidence did not bring her here, Ashby.'

'No, I fear a dashing soldier did.'

Ollenu noticed the subject of Ashby's seeming disquiet. A familiar soldier standing near to the winsome lady. 'I really do wonder what you and Mrs Lamont spent all your leisure time conversing about. Boats, flowers, the weather?

Have you spoken of your intentions towards her? Oh, now see, she pretends to admire the ship's sails.'

'That soldier is speaking to her,' said Ashby.

'Even if that soldier is reciting Shakespeare's eighteenth sonnet to her, you cannot stand back and allow him to continue,' said Ollenu. 'Just because he is handsome, a whole head taller than you, and looks most dapper in uniform does not make him a better match for her.'

'Mr Ollenu, believe me when I say that confidence building is not your strong suit.'

'Go on, Mr Ashby.'

Ashby inhaled and stared in Eleanor's direction, trying to catch her eye again. She continued to wave a delicate fan in front of her face and looked elsewhere.

Ollenu encouraged his companion, 'You can approach her. It is not forbidden.'

Ashby walked towards Eleanor Lamont followed closely by Ollenu. 'I do not require a chaperone, Ollenu,' he hissed.

'Oh, yes you do.'

Ashby cleared his throat behind the soldier. 'If you will excuse me, sir, I wish to bid farewell to Mrs Lamont.'

The soldier turned and smiled as he looked Ashby up and down, but did not stand aside.

Eleanor lowered her fan and smiled in his direction. 'Good day, Ruben. Why so formal this morning?'

'Good day, Eleanor.'

'Mrs Lamont, I wish you a very good day,' said Ollenu with a bow.

'I am heartened to see you so fully recovered, Mr Ollenu.'

'Thank you, madam. Were it not for Mr Ashby's unwavering attention, my journey to good health would be slowed.' Ollenu nodded again and discreetly turned his attention out to sea.

Pulling his shoulders square, Ashby faced the hovering soldier. 'I wonder, would you be gracious enough to leave us for a moment, sir?'

'Oh, I am so sorry, Ruben,' said Eleanor. 'Let me introduce you to Colonel Jeremy Farquharson.'

'Pleased to make your acquaintance,' said Ashby as he resentfully shook the man's hand.

'I heard much about you, Mr Ashby,' said Farquharson.

'I heard no mention of you,' said Ashby.

'Of course I have spoken of him, Ruben,' said Eleanor in some surprise. 'This is my brother-in-law, my sister Franny's husband.'

'Oh, yes,' stammered Ashby. 'Of course.'

'Of course,' repeated Ollenu with a grin, keeping his eyes trained on the Caribbean Sea.

Ashby's eyes brightened and he grasped the man's hand again, shaking with greater enthusiasm. 'Ah, I thought Eleanor said her brother-in-law was an Assembly man, a parliamentarian?'

'No Ruben, that was my deceased husband, Stanley. Jeremy has always been a soldier.'

'Delighted to meet you, at last,' bellowed Farquharson in a cheery tone. 'Eleanor purposely keeps me apart from anyone she admires, for fear I will drive them away. I cannot fathom from whence such notions bloom.'

'Indeed.' Ashby beamed. 'You are not at all frightening, and I am sure you are a credit to the regiment.'

'Thank you, Mr Ashby.' Farquharson nodded at Eleanor. 'I will leave you to say farewell, whilst I seek fresh water for the horses. Bon voyage, Mr Ashby, and to you, Mr Ollenu.' Bowing again, he strode away and was soon lost in the bustling crowd.

'Jeremy insists on accompanying me to unwholesome places, and he is of the opinion that Kingston dock is no place for an unaccompanied lady.'

'But he escorted you to the ball in Montego Bay?' said Ashby.

'Yes, and Sir Alastair's manor deserves the title of unwholesome place. So many men and women, affianced and wed, flattering each other in careless discourse.' She stared at him. 'You seemed rather entranced at the ball, Ruben. Was anyone there of particular interest to you?'

'No one at all,' said Ashby.

Ollenu cleared his throat rather dramatically.

'That is to say, no one except yourself, my dear Eleanor,' added Ashby.

A commotion was occurring further inland. Raised indignant voices, both male and female, could be heard and Ashby's attention was taken by a recognised figure. 'Hmm, I do believe a tornado is upon us, Ollenu.'

'A tornado?' Eleanor squinted and looked out to sea. 'A ship sails in, but I see no sign of any weather disturbance.'

'Not at sea, Eleanor. The whirlwind is back there.'

As Ollenu turned, a girl pushed her way forcefully through the protesting passengers and threw herself on him almost knocking him off balance.

'Rosa! Steady on, my girl.'

'Take me with you, Mr Ollenu!'

'Oh Rosa, I have told you, I regret I cannot.' Ollenu gave her a hug as she clung to him. 'Earl Cadogan was most sincere in his request for you to live on his estate, and I understand you have new friends.'

'I do not want to stay there forever.'

'Rosa, listen.' Ollenu prised her away so that he could see into her eyes. 'I have survived many horrors over the past few weeks. Both Doctor Hutchinson and Neville Kershaw failed to kill me. Coreen Ollenu will surely bring about my end should I appear on her doorstep with you. My wife is a wonderful lady, but soon she will be overwhelmed with a newborn babe. Believe me, I have been through this glorious, if trying, event twice before.'

'But I will care for the baby. Mrs Ollenu, she will not have to rise from bed.'

'Oh, she will rise,' said Ollenu with certainty. 'She is the hardest working woman that I know, whether she is attending to a baby or not.'

'I have no one.' A crestfallen Rosa stared at her bare toes. 'Nanna Della is gone. Simeon and Malachi have run to the hills to live with the escaped ones. They left me behind.'

'Your cousins would never up and leave you, Rosa.' Ollenu tried to see into bright brown eyes that stayed lowered. 'Rebellions spread across the island. I understand why they refused to stay on the earl's estate. Were I in their position, I do not know that I could remain at the mansion. You refused to go with them, that is what happened, is it not?'

Rosa shrugged. 'My new bed is soft. For a while, I stay.'

'The earl has promised you will be instructed by a tutor,' said Ollenu.

'I know of a good tutor,' said Eleanor smiling at the girl. 'She is kind and patient, Rosa. I will recommend her service to the earl.'

'I am much obliged, Mrs Lamont.'

Rosa looked uncertain. 'I can fight with gun and cutlass as the men do.'

'I'm sure you can, Rosa,' said Ollenu. 'The fight is not only for the battlefield. The fight must continue in the courts of law, and in the courts of public opinion. Study hard. Learn as much as you can. In time, your knowledge can help those in the hills to live free, and move throughout the island without fear.'

'I want to help them, for all are my people.' The young girl's face brightened. 'And I want to show Simeon and Malachi that I know much more than them.'

Ashby smiled at her. 'Without question, you will succeed in your endeavours, Rosa.'

Ollenu tugged one of her plaits. 'Without question, little lady. I look forward to reading your words.'

As he turned and watched an approaching passenger ship glide into the dock, Ollenu's expression grew sombre. The reddened face of a man at the incoming ship's bow was enough to douse all feelings of good cheer.

'Ashby, do you see who I see?'

'My word,' said Ashby. 'Jacob Dunne, as I live and breathe.'

The barrister waved enthusiastically at the men and seemed oblivious that neither man waved back. As soon as the ship lay anchor, Mr Dunne jostled the passengers and shuffled his considerable frame down the ramp. Ollenu headed towards him, fists clenched at his side. Ashby pulled away from Eleanor and Rosa, and moved quickly to catch up with him.

'Wait, Ollenu!' pleaded Ashby.

'Mr Ollenu!' shouted Jacob Dunne and waved again. 'Oh thank God, Mr Ollenu, you are alive!'

A stone-faced Ollenu stared at the man in whom he had placed so much faith, the man who had mentored him with enthusiasm for the past five years, and found him expendable when thoughts of slave money were at hand. 'I am alive.'

Ashby added, 'No thanks to you, Mr Dunne.'

Jacob Dunne shrank back, stunned. 'You cannot possibly believe I had any hand in this grave misdeed?'

'Of what grave misdeed do you speak?' sneered Ollenu.

'We do believe exactly that,' said Ashby. 'In fact, we are certain of it.'

'You and Edward Barrow,' said Ollenu. 'You sent us here under false pretences, to find three people, when the real plan was to find only one, Francis Dantry, and retrieve banknotes stained in slave blood.'

Jacob Dunne mopped his jowls with a large handkerchief. 'It is not so!'

'Edward Barrow, Heskel Wilkins, Neville Kershaw... How many of you are in this cabal? Four? Five?' blazed Ollenu.

'Surely you cannot believe this? I knew nothing of Dantry and Barrow's slave money when I agreed to this venture. I am embarrassed at my own apathy.' Jacob Dunne twisted his damp handkerchief. 'My heart was pure in thought. At first, I was hesitant to send you because of your growing family. I foolishly allowed Barrow to convince me that you would gain valuable experience as you searched for the missing. My expectation was that you would return – bruised mentally from witnessing the violent nature of Jamaica, perhaps, yet otherwise intact and possessing a much broader world view.'

'I see. This mission was for my personal benefit and growth?' Ollenu spoke in a disbelieving tone. 'Yet you furnished Kershaw with written permission to kill me, signed by chief watchman Wilkins?'

'I helped Mr Barrow draft an extremely complimentary letter of introduction,' said Mr Dunne. 'Whatever he gave Wilkins to sign could not be that same letter.'

Ashby studied the faces of both men, then retrieved the folded paper from his pocket. 'Here, Mr Dunne, read the extremely complimentary letter.'

As Jacob Dunne read he grew ashen and looked aghast. 'Upon my oath, I had no hand in this.'

Ollenu wanted to believe that the counsellor's dismayed expression was wholehearted and honest, but the heavy mistrust built up over the weeks apart refused to be erased. 'These words were not created by you, the promise that no one would be penalised for my death?'

'I would never sanction such insanity! I first learned the extent of the deceit from a beggar child who overheard Barrow and Wilkins in the Pacific Tavern.'

'Why should I believe you?' asked Ollenu.

Jacob Dunne puffed out his chest. 'You have known me for five years, Mr Ollenu. How many times have we sat and worked together inside and outside of court? Thousands. How many times have we confided secret strategies together? Thousands more. How many times have I ever lied to you? Not once!'

'At the very least, you sent me where I could die,' said Ollenu bitterly.

'That I did, but not because I meant you any ill, Mr Ollenu.' Mr Dunne pulled a document from his jacket pocket and extended his hand. 'This is a letter I recently prepared for you, written with my own hand, to be presented to you upon your return to Bristol.'

Ollenu kept his fists clenched at his sides and made no move to take the document.

Dunne continued to thrust the letter at his clerk. 'I told Edward Barrow that if you died, I would make it my bounden duty to ruin his business, and by God, I meant it.'

'Should you wish to ruin his business, I hold information that will assist.' Ashby stretched past Ollenu's tense body and took the paper. 'May I?'

'You may,' said Dunne, 'as Mr Ollenu will not.'

Ashby unfolded the page. Had Ollenu not been so infused with rage he would have noticed the slight curl to Ashby's lips as he silently read. In a stern voice the investigator said, 'Mr Dunne, surely you must be aware that the content of this missive will irritate Mr Ollenu to the extreme?'

Jacob Dunne looked perplexed. 'It will?'

Ollenu's curiosity was drawn, but he maintained a frown and rigid jaw as he stared at the senior lawyer. 'You are determined to vex my spirit.'

'I am so sorry, Ollenu.' Ashby patted Ollenu on the shoulder and said in a sympathetic tone, 'According to these words that tender scalp of yours is one step closer to suffering horsehair wigs.'

A stunned Ollenu stared at Ashby in confusion. 'What?'

Ashby waved the letter under his companion's nose. 'It states "Having successfully completed an outstanding five-year period of clerkship, the law clerk heretofore known as Mr Isaiah Ollenu shall from this day forth be known as Mr Isaiah Ollenu, Esquire, Attorney at Law upon the recommendation of Mr Jacob Dunne, Esquire, Barrister."'

Ollenu reached trembling fingers for the letter and his eyes filled with tears as he read.

'This provokes you?' said Mr Dunne.

'No, sir, it does not.' Ollenu choked and wiped wet cheeks with his cuffs. 'I know not what to say,' he whispered.

Mr Dunne beamed. 'Then say nothing and let us shake hands, Mr Ollenu.' He grabbed Ollenu's hand and pumped it enthusiastically.

As soon as he released Ollenu's hand, Ashby claimed it and shook it with vigour. 'Congratulations, my good man! Mr Isaiah Ollenu, Esquire has a marvellous ring to it.'

'Thank you, Mr Ashby,' said Ollenu. He stared at Mr Dunne. 'Thank you, sir. I cannot tell you what this means to me.'

'You deserve it, Mr Ollenu, and I believe in running a meritocracy.'

A warm smile crept across Ollenu's face as he closed his eyes and held the coveted paper to his chest. At last, he had achieved the goal that had seemed so distant all those years ago, that he had all but given up on in recent weeks. One day he would write a tale all about his exploits in Jamaica, as Sir Hans Sloane had done, for people in forthcoming centuries to read and wonder at. Perhaps he could entitle his writings *The Adventures of Isaiah Ollenu, Esquire To Be.*

EPILOGUE

Bristol, England. May 1773

Through the library window, Isaiah Ollenu watched the messenger leave Jacob Dunne's chambers on Broad Street. The young bearer closed the front door with care, not slamming it as some brazen people were wont to do. When the youth had first knocked on the door, Ollenu, could not have imagined what good tidings he brought with him.

'Hanged!' Mr Dunne puffed on his pipe happily. 'Such splendid news!'

A broad smile lit up Ollenu's entire face. 'Mr Ashby, would you agree that, as highly anticipated events go, Doctor Hutchinson's demise is right there with the Second Coming?'

Ashby grinned. 'I daresay, somewhat close.'

Ollenu wandered over to the world map that Mr Dunne had studied all those months ago, and devoted his attention to Jamaica. 'Despite the madman's capture, I feared he would find an esteemed barrister to save him from his fate.'

'He did find one; a barrister who is neither a bumptious cockalorum or an insentient coxcomb,' said Mr Dunne as he rocked on his heels. 'But the audacious murder of John Callendar, could not be excused by his esteemed counsel. Not even the best barrister on this earth – I speak of myself, of course – could have mounted a successful defence. There could only be one outcome to that trial.'

'Guilty,' said Ollenu.

'Whilst I cannot celebrate his death, I must give thanks that a murderer has been curtailed.' Ashby rose from his desk that occupied a corner of the library opposite Ollenu's. He poured wine into two goblets, and water into a third. 'For you, Mr Ollenu.'

The new attorney walked towards him, accepted the glass and nodded his thanks. Ashby had vowed never again to darken the doors of Paxten Insurance on Corn Street. Once Tredinnick and Verney, Dunne's fellow barristers, had moved out to their new chambers, Ollenu would occupy one of their rooms and Ashby the other. As Ashby conducted most of his business in taverns and in markets, his presence was not an inconvenience to the law men. In fact, Ollenu found him quite a useful person on whom to test out theories and hypotheses.

Jacob Dunne lowered his pipe as he accepted a drinking vessel from Ashby. 'You are sure you do not wish to toast with something stronger, Mr Ollenu?'

'I am determined to stay away from alcohol, sir. It has never stood me in good stead, and I believe had a hand in me hallucinating in the past. An experience I am loath to repeat.'

Ashby smiled. 'It did not become you any more than cannabis became me.'

'Raise your glasses, gentlemen,' said Mr Dunne. 'Here's to the end of the Mad Doctor's reign.'

'To the end of the Mad Doctor's reign.'

'To the end of the Mad Doctor,' said Ollenu. 'And may his soul forever remain in torment.'

'Hear, hear,' said Mr Dunne.

Ollenu sighed wistfully, 'I wish that I had witnessed him swing in Spanish Town square, red hair billowing in the wind. My presence would have so enraged him.'

'It would appear he had a large audience,' said Ashby.

'And cursed them all for daring to witness his demise,' added Dunne.

Ollenu sipped his water, his tone regretful. 'So many items of clothing were found hidden all over the castle and in that hole, yet he was never made to answer for the deaths of any of those people. Their families will never learn the real truth of their beloveds' last days.'

'It is a mercy that they never learn,' said Ashby.

'A case could have been made for further murder trials,' said Dunne. 'Nevertheless, in the end, a just result was reached.'

Ollenu nodded. 'You can hang a man once, not forty times.'

'I wonder what shall become of Edinburgh Castle?' said Ashby. 'All of the slaves abandoned the estate. Most have taken to the mountains.'

'I cannot believe anyone would wish to live in that horrible place,' said Ollenu. 'It should be left to decay. Let the bats and fireflies take it.'

'Perhaps I should encourage Edward Barrow to go live there,' suggested Ashby. 'I am informed that he continues to insist a large fortune in pounds exists on that land, despite not a farthing being unearthed.'

'The coward Barrow rants from afar,' said Ollenu. 'But he will never venture close to the environs of danger.' He looked at Jacob Dunne. 'Sir, I regret that you do not wish us to make a case against him and chief watchman

Wilkins. Even if only for misrepresenting your position on our expedition.'

Mr Dunne shook his head. 'It is best to let it be, Mr Ollenu. I have ensured that an account of Barrow's behaviour will pass through every public house in Bristol. Good citizens will shun him. Those who wish to do business with him – well, we do not wish for their custom, so we suffer no loss.'

'I understand, sir,' conceded Ollenu. 'Although we did not prove that Hutchinson killed Henry Penket or Francis Dantry, in years to come their beneficiaries are sure to petition the courts to declare them dead. I will encourage their actions. Once such declaration is obtained, Barrow will have no choice but to make the very payments he sought to avoid.'

'He will lose his mind,' said Ashby. 'On another good note, Wilkins is reduced to a lower rank and is no longer chief.'

'Yes, that I am grateful for,' agreed Ollenu. 'Though I would rather he be removed from any role in upholding law and order. I hope his replacement is someone who wants the best for Bristol, and not someone seeking merely to line his own pockets.'

'We must toast a second occasion, gentlemen,' said Dunne.

Ashby retrieved the wine bottle and the water jug, and refilled the glasses. 'To what do we raise a glass this time?' he asked.

'We are yet to formally celebrate our new working arrangement,' said Dunne. 'Whether it be temporary or permanent, it is timely to acknowledge you, Mr Ashby, as a resident of our chambers.'

Ollenu smiled to himself. He and Ashby could work well together, should another case arise, although he would insist that all investigations remain in England.

Jacob Dunne raised his glass. 'Gentlemen, here's to new beginnings.'

'To new beginnings.'

'To new beginnings. Welcome, Mr Ashby.'

AUTHOR'S NOTE

The idea for this book came about when I read a poem entitled 'Place Name: Edinburgh Castle' by Kei Miller in his Forward Prize-winning book, *The Cartographer Tries to Map a Way to Zion* (Carcanet Press, 2014). I bought the book in July 2015, at the wonderful Calabash Literary Festival, Treasure Beach, St Elizabeth, Jamaica.

Intrigued by that particular poem, I returned to it many times over the years. I had a vision of this doctor, a Scotsman with flaming red hair, raising havoc in Jamaica. A real-life serial killer. With that, I also saw a Black male hero, a person who was super smart and not subservient. Sometime in 2019, I finally sat down to write a first draft.

Although based on a true story, the majority of this tale is entirely fictional, including the main characters Isaiah Ollenu and Ruben Ashby. Doctor Lewis Hutchinson (in some archives spelt 'Hutchison') was a real Scotsman, and Edinburgh Castle, Pedro, in the parish of St Ann, is a real place. Over a twelve-year period, the Mad Doctor was a prolific murderer. Although he was a murder suspect, and did assault Doctor Hutton, no one sought to apprehend him, until he killed the yeoman John Callendar.

On 16th March 1773, Hutchinson (aged 40) was hanged in Spanish Town square, following conviction for the murder of Callendar. He had pleaded not guilty. No murder charges were ever brought against him in respect of any other victim. A subsequent search of Edinburgh Castle revealed over forty watches and a hoard of clothes belonging to a variety of deceased people. The remorseless Hutchinson demanded that his gravestone carry the inscription:

Their sentence, pride and malice, I defy.
Despise their power, and like a Roman, die.

Despite the fact that Hutchinson left money for that purpose, the authorities refused this final request.

The Scotsman is now dubbed 'Jamaica's first serial killer', and by all accounts seems to have murdered people because he could, luring some into the castle or shooting them on sight. The white planters Roger Maddix and James Walker were his real-life accomplices. The two were tried and condemned to death for participating in the murder of a farmer and of a school master.

Today, Edinburgh Castle is almost a complete ruin and carries no evidence of the Mad Master's reign of evil. Locals stay away from the area as rumours abound that duppies roam the grounds at night. In Jamaican folklore the most feared duppy of all is the dreaded Rolling Calf. So called eye-witnesses say they snort fire or steam, rattle heavy chains and shake the earth. Should you be brave enough to visit the village of Pedro, do keep an eye out for a Rolling Calf or Doctor Hutchinson's duppy. And if you see either, run.

ACKNOWLEDGEMENTS

A whole lot of people deserve my heartfelt gratitude for this book making it to publication. Firstly, thank you to my wonderful publishing team, in particular my astute editor, Craig Lye, and editorial assistant Hannah Taylor for pulling my novel out of the competition pile and recommending it to the editors.

Many thanks also to super duo Elane and Sarah, of I Am In Print, for running the Novel Award 2023 competition, without which Isaiah's voice would probably still be unheard. Ladies, I appreciate you.

As usual, warm thanks to my cheerleading team for advice, practical help and/or encouragement: Juliet (Lavern) Reid, Sharon Thompson, Gwen Thompson, Elaine (Pat) Harris, Carol Harris Simpson, Rona Harris and Pauline Johnson. Big up to my brothers Guy Lennon, Duane Lennon and John Lennon, whose requests for 'the next book' keep me writing even when I would rather sip rum punch and stare at the Caribbean Sea.

I must also give a special shout-out to the tireless folk who keep the gardens in Spanish Town Square, St Catherine in such pristine condition, providing a comfortable space to plot some uncomfortable scenes. Keep up the good work.